SHADOWS OF
BEFORE

For More Information Contact:

Three Kings Publishing
115 Canterbury Court
Princeton, Kentucky 42445
threekingspublishing@gmail.com

****

For news and upcoming books sign up for Ryan King's
newsletter at https://dl.bookfunnel.com/nm7lm5ldjy and
receive a free book.

Shadows of Before

Book IV in the *Land of Tomorrow* series

by Ryan King

For my son, Isaiah, who actually read one of my books

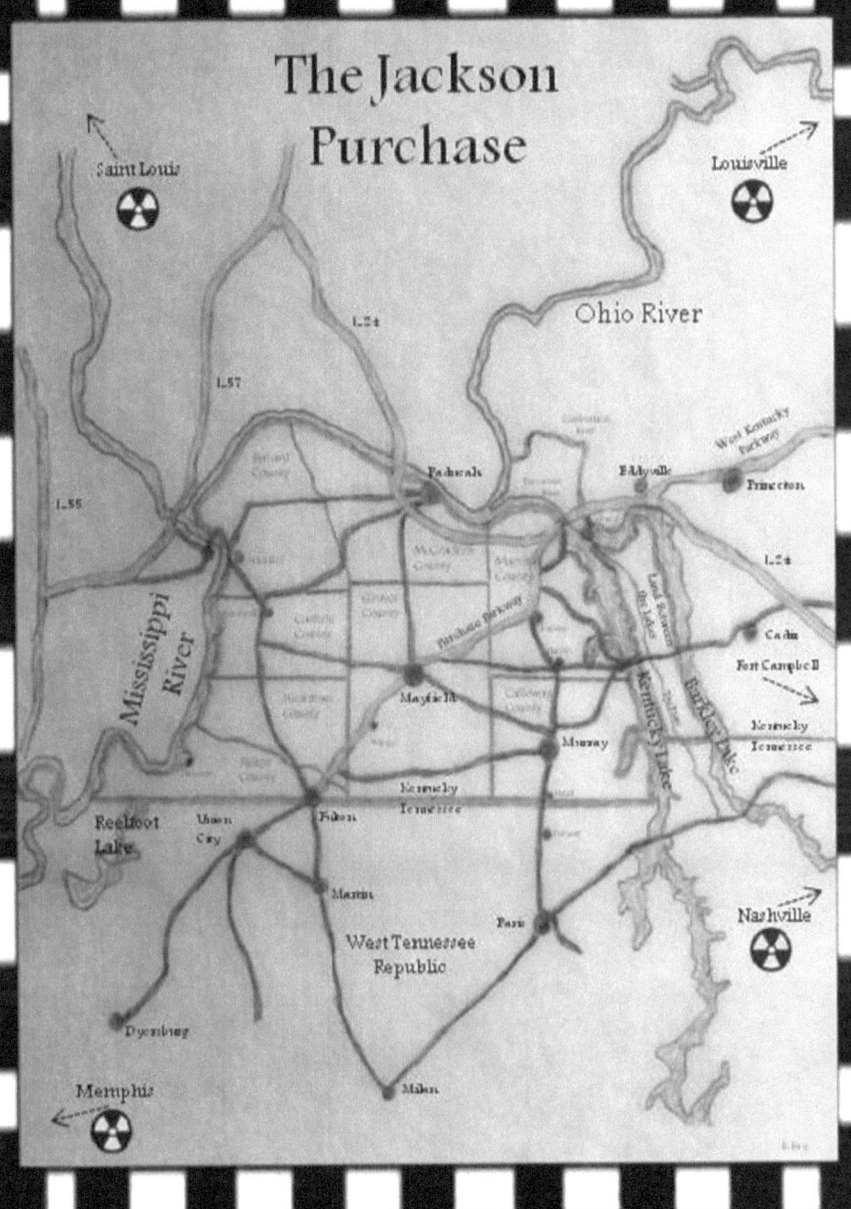

Shadows of Before

Book IV of the Land of Tomorrow Series

by Ryan King

Prologue

Simon didn't really mind the apocalypse. As a matter of fact, he rather enjoyed it. He could do pretty much everything he enjoyed before the nukes fell—eating, sleeping, and messing with computers—without someone screwing with him. No more questions like, *When are you going to start living your life?*

No, not anymore. His technical skills were what had allowed them all to function. Simon's willingness, nay eagerness, to monitor the larger situation had allowed others to go about their business.

A flurry of laughter from the other room caused him to look to his left. Normally, he didn't hear them with his headset on, but the radio intercepting traffic from the north had stopped two weeks ago and the headset lay on the console in front of him. Listening to the sporadic Jackson Purchase broadcasts had filled him with wonder, like listening to alien messages from Saturn, but then they had just…stopped. He felt that somewhere up north, where the old Jackson Purchase had been near the western Kentucky-Tennessee border, something bad had happened.

What used to be Kentucky and Tennessee, he reminded himself.

More laughter. Simon looked in that direction and could tell they were watching an episode of *WKRP in Cincinnati*. A show he actually used to liked, but seeing every episode a dozen or more times took the enjoyment out of it. Not so for the other residents of Site Conway, who laughed at the same old scenes of Doctor Johnny Fever and Les Nesman.

There were vast corridors and rooms filled with armored vehicles, weapons, ammunition and supplies, but you could only look at it all so much. Simon knew that it had been intended for the surviving remnants of the military to rally, rearm, and continue the fight, but no one had shown.

No one except Simon.

They hadn't wanted to let him in, of course. He was an outsider, and they had worked at the secret facility for decades. Lewis and Derek were the maintenance technicians, and Austin was the janitor. His entry into their supposedly secret and secure world had scared the shit out of them and their families, which they had brought into the facility against regulations after the nukes. His activation of protocols that they didn't even know existed had allowed him entry into Site Conway…and nearly gotten him shot. It was only his wits and near-magical abilities with electronics, at least in their eyes, that had won them over.

Still, he wasn't really part of them, although most of his fellow residents politely pretended otherwise. An effort he appreciated despite its futility.

The lights flickered as a bad glop of fuel choked its way through the massive generators below them. The laughter in the next room abruptly stopped. After a few seconds, the lights grew strong again, and Simon felt the tension melt away. His fellows went on in their obtuse avoidance of the larger problem lurking all around them.

We need an exit strategy, he thought. *One that doesn't involve death, torture, or slavery.*

He wondered again how much time they had left, but the truth was no one really knew. Site Conway had been fortunate to get a delivery of diesel fuel just before the end. Two tanker trucks had topped off the massive fuel reservoirs.

That had been almost two years ago, and those massive tanks were less than a third empty. No, the amount of fuel wasn't the issue, its volatility was.

It was Austin the janitor who had finally brought their attention to the issue. A former long-time gas station attendant, when the world still had such things, he knew his way around fuel. They were all eating warmed-up Meals Ready to Eat sometime in the middle of the night. In the bunker, it didn't really matter what time of the day it was. Everyone tried to stay on a normal day-night schedule, but it just didn't work. People woke up in the middle of the night and, with not much else to do, had a snack. Snack being an understatement considering each MRE had a day's worth of calories for a soldier in a combat environment. Simon chose his favorite, ham slice, and quietly joined the other men in the facility, their wives and children asleep. The four of them sat and ate wordlessly.

Lewis had finally asked how long those hundreds of thousands of MREs stacked up in hanger twelve would last before going bad. Austin had told him at least five years and Lewis insisted more. Derek had asked how old they were to begin with.

"The food isn't going to be a problem," said Austin. "We got lots of that, and besides, the fuel will go bad long before these damn things will. So much preservatives in them you could likely eat them after the next ice age."

"What the hell are you talking about?" asked Lewis. "Fuel doesn't go bad."

Austin nodded vigorously around a mouthful of eternity spaghetti. He swallowed with difficulty and wiped his mouth. "Why you think those strategic oil reserves down in Texas aren't called the strategic gas reserves?"

"Who gives a damn what they're called?" asked Derek. "And what does it have to do with us anyway?"

"Fuel is an unstable form," Simon blurted out, his mind running ahead. He was so dumbfounded by the idea that he missed the looks of amazement that he had spoken at all.

Austin pointed his spoon at Simon. "Right. Gasoline breaks down over time. Same with diesel. Mixing new fuel with old fuel helps, but when the same fuel just sits, it loses its...what would you call it..."

"Boom?" offered Derek.

"Volatility," said Simon.

Lewis, their self-appointed leader, looked at Simon disapprovingly before he turned back to Austin. "How long before the fuel starts going bad?"

"Already started. Fuel just sitting doesn't usually last much more than a year."

"But it's been almost two," said Lewis. "Why haven't the generators broken down?"

"Because I've been adding fuel preservatives," answered Austin. "There are cases of that stuff. Guess the whack-jobs who designed this place knew this would be a problem."

Lewis' face got tight and red. "And you didn't tell me?"

4

Austin shrugged and took another bite of food. "Nothing to tell really. There was a problem and I fixed it. I do stuff like that around here all the time that you all never notice."

Simon at that point had wandered away from the increasingly heated conversation. Several of the wives and children had crept into the room drawn by the raised voices. Simon wanted no part of that drama. Besides, he needed to think, and his best thinking was done alone.

And think he had. The problem wasn't getting more fuel. Whatever they found would also be going bad, or maybe already had without the fuel stabilizers. No, they needed fresh fuel, and for that, you needed oil and gas refineries. Based on the radio intercepts and reports from Cheyenne Mountain, Simon seriously doubted Shell or Chevron were busy filling tanker trucks with fresh gasoline or diesel.

The generators were going to go down. And when that happened, Site Conway would become a giant crypt. They needed a new place to go, but where?

The sudden rapid beeping startled Simon out of his thoughts. He frantically grabbed a pencil and paper and copied before he could forget the letters. He already knew who the message was from. No matter how many times he told them, Cheyenne Mountain just couldn't understand why it would be helpful if there were a greeting or alert or something to get ready before blasting their series of dots and dashes. Thankfully, Simon was very good at Morse Code.

It had been him who had fixed the digital relay and radio transmitter before venturing outside to install the antenna which had blown down in one of the storms. Lewis and company had been convinced they were all alone until Simon and his transmitter had discovered differently. Fortunately, he knew the true secret of the United States Continuity of Government Plan, putting him in extremely rare company. Lewis, Derek, and Austin knew of Site Conway's existence, and even its purpose, but none of them knew how it fit into the larger picture.

None of them except Simon. And he did not feel it was in his best interest to reveal this information to his bunker mates, nor how he had received it. So, they went on thinking rightly that he was a computer whiz, and wrongly that he was nothing else.

Simon had thrown on the headphones as he scribbled. Everyone else had gathered around him, staring at his writing with stunned looks on their faces, like cavemen watching a ballet. He almost laughed at this image and had to force himself to concentrate on what he was doing. The asshole at the other end obviously felt the need to show off by transmitting as fast as was manually possible.

Finally, the beeping stopped, and Simon pulled off the headset.

"What's it say?" asked Lewis, leaning over to look at the piece of paper.

Simon pulled it out of his sight and studied it carefully with growing alarm. He read it through again, hoping maybe that he had made a mistake.

"Come on, Simon," said one of Lewis' snotty boys. "What's it say?"

Simon sighed and was suddenly tired. He handed the message to Lewis.

"It's from Cheyenne Mountain," Lewis said, studying the message. "Says there's been a nuclear event northeast of us."

"What the hell do they mean by a *nuclear event*?" asked Derek.

"That's why the JP broadcasts stopped," said Simon.

Lewis looked around at everyone. "They want us to send someone to check it out and report back."

"Go outside?" said Austin's wife in horror.

"Don't they have satellites and drones for this sort of stuff?" asked Derek.

Simon shook his head. "Satellites can only tell so much, and the range is too far for the drones out in Colorado. They want someone to go up there and actually talk to people."

"That's freaking suicide," said Derek.

"Not exactly," answered Simon absentmindedly. "I did make my way here, after all. I've been outside dozens of times."

Lewis looked at him critically. "Yes, you have. Seems like you may be uniquely qualified for something like this."

"Now hang on," said Austin. "We can't just send Simon out there on his own. He's weird as shit, I'll give you that, but he's one of us."

"Thanks," said Simon.

"Seriously," continued Austin, "why don't we just tell those govie remnants to kiss our asses? It's not like they can do anything to us."

Simon appreciated Austin's less-than-flattering argument on his behalf, but thought he might be wrong about them not being able to do anything to them from Colorado. Part of setting up the comms and getting the digital systems online had been to allow them satellite burst transmission access as well as super administrator privileges. There had been a large number of unknown downloads and uploads. Simon had been unable to determine their purpose but suspected Cheyenne Mountain had some measure of control over Site Conway. Control they had so far not chosen to exercise.

Besides, they still needed an exit strategy. Those generators were going to die.

As if to emphasize his thoughts, the lights flickered and lurched for a full ten seconds before coming on again.

"Goodness gracious," said Derek, "this place is falling apart."

Lewis looked daggers at the man and slowly cut his eyes deliberately towards the children gathered nearby.

Derek turned his head slowly to look at their attentive faces. "I'm just joking. You know that, right? Everything is just fine. No need to be concerned. This place isn't falling apart at all."

"Anyway, maybe it's a good idea if we do send someone out," said Lewis. "We don't really know much of what is going on in the outside world except that everything is gone. We should send someone to go look and come back."

"Someone?" asked Simon. "Do we pick straws or something?"

Everyone except Lewis looked away from him in embarrassment. A long silence spread out around them.

Austin cleared his throat, and he turned to the families. "Why don't y'all try to go back to sleep now? It's late."

"Yeah, you got a big day of watching DVDs and crawling around on old tanks," said Derek sarcastically.

Lewis again looked angrily at Derek, but for once, the man met his gaze levelly. Slowly, the wives and children moved away back to their quarters.

"Maybe we should draw straws," said Austin. "I'm still not convinced we need to do this at all, but if we are, that seems like a fair way to chose."

"Simon should go," said Lewis. "That's fair. He's got the most experience topside since...Armageddon. He also doesn't have a family. The rest of us have responsibilities."

Derek and Austin looked away.

Simon wanted to be angry, but all he felt was sad. He couldn't even argue with their logic. Besides, he knew someone had to figure something out. They had to find another place to live. Without electricity, Site Conway might actually lock them all inside and slowly suffocate them in the dark.

He turned away and began pecking out electronic letters.

"What are you writing?" asked Austin.

"I'm telling them that I'm going," answered Simon.

Part I
Fading Light

Chapter 1 - Foretelling

Nathan had to force himself to stop fiddling with his hands. It had become an unconscious habit for him to try and hide the EX brand on the webbing of his right hand. Although he was no longer an exile, he felt the eyes as they lighted upon it. This was typically followed by a look of realization, or anger, or even pity.

It made him want to scream, *Yes, he was my son, and I'm proud of him. David saved all of us, don't you understand?*

Instead, he did his best to ignore the looks, and he and Bethany largely mourned in private. Between David's part in the Slaughter at the Battle of Fulton, his blowing up the gun powder factory and oil refinery at Murray State University, and his setting off a nuke at Fulton, David Taylor was not seen in the best of light.

Maybe history will be kinder. Possibly kinder to him than me, he thought, looking around at the rows of grim horsemen lining the path before him.

"I thought this was supposed to be a simple affair," said Luke Carter beside him.

Nathan nodded. "It was. The peace deal was concluded months ago right after the war ended. This was just going to be a formality."

"I guess the Creek wanted to make a show of it."

Indeed, thought Nathan. They likely wanted their people to witness the Jackson Purchase formally ceding back ancestral lands to the Creek Nation. They would see this as a pivotal moment and a redemption of sorts. *Unprecedented really*, Nathan realized. He couldn't think of any other example of indigenous people reclaiming their lands after losing them hundreds of years before.

A heavy drum started to beat slowly.

"I think that means we're supposed to walk forward," Luke commented.

"Let's not keep them waiting then." He stepped off, walking with his head and back straight, and Luke fell into pace beside him. Nathan could have done this alone, but he had hopes of finally leaving public service, and one of the oldest idioms of government work was that you had to train your replacement before anyone would let you leave. With any luck, Luke would become the next JP Chief of Defense, and then Nathan could spend more time with his family.

He saw a young woman through the line of Creek warriors to his right. She was strikingly beautiful and held a small baby that smiled innocently at the world.

Bethany had taken David's death hard, but the birth of their daughter River had soothed away some of the pain. Even so, the pregnancy had been hard on his wife, and even now, months later, she tired easily and had lost weight. It seemed she was paler by the day, although she swore she felt fine.

They would need all their strength in the days ahead. Not only did they have a baby daughter in their *mature years*, as he liked to call it, but they were soon to be grandparents. Joshua and Alexandra's baby was due in the fall.

His leg locked up, and Luke caught his arm as he stumbled.

"You okay?"

"Yeah," answered Nathan, rubbing the old wound, forcing himself to straighten and walk normally despite the pain that came and went without warning. A brief image of Joshua yanking the rusty rebar spear out of his thigh flashed in his mind, and he pushed it away quickly.

The path of Red Stick warriors curved and led them down towards a bend in the Tennessee River. Beside the river was a traditional deer-hide shelter with brightly colored tarps connecting it to a large recreational vehicle that would obviously never move again. In front of the shelter, a small fire smoldered, and several individuals waited. A boy with a large wooden drum sat off to the side, hitting the surface with a steady cadence and a look of forced solemnity.

As Nathan and Luke came into view, a middle-aged man helped a frail figure with long gray hair stand from a stool. Nathan recognized the middle-aged man as Billy Fox, the Red Sticks' chief, and the ancient man on his arm as their spiritual leader, Chicoca. Nathan also recognized Susan Rivera, Jasper Timmons, and the small girl nearby from their journey through Indiana into Kentucky together. He was a little surprised at how tall the girl had gotten and guessed she was close to eleven or twelve years old.

The drum abruptly stopped as Nathan and Luke drew near.

"Be welcome," said Billy Fox, nodding to them both.

"I didn't know this was going to be such a big affair," said Nathan.

"Of course it is a big affair," said Chicoca with a toothless smile. "Today, three hundred years of prophecy comes to fulfillment."

"And your raiding comes to an end," said Luke.

Billy Fox chuckled. "*Raiding* is a strong word. We protect these lands and punish those who do not respect our rights. How is one supposed to respond when others steal and take from you?"

"Be that as it may," said Nathan, "you agree to respect the territory of the Jackson Purchase and the former lands of the West Tennessee Republic."

"And in exchange," said Chicoca, leaning forward, "you agreed to recognize the Creek Nation's permanent rights to their ancestral lands as we have outlined."

Nathan pictured the map in his office with the Creek Nation boundaries that encompassed South-Central Tennessee along with parts of Northern Alabama and Mississippi. This had been a bitter concession to make, but Reggie Phillips had convinced him it was their best path. "We need a break from war," his friend had told him, "and there will be war if we do not give our new friends what they already feel is rightfully theirs."

There was an air of expectation, and Nathan realized everyone was holding their breath, waiting for him to speak.

"Yes," Nathan finally said, "the government of the Jackson Purchase, which includes the tributary lands of the West Tennessee Republic and the Pennyrile Communities, does from this day forward recognize the Creek Nation's ownership of these lands. It is—"

Nathan was about to go on with his prepared speech, but he was interrupted by a tumult of war whoops, spinning horses, and gunshots. The lines of horsemen had disintegrated into mad riders racing off in all directions and joyfully bouncing into each other.

"I guess it was a big deal, after all," muttered Luke.

A grinning Billy Fox beckoned them forward. "Come inside and be welcome; you are our guests and friends."

Nathan and Luke followed him into the large teepee-style shelter, along with Susan, Jasper, and the little girl. Nathan was amused to notice that the last three appeared to now be a family unit. Chicoca was seated in a large chair, which was obviously the place of honor, while the others sat around another small fire on wooden stools or cross-legged on the ground.

A woman handed Billy Fox a long smoldering pipe. "We will smoke this to seal our commitment to peace with each other."

"I always thought that was just a Native American cliché," said Luke. "You guys actually smoke peace pipes?"

"My people have always sealed peace with sacred smoke," said Chicoca, accepting the pipe from Billy who had taken a long drag. "We believe that anyone who breaks such a peace is cursed in the afterlife."

Nathan looked over at Susan Rivera and studied her carefully. She appeared to have taken on a mantle of gravity and power that had been lacking the last time they had met. She returned his gaze with neither friendship nor hostility.

"I see you remember Susan Who Saw The Fire," said Billy, handing the pipe to Nathan.

"What fire?" asked Luke.

"The fire that rose over the ashes of Fulton," said Susan. "The fire that your son brought back into the world once again. The fire that was the sign for the Creek to stop making war."

"Oh, that fire," said Luke.

"I suspect that's an improvement over your old Creek name, isn't it?" Nathan asked. "Susan Who Brought the Fire From the Sky?"

Susan didn't answer, but he noticed a tightening around her jaw line.

Nathan took a long puff on the pipe and found it fairly mild with a hint of cherry. He passed the pipe along to Luke and looked at Susan. "But the war isn't totally done, is it? Part of the lands you recognize to the south you don't yet control."

"We hope to reassess control without resorting to war," answered Billy. "Regardless, that is not your concern. It will not be war against you or your people. Between us, there will be peace."

Jasper leaned over and whispered in Susan's ear. She looked at the little girl who was staring hard at Nathan. "She remembers you from before."

Nathan smiled at her and leaned forward. "Hello, there. Do you remember me?"

She just stared back without speaking.

"Don't take it personal," said Billy Fox. "Little Lion doesn't speak much."

"Little Lion?" asked Luke. "That's a cool nickname."

"It is not a nickname," chided Chicoca. "It is her true name. One that recognizes her spirit and heart. Names are important, one of the things the white man never understood."

"Well, we understand the need for us to get along," said Nathan. "It is a time for war to be over. It is a time for peace."

"No," said the little girl.

Everyone looked at her in surprise.

"What was that?" asked Susan.

The girl stared hard at Nathan and then around at them all. "This will not be a time of peace. This will be a time of death and darkness. Both are coming…almost here."

At that moment, the pipe in Jasper's hands went out.

Chapter 2 – The Guide

Horace "Trailer" Smiley looked back to make sure the pot-bellied man and his son were still there, pulling their large handcart down the gravel road.

How is it possible for anyone to be pot-bellied anymore? he wondered.

"You sure this is the way?" the man asked again.

Horace just looked at him. He let his nearly seven-foot-tall, muscled frame do the talking for him.

The man looked away and continued to pull.

They were nearly to their destination anyway. It was getting around Memphis' smoking ruin that was the problem. After that, they could get back on the main roads and make better time, even if that did mean paying more tolls.

Trailer knew all the roads and best paths. He knew where it was safe to sleep and where it wasn't. He knew which water soothed your parched throat and which made you slowly wither from the inside. He knew which police were fighting against the chaos and which were looking for an opportunity to kill you for your boots. In short, Trailer was a guide, and his immense size meant that those he guided tended to suffer less harassment than on their own.

Most of his life, his size had felt like a curse. Trailer had grown up in central Tennessee and, naturally enough, been exceptional at basketball and earned a scholarship to the University of Kentucky. It was in his first year that he blew out his knee and had to sit out the rest of the season. The surgery was a success, but he was never the same again. Some of it was the painkillers, but mostly he had just lost his heart for the game.

At least now people didn't walk up to him and ask why he wasn't playing in the NBA. At least now he didn't have to explain how he was such a screw-up that he had missed his chance. How he had been forced to drive a semi truck all over his home state to keep himself fed. He found this ironic considering the nickname Trailer had attached itself to him nearly a decade before he started hauling them for a living.

Nobody asked that sort of question anymore, and Trailer was grateful for that. N-Day had some positive outcomes.

He had stumbled into being a guide afterwards. People were afraid to travel and with good cause. Nevertheless, there were fortunes to be made in trade. A box of light bulbs you found in your cellar could be traded for enough corn to feed your family for a month. Trailer's hulking frame and knowledge of the byways and roads meant he was a natural for his new career.

But it was dangerous. He had agreements with most of those who manned the tolls and roadblocks, but there were other dangers. Road gangs and militias still roamed about. He had barely avoided being conscripted into the WTR Army on several occasions. And then, you had to worry about getting scalped by Indians.

Who would have thought that would be a post-apocalyptic concern? he wondered.

He heard the slow *clop-clop* of a horse on the gravel ahead. Trailer held up his hand, and the man and boy behind him froze. Creeping forward around a bend in the road, Trailer saw a thickly built man leading a horse loaded down with wood. The man carried a worn ax over one shoulder.

The man stopped as well and stared at Trailer, his horse stomping tiredly behind him.

"You're a big one, ain't 'cha?" the man said, lifting the ax to hang down beside him.

"That's what they tell me," Trailer answered, resting both hands on the end of his own stout cudgel.

"You plannin' to rob me?" the man asked without apparent concern.

"Nope," answered Trailer. "Are you planning to rob me?"

"Shit," the man laughed. "Rob *you*? I couldn't even reach you. Besides, it don't look like you have much worth stealin'."

"Looks might be deceiving," Trailer added.

At that point, the pot-bellied man and boy pulled their handcart filled with valuable Kentucky tobacco up behind Trailer.

"Ah, I see. You a guide?"

Trailer nodded. "Anything up ahead I need to know about?"

The man spat and shook his head. "Open path. Tyler Creek flooded last week, but it's only marshy now. Anything up ahead I need to know about?"

"Just that Memphis is still smoked."

"Damn shame," the man said. "I used to love to go down to Beale Street for the blues and BBQ."

Trailer nodded. He missed those things as well.

"All right then," the man said, putting the ax back on his shoulder and tugging on the reins of his horse. He nodded at Trailer as he passed.

Trailer turned to look at the two beside their cart. "You're supposed to stay back when we meet anyone until I say it's safe."

The pot-bellied man guffawed. "We could tell it wasn't no highwayman. Just a woodcutter. As a matter of fact, we haven't seen much of anything of concern this entire trip. I'm starting to think we could have done this trip without you."

"Think what you want," said Trailer. "The payment is the same whether it's a milk run or we have to fight our way through."

"How far from the Border Market?"

"Couple of miles. Figure we'll find a place to camp once we get there. You should be able to sell that tobacco at a good price in one day. Then we can head back."

The man rubbed his face. "Yeah, I don't think we're going to need you on the way back."

They always think that, thought Trailer. *They see the path and think they know the way. I'll probably see their bodies in a ditch soon.*

"I'm not sure about that, paw," said the boy.

"You shut your mouth," the man said, and turned back to Trailer. "I'm still willing to pay you half of what we agreed to. That seems fair given that you'll only be taking us halfway."

"We had an agreement," said Trailer.

The man licked his lips nervously. "I'll give you two pounds of prime tobacco."

"You're not *giving* me shit," Trailer said. "I earned what I earned, and two pounds isn't enough."

"That's more than fair. Two pounds is half of the four we agreed to."

Trailer lifted up his cudgel and laid its tip on top of the cart's load of tobacco. "As impressed as I am by your superior math skills, we had a deal. It's not good business to go back on an agreement."

"But it should make no difference to you."

Trailer sighed. "The difference is that I have no business down here. My next job is up in the JP, bringing people down. Why should I walk north for no pay when I can walk north with you two for full pay?"

"Because we don't need you," the man said, lifting his chin.

Trailer fought the urge to crack the man's skull. The old Trailer, drunk and high on pills, wouldn't have hesitated, but those days were a distant memory.

Instead, he poked the man in the chest with the cudgel for affect. "I tell you what...you give me three pounds right now, and I'll walk away. We'll all be good."

"Three pounds? The full two-way trip only costs four."

"You should have been an accountant, my friend."

The man shook his head stubbornly. "I won't do it. Why should I?"

Trailer pushed forward on the cudgel, leaning the man back against the cart. "Because if you don't, I'm going to beat you senseless and take the whole lot."

"But that ain't fair!" the man wailed.

"You went back on our deal." Trailer smiled. "Believe me, you're getting off lucky. A lot of guides would kill you for that. You'll still make a huge profit and enjoy prosperity back home...presuming you make it back home."

The man hesitated for a few seconds, but then, with a curse, he turned and starting digging through the trailer. Finally, he turned back with several tightly packed bundles of dried tobacco and handed them over.

Trailer hefted them experimentally and found the weight satisfactory. He then lifted the bundles up to his nose and inhaled deeply. "Good stuff."

"Where will you go?" the boy asked.

Trailer turned to him with a smartass reply, but saw the boy was just curious. He had determined long ago that the lad was good-natured, but not playing with a full deck.

"Been thinking about that for the last minute," Trailer explained. "I learned as a driver you never want to make a trip with an empty load. In my line of work, that means going too far without someone to guide. Mississippi is probably the best bet to pick travelers up to take north. I hear the rice harvest has come in. Plenty of people will be wanting to go north to trade it."

The pot-bellied man looked at him in astonishment. "Tunica? You're going into that hell-hole? You're plain crazy."

The same thought had crossed Trailer's mind. After N-Day, most of the levies around the Mississippi River had broken with no one with the manpower, technology, or inclination to fix them. This had resulted in vast, shallowly flooded fields. Someone had gotten the idea to plant rice just as plantation farmers had in centuries past, and it had flourished. It wasn't long before Arkansas raiders were coming across the river to steal and murder from the fledgling communities. Soon after, strong warlords had moved in to take over the fields. They provided protection, at an extraordinary cost, to all the sharecropper farmers. These warlords and their retinue had grown wealthy off the rice and the backs of those they were protecting.

Tunica had since sprung up in the middle of these plantations as a hub of trade and vice. Gambling, prostitution, homemade alcohol, and drugs abounded, as well as unchecked violence. Trailer had been there before, but the experience had left its mark...literally. He rubbed at the knife scars on his arm. Trailer had thought he was going to die that night, and after escaping, he swore he would not go back. It was an oath he had planned to keep.

He also knew he would have to pay a 'toll' from his tobacco to the local sheriff right away to avoid any institutional trouble, but he didn't see any other good option. It was never easy to find a fare to guide, even in such a dangerous world.

Trailer pointed down the road they had been traveling. "Continue on this road for a quarter of a mile. When you get to a blacktop, turn left and follow it on into town. The market will be in the middle by the courthouse. Gives the guards at the town edge my name and they'll let you pass."

"You're leaving us?" the man asked.

"Good God, man," said Trailer in exasperation. "Isn't that what you wanted? What have we been talking about for the last ten minutes?"

"I said we didn't need you on the way back. You could at least take us the rest of the way in."

Smiling, Trailer shook his head. "I got places to be. Tunica is where I have to get to now, thanks to you. Besides, anyone who can make it from the Mississippi border back to the JP without a guide certainly doesn't need my help walking into a peaceful town."

"But we had a deal," the man protested.

Trailer laughed and turned his back on the two. He began walking back up the gravel road they had come. There was a trail up ahead that would cut over to the main state highway leading south and be much better time.

"Fuck you, nigger!" the bellied man screamed after him.

He just lifted his hand and waved behind him. It was good to see that some things didn't change, even after the apocalypse. The warm sun shined down on Trailer, and he began to whistle.

"Hey, mister," the boy called.

Trailer stopped and turned around to see both of them staring at him. The man with a red face, but the boy's calm and curious.

"Yeah?"

It took the boy a few seconds to spit out his questions. "How come you're not in the NBA?"

Trailer turned around and began cursing under his breath as he walked.

Chapter 3 – Letting Go

President Reggie Phillips could only stare in at the ravaged and partially burned WKPO studio. In the last months of Ethan Schweitzer's presidency-turned-dictatorship, he had ordered the radio station shut down. Evidently, those that executed his will had done so with a great deal of vigor.

What stunned him more than the sight of the station was the sight of Tim Reynolds, who had run the station for nearly twenty years. After N-Day, they had collaborated on weekly news broadcasts to calm residents and disseminate information. It had been a huge hit among the JP residents and even those outside their borders. Reggie had gotten to know Tim quite well and found him to be eternally positive, tireless, and with an ever-present smile upon his expressive face.

That was not the same Tim Reynolds he saw now.

The man was pale and gaunt, even in the dim light of the lantern in the dark room. Most of his hair had turned white, and Reggie was shocked when he caught a glimpse of them both in a shattered wall mirror. Both appeared to be the same age, even though Tim was two decades younger. Reggie had heard how Schweitzer ordered Tim hunted down and arrested after his unauthorized news broadcasts, but he hadn't fully understood the consequences.

"I apologize, Mister President," said Tim, fumbling with keyboard switches. His hands shook and recoiled from any surface they gingerly touched. It was obvious that the removed fingernails had not regrown properly and were a source of constant pain.

"Please don't apologize to me," Reggie said, fighting to keep his voice even. "It is I who should apologize to you."

Tim looked up in genuine surprise. "Whatever for?"

Reggie swallowed. "I believe I at least played a part in"—he pointed to the man's hands—"what happened to you."

The gaunt man looked at his hands in surprise and laughed nervously. "This was the least of it, believe me."

"That doesn't alleviate my guilt."

Tim nodded while looking at the floor. He was silent for a long time before looking back up. "It wasn't in either of our natures to keep quiet in the face of wrong; you were just smarter about getting away. Let's call that whole ordeal a learning experience for me."

"One you'd not like to repeat," said Reggie with a hint of smile.

Tim smiled back. "Nor talk about further if you don't mind."

"Of course. I'm sorry." Reggie drew himself up and looked around the studio. "Does this place even still work?"

"Sure, it needs some TLC, but the important parts have been repaired and are in good working order." Tim looked at his watch. "Let me go fire everything up, and we can get started at the top of the hour."

Reggie watched as the man slowly and carefully lifted himself out of the chair and walked out of the control room. He watched the man leave and then peered around at the small, shadowy space. Reggie had recognized and taken stock of people and things that had been lost, but he now realized there were likely many other rooms out there like this one and many other people like Tim. Those who had suffered the hardships of the past war and did what they could to carry the resultant scars with dignity.

His thoughts were interrupted by the sudden burst of electricity that until recently he had taken for granted. Now it bordered on magical. Nearly everyone had gotten into the habit of throwing their breakers when not actually using electrical devices.

Tim hobbled back in, and his appearance was even worse in the bright lights, something Reggie hadn't thought possible. Tim carefully extinguished the lantern.

"We can wait, you know. Are you sure you're ready for this?" asked Reggie, placing his hand over Tim's.

The man jerked his hand back from Reggie's with the speed of a startled animal. He panted with his hands held protectively near his chest. After a few seconds, he appeared to recover himself and attempted to smile.

"Seriously. This can wait. There hasn't been a broadcast in months. The people will wait another few days. More, I suspect."

Tim shook his head. "No. I thought about this in that dark, wet cell. All the things I would say and talk about once I got out. All the injustice I would expose and truth I would tell. That all seems so naive now. I'm just grateful to be here."

"I can understand where you are coming from. Things were pretty dark for a while."

"Yes, and this broadcast is redemption for you, Mister President. It tells the people that they do still have a say and it is their government." Tim paused in thought. "Maybe it's a redemption for all of us. At the very least, it signals a new start. I think what I'm trying to say is we all need this...even me."

"Then by all means"—Reggie nodded gravely—" let us proceed."

Tim picked up a prepared script and looked again at his watch. "We are really close on time. I can try and run through these with you quickly if you want."

Reggie shook his head. "Let's wing it. I trust you and believe we can play off each other. After all, this isn't our first time doing this."

The man grinned weakly. He stared at his watch and reached out to pull the microphone close. His hand shook wildly, and he clenched it into a fist.

"Are you sure?" asked Reggie.

Tim nodded and then pulled the microphone closer, putting on headphones and motioning for Reggie to do the same. He hesitated for a second more and then flipped a few switches. The broadcast light turned from red to green, and there was a quick hiss of static in the headphones.

The man sat frozen and silent.

Reggie leaned forward about to speak, but Tim held a flat palm out towards him. Tim closed his eyes and took several deep breaths. He then opened his eyes, smiled, and moved his face near the microphone.

"Good afternoon, citizens of the Jackson Purchase, West Tennessee Republic, Pennyrile Communities, and all you good people out there. This is Tim Reynolds of WKPO Radio, bringing you the *Voice of the Jackson Purchase*."

Reggie smiled and nodded to Tim approvingly.

31

The man turned to Reggie. "We have the pleasure today to welcome the President of the JP, Reggie Phillips, a man I for one am extremely happy to have back in that position. Welcome, Mister President."

"Thank you, Tim, and please just call me Reggie."

"Reggie it is. Why don't you start by giving the people a quick recap of what has happened over the last few months. Many of course know, but there are countless rumors and false stories floating around."

"Yes," said Reggie, coughing to clear his throat. Here it was, the elephant in the room. "As you know by now, the Second KenTen War ended recently with the death of Ethan Schweitzer, a man who illegally usurped the position of JP President."

"Yes, we're glad to see that bastard gone," said Tim. "And by death, you do mean blown to smithereens with a nuclear bomb?"

"It was a tactical nuclear device," Reggie admitted. "In fact, it was one of the devices Schweitzer tried to infiltrate into the JP in order to destroy Kentucky Dam and deprive us of electricity."

"Well, I'm grateful he's gone, but how do you respond to those who feel that David Taylor, the son of your Chief of Defense Nathan Taylor, sent his own son on a suicide mission? That seems pretty ruthless, even under the circumstances."

Reggie's lips tightened over the memory of his friend's grief. "Nathan Taylor had no knowledge of his son's plans, I can assure you. He was as surprised as the rest of us."

"I see," said Tim. "Some have said that David Taylor was out of control even before setting off the nuke, considering he was responsible for the Murray State bombing and even played a role in the Battle of

32

Fulton Massacre. How can someone like that be invested with authority?"

"I don't believe he was out of control. I believe he was a man trying to do what was right. You could even consider his actions selfless. Making tough decisions for the good of all. Let me remind you and everyone else, there were no easy choices in any of those cases."

"But a tactical nuke?" Tim asked. "Doesn't that seem extreme?"

Reggie felt his heart racing in anger and had to force himself to calm down. "We were beat. I was in hiding. Our delegation was in Fulton to present our surrender. If there had been any other option, we would have considered it. If David hadn't have done what he did, we would all still be under that madman's rule."

Tim started to ask another question and stopped when the microphone was roughly pulled away from his face by Reggie. The two stared at each other, and comprehension seemed to dawn on Tim's face. He reached out and pulled it back in front of him.

"I'm sorry, Reggie," Tim said more softly. "You are, of course, right, and I know that as well as anyone else. You could even say David Taylor's name should be added to that long list of honored dead who have fallen in the defense of this nation."

Reggie nodded. "I agree. I know people are upset about what he did, and frankly scared. We all lived through a nuclear apocalypse, and no one wants to ever experience that again. But David's actions saved us. I stand by that."

"Very good," said Tim. "Let's shift gears a little bit and talk about the upcoming elections."

"Well, as you all know I am actually filling the position of Interim President. Paul Campbell was the last elected JP President. He resigned that post to Ethan Schweitzer, now deceased. As no one has been able to locate Paul Campbell, I was asked by the Executive Council to fill in until elections can be held next month."

"I'm assuming you will be running?"

Reggie nodded. "I will. When I lost my last election, I had no intention of ever running again, but I still think there is work for me to do."

"It also does not appear anyone else is running against you," chuckled Tim.

"Currently, that is the situation, but there is still time for a candidate to add their name to the ballot."

Tim pulled out a piece of paper. "Even as Interim President, you have orchestrated an impressive series of actions: the Creek Nation Treaty, resettlement of Paducah, the agreement with the Pennyrile Communities, and the Fulton relief effort. And all of that during a particularly harsh winter that featured a number of electricity disruptions. I think you have done a particularly good job, but how would you respond to those critical of your executive order to grant full pardons to all those who collaborated under Ethan Schweitzer's regime as well as citizens of the WTR?"

"I believe in my heart that the vast majority of those people who were pardoned were not collaborators but victims. They were in a difficult position. To resist would have meant imprisonment or death for them and their families. The stories of those who passively resisted and helped our forces behind the scenes will in time become legend."

Tim looked troubled, and Reggie thought he was likely comparing his own recent circumstances with those who had not resisted or been imprisoned.

Reggie continued, "We also need to move beyond neighbor fighting neighbor. It is time for us to pull together. I am particularly concerned with several increasingly bloody feuds that have erupted between a number of families. I urge everyone to continue to rely upon the rule of law to settle disputes and not resort to violence. We are all in this together."

"How do you plan to respond to the continued refugee crisis and the growing violence from gangs, not just inside our borders but from across the Ohio and Mississippi Rivers?"

"It is all about defense," answered Reggie. "Refugees have been a part of our lives from day one and will continue to be so as long as we have it better than everyone else. It's a pretty good problem to have, and we should remember that we have benefited greatly by the influx of talents and knowledge that these refugees have brought. When refugees stop trying to get in, that's when it will be time to worry.

"Nathan Taylor, my Chief of Defense, has been working with the military forces and local sheriffs to try to curb violent gangs and brigands. We have a growing trade with our neighbors, but it cannot thrive until it is safe to travel the roads.

"As far as outside influences, we are working on that issue. Most of you likely know of our recent successful military campaign against the operating base of a group that called itself the Pirates of the Mississippi. This group has been raiding, murdering, and pillaging up and down the river unchecked for months; it is now destroyed. We are working on similar plans to curtail various groups who periodically cross into our borders."

Tim looked at Reggie and tapped his watch. "We are almost out of time. Is there anything else you would like to tell our listening audience?"

Reggie almost said 'no,' but the image of David Taylor came to mind. "Yes, I would. I would like to have a moment of silence for all of us to remember those who have fallen for our nation's sake since N-Day. Men like Clarence Anderson, Butch Matthews, Harold Buchannan, Jim Meeks, Doctor James Bryant, Timothy Brazen Walker, Beau Myers, Pastor Gary Lancourt and...David Taylor. I would like us to remember all who have suffered, especially those at Fulton and Paducah. Everyone has lost someone. Everyone, and no one is to blame. The only way forward is forward. Let us honor their memory by remembering them and building again...as they would want."

The silence dragged on as Tim looked at him. Reggie realized that a minute of silence on the transmitter meant a minute of unused electricity not only for the radio station but also for thousands of radios among thousands of home. Valuable electricity just leaking uselessly out into the air.

Not useless, thought Reggie. *It is an offering. This moment of silence means even more because everyone recognizes the cost. Let us hope we can let go and move forward.*

Tim cleared his throat. "Thank you, Mister President, and thank you listeners for your time. Please check back this same time next week. Until then, stay strong, my friends." He then flipped the broadcast switch, and the light went back to red. Tim immediately pulled the headphones off his head and walked out of the booth.

Reggie followed him downstairs and outside where Tim stood with his eyes closed and the sun on his face.

"You okay?" Reggie asked.

"Just needed to get out of there for a minute. Some bad memories came bubbling up, and I'm not real fond of small spaces anymore."

Reggie looked at the man and wanted to comfort him somehow. If it were someone else who hadn't endured such horrific abuse, he would have put an arm around them or at least given him a manly pat. It was hard for Reggie to stand there and do nothing.

"Do you really think people can just let go and move on?" Tim asked.

Reggie looked over and saw it wasn't a rhetorical question. The man was sincerely curious, and his face looked even tighter than before. "I do. It is the only way forward. All other paths lead to destruction and more death, I'm afraid."

Tim nodded minutely.

Reggie stepped around until he was in front of Tim. "You need to let go for your own sake, otherwise things are going to eat you up."

The man stared at him hard for several long seconds with hallow eyes. When he finally spoke, it was nearly a whisper.

"I'm trying."

Tim turned his back on Reggie and walked back into the radio station.

Chapter 4 - Tunica

Simon made his way northeast along roads he knew well. He had traveled most of them on the way to Site Conway nearly two years before. He wasn't sure how to get into the JP yet, but he had decided to start on familiar territory. When he had fled from his hometown of Tunica, Mississippi, its survivors had been like a warren of scared rabbits looking to the sky for the hawk. Simon wasn't judging; he had been one of those rabbits.

It had been easy for him to leave because there was nothing to keep him there anymore. He had in part at least left the army due to his ailing mother who died over a year before N-Day. Even if his mother had been as healthy as a goat, he knew he was not a good fit in the army. It had always been a means to an end. It had paid for his college degree in electronics engineering from Tulane University.

His first days in the army had been rather overwhelming. Simon had barely made it through Signal Officer Basic Course, not because he couldn't understand or grasp the concepts taught—there were plenty of others in that boat—no, he had almost been dismissed for his failure to bond with his fellow officers. Simon didn't intentionally set out to keep himself removed; he had simply never seen the need to bond with others.

Simon knew enough about psychological disorders to know he did not suffer from a psychopathy or some sort of disassociation disorder. He recognized and understood the feelings and worth of others. Simon did not believe himself some sort of superior being or want to harm others. He just liked being alone, and he had discovered for the most part the world was kind enough to oblige him...except in the army.

His first assignment had been in the 3rd Infantry Division at Fort Stewart, Georgia. As a signal officer, he was assigned to an infantry battalion where was incorrectly labeled as gay and correctly as antisocial. It hadn't mattered that he was good at his job and did all that was required of him; he didn't fit in and everyone could see it.

So it was with relief that Simon was informed by his superior officer that he was beginning chapter paperwork to separate him from the military under the ambiguous "failure to adapt" clause. His commander had informed him of all his rights to fight this decision, but Simon had eagerly waived said rights. When asked why by those few who still talked to him, he told them it was because of his sick mother, but truth be told, he felt like he was escaping a prison.

Simon froze on the highway. He thought he had heard something. After a tense minute, he realized it was just a rabbit in the brush. Several times during his journey, he had hidden along the side of the road as others passed. They may have been simply harmless travelers like himself, but even before N-Day, Simon would not have wanted to talk to them.

As he looked both ways again, he saw the small, octagonal, blue decal on the back of a road marker nearby. He had followed signs like this all the way to Site Conway. Signs with secret messages hidden in plain sight. Messages that he understood. There were few who did.

Simon had learned about the signs by happenstance. It was an annual army requirement that each combat brigade send one officer to the Continuity of Operations course at Cheyenne Mountain, Colorado. Since the course sounded lame and was classified so those that went could not talk about it, everyone assumed it was one of those meaningless military training requirements. Although Simon was getting out of the army, it took a few months to process his discharge, so his command decided to get some use out of him before then. Sending Simon kept them from having to lose one of their "real officers."

He had arrived at the reporting location on Fort Carson, Colorado with about a dozen other junior army officers. They all signed threatening non-disclosure agreements and were forced to give up their phones and cameras before being bused north.

The Cheyenne Mountain complex had been impressive, and Simon was fascinated with everything about the facility. Its huge blast doors designed to withstand a direct nuclear strike. Its football field-sized rooms sitting on concrete slabs supported by giant springs to withstand earthquakes. Its underground geothermal and hydroelectric systems. Everything about it had been designed to last...well, forever. But the point of the course wasn't to see this massive facility; it was to prepare them for the day when it would be needed.

No one knew when or if any such end would come along, but the U.S. Government believed in being prepared. Part of that meant having contingency plans should the United States suffer a series of debilitating nuclear strikes that decimated the national leadership. In such an occurrence, the remnants of the military were expected to get to one of dozens of giant secret bunkers spread across the country filled with weapons, supplies, vehicles, and everything else needed to carry on the good fight against terrorism, communist, or Martian aggression.

The problem was those remnants would not know where the bunkers were. No one could, other than a select few, otherwise those bunkers would also be targeted with nuclear strikes. So, in theory, every combat unit had at least one officer who could lead his unit to one of these locations.

When Simon and his new conspiratorial buddies left Cheyenne Mountain after several weeks, they hadn't known where the bunkers were either...but they knew how to find them and get into them. After his discharge from the army, he had promptly forgotten about the crazy contingency plan and gone about the business of making his dying mother's last days as comfortable as possible.

After she died, he had felt lonely for the first time he could remember. Simon floated around the family house, fiddling with electronics, and worked at a local Radio Shack to earn food and gas money, but he recognized that in essence he had become unmoored and was adrift in a world where he did not fit in. He supposed he would have gone on like this until he died, through natural or self-inflicted causes, if N-Day hadn't have happened. Those catastrophic events had seemed to clear the fog from his mind. Simon had rushed home, barricaded their house, collected supplies...and waited.

After N-Day, Simon had laid low for a week and then started looking for what he knew was out there. He rode his bicycle along packed highways, doing his best to avoid the throngs of panicked survivors. He gazed at the roadside light reflectors longingly. If he had the right type of encrypted radio from a combat unit, it would be easy to vector into one of the secret sites since those reflectors were actually tiny radio relay transmitters, but as a civilian, he no longer had access to such things. Simon was forced to look for the hidden signs.

He rode for several days along the left-hand side of the road instead of the right. Whoever had designed the Continuity Plan for National Continue the Fight had thought it made sense for the military to travel along the left side of the road instead of the right. Simon now realized that neither side would have worked very well since masses of survivors had taken to the roads after N-Day to get anywhere but where they were.

He had nearly fallen off his bike when he had seen the first sticker on the back of a road sign. It told him there would be another one nearby. A different color one told him to turn right, another to turn left. Soon he was off the highway and making his path down smaller and smaller roads until he found himself at the end of a dirt lane at the foot of a small mountain. An unassuming gate with a "No Trespassing" sign barred his way.

Simon had felt a moment of doubt then. Maybe there really wasn't anything here. Maybe it had all been a farce or budget cuts had cancelled the massively expensive doomsday bunkers. But then he had looked down and seen deep imprints of many wide tires. Recent imprints.

Why would semi trucks be coming down this road? he wondered and climbed over the locked gate.

Within a hundred yards, the path had become paved again and led to a concrete pad with several large pipes sticking up. Pipes for giant fuel tanks below ground.

He knew he was in the right spot.

It took him nearly an hour to find the entrance behind a tall hedge. There, a gray steel door without a handle greeted him. Nearby was a spin dial like on a bank vault under a metal plate that said, "Site Conway."

Simon chuckled. He had heard during the course that the man who established the sites had been a big fan of country music. He imagined there was likely a Site Waylon, Site Willie, and Site Johnny out there, along with many other first names of country music legends. As long as their name had exactly six letters.

He imagined an old telephone keypad with the letters on them. Conway corresponded to 26-69-29 which one might figure out was the combination if one were exceptionally clever. But the designers of the facilities had foreseen this and liked to change the combos regularly, monthly in fact. Since N-Day had been in the middle of August that meant that he would need to subtract 8—the number of the month— from each digit, making the combination 18-61-21.

Of course this would only work if whoever ran the facility had changed the combo as they were supposed to. If this combo didn't work, he could start working back by months, but after three wrong tries, he would be locked out for an hour before he could try again.

"It's not like I'm in a hurry to get anywhere else," he had told himself and began to spin the combination dial. He was surprised when the combo stopped showing numbers and instead said OP, and the door clicked electrically, opening the heavy door a fraction of an inch. Simon had slipped his fingers in the opening and pulled the door open. Inside was a small sterile room lit by an emergency light. There was another door on the opposite wall and this time an electric punch keypad.

He knew from the training course that this was mantrap and that the opposite door could not be opened unless the door he had just pulled wide was secured. The danger was that if someone inside did not want him to enter, they could prevent it. Actually, they could seal both doors, locking him inside until he died of dehydration or lack of oxygen.

Simon looked up towards the ceiling and saw a camera there. He almost waved but did not know if anyone was watching or even if those potential watchers were receptive to friendly waves.

What if I lock the vault door and am then trapped in here? He examined the inside of the door and saw a handle to pull it shut behind him, but no mechanism for opening the vault door. *Going out must be controlled from inside*, he realized.

After a few minutes of deliberation, he pulled the massive vault door shut behind him, flinching at the heavy boom sealing him inside the small room. Simon walked over to the keypad. He knew this one would only open with five numbers which were randomly assigned to the digital buttons when he pressed the square marked START. Unlike the outer door, this combination was specific to him alone.

Simon thought back to the course. They had been instructed to pick a five-digit combination that they were unlikely to forget. Supposedly, those numbers had then been entered into a secret database that controlled entry and exit from these facilities. Someone, somewhere was likely supposed to delete Simon's combination once he left the military. In fact, they might have done so. Or forgot to upload it to begin with.

Just try it, he told himself. Simon hit the START button, and a standard ten-digit keypad appeared, but with the numbers scrambled. He had punched in the five-digit code from years before without effort: 38676. It was Tunica's zip code.

The keypad beeped, and the door in front of him clicked. Simon pushed open the door and stepped inside. Heavy springs on the door pulled it shut automatically behind him.

The first thing he noticed was how cool it was inside. Either the facility went deep underground and cooler air drifted up, or they had the air conditioning working overtime. The next thing he noticed was a heavy, not unpleasant smell of machine oil and grease. Dim light drifted towards him from down a narrow hallway.

"Thank the Lord that stopped," an unseen voice said from the other end of the hallway. "I don't know what was causing that confounded alarm, but I'm glad it finally stopped."

Simon walked carefully down the hallway past closets and small rooms on either side.

"It must have meant something though," said another voice. "Alarms don't go off in this place for no reason."

Simon peeked around a corner into a small control room from the hallway. Three men in nearly identical gray coveralls stared at a control panel with what looked like millions of lights, dials, and switches.

"It went off because you had someone coming inside from the outer door," Simon said as he stepped into a larger room with the three surprised men.

45

They all spun in his direction and stared at him. One of the men that Simon soon came to know as Derek reached down frantically to his hip. When he didn't find what he wanted, he looked down and began to pad himself.

"Goddammit!" Derek yelled. "I took my pistol off when I went to take a shit."

The other two men looked at him and then at each other before turning back to Simon, who held out his hands in front of him.

"You're not going to need a gun. Not for me."

"Good, get the hell out," said the Derek, with obvious trust issues.

Simon shook his head. "I can't do that. I'm here as part of the Continuity of Operations Plan. I'm supposed to be here."

"See, I told you," said the man Simon would soon learn was named Lewis. "Eventually, someone would show up."

"You got more with you outside?" asked Derek, his eyes narrow.

Simon shook his head. "It's just me."

The first man stared at him silently, his jaw working. "You aren't supposed to be here, are you?" he finally said.

There was a squeal of small girl several rooms away.

"Damnit, Austin, tell your woman to keep those kids out of sight. We're dealing with a situation here."

Austin left the other men and walked past Simon further down the hallway. Sounds of other children playing could be heard.

Derek turned back to Simon. "Tell us the truth. You'd be here with more people if you were official."

"No," answered Simon. "I'm no more supposed to be here than they are." He pointed in the direction of the children.

It had taken some convincing, but eventually, they had allowed him to stay. It had helped that he could get most of their electronic surveillance cameras to work as well as re-establishing the communications links. Although they had never really become close, over many months, Simon had gotten to the point he felt comfortable around his fellow Site Conway inhabitants.

And now they've voted you the one to pursue a dangerous, possibly suicidal mission, alone.

Simon pushed down the sense of sadness this thought brought forth. He continued to trudge along abandoned highways, sleeping in abandoned cars, eating MREs, and drinking water using the pump filter from the bunker. He also carried an assault rifle, which he knew how to use from his time in the army, but he couldn't imagine himself actually firing at anyone.

He began to see vast lakes of shallow water being worked by a multitude of thin figures bending down into the ankle-deep water. Here and there, men on horseback with rifles watched over them. Simon instinctually made sure to avoid these people as much as he could. After a week, he was walking through the burned-out neighborhoods where he had once lived.

Simon stopped on the sooty street and stared up at the only home he could ever remember. It had been a modest Tudor home his dad had bought before dying in an accident at the electric company. He and his mother had taken care of each other there. This had been their refuge from the world and its people.

Now it was nothing but a burned-out husk.

Turning away, Simon continued walking towards what had once been the center of town. He saw more and more people, but his rifle seemed to give them a reason to keep their distance. Almost suddenly, he found himself on a busy and dirty street. Laughter and music wafted out of open windows and doorways. Small tables lined much of the street, selling everything from half-rotten potatoes to compact music disks. Abandoned cars sat where they had obviously sat since running out of fuel shortly after N-Day.

He remembered this street as being wide, straight, and stately. The town's courthouse sat at the end of the lane, and as a youngster, Simon had thought it as grand as the Lincoln Memorial. Now it looked like a tacky garish prop against all the filth, discord, and bustling humanity.

Simon stopped and fought the urge to go back to Site Conway. He could do it, he realized. Despite sending him out, they would let him back in, even if they did think him weird. But what would happen when the fuel all went bad?

"What you looking for?" asked a voice nearby.

Simon turned to find a small man in a dirty apron leaning heavily on one crutch. "Excuse me?"

The man shrugged. "What you looking for, young fella? You obvious want something. Ain't seen you here before, so what brings you to Tunica? You want to buy rice or salt?" His eyes got a mischievous look. "Or maybe it's something else. Young man like you is looking for a nice piece of ass I bet? Maybe some booze or weed to go along with it?"

"No," answered Simon, taken aback. "I'm trying to get to the JP."

The man laughed. "Hell, ain't we all. That's the promised land. They got electricity; still comes out of the walls, they say. Trouble is, you need a guide to get you there, and even if you make it without losing you balls or your scalp, they won't let you in."

"Why not?"

"Because you ain't a JP citizen, are ya'?"

Simon shook his head.

"There you have it. Might as well enjoy yourself while you're here. Everybody does." The man looked him up and down. "You just tell Ole Jonesy what you need, and I'll make sure you get it. Best deals for my new friend."

"Where would I find a guide to the JP?"

The man smiled again and couldn't stop looking at Simon's rifle. Finally, he pointed up the street. "Go into Miller's Hardware. It's not a hardware store anymore."

"What is it now?"

"You'll find out. Just go in there and ask for Tiny and Coon. They don't look like much, but those boys are the best guides you're likely to find, mark my words."

Simon nodded. "Thank you kindly. I appreciate it." He reached into his pack and handed the man an MRE. "For you help."

The man's face had become slack. He reached out and snatched the MRE away and hid it under his baggy shirt so fast it looked to Simon like a magic trick. He then looked around to see if anyone had seen before turning back to Simon. "Where'd you get that?"

"Just found it, that's all."

"Got any more of them?"

Simon shrugged. "Thanks again. Tiny and Coon, you say?"

Ole Jonesy nodded and gave him the biggest friendliest smile Simon could remember seeing.

Simon turned and began walking down the street.

The smile vanished off the man's face and was replaced by a look that would have given Simon pause if he had seen it. Jonesy lifted the crutch from under his arm and ran around to an alley that bordered the rear of all the shops on the street.

He reckoned he needed to talk to Tiny and Coon before that rube did. He wanted to make sure he got his fair cut.

Chapter 5 – Vision in the Flames

Susan hesitantly approached the old camper sitting by the river like a giant abandoned toy. Billy Fox stood outside smoking a home-rolled cigarette. He looked as nervous as she felt, but he nodded to her agreeably enough as she approached.

"He's been asking for you," Billy said.

"I'm sorry, one of the pregnant mares was breech. Stayed to help."

"Healthy foal?"

Susan nodded. "Our herds are growing. This place agrees with them."

"I like how you say 'our herds.' You wouldn't have done that when we started this journey."

She stared at him levelly. "Jasper and I have been accepted into the tribe. We're Creek now. I took that at face value. This is our home now too, isn't it?"

Billy Fox nodded and tossed his cigarette into the river. "It is, but it's good to hear you say it."

"How's Chicoca?"

He tilted his head toward the camper. "Dying...still. Taking his sweet time about it, but doesn't seem to be in much pain. Sleeps more and more as the end gets near."

"That's good at least."

Billy put his hand on her arm. "He's dying at peace. None of us ever thought we would make it back here, especially after World War Three. We gave that to him. *You* gave that to him."

Susan started to reply, but a young brave stepped out of the camper and looked at them with a look that was both murderous and calm. A look Susan had learned to associate with the Creek when they were trying to be respectful or polite. "He's awake."

"Come on," said Billy. "Not sure how much more awake time he has left."

Hesitating, Susan followed him inside, stepping up the thin stairs. She was not a stranger to death, but didn't like it all the same. Expecting the worst, and picturing her parents' last days in an intensive care ward, she was pleasantly surprised.

The windows and curtains were open so a gentle breeze ruffled the wildflowers arranged in glass jars around the old man. Warm sunlight rested on his parchment skin, and thin ribbons of incense smoke drifted lazily through the air.

"Come," whispered Chicoca to Susan, and his eyes indicated the chair beside him.

She moved forward carefully and slid down into the seat beside him, being careful not to touch anything. Chicoca looked so fragile that she was afraid any impact on her part would scatter the remaining life force within him like a house of cards. Even a floorboard creak might make one of the old man's body parts fall off.

"Don't look so afraid, child. It's just death," said Chicoca. "You have been through much worse than this."

Susan tried to smile. "This is not a good time for you to leave us. What about the Creek? Who will lead them?"

"Billy here will, just like he has been," said Chicoca. "He is the chief. I am just his advisor."

"You are more than that," said Billy.

"At times, that is true. Other times, I have been even less than an advisor. I am whatever the people need me to be."

"But who will take over once you...are no longer here?" Susan asked.

The old man reached out and took her hand in his. "You will, Susan. You will be their prophetess. You will give them wisdom and understanding in the uncertain days ahead."

Susan pulled away and stood, shaking her head. She finally laughed. "Thank you, but I think you've got this wrong. I'm not even a Creek."

"I thought we just established that you were," said Billy.

"You know what I mean," said Susan, not taking her eyes off Chicoca. "Besides, I'm a woman. Will all these braves listen to me?"

"Of course they will," said Chicoca. "We are not as male chauvinist as you take us to be. My predecessor was a woman and a better guide than I. How she would have loved to see this day."

Susan looked back and forth between the old man and Billy. "This doesn't make sense. There are thousands of Creek out there and you're telling me *I'm* the best person for this job?"

"You have something none of them have," said Chicoca.

She felt like crying now. "What, guilt? That feeling of pushing the button that ended the world?"

"The world is still here, just moved on," answered Chicoca gently. "If you had not pushed that button, the Creek may never have regained their homeland. It was a terrible thing, and you will carry that burden all your days. That burden gives you wisdom."

"That's all it takes to be the wise man…person of the Creek Nation?"

"No." He smiled. "There are plenty here with their own burdens. You must be our guide because you have the gift of prophecy."

Susan sighed and dropped her head. "You know that's not true. I told you I made up the stuff about the fire in the west and it being a sign to stop making war. I just wanted to stop the bloodshed."

"And I believe you, but you have the gift nevertheless."

"Well, shouldn't I see visions or something?"

"Maybe, but the Creek believe that a prophet's primary gift is the ability to see a wise and safe path through the dangerous forest of uncertainty ahead."

Susan threw her hands up in exasperation. "What do I know?"

"You brought us here, didn't you?"

"Me? It was your damn Red Sticks story that did it. Tecumseh and all that. Speaking of which, I can't do your job because I don't know all the stories. You'll need to find someone else."

Chicoca sighed and closed his eyes. "There are plenty who know the old stories. You will live new ones."

"It is what he *wants*," said Billy, staring at her with a hard look.

Susan sighed. "Is there some sort of initiation or something?"

Chicoca nodded. "You ever see *A Man Called Horse*?"

Susan's eyes got wide. "You mean the movie where they put ropes through his chest and lifted him up off the ground?"

"Yeah, it will be nothing like that."

"Thanks."

"Now, I'm afraid I must rest," Chicoca said, closing his eyes.

Billy gently grabbed her arm. "We should go."

She resisted looking at Chicoca. "Are you afraid?"

He opened his eyes to peer at her. "Afraid of what?"

"Dying?"

The old man closed his eyes again. "I am afraid of many things, but dying is not one of them. I know I am soon going to see my friends and family and ancestors that have gone on before me. You should know by now that this is not the only world there is." His breathing slowed, and his chest rose and fell.

She turned and followed Billy towards the exit.

"Susan Who Guides the Creek," a faint voice said behind her.

Susan turned to see he had opened his eyes once more.

"You will not see me again in this life, but know that I will be watching you." He then closed his eyes for the last time.

They walked outside into the warm sunshine.

****

Cremation had gone out of style with the Creek hundreds of years before, but Chicoca had asked to be buried the old way. His body would be burned on a giant pier at sunrise and then his ashes collected to be scattered to the Four Winds at sunset. The entire Creek Nation would gather around and not eat or drink anything during this time. They would honor him and witness his soul moving on to the afterlife.

Susan stood watching. Any further talk about her not complying with Chicoca's wishes regarding her new role had been met with silence. It was one thing to humor an old man's crazy ideas so that he could die in peace. It was quite another to go through with those crazy ideas after he was gone. She had wanted to scream at Billy and the other leaders in frustration, but knew it would do no good. They would adhere to Chicoca's dying wishes, no matter how idiotic they were and even if it got all of them killed.

Maybe it was really all about guiding them through potential dangers ahead, she thought. Maybe this whole prophetess business was nothing more than an advisor who specialized in contingency planning. She had learned such things in the Air Force and could certainly introduce some flow charts and graph diagrams at the next tribal meeting.

She felt her head grow light and swayed in the sun. Little Lion had at some point come up beside her, and now took Susan's hand to steady her. She looked down at the little girl in gratitude and smiled.

The sun was nearly straight up in the sky by now, and Chicoca's remains smoldered. Smoke billowed in the soft wind, sometimes blowing in Susan's face. She tried not to cough, but shuddered thinking that she was likely inhaling part of the old man's ashes. In fact, everyone there probably was. Maybe in some way that was the point of the ceremony.

She heard a strange sound from the bier. It was that of fire, but somehow different, bad in some indescribable way. Staring at the smoke and fire, Susan imagined she saw swirling shapes and figures. A face here and horse there. Figures running...and screaming.

Susan shook her head and looked around. The faces remained solemn, but none appeared to be seeing what she was seeing. She gazed up at the sun and wondering if she were suffering from heatstroke.

A series of soft pops drew her attention back to the fire, and there through hazy smoke, she saw a blackened field coved in bodies. The sky was darkly overcast, and pitiful figures walked through the dead landscape. Dogs and crows fed on the mounds of dead. Fighting in the distance could be heard faintly, and bodies floated downstream and piled up at a bend in the mighty river beside an abandoned camper.

She didn't feel herself strike the ground, but heard voices from far away. Water was pressed to her lips, and the sun was blotted out as others stood over her.

"Give her some space," said Billy Fox, coming close. After most had stepped back, he knelt down close beside her. "You saw something in the fire. What did you see?" he asked in a whisper.

Susan shook her head and looked away.

"Tell me," he insisted. "What was it?"

"Death," she rasped, and a tear trickled from the corner of her eye.

"Whose?"

Susan looked around at the concerned Creek faces. "Everyone's."

Chapter 6 – The Deal

Horace Trailer Smiley sat with his back in a corner, carefully watching the other miscreants like him who filled the room. Places like this were why he didn't come to Tunica until forced by circumstances. The room was filled with violent and desperate people, either stoned or drunk, and all of them were certainly still living in a state of shock. Many things could happen here, and hardly any of them were good.

Despite his misgivings, Trailer knew this was where he needed to be to get work. He could have gone back north without a fare, but being a guide had a very tight profit margin. Showing up at a toll without enough bribe money was likely worse than encountering trouble in this particular cornucopia of misdeeds.

He took a sip of the homemade beer they brewed in this particular hardware store turned bar/brothel/gambling den and regretted the decision immediately. Trailer had drunk a good deal of homemade beer in the last two years. Very little of it had been what a sane person would call good, but what he was drinking tasted so bad it made his stomach seize and his teeth lock down in revolt.

Trailer kept watch on several people around him. He had learned the hard way to distinguish between the blowhards and the genuine murderers. The key was often in their eyes and their hands when they thought no one was looking. The small weasel-looking man across the room that Trailer was watching now kept looking at a whore engaged with another man, but his hands were locked together near his waist, obviously imagining himself chocking her to death.

What the hell happened to the world? he thought. *Maybe we would have been better off if those nukes had just wiped us all off the face of the planet.*

He had put the word out in all the usual places that a guide was available to take people north for a fair price. No one had approached him yet, but he knew these things often took time. Trailer was prepared to sit there all night if need be, but had decided he would milk his current beer until he left. One of those bad boys was enough to last a lifetime.

Two scoundrels he had been watching earlier stopped their intense drinking to talk to a small man who appeared to have come in the back entrance. A giant goon mostly listened while the small mousey man with long hair did all the talking and asked questions of the newcomer. Trailer thought that if John Steinbeck had seen these two, he would have instantly pegged them as George and Lenny from *Of Mice and Men*. The conversation was tense, then confrontational, then cordial, and finally friendly. All shook hands, and the man vanished out the back of the bar.

Something tells me that conversation is going to lead to more evil in the world.

A small girl with an empty tray walked over to Trailer and pointed at his still mostly full mug. "You want another?"

"Good Lord, no! Are you trying to kill me, girl?"

She put her hands on her hips and frowned at him. "Whatever. I was just asking." She then turned and stomped away.

Trailer noticed that George and Lenny had stopped drinking and were now both watching the front door. Whatever was going to happen would happen soon.

Within a few minutes, a strikingly clean fellow wearing nearly new clothes walked in and looked around as if he was lost. Nearly every eye in the establishment turned in his direction. It wasn't just his appearance that drew attention; it was the assault rifle he carried casually over one shoulder, as if he were headed down to the river to plink cans. Anyone with a weapon like that now knew to keep it hidden or in both hands ready to defend its possession.

Mister Man Out of Time and Place finally asked a nearby drunk a question. The drunk pointed over to George and Lenny, and the man thanked the drunk politely.

Where in the hell did this cat come from? Trailer wondered.

The man walked over to George and Lenny with a pleasant yet naïve smile on his face and spoke in a far too loud a voice. "Hello, gentlemen, my name is Simon. Ole Jonesy outside said I should talk to you two about guiding me north into the JP." He turned to Lenny. "I presume you are Tiny," and then up to George, "and you are Coon?"

"You'd presume wrong," said the smaller man. "I'm Coon and the big guy's Tiny."

Simon looked confused and thrown off his obviously prepared spiel.

"The name is ironical," hollered out Trailer helpfully.

All three turned in his direction, sizing up his massive frame.

60

"Mind your own damn business," said Coon, before turning back to Simon. "The roads up to the JP are dangerous and long. You got a way to pay?"

"I do," said Simon and started to pull his pack off his shoulder, but Coon stopped him.

"That's good, but not here. This place is full of thieves and murderers."

Trailer laughed. "He's not lying."

Coon pointed a finger at Trailer. "I told you to mind you own damn business."

"What? I'm sorry I didn't hear you."

"I said, mind your bus—" the long-haired man began to threaten.

"Still can't hear you. I'm really sorry, ma'am, but I have to say you're the prettiest girl in this place. How much for a blowjob?"

Several drunks around the room laughed, but Coon only got red and started to shake. He slapped Tiny on the arm and strode over to Trailer, Tiny close behind him.

"Say that again."

Trailer looked at the small man and smiled. "Damn, you've got a pretty mouth, too. I bet you make a killing in here sucking all these boys off."

Coon reached behind his back and pulled out a small revolver. Tiny looked surprised and then reached around to his back and pulled out a larger automatic.

"You're a dead man."

Trailer held his hands out in front of him. "There has obviously been a mistake. I apologize, blowjobs are obviously not your specialty. What services *do* you provide a lonely cowboy?"

Coon was shaking his head and was so angry there were tears in his eyes. "You messed up, coon. You messed up bad."

"Wait, I thought *your* name was Coon?"

"Let's everyone settle down now," said a commanding voice from behind them. They all looked behind them to see the bartender in an apron holding a shotgun in their direction.

"Put you guns away," the bartender said. "You can do whatever you want to each other once you leave my place, but I don't want any blood on my floors, you understand? Take it out into the street if you really need to."

Coon slowly slid his pistol back into the back of his pants. He nodded to Tiny, who did the same. Coon then looked at Trailer and smiled. "We're not done here."

"Looking forward to it," said Trailer. "Let me know when you get a break from sucking on scrotums. We'll hook up."

Coon and Tiny walked back over to their normal spot and began to drink even more heavily than before.

"You too, big man," said the bartender.

Trailer smiled innocently and put the large automatic pistol that had been resting in his lap under the table back in his thigh holster.

The bartender lowered the shotgun. "Remember, not in my bar, but it wouldn't break my heart if something happened to those two." He then turned and went back behind the long makeshift counter made from old wooden pallets.

Simon stood still in the middle of the room, evidently forgotten by Coon and Tiny in their rage and plans for vengeance against Trailer.

"Hey, Mister Clean," called out Trailer.

Simon looked over, startled, and actually pointed at himself.

"Yes, you see anyone else in here that doesn't look like they've lived out of a trash heap for the last decade?"

"Uh, what?"

Trailer kicked one of the chairs at his table out. "Come on, have a seat."

Simon backed away a little. "I'm not sure that is such a good idea."

"Actually it's the best option you got going right now. You do know those two clowns were getting ready to take you out back, slit your throat, and walk away with all you stuff?"

Simon's head snapped around to look at the two speed-drinking fellows. "But Ole Jonesy—"

"Came in here a few minutes before you arrived to make a deal with them. You were set up, my naive little babe in the woods friend."

Simon still looked confused. "Then why did you...?"

"Because, unlike those two turds, I actually *am* a guide. Taken people north plenty of times, and you look like you can pay."

Hesitating a few seconds more, Simon walked over slowly and sat in the chair on its front edge, not bothering to take his pack off.

"Want a beer?" Trailer asked.

Simon shook his head. "I don't drink."

"Well, you can't drink the water around here; it'll give you the grips. Gotta be something fermented." He waved for the girl who had offered him another beer earlier. "One more over here, dear."

"Who are you anyway?" Simon asked.

"My apologies. Name's Horace, but everyone calls me Trailer."

Simon gingerly reached out to accept the big man's handshake.

The girl came back and set a mug of beer down hard enough that it bounced. "I wish you'd make up your goddamn mind."

"Thank you," yelled Trailer after her before turning to Simon. "What a sweetheart. Main reason I come here."

Simon stared in horror at the glass before him. It appeared there were bits of leaves and newspaper floating in a liquid the color of old urine. "I really don't want this."

"Go on anyway," said Trailer. "Consider it a test. Will tell me if you are a man to be taken seriously."

Simon gingerly picked up the mug and placed the dirty glass to his lips. He then tilted the mug back and allowed a long swallow to go down his throat. He immediately slammed the mug back down and started coughing and retching.

"Oh, that's terrible! How can anyone drink that?"

Trailer nodded approvingly. "Okay, you passed. So tell me how you plan on paying to get north."

Simon looked suspicious. "How do I know you're not going to rob and murder me?"

"Now you've got the right attitude. Well done. You don't, to answer your question, but that's the same position you're going to be in with any guide you pick. It's not exactly like you can go to the Better Business Bureau and check out my references. Now tell me...don't show me...what you got."

He looked around, obviously thinking through his situation. Finally, Simon sighed. "I got batteries."

"Not dead ones, I'm presuming?"

"No, even got a battery meter to verify."

"What sizes?"

"D's, C's, and lots of double A's. Better yet, they're rechargeable, and I got chargers, too."

"Seriously?"

Simon nodded. "How many will it cost me to go to the JP?"

"First, I can't guarantee they'll let you in the JP, I can only get you there. Second, it'll cost all your batteries."

"All of them? I thought batteries were super valuable."

Trailer nodded and sat back. "I'm guessing you've got plenty more where those came from. Consider it me doing you a favor. Batteries are heavy; you don't want to be carrying them around."

Simon considered for a moment. "Okay, I guess."

"No, damnit," said Trailer. "You're supposed to negotiate. I name a price, you offer half, and we meet somewhere in the middle. Where have you been the last two years, living in a hole?"

"Okay, half the batteries."

"Too late. I now know you'll give me all of them. You'll need to provide them before we start."

"Give them to you now or outside?"

Trailer sighed heavily and shook his head. "You are one lucky bastard to find me. Don't ever give anyone the full payment upfront. What would keep me from running off after you paid me? Half upfront

65

and half when the job is done. And keep an eye on them in case I try to pick your pocket."

"I think if you were trying to rob me you wouldn't have told me those things."

"Maybe I'm just not a very good thief, you ever think of that? Looking to turn my luck around with you."

Simon looked like he wasn't sure if he wanted to stay or go. "So...I should trust you or not?"

"You shouldn't trust anybody; haven't you been listening? Also, hide that damn assault rifle; you're drawing stares."

After breaking down the rifle into two parts and stuffing them in his pack, Simon sat back up and looked at Trailer's massive form. "What now?"

Trailer took a small sip of his beer and grimaced. "I wait here until tomorrow and see if anyone else needs to go north. We'll get started at first light."

Simon looked outside and saw with dismay it was getting dark. "Is there a working hotel around here anywhere?"

Slapping an enormous hand against his forehead, Trailer groaned. "Just follow me. I'll show you a place where we can bed down for the night without getting sodomized or eaten by mutant bedbugs."

A thin shaven-headed man with tattoos on his neck and arm walked in and looked around. A small dark-haired girl followed in slowly behind him. He locked eyes with Trailer and stepped forward. "You the guide?"

"I am. You need to go north?"

The man turned to point at the girl. "My daughter here does."

"What for?"

"That's my business, ain't it?"

Trailer shrugged. "You're right. See you later."

The man frowned for several long moments. "She'll be taking a load of our rice north. I've heard they trade there for tobacco or salt."

"Aren't you supposed to only sell your rice here at the co-op? Does your landlord know about this?"

The man's face turned red, and he fists clinched.

"Relax," said Trailer. "It's nothing to me; just like to know what's going on. I'll take her north and back for a tenth of what you trade for."

"A tenth? Half of that at most."

Trailer looked at Simon and pointed approvingly at the man. "See, that's how you negotiate." He turned back to him. "Normally, I would counter-offer, but I'm in a generous mood. One twentieth is satisfactory. We'll leave tomorrow morning."

The man nodded. "Where should she meet you?"

"In front of the town courthouse at dawn." Trailer looked at the woman behind the tattooed man he had initially mistaken for a girl. "It's a dangerous trip at times. You sure you want to send your daughter?"

He yanked her roughly forward. "She's tougher than she looks."

Trailer gazed at the man's arm that had come uncovered when he pulled the girl forward. In addition to the other tattoos, there was a large Nazi swastika. He pointed at it. "Is that going to be a problem?"

Looking down at the tattoo as if he had forgotten it was there, the man shrugged. "Not anymore. I still don't care for the darkies, but you treat me fair, I'll do the same with you."

"I like it." Trailer smiled. "Interracial harmony, right here in Tunica."

"Let's not push it," the man said.

Trailer laughed. "Right, anyway, have her at the courthouse at dawn." He turned to the woman. "Wear good boots. We're going to walk a lot. Pack for hot days and cold nights and maybe a little rain. We'll find water and trade for food along the way, so don't worry about that. You got any questions, darling?"

"No, she don't," said the man, pulling her close to him. When he did, Trailer could see old and new bruises along her arms.

"All right then," said Trailer, turning away from them and picking up his beer again.

The man walked out, dragging the woman behind him. Just before she left the room, Simon locked gazes with her and realized just how deep and dark her eyes were. They were the sort of eyes that made him forget the squalor around him.

"I agree," said Trailer. "She's hot."

"Excuse me?"

"Oh, nothing."

They sat silently for about an hour before Coon and Tiny walked out the front of the bar without looking at their table. Trailer killed his beer in one long gulp and then stood.

"Order me another beer," he told Simon while picking up the large wooden cudgel leaning against the wall.

"Wait, I'm staying here?"

"You'll be okay now with those two gone," Trailer said. "I'll be right back, and then we can see about getting some shuteye...after I finish my beer of course."

"But where are you going?" Simon asked.

Trailer smiled and nodded his head out the door. "Those two promised me this wasn't over and I believe them. They've been working on a plan for the last hour and are now just drunk enough to think it will work."

"What plan?"

"To spring an ambush for me when I walk out of here tonight."

Simon looked towards the back door leading to the alley. "We could go out a different way, avoid them."

"Now why would I do that when I have the opportunity to do the rest of humanity a solid by getting those two off my planet? Besides, I don't want us looking over our shoulders the whole way north."

"Okay, I guess."

"Stay here," said Trailer, walking towards the front door, swinging the massive cudgel lightly. "And don't drink my beer."

He ducked his head, and he went out into the night.

Chapter 7 – Razor's Edge

"I have to say I'm impressed," said Nathan.

"At what?" asked Reggie without looking at him.

"Your ability to handle a horse and buggy. When you invited me to ride with you to the Executive Council Meeting in Paducah, I didn't imagine it would be like this."

Reggie smiled and flicked the small whip near the flank of a sleek horse. "How do you normally get around?"

"Bike mostly. Sometimes horse."

"So, not by car, I take it?"

Nathan shook his head. "It's getting too hard to find gasoline. What little we have we want to save for emergency situations. Besides, that's the security for our currency. Many people still don't trust it, but JP dollars are getting more popular."

"Too bad we didn't have any electric cars before N-Day. We could have charged them from the dam's electricity."

"Lots of people are still using their golf carts, but they're rather slow and best on level ground."

They were silent again and watched the wide fields around them. Farmers were just getting out to plow fields. There were a few tractors, but most of the plowing was now done by hand with horses and tackle obtained from the Mennonites.

"I was worried there for a while," Reggie said. "Wasn't sure we would make it through the winter without things breaking down."

"I don't think it was comfortable for anyone."

"It never has been, except for the last hundred years or so," Reggie said. "Between harvest and spring most people in the western world practiced a near-starvation diet. Stayed indoors and slept in a sort of semi-hibernation in order to burn as few calories as possible and survive until the snow and ice broke."

"That may be our future," Nathan said, looking around. He turned to Reggie. "I heard your broadcast."

Reggie's smile slipped away. "I'm sorry about the David talk. Tim didn't mean—"

"I know. Tim has been through a great deal. If we had psychiatrists anymore, he would likely need to be admitted for trauma recovery."

"Maybe not just him."

Nathan leaned back on the wooden seat. "He was only repeating what others are thinking. In a way, it was good to get it out there. What you said meant a lot to Bethany and me. Thank you."

"You don't have to thank me. I only said what I thought."

Nathan leaned forward again. "Yes, I do. Not just for that, but for everything. There are still a lot of people who look at us as outsiders."

"Damn fools, don't listen to them."

"I don't, and that's not my point. You've been like family to us, and we appreciate it. Just wanted to tell you."

Reggie snapped the reins on the mare's flanks, as they were climbing a small hill. "Sounds like you've been a bit introspective lately."

"Between David and little baby River, I've had cause to be. Not counting all the other normal craziness that evidently isn't unique to living in the end times. I'm also worried about Bethany."

"She okay?"

Nathan shrugged. "Hard to tell. She says she's okay, but I'm not so sure. She seems so tired and lethargic all the time."

"She has cause to be on many fronts. Maybe give her some time and have one of the doctors take a look at her. She could be suffering from some complication from the birth. None of us are spring chickens anymore."

"True. Speaking of none of us being young anymore, you know this meeting is going to be a rough one, right?"

Reggie nodded. "I hate to say it, but David setting off that nuke really shook everyone. I'm saying that knowing it was the right thing and was a selfless act that saved countless lives, but not everyone feels that way. Plenty of people have relatives down there, and Hickman and Fulton Counties have suffered some radiation effects. I'm not even going to go into the problems with the West Tennessee Republic."

"That's something we need to figure out as well," said Nathan. "We need to either rule them directly or get them to hold elections. Maybe they'll end up with someone running things who's sane. Just having them pay us tribute, but still be disorganized, is dangerous. Either someone with fill the vacuum, or it will continue to get more and more chaotic."

"What do you recommend?"

"We annex it outright. Don't even ask. I doubt anyone in the WTR will resist or care. As long as we bring stability, a little food, and occasional electricity, they'll be happy."

"That's going to be a tough sell to a lot of people, especially before an election. They'll see it as spreading scarce resources even further."

"Fine, put it off until after the election, but once you're re-elected, it needs to go to the top of the agenda."

"Don't you mean *if* I get re-elected?"

"No, I can't imagine anyone even wanting the job. You'd have to be insane to run."

"Thanks."

"Seriously. That was always my problem with our old U.S. politics. I always said the exact sort of people we needed running our government were the sort who would never want those jobs."

Reggie glanced over at Nathan. "You do know I'm a lifelong politician."

"Okay, I'm sure there are exceptions, but I hope you get my point."

"What about you?"

"What about me?" asked Nathan.

"Like you said, I'm not a spring chicken. Someone is going to have to take over for me eventually. I'd like you to run as my vice presidential candidate for this election."

Nathan looked at Reggie, trying to determine if he were joking. "That would be really dumb."

"Why?"

Nathan sat still for a moment. "Because of David and what he did. I love him still, but as his father, I'll be political baggage you don't need. As a matter of fact, I was planning on stepping down as the Chief of Defense soon."

"I don't think now is the time to step away from anything. Besides, who would replace you?"

"Luke Carter is ready."

"Okay, maybe, but we have too many needs right now. New Harvest County has been leaderless since Harold Buchannan died, and I'll still need a vice, even if I am re-elected. Also, I thought you had talked about wanting to re-establish some sort of intelligence and security apparatus."

"I do, but I also want to focus on family."

"We all do," answered Reggie, "but if we don't find a way to make this whole thing work, our families are going to be in a world of hurt."

"I hear you."

Reggie turned and put his hand on Nathan's leg. "I can't do this alone. I need help. Please just think about it."

Nathan saw how tired his friend was. He also spotted a hint of fear that caused his stomach to drop.

"I will," Nathan promised.

****

The meeting went pretty much as they had expected. There were plenty of temporary positions being filled. Most of the mayors or chief executives who had died in the Second KenTen War would be replaced in the upcoming elections, along with the JP President. Until then, there

74

was a hodgepodge of people with various degrees of competence with their own axes to grind.

Nathan did his best to ignore all the looks he received and pointedly did not participate in the discussion regarding the Fulton relief effort. No one actually brought up David's name, which Nathan supposed was because he was here. It was the elephant in the room that everyone clumsily stepped around.

There was discussion about plenty of problems that they could do nothing about. Refugees were still leaking in. Sewage, gas, and water lines were breaking down. Power lines were failing. They didn't have enough of anything, and far too many people were fighting for what was left. Regarding those topics, they all decided to do the only thing they could: table them until the next meeting in hopes the situation would be better...or at least different.

Nathan provided them an overview of the military and threat situation. Although things were mostly quiet, there was growing lawlessness, especially in the WTR areas. There were also growing rumors and indications of a community in Huntsville, Alabama centered around the military base and NASA rocket research facility. Everyone had assumed the important facility had been nuked, but it was possible this was not the case. Plenty in the room got excited about the idea of the U.S. Government in any form still existing.

They're still waiting for someone else to come save us, thought Nathan.

In the end, he agreed to send a reconnaissance element to try and find out more. In fact, he had already dispatched them, but letting those folks think he was doing it at their behest at least gave them a sense of control.

The meeting was nearly over when John Downing, the man in charge of the Kentucky Dam, stood to speak. Most everyone in the meeting was shocked that he was there and hadn't noticed him until he had spoken.

"I'm afraid I have some bad news," he said.

"What's wrong with the damn dam now?" asked James Harping, the county executive from Ballard County.

"Plenty," answered John, "but that's not the bad news. Yesterday, I was in Benton, so I decided to visit the fuel depot. They were having issues getting the vehicles to start using the strategic reserve fuel."

"They're not supposed to be *using* it anyway," said someone from the back. "That's our money."

"They had a valid requisition," said John. "The issue is the fuel didn't work."

"How does the fuel not work?" asked James.

John sighed. "We should have seen this coming. Fuel in itself is not a stable form. It breaks down, making it no longer able to burn. No one thought to check with everything else going on."

"So the fuel is going bad?" someone asked.

"Yes," answered Downing. "A significant amount is likely already bad."

"Are you saying all that fuel is worthless?" asked Reggie.

John nodded. "For running engines, yes. We have twenty-two large fuel tankers down there. All but three of them full. Might be able to use the stuff as a cleaning solution."

"And it's all gone bad?" asked Nathan.

"Most of it, around a half million gallons, best I can tell."

Everyone looked at each other in shock.

"How are we supposed to get around or farm?" asked James.

"That's what our money is based on," cried Leslie Mitchell, the Paducah mayor. "People trusted that their money would be good."

Everyone started talking at the same time. Voices became raised and heated. Lots of fingers were jabbed angrily at others.

"Please," yelled out Reggie. "Calm down. Let's just calm down."

Most in the room ignored him.

Nathan walked over and picked up a folding metal chair that was against the wall and then began to pound it loudly against the surface of a table.

The cringingly loud noise shocked everyone into shutting up. After a few seconds, Nathan dropped the chair. "Thank you," he said and turned to Reggie. "Mister President."

Reggie rubbed a hand through his hair. "Listen, everyone. This is a shock to all of us, but we'll figure it out."

"I don't see how," said someone.

"Me neither," answered Reggie. "Not yet, but I'm sure we will. The important thing is to not start a panic. This information has to stay in this room until we can do what we can to find a solution."

"That's going to be difficult," said John. "Word is spreading down at Benton. Besides, people will know soon enough when their tractors or cars won't work."

"I understand we're working on limited time," Reggie said. "All I'm asking is that we keep this as quiet as we can. Let's end on that point, and I recommend we meet again in three days to see what we can come up with."

There was grumbling, but everyone in the room agreed and slowly filed out of the room buried deep in the underground facility.

"Sorry to drop that on you," said John, before he walked out with everyone else.

Finally, only Nathan and Reggie were left in the silent room.

"You do know there is no solution to this," said Nathan.

Reggie nodded. "Yes, there is only managing the situation as best we can. It appears the razor's edge we were balancing on just got thinner."

Chapter 8 - Vivax

Bobby Wilson, like most doctors, had always wanted to help people. The medical field was a self-excluding profession. It was just too damn difficult a process to become a doctor unless you really wanted it.

He now wished he were anything else. It was the curse of a healer to look into the eyes of those seeking hope and have nothing for them. It was a relief to get away from those eyes, even for a few hours. Out into the world of the living. He would have to return to the Murray Hospital soon, but for the next hour, he was free.

Glancing over to his left, he saw what had once been the Murray State University basketball arena. Before it had been destroyed, it had contained a small oil refinery and factory to make gunpowder and ammunition. Now it was nothing but a crumbling blackened ruin with safety cones and barriers ringing it.

Bobby turned away and walked purposefully to the biology department building. The MSU President had asked him to meet her there, and Bobby already suspected what this was about. He walked past students hurrying to and from class. On the wide grassy area between buildings, young men and women slept or read or talked with each other, not much different from what students had been doing here before N-Day.

This is our best hope, he thought and wished he were one of them.

He walked into the cool stone building and went down a set of stairs into the basement. He saw the MSU President coming down the dim hallway lit with the bare minimum of electrical lighting.

"Bobby, glad you're here. I asked Doctor Henry to look at those blood samples you brought in. Do you know what's in them?"

"I know lots of things that could be in them," Bobby answered.

"Well, come on in," she said, holding a door for him and pointing to a man in a lab coat looking into a microscope. "Meet Doctor Scott Henry, the head of our biology department."

"Before you say anything," began Scott abruptly, turning towards them, "where did these samples come from?"

"The hospital here in town," Bobby answered. "We have a whole ward with the same symptoms. High fever, bouts of chills, headaches, stomach gramps. They also seem to have an enlarged spleen although it's hard for me to tell without an invasive exam. The worst of them have trouble breathing and staying conscious."

"Them? How many are we talking about?"

"Twenty-six so far," Bobby answered. "I've heard reports of similar cases in Mayfield, Paducah, and Benton."

Scott looked back at the microscope and then at Bobby again. "Were these patients new to the JP? Maybe coming in from somewhere down south?"

Bobby shook his head. "All the ones we have are locals."

"I was afraid of that," Scott said.

"What is it?"

The biologist took a deep breath as if preparing to give a lecture. "The blood contains a parasite known as *plasmodium vivax*. It is carried in the saliva glands of its most common host in the American Southeast by various members of the *culicidae* family."

"Malaria," said Bobby with a sense of dread.

"Yes," continued Scott with a smile. "Well done. Used to be called Tertian Fever from the Latin word for three. The fever comes and goes in three-day cycles most of the time. As you likely know, malaria was endemic in most of America until after the Great Depression. It was mostly wiped out with mosquito eradication programs in the forties."

"But there's no one to spray for mosquitoes anymore," said Valerie. "I also suspect there's more standing water around for them to breed in, with levies breaking all over. Do we have any medicine for malaria?"

Bobby shook his head. "We don't have the antibiotics to treat *vivax*. Hell, we don't even have the tree to make quinine, I bet."

"*Cinchona officinalis*," said Scott. "No, the cinchona trees are tropical."

"What did they used to do to treat malaria back then?" asked Valerie. "When it was a permanent part of life...endemic, as you say?"

"They didn't do anything but endure it," answered Scott. "Everyone got malaria at some point in their lives and built up various degrees of tolerance and immunity. At least we're dealing with *vivax* and not *plasmodium falciparum*. It gets too cold here for that deadly little bastard."

"*Vivax* is bad enough," said Bobby.

"True, especially for those with lowered resiliency," Scott said. "The young, old, and pregnant are going to be particularly hard hit, although everyone is going to get it at some point"

"Everyone?" asked Valerie.

"Unless they can somehow manage to never get bitten by a mosquito," said Scott. "Either that or move sufficiently far north and hope that the winter freeze lasts long enough to kill *vivax* eggs."

"What are we going to do?" Valerie asked.

Bobby saw that she was looking at him. "There's nothing much we can do except try and help people."

"And hope we don't get malaria's close friend," Scott said.

"I don't even want to think about yellow fever," Bobby said.

"Guys," Valerie said. "We've made gasoline and gunpowder and all sorts of other things. Bobby, surely you can get all the other doctors together and come up with a way to make antibiotics for this."

Bobby felt suddenly very tired. "Valerie. I was a *prison* doctor. Do you know what that means?"

"I guess it means you treated prisoners."

"Exactly right. But if I were a good doctor, I wouldn't be treating angry and dangerous prisoners for less pay than a good plumber makes. I went to the Dominican Republic for medical school for God's sake."

"So?"

"So," Bobby sighed, "none of these real doctors are going to listen to me. The only reason anyone does is because I know Nathan Taylor and Reggie Phillips."

"Go with that then," said Valerie. "Use what you got. At the very least, people need to do what they can to prevent getting bitten by mosquitoes."

"They need to use screens on their windows and doors," Scott said. "Especially at night."

"And what about an antibiotic?" Valerie asked. "Can you make one?"

Bobby shook his head. "Not my field by a long shot. I'd be afraid what I cooked up would poison someone."

"I might be able to," said Scott hesitantly.

"Really?" asked Bobby and Valerie at the same time.

"Maybe," he said, sounding even less certain.

"Good enough," said Valerie. "You're pulled from all your classes and duties. This is your focus until further notice."

Scott looked at his watch. "I got a lecture in ten minutes."

"Not anymore you don't. Find someone else to do it and get to work."

Valerie smiled at Bobby, and he simply shook his head.

"We're all in this together," she told him. "You're not alone."

Bobby closed his eyes and walked away. He didn't want to go back to the hospital, but that was where his feet led him.

Chapter 9 – Right Man for the Job

Director Erik Sessions was surprised he was still around. It had been nearly two years since N-Day and there had never been a single day devoid of the threat of extinction for him and his people. As the NASA Site Director for Redstone Arsenal in Huntsville, Alabama, he had never expected to be in this position, but here he was.

Redstone Arsenal was the hub of U.S. rocket development and research. Huntsville itself had more PhD residents than any other city in America because of this. Everyone had pretty much assumed that Redstone was on everyone's nuclear pre-target index.

Yet, when they had awoken that fateful morning to find themselves still alive, it had not been the soldiers and police that had picked up the pieces, but the scientists and researchers. The Redstone Commander Lieutenant General Claster had blown his brains out before the heavier radioactive particles had even finished settling out of the atmosphere. Most of the other military folks had taken to the hills, as had a significant portion of their civilian counterparts.

Erik had been humbled when he arrived at work to find most of his fellow techies where they had been the day before...on the job. He had quickly formed various research committees with assigned tasks, and they had organized.

There, of course, had been problems. They had suffered losses in lives before it became apparent they needed to focus on physical security and defense. What few soldiers were left had been pressed into service to recruit and train Huntsville civilians to secure the hydroelectric dams at nearby Guntersville and Wheeler, as well as the twenty-three kilowatt solar array at the Huntsville Botanical Gardens. This had at least kept the electricity, sewage, and water running.

They still suffered attacks. Most recently from horsemen from the north. Everyone was calling them Indians, but Erik knew that had to be simple hysteria talking. They had been forced to open their city borders to people with any type of military or law enforcement experience, and they pressed them into service. Most had come with limited skills, but they had gotten lucky in a few cases.

There was as knock on his office door. "Come in."

A tall, thin, blond man stepped towards him with the grace of a cat.

"Ah, Vince, thank you for coming. Please sit down."

The man sat in the chair across the desk from Erik. He neither slumped nor sat forward. He appeared at ease while at the same time ready for anything. It appeared his ice-blue eyes missed nothing.

"Vince, you've been here, what, six weeks?"

"Seven."

Erik nodded. "I have to say everyone has been extremely impressed with you."

"Thank you, sir."

"I'm serious. You have completely reworked our security training program. Our defense forces are better organized and capable, and everyone respects you. You're obviously smart, capable, and know what you're doing."

Vince smiled lightly. "I do my best."

"Indeed you do." Erik pointed out his window. "This was a military post, yet all the military ran when the leadership...let us say...checked out. It was the scientists and engineers who were left to figure things out, and I think we've done a pretty good job, but scientists and engineers better than most understand specialties. Physical defense and security is not our specialty.

"I've spent thirty-two years at NASA. Started as a physicist right out of college working on the early Mars Orbiter programs. I've risen through the ranks because I know my limitations and how to get things done. And the best way to get things done is to find good people and empower them to accomplish a task."

"I couldn't agree more, sir," said Vince.

Erik nodded. "I'm sure you have heard the rumors of a nuclear explosion near the western Tennessee-Kentucky border as part of some war between leftover remnants?"

"I have. Even spent some time passing through there myself."

"Well, that sort of thing worries me. We've been able to fight off small bands and raiders so far, but what if there is something stronger than that out there? What if they want what we have? Our food, our electricity, our fuel refineries, our know-how? Would we be able to deter them?"

Vince kept silent.

"If you were in my seat," Erik asked, "what would you recommend?"

He answered without hesitation. "Obtain the means for us to defend ourselves."

"Sounds good, but how?"

"Those warring parties you mentioned earlier are currently in a slight state of discord from my understanding," said Vince. "I happen to know there is a military depot only one day's drive from here."

"Does it have what we need?"

Vince nodded. "Plenty of weapons, both light and heavy. Artillery, vehicles, ammo supplies, equipment."

"And you could go get it?" Erik asked.

"If you give me the authority and the resources I could. I would need control over the security forces, access to vehicles, fuel, and weapons, and freedom to come and go. Give me that, and I can get us what we need."

"How quickly could you make it happen?"

Vince appeared to think, his blue eyes up towards the ceiling. "A few days to provide specialty training, a few days to prep equipment and rehearse contingencies, a day to plan. At best, we could accomplished the mission in a week."

Erik chewed a lip and then made a decision. He pulled out a piece of paper with his letterhead on the top and wrote furiously for nearly a minute. He then handed this to Vince. "Show this authorization to any department head, and they will give you what you need. Come see me again before you go."

"Yes, sir," said Vince, rising.

"And, Vince," said Erik, "thank you. I know I have the right man for the job."

"It is my pleasure, sir."

Vincent Lacert—former head of the Missouri Alliance and orchestrator of mass torture, slavery, and murder—walked out of the office and down the hall.

If Erik had seen the cold smile on the man's face, it would have given him chills.

Chapter 10 – A Ghostly Visit

Ernest Givens yanked the drawer out of the dresser and dumped the contents on the floor. He kicked through the rat's nest of discarded and forgotten items and then threw the empty drawer against the wall in frustration.

"Where is it?" he moaned.

Walking across the room, he flipped up seat cushions off the couch and then got down on his hands and knees to look under the living room's furniture. He then stood and peered around, trying to control the panic that was rising within him.

Closing his eyes, he struggled to remember where he could have put it and realized in a detached way that his hands were shaking. He had a sudden thought, and his eyes flew open. Ernest raced back into the bedroom and lifted up the mattress and cried out in triumph. He grabbed the bottle and spun off the cap, letting it fall to the floor. Before it had hit the stained carpet, he was tilting the mostly empty bottle to his lips and letting the fiery liquid pour down his throat.

He drank like a heat-stroked man in the desert. His Adam's apple bobbed up and down until the bottle was empty. He then licked the rim to get the last drop out. Closing his eyes, he felt warm and calm, and goodness flowed through him. When he opened his eyes, he was startled by the stranger staring back.

It was a dirty haggard man with long hair and a scraggly beard. The man had on a pair of boxer shorts and nothing else. Ribs tried to poke through the skin. The apparition held the empty liquor bottle tightly in both hands.

Ernest screamed furiously and hurled the bottle at the mirror; both shattered.

He closed his eyes and took deep breaths. It felt like he wasn't really here. Like this wasn't him. Someone else was in his body, or he was witnessing someone else's life.

Opening his eyes, he saw the mirror. The shattered remnants were attached to a dresser that had been one of the first pieces of furniture he and Melanie had bought together after getting married so long ago. Back before.

He thought of Melanie and the girls. They had a life together once. Back when he had been in the army. Had been a success. A Sergeant Major leading men and women. A loving father and husband. A man to be respected. But, one day, he had turned around, and they were gone. He couldn't even remember the exact point they had left, just that Melanie had taken them to live with her parents in Galveston.

Then the world had ended and people had turned to him. It had seemed natural, and he had always been a leader. Done for his soldiers what he couldn't do for his family, be there for them. He had fought and won. He had served with some good leaders in his career, even after N-Day. General Clarence Anderson and Major Beau Myers came to mind often. But then, they were both gone.

It was only him and huge masses of civilians fleeing certain death in Paducah. All those lives on his shoulders and he had brought them through to the other side...safe. When the resistance called, he had stepped up again. Leading them against evil and oppression until the fight was won.

"We've won every time," he said.

But he wondered why he felt so lost now. Why, when he slept, the faces of those now gone came to mind. The faces of those who he had killed.

He shook his head to clear the image. Ernest didn't want to think about Brazen's man. The one he had made an example of with the bloody eagle. He couldn't even remember his name, Jinx or Jake or Juke or something, but he couldn't forget his face or screams.

"Son of a bitch deserved it."

Of course he did, he thought. *So why do I keep thinking of it? Why can't I seem to find a way out of this?*

Ernest looked over at the end table. The one that sat beside his favorite chair. It held a lamp that didn't work, several dirty and empty glasses, and his service pistol.

There's your way out, a voice said in his head. *It's the only way out you're going to get. What do you have to live for anyway? You really want another day of this?*

Walking slowly, Ernest approached the table and gingerly picked up the pistol. It felt good in his hand. .45s always had. Berettas and the new fangled handguns that tried to cram as many rounds into the magazine as possible had never appealed to him. It made the butt of the pistol too large. Unless you were a freaking wookie, you couldn't really control a pistol with a butt like a can of corn.

But a .45 was different. It fit into your hand like a caress. Maybe even like an old friend.

There was a loud knock on the door.

Ernest turned slowly towards the door and clinched the pistol tightly at his side.

"That better not be you, Dale," Ernest yelled, striding towards the door. "I told you not to come back here. No one's getting any damn taxes from me. Not now, not ever again."

He yanked open the door and pointed the pistol in the face of a dead man.

There stood a bald, slumped figure with hallow eyes. He didn't even react to the pistol in his face.

"Who the fuck are you?"

The man licked his lips and coughed. It was obvious that talking was painful to the man. "Sergeant Major Givens."

"Yeah, do I know you?"

This resulted in a slight smile. "It's me. Sergeant Booker."

It took a minute for Ernest to place the name. He had known a Sergeant Booker. The man who had fought with him in Paducah and helped him take the refugees across the river and then back into Kentucky, but that couldn't be this man. This man was one hundred and fifty years older and twelve suit sizes smaller.

The man nodded as if he could read Ernest's mind. "It's me." He then walked straight ahead at Ernest without asking to be let in, and Ernest was forced to step aside to keep the man from running into him.

Ernest looked after him in disbelief. He could now recognize the face somewhere down deep in there, but Sergeant Booker? He realized that all the time he had spent with the man he didn't even know his first name. Or maybe he did and had just forgotten. If Melanie had been here, she would have told him that was typical.

Booker pulled out a kitchen chair and sat down in the small kitchen.

Closing the front door, Ernest laid the pistol back on the table beside his chair and went to sit across from Booker.

"You want some water or something?"

He waved the offer away.

"What happened?"

"Radiation poisoning," Booker said. "After we made it back across the river into Kentucky, I went down to see my mom near Fulton. We were far enough away that the blast didn't get us, but the radiation did. Probably from drinking the water afterwards, they say, but the truth is no one knows."

"And your mother?"

"She's gone. Didn't go very nicely either. Radiation sickness is a very bad way to go."

"Shit, I'm sorry. What are they doing for you?"

Booker's mouth tuned up with the barest hint of a smile. "There's nothing anyone can do. Probably only got a few weeks left, and those won't be very pleasant days. The nurse who was seeing me was an angel and gave me a killer dose of morphine. Said it was the last she had. I'll hold out as long as I can, but won't go like my mom did."

Ernest sat there, uncertain what to say or do. "I'm sorry," he said again.

"Believe it or not, I'm not the only one. There're hundreds like me. Down in camps around Fulton."

"Really? I didn't know."

"Most don't. It ain't pretty, and there's not much people can do about it now. Not after our own did this to us."

Ernest sat quietly. He knew what David Taylor had done. Everyone assumed it was Nathan who had sent him. You had to be one cold-hearted bastard to send your own son to do something like that.

"Is this what we fought for?" Booker asked, looking around the room. "This?"

Looking around the trashy room, Ernest saw it as it really was for the first time in weeks. He remembered now that he was nearly naked and felt embarrassed, but didn't want to leave this man to go put on more clothes.

"Yeah, it sucks, but what are you gonna do?" Ernest asked.

"Change it. Find a way to make it better. At least take the power away from those who don't deserve it."

"What do you mean?"

Booker sighed and looked at Ernest with those hollow eyes. "There's a lot of people who remember what you did for them, and they're grateful. Thousands would have died if you hadn't saved them. What has Reggie Phillips ever done? What has Nathan Taylor ever done?"

Ernest shook his head. "I'm afraid I still don't know what you're talking about."

"Lots of people aren't happy about what is going on. They feel it's time for a change, but there just aren't any other valid options. As it stands now, Reggie Phillips will win the new presidency in a landslide, and then Nathan Taylor will take over for him in a few years. They'll keep using us all and looking out for themselves long after the both of us are gone."

"I'm not sure that's entirely fair. I've been a leader myself and know it sometimes takes tough choices."

"Don't talk to me about fair," said Booker with a hint of anger. "Go down to those camps around Fulton and talk to them. Talk to my mother or Major Myers or the hundreds of children dying by inches. I mean, what did they all die for? So one man can rule us unchecked?"

Ernest stood and went to the sink. He looked for a clean glass and couldn't find one in all the mess and felt revolted by his own home. He finally settled on what looked like a mason jar that wasn't hideous and filled it with water from the tap. Ernest drank slowly, staring out the window at his small backyard.

"Even if you don't agree with me...with all of us...about what they have done, do you really think it's a good idea to have an election with only one candidate?"

"Of course not," said Ernest, turning, "but look at me. Do I really look like the man for the job?"

"Not at this very moment, no."

"So?"

"So, you get your shit together. Stop feeling sorry for yourself. The Sergeant Major Givens I knew was better than this. Do something."

Ernest stood there, looking at the shell of the man in front of him, and wanted to be angry, but couldn't. "Excuse me," he finally said and walked into his bedroom and threw on a t-shirt and some jeans. As he was leaving, he saw the broken mirror and glass bottle.

I am better than this. Oh dear God, please let me be better than this, or I'm going to die in here.

He walked back in and stood at the sink again, gazing absently out the window. "What exactly is it you're asking me to do?"

"We're asking you to put your name on the ballot to run as JP President. That's all. Others will take care of the rest. It may also help if you made some effort to win."

"Against Reggie Phillips? Like that's going to happen. That man is a god around here."

"Maybe that's the problem. You don't think he's made mistakes? Did you listen to his last radio broadcast?"

Ernest shook his head.

Booker looked like he wanted to say something else, but just sort of deflated. He stood slowly, with difficulty, and turned towards the door.

"You leaving?"

Booker nodded. "Not much time left now, and I did what I set out to do."

Ernest opened the front door for him, and now saw a group of people waiting by the curb with what looked like a bed on wheels.

"Let me know if there is anything I can do for you," Ernest said.

"I already have," answered Booker. "Goodbye, Sergeant Major. It cost me a lot to come up here; please don't make it have been in vain."

Ernest watched the dead man who used to be one of his soldiers slowly shuffle away.

Chapter 11 – Dangerous By-Ways

The next morning, Trailer roused Simon from the corner of the small shed they had rented for the night. Simon offered to split an MRE with the big man, who eagerly accepted. They then packed their belongings and walked down to the courthouse square.

The street was quiet and filled with shadows from the barest hint of the sun to the east. Simon thought his town looked almost normal in this light. He could imagine that it was maybe the morning after the annual peach blossom festival or possible following a few small tornados.

"We're early," said Simon, looking to the east. "You told the girl dawn."

"She'll be there anyway," Trailer said. "Probably been there for hours already."

"How do you know?"

"Didn't you see her? She'd welcome anything different at this point."

"That's a common feeling I've noticed."

The big man was right. They saw a small two-wheeled handcart loaded down with what were presumably bags of dried rice, covered by a ragged piece of blue tarp. The cart rested on its two long pull poles. The small woman sat under the cart, her back resting against a small pack, and she looked out at them.

"Good morning," said Simon.

She just glared back at them.

"Guess your daddy didn't feel the need to come see you off," said Trailer.

The woman climbed from under the cart and pulled the pack out behind her.

"What's your name, girl?" Trailer asked.

"What's yours?" she asked back at them, strapping her pack to the side of the cart.

Trailer shrugged. "Fair enough. I'm Horace, but everyone calls me Trailer, not sure why. And this is Simon."

"I'm Jessica," she said.

"Excellent," said Trailer, pointing with his stick east. "Let's get started."

"Aren't we supposed to be going north?" Simon asked.

"Only if Mud Island is your destination," the big man answered.

Simon watched the big man stride away and then turned to see Jessica struggle to lift the wooden pull tongues off the ground and work herself into a leather harness. She then leaned all of her weight forward with the cart wheels moved ever so slightly.

He went around to the back and gave the cart a helpful push that speeded her along.

"What the hell are you doing?" she asked without stopping. Her legs were in motion and the cart was moving surprisingly fast now.

Simon jogged to catch up to her. "Just helping."

She cut her eyes at him, her face straining. "And just what do you expect in return for helping me?"

Taken aback, Simon stopped walking for a second and then had to jog again to catch up to her. "I don't expect anything, just helping."

Jessica chuckled and pushed a strand of black hair out of her face. "I may not have traveled all over like you two, but I know enough to know help is never free."

Sure it is, Simon almost said, but then thought. Did he want something from her? Sure, he thought she was pretty. Would he help her if she were an old hag? Probably, but that didn't change that he was interested in her. Being interested in another person was a new sensation for Simon, and he liked the feeling.

"How old are you?" he asked abruptly.

"Not as old as I feel," she sighed. "How about you?"

Simon had to calculate in his head. "I turned twenty-six last month."

"Congratulations," she said. "Living another year is a bigger accomplishment than it used to be."

He looked at her again as she strained against the straps attached to the cart. "Why didn't your father come instead of you?"

"He's not allowed to depart our field this time of year. Besides, we couldn't leave our home unguarded. Someone would come in and take it. If he had come and I stayed, that would just invite people to...bother me."

"Are you going to miss your father?"

"No," she answered.

"Why not?"

She didn't answer and then began to pull harder. "Just shut up for a while, will you?"

Simon did and walked beside her.

****

After several hours of walking east, they turned north at an intersection. The roads north passed through several small towns, some completely abandoned and picked clean, others occupied with various degrees of neighborliness towards outsiders. In each case, Trailer did all the talking and appeared very adept at soothing suspicions and calming itchy trigger fingers. Most of the big roads were still packed with stalled cars, and it was at times difficult to get the handcart down the middle path between abandoned cars or on one of the road shoulders. Despite her declaration of not needing any help, both Simon and Trailer at times had pushed the cart through particularly rough patches.

Trailer avoided the big roads most of the time, and they followed a bewildering maze of turns and twists from hardtop to gravel to dirt back to gravel and so on. Once they saw a long line of men and women attached to each other by a chain connected through padlocked dog collars on their necks. Most were in rags and had their hands tied together in front of them. Their eyes were downcast and steps shuffling.

"Are those actual slaves or something?" Simon asked.

"Criminals," said Simon. "No one can afford to run a jail or prison where people just sit on their ass and eat free food all day. If that were the case, we'd all find a way to get in there. They'll work for awhile and then be released. The chain boss there probably had to pay a good deal to get ownership, and now he gets to keep any proceeds from labor they earn."

"How dangerous are they?" asked Jessica.

101

Trailer looked after them. "Probably not too much. Thieves and vagrants mostly. The dangerous ones they just execute."

Occasionally, there was a road block with armed men where they would demand a toll or safe passage payment. Sometimes, Trailer was able to talk his way through without paying, but most of the time, he would turn to Simon or Jessica and tell them to give him something from what they had for the payment.

"Don't you have anything to give them?" Jessica asked once.

Trailer smiled, measuring out a cup of rice from an open bag on her cart. "They don't want anything I got."

They camped at night in abandoned gas stations or homes or just out in the open if they had to. Trailer was careful about banking their fire so it couldn't be seen from very far away. The first night Jessica had said she needed to go into the woods to go to the bathroom.

"I'll come with you," Simon had offered.

"Do I follow you around and watch *you* pee?" she asked him.

Trailer chuckled. "She's got you there, I guess. Just don't go far, and if you're not back in five minutes, *I'll* come looking for you."

Over a number of days, they seemed to settle into a routine that involved mostly mind-numbing walking and then exhausted sleep at the end of the day. Simon had woken up once in the middle of the night to see Trailer sitting by the fire leaned against his pack. His stick was beside him and a pistol rested in his lap. The big man was staring right at him with unblinking eyes.

"Don't you ever sleep?" he asked.

Trailer appeared to rouse himself. "What? What is it?"

"I asked if you ever sleep?"

"Hell, I *was* sleeping till you woke me."

Weird, Simon thought, and rolled back over to try and rest but found himself staring at Jessica's sleeping form. He realized it was difficult not to look at her face, especially when she was sleeping and not on guard. Her dark hair fell around a petite, almond-shaped face with full lips, narrow nose, and large eyes. When she breathed, she let out the very faintest of snores. Simon thought it would be impossible to sleep while looking at her, but the next he knew it was sunrise and Trailer was kicking them all awake.

They saw a few other travelers on the road, some of them even in the company of their own guides. Trailer either exchanged greetings or insults with these as they moved in opposite directions.

Trailer appeared to get more nervous the further north they proceeded. Several strange painted symbols on trees or buildings seemed to particularly concern him, and as often as not, whenever Simon or Jessica said anything, he would tell them to shut up in a hushed voice.

"What are we worried about, exactly?" Simon asked Trailer one night around a fire.

Trailer looked up from where he had been staring into the fire. He stared at both Simon and Jessica's expectant faces and sighed. Pointing west, he said, "Memphis is that way. Still a little hot. No one knows how much, but its best to steer clear." He then hooked a thumb over his shoulder east. "Over there is the Creek Nation. Haven't run into them myself yet, but word is they take it very badly if you're caught on their land. That leaves us a very narrow corridor."

"It seems okay so far," said Jessica.

"You seen those signs?" Trailer asked. "The ones with the pentagrams and those with what looks like a knife?"

"I thought that was an upside-down cross," Simon said.

"Well, none of them are good artists. They're rival gangs, the Road Devils and the Cossacks, in a turf war over this valuable little corridor. They were both motorcycle gangs at one time, but now there's not enough gasoline, so they roam on foot, which makes them more dangerous."

"Why's that?" Jessica asked.

"Because you used to be able to hear their motorcycles coming."

"Can't you pay a toll and get through?" Simon asked.

"Used to, when only one group was in control, but now that neither really owns the roads, each feels the need to take everything they can from a traveler knowing the opposing group will do the same. I used to go east around them, but the Indians have that locked up now."

"So we're trying to thread the needle between two dangerous elements that will both likely rob us or worse if they catch us?" Simon asked.

"That's about right," answered Trailer.

Simons dug into his pack and pulled out the two parts of his assault rifle, putting them together, and then loaded a magazine. He looked up to see Trailer looking at him appreciatively. "Maybe we should start pulling watches in the night."

"Look who's a soldier boy now," Trailer said.

"As a matter of fact, I was a soldier once," Simon said. "Not a very good one, but I learned a few things."

"So you didn't just steal that rifle?" Trailer asked.

104

"No," Simon answered. "I can take the middle watch if you like. It's the worst time if I remember correctly."

"I'm a morning person," Trailer said. "Wake me up when it's my shift." He then settled down and stared into the fire without blinking in a way that they had come to know meant the big man was asleep or headed that way.

"I guess I'm first," Jessica said. "I'll need you rifle."

Simon hesitated, but realized it only made sense. "You ever shoot before?"

"Yes, but not a gun like that. Shotguns mostly for hunting before...you know."

"Yeah, I know." He sat down beside her and dropped the magazine, clearing the chamber before giving her a quick class on how to shoot and clear malfunctions. He then showed her how to load the rifle and handle it safely.

"It's heavy," she said with appreciation. "With something like this, no one would ever mess with me again."

"That's not how guns work," Simon answered. "It's just a tool. The person behind the gun is what matters."

"What do you know about it?" she asked, her earlier smile a distant memory. She stood, taking the rifle with her. "I got first watch. Better get some sleep."

Simon did.

****

"Hold up," Trailer whispered, and they stopped. The big man turned his head back and forth as if trying to get a scent.

"What's wrong?" Simon whispered, coming up beside him.

"Not sure. I thought I heard something, and it just feels...off somehow."

Simon looked back at Jessica behind them attached to the cart. He made sure to keep the end of the rifle pointed away from either of his traveling companions. "So, what now?"

"We keep going, but stay alert."

They walked down the paved two-lane road that a local sign declared as State Route 76. In the middle of the road, there was a naked form covered in blood. Flies had started to collect on the dead man's face and wounds to his chest.

Trailer bent down and put his fingers to the man's forehead. "Not cold yet." He stood and looked both ways along the road alertly. "We have to get off this road."

"Which group did this?" Simon asked.

"Does it matter?" Trailer asked angrily.

Simon saw with surprise that the big man was afraid and realized he should likely be afraid as well. He peered back and saw Jessica staring at the body in the road calmly.

Trailer looked at the handcart and then at the side of the road. "Follow me, quickly," he said, walking towards a wider path leading into the woods.

Simon helped Jessica get the cart down the embankment without it crushing her and then pushed to get it going. He noticed she didn't complain about his help as she once had.

They walked slowly for nearly an hour. Simon turned to scan their rear every few seconds, as he had been taught in light infantry tactics years ago, and was surprised how quickly such things came back.

"We'll stop here for the night," Trailer said as they pulled off the trail and into a natural large depression in the ground surrounded by trees and thick brush. "No fire tonight."

Neither Simon nor Jessica complained. Simon felt bone tired with a need to sleep and understood this was a post-adrenaline rush reaction. He sat heavily on the ground and breathed deeply.

Jessica struggled out of the straps and set the tongues of the cart down. "I gotta go pee."

"I'll go with you," said Simon, struggling to stand.

"Remember, we had that conversation already," she said, walking out of the depression.

"Don't go far," said Trailer sternly.

Simon relaxed, and Trailer sank down to one knee across from him.

"Who do you think he was?" Simon asked.

"Hard to say. He was picked clean. Could have been locals that did him in, but I would guess one of the gangs."

"So they might be close?"

"They've been close for a good while," Trailer answered. "That's what I was trying to warn you about. This is the worst part of the trip."

"Is it always like this?"

"Not usually. I'm always on edge around here, but most of the time I'm able to get through without any cause for concern. Maybe something has gotten the Devils and Cossacks stirred up. Hell, for all I know, there could be a new player in the area causing trouble. I just wish one side would destroy the other so that they can go back to simple extortion."

"Is one worse than the other?"

"Doesn't matter. Any state of chaos is almost always worse than any state of order."

"That's pretty deep," Simon said. "Who said that?"

"I did, just now. I'm a deep thinker if you hadn't noticed. Studied philosophy back when people did such things."

"Maybe that's the only thing worth studying anymore," Simon said.

Trailer held up his hand. "You hear that?"

Simon listened but didn't hear anything. He turned, and his eyes alighted on the handcart. He sprang to his feet. "Jessica's not back."

Trailer grabbed his arm. "We'll go find her, don't rush. Also realize that if you catch her in the middle of taking a dump, it *will* put a damper on that puppy-love you're feeling."

"I'm not worried about that; remember the body in the road?"

The big man began walking carefully down the path he had seen Jessica take using his cudgel to quietly clear the way before them. Within a few minutes, they could hear voices and crept cautiously forward.

"She's a pretty little one, ain't she?" said one voice.

"Don't even think about it," said another voice. "You know the rules. Scratch gets first taste of any sweets we bring in. After that, we can all get our fill."

There was a sound as if Jessica were struggling.

"Doesn't mean we can't sample the goods, at least a little bit."

Simon started to move forward, but Trailer put his hand up to block him.

"No guns. There could be others nearby. Sling the rifle and take this." Trailer held out a large hunting knife.

Taking the knife, Simon slung the rifle over his shoulder beside his pack as silently as possible.

Without warning, Trailer raced forward.

Simon heard a few gasps of surprise and then ran after him.

One man was already in the ground with his skull cracked open. Blood and brain matter oozed out into the ground. Trailer had his back to this one and his cudgel held out menacingly in the other direction.

"Don't move," said a wiry man with a tattoo of a snake running from his bare chest up around his neck. He had Jessica by the hair and was holding a pistol against the side of her head. He looked wildly from Trailer to Simon to his dead friend. The man pointed the gun at Trailer, but then Jessica began to struggle, and he had to hold the pistol on her again to keep her still.

"So, we're not moving," said Trailer. "We just want to be on our way. Let our friend go, and everyone can just continue with their lives."

The man shook his head and nodded towards the nearby body with the split skull. "I got a better deal. You trade me the girl for your freedom. That's fair for you killing Sax, I would say."

"Not going to happen," said Trailer. "You hurt the girl and we jump on you. You shoot one of us and the other one jumps you. You let her go and we all go happily on our way."

The man appeared to consider the situation anew. "You got anything to sweeten the deal?"

"Sure," said Trailer, hooking a thumb over his shoulder. "Back a hundred yards is our campsite. Sitting there is a cart filled with about three hundred pounds of dried prime Tunica rice."

"Seriously?" The man smiled.

"No!" yelled Jessica, struggling and trying to pull away.

The man with the tattoo was forced to look away from the two men in order to regain control of the woman in his grasp. When he did, the pistol came away from her head for a fraction of a second and was out to his side.

Lightning quick, Trailer stepped forward and brought his heavy cudgel down on the wrist that was holding the pistol. There was a loud sickening crunch and then a gunshot as the man squeezed the trigger reflexively.

He screamed in pain and dropped the pistol.

Jessica scrambled on the ground and grasped the dropped pistol. She rolled over on her back to point it at her former captor.

Trailer was already in full swing. His cudgel connected with the side of the man's skull with the sound like a baseball bat hitting a melon. The man crumbled.

"Are you okay?" Simon asked, helping Jessica to her feet.

They could hear yelling in the distance.

"We have to move fast," Trailer said, turning east. "Follow me."

"The rice!" Jessica said.

"Leave it," Trailer ordered. "With any luck, it will distract them long enough for us to get away."

"I can't leave it," she said. "My father will kill me."

Trailer pointed at the sound of the voices. "Believe me when I say they will do much worse than kill you if you don't leave it."

Jessica seemed torn.

"Suit yourself," said Trailer, taking off at a run. Within seconds, he was out of sight.

"Come on," said Simon. "He's right. We'll never be able to outrun or even hide from them with that cart."

With a cry of frustration, she sprinted after Trailer, and Simon followed.

Chapter 12 – Going South

Joshua led his detachment of reconnaissance personnel south on a motley collection of bicycles. Most were mountain or racing bikes except for one large three-wheeled bicycle that carried most of their supplies.

He shifted the large pack on his back and checked that the assault rifle was still securely attached to his handlebars. As the commander, he rode in the middle of a large dispersed formation that would have probably fit within a standard football field.

They hadn't had any trouble so far, but he knew that was no reason to get complacent and bunch up. All it would take would be one ambush with a machine gun or IED and they would be in a world of hurt.

That made him think of his new wife Alexandra and their expected baby. Joshua and his wife had argued the morning he left. He didn't like that she still went out into the forest to hunt alone with her crossbow. He had told her that as an expectant mother she had responsibilities and needed to not just think of herself. Alexandra had retorted his argument played both ways and that maybe he shouldn't be going on a dangerous mission now that he was a soon-to-be father.

He had told her he *had* to go, but that wasn't the truth. Joshua was senior enough he could have sent others on the mission. One of the things he loved and hated about Alexandra is that she couldn't be bull-shitted and she had seen right through his hypocritical argument. He hoped she understood it was because he cared far more for her life than his own.

She also accused him of being withdrawn lately, and he couldn't argue with her. Ever intuitive to people around her, she had understood it was guilt and grief over losing David. Not simply his brother being gone but all the distance between them left unreached. All the things left unsaid and undone forever.

The sun broke free of the clouds, and Joshua adjusted the hat on his head. He rolled the sleeves down on his shirt. His burn scars were light sensitive, and he had been told they probably always would be. Joshua had taken to covering them even when the sun wasn't out, because he didn't like the whispers and the pointing. He didn't draw attention because of the scars themselves, but because he was easily identified as the brother of the man who had done the unforgiveable: setting off a nuclear bomb after N-Day.

Conrad McKraven rode up beside him on a mountain bike with the seat and handlebars at their maximum extension. Even so, he looked like he was on a child's ride.

"We're not far now," Conrad said. "Another few miles and we'll hit Creek Territory."

Joshua nodded. "I've been wondering something."

"What?"

"Why are you here? I mean, I like having you, but recon isn't really your thing and you're in the middle of a new soldier training class. Seems to me like the best place for you would be back at LBL with you recruits. And don't tell me again how you're bored and looking for some excitement; you just got back from that campaign against the Pirates of the Mississippi."

Conrad smiled to himself and weaved his bike back and forth on the road like a racecar driver trying to warm up his tires. "You're a smart guy. Why don't you tell me why I'm here?"

Something about the way he said it made the pieces fall into place in Joshua's mind. "You're here to watch over me," he said in disbelief.

"More like watch out for you."

"Did Colonel Carter put you up to this?"

Conrad nodded. "Yeah, but I got the impression it came from higher."

"My father?"

"If I had to guess, I would say so. Don't be too angry about it. My father never gave a shit about what happened to me. Thankfully, I had a grandfather who did."

Joshua rode in silence for a few minutes.

"He's just worried, that's all," Conrad finally said. "Just be lucky you were allowed to go on this mission."

"Allowed? This is my job, I'm..." Joshua trailed off. "That was why I was sent north to recon during the Missouri and Arkansas campaigns. To keep me safe."

"Hey, you didn't get that from me," said Conrad, realizing he had maybe gone a bit too far. "And let's face it, you have been different since David died."

"Yeah," Joshua said. *David.* Even though his brother was gone, his ghost seemed to be everywhere.

"So you're supposed to be my wet nurse?"

"In a sense, but not just for you sake, but for theirs as well." Conrad waved his hand in the direction of the men and women around them. "I can step in if you go off the deep end. Break down crying in the corner or something like that."

"So, let me get this straight. The man responsible for overseeing my torture is now watching out for me?"

Conrad grunted. "The irony isn't lost on me either. I judge your mother had no part in that decision. She would still skin me if she got the chance."

The riders at the front of the formation held up their hands and began to stop. The sign was passed back, and soon the whole group was sitting still on their bicycles. Joshua and Conrad rode forward to find two tanned men sitting casually on horses.

"How?" said Conrad, holding up a hand to the side of his face.

"Very funny, paleface," said one. "You the group Nathan Taylor said would be coming down to go check out Huntsville?"

"That's us. I'm Joshua Taylor, and this is Conrad McKraven."

"I'm Don," said the first rider, who nodded towards his companion, "This is Jimmy."

Jimmy stared down at them in distaste. "Don't you assholes have horses?"

"Good question," said Conrad, turning to Joshua. "Why *don't* we have horses? It feels like I'm on the goddamn Tour de France."

"What the hell would you know about horses anyway?" Joshua asked Conrad. "You barely manage to keep air in your bike tires and oil on the chain. You'd be a disaster with something that actually needed to be fed and watered."

"We could always help you out with that," said Don. "We have plenty of horses."

"That's mighty kind of you," said Conrad. "It's not anyone who will just give you a horse."

"*Trade*," said Jimmy, pointing at their rifles.

Joshua shook his head. "These aren't ours to trade. We'll stick with our bicycles for now."

"So be it," said Don, spinning his horse around. "Follow us and try to keep up."

The two horsemen galloped south, and Joshua's group was forced to pedal hard to stay with them.

Chapter 13 – Conflicting Duty

"You're going to do *what?*" Bethany asked.

"Please don't say it like that," said Nathan.

She threw her hands up in the air. "How am I supposed to say it? You're going to be the vice president?"

"Going to *run* for vice president. Reggie asked me, and I don't feel like I can say no."

"It's easy," said Bethany. "Here, let me show you. 'Reggie, I'm flattered by the offer, but I've promised my wife I would spend more time at home now that we have a new baby. I've spent much of my military career away from home and missed a lot of the boys growing up and my family needs me. Please accept this as my final answer.' See, what's so hard about that?"

Nathan turned away and walked over to look out the window towards the lake. It was peaceful here. He could see Joshua and Alexandra's cabin down towards the shore as well as his mother's small cabin to his left. It had taken some convincing her to move from Mayfield, but once she settled here, she loved it. "I always wanted a lake house," she kept saying.

Bethany walked up behind him and put a hand on his shoulder. "I know you want to help and it's never been in your nature to refuse those that ask for it, but *I'm* asking for your help now. I need it."

"I can get my mother to come help more," Nathan said.

His wife turned away in frustration. "You're missing the point. I don't need someone else to help me do *stuff*. I need my husband and friend here to share this life with me. Who knows how long we have together or with the children."

"Is this about David?"

"No...yes...maybe, I don't know. And now you've gone and sent our only surviving son off on a dangerous mission to the south. Aren't their others who can do that?"

"Who told you?" he asked.

"Alexandra."

"Who told *her*? It was supposed to be a secret mission."

"I don't know," she answered. "I guess some husbands and wives talk about things. It may seem strange to you at first, but give it a shot."

"I hate it when you get this way."

She glared at him. "Well, I'm not capable of being any other way right now. I'm tired and my head hurts. We talked about you pulling back, doing less. Then you go and agree to run for vice president without talking to me, and oh yeah, we both know that will not be the end of it. You'll be president after Reggie until you either have a heart attack or are assassinated."

Nathan shrugged. "He needs me."

Bethany walked over and grabbed his left hand in both of hers. She touched the wedding ring. "This means I need you, now." She reached for his right hand and touched the EX brand. "This means you've done more than enough." Her eyes grew sad. "Don't you understand? When they sent you away, I didn't think I'd ever see you again, or Joshua. I was going to raise our daughter without you. All I thought about was

118

how many things I had gotten wrong or not done, and I wished I had another chance. Now we have that chance. It may be our last one. Let's make time to be happy together. To raise our daughter."

"I am happy," Nathan said. "Aren't you happy?"

She let go of his hand. "Sometimes. Mostly I'll settle for being content and safe. Other times, I think of all we've been through and what we've lost and I just need you and you're not there."

Nathan stared at her, not sure what to say.

"Don't you look at me like that," Bethany said. "I'm not some delicate flower of a woman. I've kept our family going while you were off in warzones around the world, and I've dealt with things you'll never know. I survived that horrific march from Maryland here. I'm not having a weak moment. Please, let go, for me."

"Who will do it if I don't?"

"Someone, I promise you, someone will. Nathan, I love you, but listen to yourself. Aren't you the one who always said no one is irreplaceable?"

"This is different. Ernest Givens is a serious challenger; he might even win."

"Would that be such a bad thing? Reggie could stand to spend more time with Janice as well."

"Am I just supposed to retire and do nothing? With everything that's going on? I'm not old, and I'm able to help."

"You could do something that keeps you around here," she offered. "The New Harvest County Executive is still vacant. We need someone good there. It hasn't been the same since Harold Buchannan died."

The thought of Harold gave him pause. She was right in a sense. There were needs closer to home.

River wailed from the adjacent room. Bethany's face dropped, and Nathan noticed how exhausted she was. He hated himself for being so self-absorbed as to not notice it earlier. She moved towards their daughter.

He grabbed her by the arm. "I'll get her. You go lay down for a bit."

She smiled back at him in gratitude. "Maybe just for a little while. I can't seem to shake this cold, and I feel the fever coming back."

"Have you taken any aspirin?"

"You know we're all out; everyone's out."

"Sorry," he said. "Just a habit to ask. Go lay down. I've got this."

Nathan went in and picked up their daughter, and she grinned and laughed at the sight of him. He realized she was wet and reached for one of the cloth diapers nearby. He supposed changing a diaper was like riding a bicycle.

He picked his daughter up and bounced her around the house. She didn't seem hungry, which was good; he didn't want to have to wake Bethany to feed her. After a while, River started to nod off again, and he gently placed her back in her crib.

Walking into the bedroom, he found Bethany sleeping fitfully. He touched her forehead and found it both hot and clammy. She tossed away from him.

There was a heavy knock on their front door, and he rushed towards the sound before someone woke either Bethany or River. He pulled open the door just as a soldier in uniform was about to knock again. Surprised, the soldier snapped to attention and saluted Nathan while handing out a piece of paper.

Nathan returned the salute, then took the letter. The man spun on a heel and was striding purposefully away when Nathan called out to him. "Soldier?"

The man halted and turned again, attentive. "Yes, sir."

"I need you to go to that cabin right there"—he pointed at the adjacent cabin—"and tell the nice lady that her son needs her. Can you do that?"

"Yes, sir," the soldier said and took off at a brisk walk towards the cabin.

Nathan tore open the letter and sighed in frustration. It was always something. He would have loved nothing more than to stay with Bethany and River, especially now, but he already knew duty called. Like a good man had said before, there was never an acceptable excuse for not doing one's duty.

Thank God my mother is here, he thought. *She can take care of things while I'm away.*

Reading the letter, he sighed and hung his head before going back into the house. He began to pack and make plans for what lay ahead.

Unfortunately, what lay ahead was worse than he could imagine.

Chapter 14 – Tax Day

Trailer heard one of his companions fall again behind him. Looking back, he discovered it was Simon this time. Jessica had stopped beside him as well, her hands rested on her knees as she sucked in air.

They can't go much longer, he realized.

Simon struggled to his feet slowly.

Trailer walked over and took the rifle from Simon's hand, handing him his cudgel in return. Simon looked at the stick as if he didn't know what it was.

"Stay here," Trailer said and pointed to some bushes off to the side. "Hide there until I come back."

"What are you going to do?" Jessica asked.

"Go see if we're being followed."

"And if we are?"

"Take care of it," Trailer said and began walking back the way they had come before there could be any further talking.

The assault rifle felt awkwardly small in his hands, like a child's toy, and he hoped he didn't have to use it. After walking a couple of hundred yards, he stopped and took a knee beside the trail. Trailer looked around and then closed his eyes to listen.

He heard nothing except the wind and the birds.

Good enough, he thought and stood to head back to his companions. He found them where he had left them and traded the rifle back for his cudgel.

"Are we safe?" Simon asked.

"Relatively so, yes. At least for now."

"Can we go back for the rice?" Jessica asked.

Trailer looked at her sadly. "You already know the answer to that."

"That's your payment too, you know," she told Trailer. She looked like she might cry. "I can't go back home. Not after losing everything." A curious look appeared on her face, the panic transforming into realization.

"Sure you can," said Simon helpfully. "I'm sure your father would understand. You can go back if you want."

She stared at him with burning intensity. "But what if I don't want to? It's not like he can come looking for me."

Simon's face scrunched up in confusion. "But won't you miss your family?"

"What family? My father hasn't been the same since my mom died, and the lady he married is a whore."

"I'm sure she's not that bad," said Simon.

"No, I'm serious," Jessica said. "He met her at Spencer's where she worked as a whore. Still does."

"Well, every family's got its peculiarities, I guess," said Trailer.

Jessica shook her head stubbornly. "I'm not going back. Not ever. I'll start a new life somewhere else."

"Let's not get ahead of ourselves," said Trailer. "We're still working on not being dead. There's some work to be done in that department."

"Do we have to keep running?" Simon asked.

Trailer thought for a moment. "I don't think so, but we'll need to move with a purpose. I'm going to try to cut north if possible. Maybe we can avoid the Creek Nation. I just wish I knew where we were exactly."

"What?" asked Jessica. "Aren't you the guide?"

"Doesn't mean I know every square inch of ground. Don't worry. As long as we head in the general right direction, something will become familiar."

He looked around at where they were. "We should probably start by getting out of this little creek bottom and back up on a road. Take a few more minutes to catch your breath, and then we need to move."

After passing around a canteen, they stood wearily and followed Trailer north. After about half an hour, they stumbled out onto a gravel road and turned northeast. They walked for several hours through fields and small farms under a gray overcast sky. At times, they would see someone through a window or working in a garden, but no one greeted them.

Simon caught Jessica smiling. "What's so funny?"

She looked at him surprisingly, and the smile vanished. "Nothing, what are you talking about?"

"You just looked happy, I guess. Something's evidently changed."

Jessica walked silently beside him for a few minutes before speaking. "You know that cart of rice was heavy. It pulled me all over the place. Pulled me back going uphill and pushed me forward going downhill."

"You probably feel like you're floating now without it."

"Exactly," she said. "And it's not just the cart. Other burdens lifting away as well."

They rounded a corner and came upon a small house set back among a group of trees. A man, woman, and two small boys stood on the front porch looking in the direction Trailer was walking. When they saw him, a look of surprise registered on their faces.

"Howdy, folks," called out Trailer in his most jovial voice. "Would you mind telling me where this road leads to?"

The woman looked down at their feet, and Trailer saw there were sacks of vegetables and what looked like dried corn.

"To another road," the man said curtly.

"Very helpful, but could you be more specific?"

The woman looked at them incredulously. "If you ain't from around here, you picked the wrong day to be lost."

"What do you mean?"

"It's Creek Tax Day," the man said, pointing at the bags at their feet. There was a sound of hooves on gravel coming down the road. "I suspect that's them now."

Before Trailer could react, three riders cantered into sight behind them. They pulled a long trail of horses on lead ropes packed with what Trailer assumed were other collected taxes. They pulled up in the front yard and surrounded Trailer, Jessica, and Simon.

"They're not with us," the man on the porch told the Creek. "They just walked down the road a few minutes ago. Our tax is right here, down to the last kernel of corn."

An Indian in front wearing a cowboy hat turned to Trailer. "Is that true?"

"How should I know? I haven't counted their corn."

He leveled the lever-action rifle he had been holding on his saddle horn at Trailer. The other two riders did the same.

"Go inside now," the man on the porch told his family, and they complied.

"Easy now," said Trailer. "No need to get upset. We're just passing through."

"There is no 'just passing through' Creek lands without permission."

"I've heard that, but it was an accident. We were attacked west of here by the Cossacks or Devils or someone and had to run."

"Where you going?" the Creek asked.

Trailer pointed at Simon and Jessica. "North to the JP. I'm a guide."

"Not a very good one evidently," said one of the other Creek.

"Hey," said Trailer, "you got any openings in the Native American IRS? I'll be glad to apply. Otherwise, I do what I can."

The Creek looked at Simon and Jessica before pointing at Simon. "You. What's your story? You're different from those new clothes to that clean rifle. Where'd you come from? Tell the truth, or we'll kill you and leave your bodies for these good folks to bury."

Simon thought about lying, but couldn't think of anything to say except the truth. Besides, the man looked as if he could see right through Simon.

"I'm looking for a place to settle down. For me and my friends."

"These two?" asked the Creek.

"No. About twenty more," Simon answered. "We can't stay where we're at any longer."

Trailer and Jessica were looking at him curiously.

"And where are you living now?" he asked.

"Would you believe me if I said an underground government bunker?"

The three Indians appeared startled and looked at each other. "Like from her story," one of them said.

The lead Creek stared at Simon with deep dark eyes. "They're more rifles in this bunker like the one you're carrying?"

"Yes," said Simon. "Thousands of them."

"You'll come with us," the Creek finally said, lifting his rifle to rest again in his pommel horn. "The prophetess may want to talk to you...and we need guns."

"Who doesn't?" asked Trailer.

Two saddleless horses were led forward on lead ropes and indicated that Simon and Jessica should climb up on them. The Creek then counted the tax on the front porch, wrote something in a notebook, handed the man what might have been a receipt, and then loaded the corn and vegetables into a horse.

"What about me?" asked Trailer.

"You're too big," the head Creek said. "You'd make a good horse swaybacked. You'll have to run along beside us...or be on your way if you like. I doubt the prophetess would be interested in a simple guide."

"I can just go?" Trailer asked.

"Sure. Better be out of Creek territory by nightfall though. That dark skin of yours would make a pretty saddle cover," answered the Creek, and turned heading down the road they had just come. The other four riders followed along with string of pack horses.

Simon and Jessica looked back at him, and the girl finally gave him a small smile and a wave.

Trailer watched them until they were out of sight. His thoughts were interrupted by the sound of a pump shotgun chambering a round.

He turned to find the man still standing on his porch, now leveling a shotgun in his direction. "Get off my property, now."

Trailer slowly backed away to the edge of the road. He then turned and looked north and then south.

"Oh, damn it to hell," he said and started running south after the horses.

Chapter 15 – Milan Depot

Vincent Lacert was disappointed they hadn't encountered any resistance on the way to Milan Depot. The West Tennessee Republic forces were no more and JP elements were far to the north. The few criminal gangs along their route got one look at the heavily armed convoy and fled.

Near Milan Depot, Vincent sent a small reconnaissance element forward, which returned to tell him that twenty JP soldiers guarded the facility. None of them appeared very alert and many were asleep.

"Attack fast and without hesitation," he told his commanders. "We can't allow them to barricade themselves in the facility. I also need prisoners, so don't start executing people until we're done with them."

Several of the commanders looked at each other at the expectation of executing prisoners, but none said anything.

They left all the vehicles under a security detachment and made their way forward on foot in three groups. Vincent stayed to the rear where he could control all the elements. Once they were all in position, Vincent ordered the assault. After several short minutes of intense shooting and explosions, it was over.

"Reaper 6, this is Reaper 3, over," said Vincent's radio.

"This is Reaper 6, go ahead."

"Objective is secured."

Vincent motioned his driver forward, and they raced down the paved road and through the chain-link barrier his men had blown open.

The vehicle screeched to a halt in front of the depot. A line of stunned men, several of them wounded, were on their knees in front of armed guards. A small stack of bodies were being piled up to the side.

He stepped out of the vehicle and walked up to the kneeling men. "Who's in charge here?"

"I am," said a voice to Vincent's left.

He walked over to a gray-haired man with strong features. "What's your name?"

"Captain Rueben Bonnett."

"Captain, I presume you know the codes to access the secure locations within the depot."

"I do," Reuben said and then looked up at Vincent. "And you're not getting them."

Vincent pulled the pistol from its holster at his hip and placed the barrel on the captain's forehead. The man looked back impassively.

Moving the barrel of the pistol to the right, Vincent shot the next man in line in the head. Droplets of blood splattered on both Reuben and Vincent. The body toppled over slowly to the ground.

"How about now?" Vincent asked.

"You bastard."

Vincent stepped to the left and shot the man on the other side of Reuben.

"Stop it!" said a voice to the right. "I know the codes. I'll give them to you."

"Shut your mouth, Sergeant!" yelled Reuben.

Vincent backhanded the captain with his pistol, feeling the cheek and eye bones cave in. He walked down the line to stand in front of the man who had spoken. "You're telling the truth?"

The man nodded. "I'll tell you, just let us go."

"That's all I want," Vincent said and pulled the man to his feet. He walked him towards the depot and up to the front entrance.

"The front's just secured by a key," the sergeant spoke hurriedly while staring at the bloodstained hand gripping him. "I have one and Captain Bonnett has the other. Mine's in my pocket."

Vincent holstered his pistol and pulled out a knife, which he used to cut the bonds restraining the man's hands behind his back. "Open it."

The sergeant massaged his wrists before reaching into his pocket with a trembling hand. He brought out a massive key ring, which he used to open the door.

Vincent saw the large adjacent doors on a loading dock. "Open those as well."

The man did so.

"Bring the trucks up," Vincent ordered his men. "Start loading up as per the priority list. Anything we can't take with us drag outside. We're going to destroy it."

Vincent walked the JP sergeant back past rows of mortars, claymores, grenades, and rifles. Pallets of ammunition and equipment filled the rooms. Most of the depot's supplies had been used in the last two years by the WTR and JP, but there was plenty left over.

"Where's the Class F explosives storage area?" Vincent asked.

The man looked at him, confused, and shook his head.

Vincent tapped the man on the chest with his knife. "We had a deal. I know they're here. This used to be *my* facility, after all."

The sergeant turned and walked through several rooms, hitting light switches as he went.

"I see there's still electricity down here, that's nice," said Vincent.

Approaching a large metal door, the man strode over to a keypad and placed his thumb on a scanner until it beeped. He then punched in a code and pulled the heavy door open, turning on the light.

Vincent followed him inside the small room and saw several racks containing large square suitcases approximately three feet across. All the spaces were filled except for one, which was vacant. Each case had a lock and keyhole.

"Keys," Vincent said.

The man walked over to a safe set against the wall and began to spin the dial a few times. He then opened the drawer with a loud clang and stepped back.

Vincent leaned over and saw about two dozen small black boxes, with one hole missing. He pulled out one of the boxes and opened it to find a hex key with a number on it: 6. Vincent walked over to the space marked 6, pulled the case out onto the floor roughly, and opened the case. Inside, he found a large backpack with several manuals attached.

He immediately noticed something wasn't right. There were raw wires sticking out where electrical components were supposed to be, as well as a vacant space where the control module had sat.

"What's this?" Vincent asked, pointing with his knife.

"General Taylor ordered them all rendered inoperable after Fulton."

"All of them?" Vincent asked incredulously.

The man nodded.

Vincent stepped away towards the door and stared vacantly at the wall.

How could a leader make such a stupid decision? Vincent wondered. *He might need those nukes in the future. Just goes to show you some are unfit for the burden of leadership.*

He then turned swiftly and slashed the man across the throat with his knife. The sergeant grabbed his spurting neck and crumpled to the floor with a look of amazement. Vincent bent down and cleaned his knife off on the dying man's shirt sleeve.

"Sir?" said a hesitant voice at the door.

"Yeah?" Vincent answered without turning.

"We'll be loaded soon."

"Good," said Vincent, standing and putting his knife away. "Get some people in here to load up everything; don't forget the keys in the safe."

The man looked at the body on the floor. "What about the prisoners?"

"What do you mean?"

"Are we turning them loose or taking them with us?"

Vincent laughed. "Just kill them. They're no use to us anymore."

"You mean...just kill them?"

"That's exactly what I mean," said Vincent. "As a matter of fact, I want all leaders to execute at least one prisoner personally. Anyone who refuses will be brought to me, understand?"

"Yes, sir," the man said and departed.

"This is very disappointing," Vincent said, looking at the open case at his feet. Still, those scientists at Huntsville were wicked smart. Maybe they could figure out a way to salvage the tactical nukes.

Vincent smiled as he started to hear individual pops from outside.

****

Back in Huntsville, Vincent's forces moved swiftly once past the security barriers. All of the leaders had agreed to kill one of the prisoners except for two, which Vincent had then executed. Those that were left were tied to him by the bond of shared atrocity. Who else would accept them now?

Those forces moved swiftly and efficiently, taking control of key areas and personnel. Most people didn't even realize that a coup was occurring until it was over.

Vincent marched into Director Erik Sessions's office without knocking.

Erik was standing behind his desk looking out the window. He turned as Vincent and two soldiers walked in. "Vince, what is going on?"

"The mission was a success," Vincent said. "We are now better prepared to resist future aggressions."

"That's...good," said Erik, looking worriedly at the two soldiers flanking Vincent. "Why are they here?"

"In case we need to remove your dead body. You can't expect *me* to do it."

"My...body?"

Vincent walked up and sat on the edge of Erik's desk. "I'm going to give you a choice. Like you, I recognize talent and see some good qualities in you. You know how to talk to these geeks around here, yet can stay on task. Get the mission accomplished. The key question is can you work for me?"

"Work...for you?"

"Sure," said Vincent. "Call us partners if you like, as long as we both understand I'm in charge. You keep your same position and keep doing what you're doing, just make sure to run everything by me, understand?"

Erik looked at the two soldiers and noticed one of them was carrying what appeared to be a body bag while the other had pushed in a mop and bucket filled with dirty gray water.

Erik forced himself to smile. "Sure. Why not? We're all on the same team, right?"

Vincent stood and grinned, holding his hand out to Erik. "Very wise choice. I knew you were a reasonable man."

Erik shook his hand.

"We'll talk later," Vincent promised and then turned to the two soldiers. "Come on, boys. We have a very busy day."

They walked out of the room.

Erik slowly walked across the room as if in a trance. He closed and locked his door and then returned to sit heavily in his chair.

He stared at the body bag and mop bucket the two soldiers had left in his office.

Chapter 16 – The Memorial

"It's ugly as hell," Nathan said.

"Shush," Reggie said out of the corner of his mouth. "People are watching."

He looked around. Indeed they were. The crowd was much larger than he had expected, but then again, the event would resonate with a great many people. All the seats were filled, and throngs of people lined the riverfront for as far as Nathan could see.

They were there to commemorate the Paducah Memorial, but people were already calling it the Brazen Memorial because the giant piece of concrete and steel had been placed right at the spot where the man had been crucified. A jagged hole had been dug into the concrete embankment to rest the base of the wooden cross. Now, that hole had been covered by a large portion of the bridge foundation that had been destroyed when Ernest Givens fled with several thousand citizens. The names of all those who had died in the defense of Paducah were inscribed in the concrete.

Nathan knew who some of those names were without having to look.

Paducah Mayor Leslie Mitchell stepped to the podium to polite clapping and some grumbling. It was rumored that when Ethan Schweitzer's forces had encircled Paducah, he had fled, which was why Brazen was in charge of the city's defenses. Most thought Mitchell would not be re-elected.

"Good afternoon," Mitchell said into the microphone. "Thank you all for coming here today. As you know, nearly six months ago, this city was under siege and threatened with annihilation. Through the brave actions of many, we were saved and are still here today. Many of you were among those who fought in its defense or were forced to make the long exodus across the river.

"It is important that we remember the sacrifices of those who died. Their names are inscribed on this memorial. Names like Beau Myers, Gary Lancourt, and Timothy Walker."

There was a murmur of "Brazen" that flowed though the crowd.

A lot of good people have died so that we could be here today, thought Nathan, *yet the one everyone immortalizes was the biggest scoundrel of them all. Maybe there's a lesson in that.*

"I could talk more, but I thought it appropriate that someone who lived through those experiences should address you today and have the honor of commemorating this memorial."

Nathan turned to Reggie with a questioning look. Reggie shrugged.

Mitchell smiled to someone off to his left. "It is my pleasure to introduce to you a man that many of you here know well, the hero of the Long Walk, Ernest Givens."

There was wild applause from the masses along the river. Nathan looked back and saw several people were crying.

"Oh, hell," said Nathan, "this is bad. Everyone here loves that man. He brought them back home."

"Just smile and make the best of it," Reggie said, clapping.

"Thank you, Mayor," said Ernest, stepping to the podium. He started to say more, but stopped and gazed at the memorial behind him.

137

He turned and placed his hand on the concrete and lowered his head for nearly a full minute. When he returned to the podium, he wiped his eyes with a handkerchief.

"Damn, he's good," whispered Nathan.

"Don't be so jaded," Reggie said. "He's not faking anything, just using what's there. It's sincere."

"Sorry for that," Ernest said, and there was clapping, which rose again to a loud roar. Once it settled down, he began again. "I cannot tell you how much of an honor it is to be here today, how humbling, how...terrifying it is."

There was a wave of laughter and someone yelled, "We love you, Ernest!"

"Thank you," he said with a smile. "I'm terrified because I wasn't sure how I would feel about this. I've talked to many of you about our shared experiences. Most of you have thanked me, but it is I who should be thanking you. We made it through that awful ordeal because of each other."

He turned and pointed at the memorial. "This represents those who made our survival possible. They died so that many could live."

"He's not using notes," Nathan muttered.

"That's because he doesn't need them," said Reggie. "He's just talking to a bunch of friends."

"Major Beau Myers was my commander and my friend. Right before the enemy forces were about to break though, he ordered me and others to get everyone across and to blow the bridge. He knew what that meant, but he did it anyway.

"Sacrifice," Ernest paused. "That is the essence of our survival. It always has been. Putting the welfare of others above that of one's self." He looked at Reggie and Nathan suggestively.

"We all want the same things. It was the same things these men and women behind me who have fallen wanted. To live in peace and provide for their family. That's all. That was the hope of the Jackson Purchase. That was the only thing we asked for. Yet, after only two years, we have had two disastrous wars, rampant crime, food and power shortages, and now we're hearing that our money is no good because the fuel is gone."

There were cries and murmurs among the crowd.

"That son of a bitch," said Nathan. "Someone told him."

Reggie put his hand on Nathan's leg. "Do not react to anything that is said today. Every eye is on us. If there isn't a riot, consider it a win."

"And what about Fulton?" Ernest asked. "Not fifty miles from here is a radioactive wasteland. It used to be filled with families, people just like you and me, trying to survive. Now they're either sick or gone. Some of them were my friends, and no one speaks for them. Where is their memorial?"

There were angry cries from behind Nathan.

"I don't have all the answers, folks. No one does. That's why it's so important for decisions to be made in public. So we don't have nuclear bombs going off, so we don't have all our money stolen from us, so we aren't putting control of things that belong to all of us by right"—he looked at Reggie and Nathan again—"into the hands of a very few."

Several spectators started clapping.

139

"I guess the question we have to ask ourselves, that we should have been asking all along, is…what type of world do we want to live in?" He turned and pointed at the memorial. "What type of world did they die for? The good news is the answer is in all of our hands. We live in a democracy, at least in theory. We have the power to change things if we want to."

Ernest paused and looked out over the crowd. "I've had a tough time of it since we got back home. I'm sure some of you are in the same boat. I've recently come to realize we can't give up and just let things flow around here. We have to decide, or things will be decided for us. That's why I'm running for president, because we're all in this together."

He smiled and waved to the crowd. "Thank you all," he said, and then turned and put his hand on the monument.

There was loud cheering, and everyone in their seats rose for a standing ovation.

"Stand," said Reggie, rising.

"Are you serious?"

"Yes! Get up," said Reggie, clapping. "The political damage has been done, but if this crowds turns on us, it could get ugly for everyone."

Nathan stood and began to clap slowly.

After Ernest spoke, they played taps and had a moment of silence. Then, a number of people, including Reggie and Nathan, laid flowers at the foot of the memorial. It ended with a prayer.

"Where are you going?" Reggie asked Nathan, seeing him head towards Ernest.

"I'm going to talk to Mister Givens."

Reggie held his arm. "It's not the time. And since when did you become such a hothead?"

Nathan opened his mouth to answer that he wasn't a hothead, when a soldier ran up out of breath. "General Taylor, sir?"

"Yes."

"There's an urgent landline call for you over at the court house."

"Oh. hell, what now?" Nathan motioned to the soldier. "Lead the way."

Nathan and the soldier ran to the court house a few blocks away, and Nathan picked up a phone on the county clerk's desk. "Hello?"

"Where in the hell have to been?" an unmistakably raspy voice asked. "Do you know how long I've been trying to call you? I had to threaten some dumb soldier to go find you."

"Mom?"

"Yes, who did you think it was?"

"What's wrong?"

She paused. "It's Bethany...she's real bad."

"With what?"

"Fevers, chills, delirium. Keeps losing consciousness."

"What does the doctor say?"

"Doctor Wilson is evidently covered up right now with some sort of epidemic, but he sent one of his nurses over here."

"So what does the nurse say?"

"Malaria," his mother answered. "Evidently, lots of people are getting it."

Malaria? he thought. *That shouldn't be too difficult to treat, just a round or two of antibiotics to... Oh, no.*

"What's the treatment?" he asked.

"There is none. You need to come home, son. She's either going to pull through on her own or she won't, but you need to be by her side regardless."

"I'm on my way," Nathan said. "Tell Bethany that I love her and I'm on my way."

He dropped the phone and ran.

Chapter 17- Compromise

Joshua and Conrad sat on small stools by the Tennessee River with warm cups of chicory coffee in their hands. Billy Fox and Susan sat across from them.

"This is good," said Conrad, sipping the cup.

"We try," said Billy. "Maybe the JP would be interested in trading chicory for tobacco?"

"That's the second time today someone from the Creek Nation has tried to work a trade deal with us," said Joshua.

Billy spread his hands out at his side. "We are friendly neighbors. It only makes sense for us to trade."

"I agree," said Joshua, "but that is not our purpose in coming here."

"Your father said you would be coming through in order to look at the people to the south," Billy Fox said. "You must be talking about Huntsville."

"We are," said Conrad. "What do you know?"

Billy shrugged. "Not too much. They have a walled community south of here. We trade with some of their adjacent towns. They also have electricity."

"Electricity?" said Joshua.

Susan nodded at him. "Seems like the JP is not the only power player in the area."

"They're also organized and well armed," said Billy Fox. "Especially after Milan."

"What about Milan?" asked Conrad.

Billy looked at them quizzically. "You don't know?"

"We've been traveling. It's not like they could call us on a cell phone."

"We just presumed the JP knew about the attack," said Susan.

"What attack?" asked Conrad.

"They hit the Milan Depot," said Billy. "Killed all your guards there and burned everything they didn't take with them."

"Who did this?" asked Joshua.

"We talked to some people afterwards," Billy said. "Indications are that it was a convoy from Huntsville. Some of their vehicles actually had Huntsville stickers or decals on their plates."

"They took everything?" asked Joshua.

"What they could," answered Billy. "The rest they doused in fuel and set alight. There was a huge fireball that burned for several days. Thankfully, they took all the ammo and explosives instead of burning it. People in the area had to come and put the fire out before it burned the forests and fields around there. If not for the fire, it probably would have been longer before anyone knew."

"People said they saw a tall blond fellow leading them," said Susan. "There's been rumors of a new military leader down there. Someone capable and ruthless. They call him Reaper."

"Tall and blond, you say?" said Conrad, looking at Joshua expectantly.

"So, if I understand correctly," said Billy, "your government is trying to discover if Huntsville is a threat to you."

"That's about right," answered Joshua.

"And what if you decide it is? What then?"

"That's for the leaders to decide," said Joshua. "I just gather information."

"Well, if there is to be another war," said Billy, pouring himself another cup of chicory, "tell your leaders not to just expect to come through our lands or get our support for nothing. We're allies, but that only goes so far."

A rider raced up and stared at them meaningfully.

"Yes, Don?" said Billy.

"We found some people we think you're going to want to talk to. The prophetess especially. One of them knows about a government bunker like the one she came from in North Dakota."

Billy looked at him in exasperation and cut his eyes to Joshua and Conrad.

Don seemed to notice the visitors for the first time. "Oh, sorry."

"I'd love to hear what they have to say," said Conrad.

"Me too," said Joshua.

Billy sighed. "Bring them here."

Within a few minutes, a small dark woman, a serious man, and a black giant were escorted up to them.

"Holy sasquatch," said Conrad, staring at Trailer.

"Look who's talking," answered Trailer, glaring back at him.

"Welcome, I am Billy Fox, Chief of the Creek Nation." Billy turned to the others. "This is Susan, my advisor, and Joshua and Conrad, two visitors from the JP."

"The JP?" said Simon. "That's where we're trying to go."

"First things first," said Billy. "Tell us your story and start with who you are."

They each introduced themselves, and Simon then told them about the bunker and the people there. Simon told them how he knew about the bunker and Cheyenne Mountain. He described their situation and the need to find a new home before the fuel ran out.

"He said they have lots more rifles like this," said Don, holding up Simon's assault rifle.

"Is that true?" asked Billy.

Simon nodded. "Not just rifles. Everything."

"Where is it?" asked Joshua.

"Don't answer that," said Trailer. "Remember how to negotiate."

"Maybe you should stay out of this," Conrad told Trailer.

"Maybe I should," Trailer answered, leaning forward on his cudgel, "but I won't."

Joshua stared at them each in turn. "So you're looking for a new home for about twenty people and, in exchange, you'll let us have what's in your bunker?"

"Twenty-two," said Simon. "The deal has to include Jessica and Trailer as well."

Jessica turned to him in surprise and put her hand on his arm.

"That's mighty kind," said Trailer. "I'll need to check out the nightlife there before making a final decision."

"Why not come live with us?" said Billy Fox.

"What?" asked Simon and Joshua at the same time.

"Why limit your options?" asked Billy. "We can give you a new home as well. Offer us the same deal."

"Now just wait a minute," said Joshua. "What are you trying to do here?"

"What are you trying to do?" asked Billy. "You are our guests sitting on Creek land talking to Creek prisoners."

"Is that what we are?" asked Jessica.

"Are you threatening us?" asked Conrad.

"Everyone!" yelled Susan loudly. "Let's all relax and talk this through. I'd like to propose a compromise."

"Sure," said Joshua.

Billy Fox nodded.

"Why don't we leave the choice up to our guests, but...we agree ahead of time that no matter what the decision is, we will split everything evenly. It sounds like there is plenty for everyone...assuming their story is true. Also, you're going to probably need the Creek to help you transport everything anyway. You're not going to get an eight millimeter mortar's base plate a hundred miles on a ten speed."

Conrad whistled. "Look who knows her artillery."

"I was a military officer," Susan said, glaring at Conrad. She turned to Joshua. "What do you say? I think it's more than fair."

Joshua looked at Conrad, who shrugged. He turned back to Billy and Susan. "I'm not really in a position to obligate my government to anything."

"You better be," said Billy, "or we'll take it all."

Joshua sighed. "Okay then, I guess we've got a deal."

"Okay," said Billy, nodding.

"If we're done with all the haggling," said Jessica, "I for one want to go to the JP."

Simon looked at her for a second. "Me and my people as well."

"Can I do both?" asked Trailer. "I am a guide, after all. It would really make things easier for me."

Billy shook his head and sighed. "Sure."

"Really?" asked Trailer, smiling. "I was just joking. I didn't expect you to agree. Does that mean I'm a Creek now?"

"We should all go together to Simon's bunker as soon as possible," Billy said, ignoring the big man. "It sounds like those people there would be in a very dire situation the minute the fuel goes bad."

"And we might not be able to get in and get the goodies once the power goes out," grumbled Conrad.

"We still have a mission," said Joshua, looking at Conrad. "Huntsville?"

"I'd say that's on hold for now," said Billy. "You can always check it out when you get back...unless you're okay with us going to the bunker without you."

Joshua hesitated before finally answering. "No, Huntsville can wait."

"Okay," said Billy, "I suggest everyone leave first thing tomorrow for Mississippi."

"I'm not going back there," said Jessica. "You all can go if you want, but not me."

148

"I have to send some of my men north anyway to report this," said Joshua. "You can go with them if you want. You'll be safe."

The girl nodded to him gratefully.

"What about you, big man?" said Conrad, looking at Trailer. "What are your plans?"

Trailer smiled. "I think I'll ride this out. It's starting to get interesting. Besides, I bet they got new clothes in that bunker in even my size."

Everyone agreed and moved away to plan for their various trips.

Billy Fox turned to Susan. "I knew Chicoca was right about you."

She hardly heard him. It was visions she had seen in the smoke that kept haunting her mind.

Chapter 18- Innocence

Nathan burst through the front door of their home in New Harvest. He had managed to find someone with a functioning vehicle willing to drive him. Even so, it had been nearly two hours to get home since he had talked to his mother.

"Where is she?" he asked.

His mother and Alexandra looked at him with blank faces.

"Is she in there?" he asked, pointing towards their bedroom. When they didn't answer, he began moving in that direction.

His mother stepped in front of him. "Son."

"Just let me see her, please."

She dropped her head and stepped aside. Nathan walked into the bedroom they had shared since surviving the trek back home from Maryland.

Bethany lay there. Still and lifeless. Somehow beautiful even in death but obviously not there anymore.

"No." Nathan backed away, shaking his head.

His mother put her hand on his shoulder. "Son, you need to—"

He slapped her hand away angrily. "Don't touch me!"

Nathan strode through the house and out the front door. He walked down to the waterfront and just stood there, staring out over the water. It felt as if a weight pressed on his chest and he couldn't catch his breath.

Nathan remembered how they first met and the birth of each child. Their wedding day and when they would lose their first baby, Caleb, together. All the deployments and hardships and worry and loss they had been through together and how they had loved each other. Their last conversation started playing itself in his head. He remembered how she had asked for his company and his comfort—hell, simply his presence—and he had dismissed her. His wife and friend, who he had counted on for most of his life, who had never let him down, had died without him. Because of what? Vanity? Self-importance? Putting others before his family?

He drew in breath and screamed as loud as he could out over the water. Drawing in breath, he did it again and felt like he could now breathe. Nathan sank down to his knees and cried.

His mother's arms were suddenly around him, and he didn't push her away this time. They cried together and held each other for a very long time.

Finally, his mother said, "I know it's hard, but you need to go in and say goodbye to her."

Nathan shook his head. "I don't know how."

"Yes, you do," she said, pulling him towards the house. "I'll be with you. Come on."

He walked carefully into the house and then their room. Even in the time that he had been away, she had seemed to diminish and no longer had that essence of residual vitality. She now looked dead. It was the body of his beloved wife, but it wasn't her. Bethany was no longer with them. Just a stack of inert mass: decaying muscle, organs, and bones.

His Bethany was gone.

"I'm sorry," he said. "Not just for this, but for everything. I'm so sorry." He wanted to cry again but found that he couldn't.

He turned to his mother. "Did she suffer?"

She shook her head. "I don't think so. She was in and out of consciousness and delirium most of the time."

"Did she say anything?"

"She said plenty of things."

Nathan closed his eyes and breathed deeply. "Did she say anything for me?"

His mother took his hands in both of hers. "She said, 'Tell Nathan to take care of the family.'"

"That's all?"

His mother nodded.

Nathan turned to find Alexandra holding a sleeping River. She handed the baby over to Nathan, who took her gently.

He gazed down into the sleeping innocent face. Some of the pain and emptiness slipped away as he held his daughter.

What is it about babies and little things that call out to our hearts? he wondered. He stared and realized it was their innocence. *Innocence in all its forms is beautiful to us. It is the purest form of beauty and goodness. That is why it should be protected.*

"I'm here for you," he whispered to River. "I'll always be here for you. I promise."

His mother pulled the sheet up to cover Bethany's face.

Part II
Approaching Night

Chapter 1 – The Monster

The last week had been a nightmare for Erik Sessions. Who would have thought things could be worse than the problems they were already experiencing…before Vincent Lacert.

You caused this, he thought and pushed the thought away. Not because it wasn't true, but because it wouldn't help them at this point.

Vincent Lacert is a monster, he found himself thinking with surprise. *I invited a monster to take over.*

But he took great pains to hide those thoughts. It was imperative for their survival, as he saw it, that Vincent believed he was a cowed dog. Which he was most of the time, he admitted, but he did have his moments.

It had been only a few days since Vincent's coup. Erik had heard rumors of executions but didn't know if they were real or not. He suspected they were. Vincent had not been acting when he came into his office that day with the body bag and mop bucket. Tensions were high when Vincent explained to him the problem with his several dozen tactical nuclear weapons. They wouldn't go *boom*, and he needed to find a way to make them operable again.

"Of course I will help," Erik had told him. "I'll put my best people on it."

And he had. People he could trust. They had determined that it would be a relatively minor affair to fix the bombs. The intricate firing mechanisms based on multiple safety procedures was missing, but it would be simple enough to design a rudimentary explosive trigger to start the catastrophic chain reaction.

"That's not what we're here to do," Erik had told them in a whisper, even though they were alone. "We can't allow that madman to get his hands on a nuclear bomb. We need to render them all permanently inoperable. Then, we need to give our very best acting performance and explain why they were already too far damaged to fix. Everyone understand?"

They did. Now it was time to play their parts. He had given them three days and that time was up.

Vincent sent a soldier to get Erik from his office, who escorted him to Laboratory 5A. It was actually more like a very sterile airplane hangar with lots of work benches and sophisticated machinery. Twenty-three tables sat in the middle of the hanger, and on each of them rested a dissected tactical nuke.

Turning from one of the tables as Erik walked in, Vincent pointed an angry finger at him. He looked calm, but his lips were tight and his eyes flashed even icier blue than normal.

"This is not what I expected," he said, his voice rising. "This is not what I *wanted*."

"What's wrong?" asked Erik as innocently as he could.

"What's wrong?" Vincent pointed at the host of pale-faced scientists and engineers around him. "They're telling me none of these can be made to work again."

"Is that true?" Erik asked them, and they nodded.

Erik sighed and shook his head. "Nuclear devices are sensitive. It doesn't surprise me that they couldn't be repaired. They're not made to be messed with once assembled."

"You told me you would put your best people on this."

"I did. These are the best of the best."

"Really?" Vincent walked over and grabbed a small thin man by the lapel of his jacket. He dragged the man to stand near the nuclear carcass on the nearest table. "Tell me exactly what it was that you did. Tell me why it is impossible to make it work. Use small words for an idiot like me."

The man tried, but there was a reason Einstein wasn't a Hollywood star except for the hair. The technician stammered and kept looking at Erik for help.

"Come on," said Erik, stepping forward. "You're scaring the snot out of him. He can hardly even talk."

"Don't move!" yelled Vincent, pointing at Erik.

Erik heard shuffling around him and turned to find there were soldiers in the corners of the room. *This is not good.*

Vincent stared at him, hard. He then looked at the other scientists around the room. He noticed the tight faces that kept coming back to Erik. He saw the beads of sweat rolling down faces in the cool hangar.

"You have good cause to be scared," Vincent whispered to the man in his grasp. "I'm not fond of my people failing me. That really makes me angry, but there is something that is far worse. Something that I simply cannot tolerate. Do you know what that is?"

The man shook his head.

"Disloyalty," Vincent said while looking at Erik. He then turned to gaze around the room. "I'm going to give all of you one chance to tell the truth. There will only be one, and the consequences for lying to me will be dire. Not just for you, but for your families."

"Vince," said Erik, stepping forward, "what are you doing?"

"My name is not Vince!" he yelled at Erik, stopping the man in his tracks.

He turned back to the scientist in his grasp and pulled the knife from his belt. He laid it casually just beneath the man's left eye. The small figure began to tremble and whimper.

"Nod up and down for yes and left to right for no," said Vincent, looked at the scientists gathered around him. "Anyone who doesn't answer, or hesitates in answering, will lose an eye. Everyone understand?"

Twenty heads went up and down.

"Did Erik Sessions tell you to sabotage these bombs?"

No one answered immediately.

Vincent pressed the edge of the knife under the man's eye and he screamed. "Yes! Yes, he did!" He pushed the sobbing man to the floor and looked around at the scientists meaningfully.

They all began to slowly and shamefully nod.

Vincent turned to Erik and shook his head in astonishment. "Why?"

"Why? Why would I not provide a crazy madman two dozen nuclear weapons? Isn't it obvious?"

158

Vincent pointed his knife towards the outside. "The world is already trashed. What's a few more nukes matter? I might not even use them."

"You would use them," Erik said. "Your type can't help themselves."

"That's true," said Vincent with a smile. He looked around the room, and his eyes settled on a thick insulated cable about an inch thick and six feet long. Each end contained a metal coupler. Vincent pulled it off a rack and walked towards Erik.

The director began to back away but bumped into several soldiers. They grabbed his arms and held him in place.

Vincent swept the remnants of a tactical nuke roughly onto the floor. "Right here's fine," he told the soldiers. "Tie him down."

Erik struggled as they bent him over the table and tied his wrists to the far edge of the table and his legs to the supports nearest him.

The madman bent down until his face was inches from Erik's. "I really do regret this, but you forced my hand. We could have worked together, maybe even been friends, but you had to do this." Vincent sighed. "What's about to happen is on you."

He pointed to the scientists. "Make a single file line behind the director. Come on, move quickly now, we still have work to do."

They all lined up nervously, soldiers standing nearby watching.

Vincent handed the first man the cable. "Three lashes from each of you. Each strike needs to be as hard as you can, or it doesn't count."

The first man looked at Vincent in shock. "I can't do that."

"Really?" asked Vincent. "Do you really want to know what will happen if you don't?"

After a moment's hesitation, the man took the cable.

"I'm sorry, Erik," he said.

"Don't be sorry," Vincent said. "He brought this on himself. Now get to whacking."

The man hesitated several times before he lifted the cable up and brought it down on Erik's back with a loud thump. The metal coupler slashed a gouge in his scalp. Erik cried out and began to bleed.

"No, no, no," said Vincent to the man with the cable. "You have to put some feeling into it." He turned to two soldiers nearby. "Grab him and hold him down."

Two soldiers grasped the struggling man and dragged him over to a table. They didn't bother to sweep off the nuclear backpack, only bent him over it. They jerked the cable from his hand and held it out to Vincent, who took it.

"This is how you do it, people." Vincent took a small running start, whipped the cable back over his head, and brought it down with all his might. His feet came off the floor at the moment of impact.

There was a loud sickening thump, and the man screamed.

"Sha-zam!" said Vincent, grinning. "That's what I'm talking about. Now who's ready?"

He tuned to the whimpering man bent over the backpack. "I'll give you a moment to recover." Vincent then turned to a tall thin woman next in line and held out the bloody cable to her. "You're up."

She stepped forward with horror in her eyes.

"Come on now," urged Vincent. "It's easy, believe me. And let's be honest, you've secretly wanted to do this for some time, right?"

The woman was crying and hyperventilating at the same time. Gripping the end of the cable with white-knuckled hands, she let out a piercing scream and then brought the cable down savagely on Erik's back.

"That's what I'm talking about!" said Vincent with a big grin. "That is the can-do attitude and go-get-em-ness I expect."

They all did what Vincent wanted.

When it was done, there was a large pool of blood under Erik's table. He had thankfully passed out long ago.

"Okay then, job well done, people," said Vincent. He turned to the first man who he had struck. He was sitting on the floor under the table he had been bent over. "What's your name?"

"Jeff."

"Well, Jeff, you didn't pull your weight. Everyone here did their jobs, but you didn't. That means you have to make up for it."

Jeff reached for the discarded bloody cable lying on the floor.

"No, no, it's too late for that," Vincent said. "Stand up and come over here."

He slowly and hesitantly climbed to his feet and walked over to stand beside Vincent near Erik's head.

Vincent held out a large knife and spun it in his hand until the handle was pointing towards Jeff. "Take it."

Jeff slowly grasped the knife and found that Vincent had a gun to his head. "Cut his throat."

"What?"

"Do it."

Jeff looked to the others for help, but none would meet his gaze. "I...I..."

"Do you have a family, Jeff?"

He nodded.

"Any children?"

Jeff nodded and stammered. "Boy and a girl."

"What ages?"

"Six and three."

"Oh, those are great ages," gushed Vincent. "Lots of fun then. Still so happy to see Daddy walk through the door at the end of the day. Do you enjoy that moment, Jeff?"

He nodded.

"Do you ever want to enjoy it again? Think about how your children would feel if they never saw their daddy again… Well, except for your severed head delivered to them. Think of what that would do to a six- and three-year-old. They might never recover, I fear."

Tears crept down Jeff's ashen face.

Vincent sighed and patted Jeff on the chest with the hand that didn't hold the gun. "It's okay," he said softly and comfortingly. "He's going to die anyway. You know that right? What does it matter if you do it or someone else?"

He stared at the knife in his hand.

"Like Jake Spoon said in *Lonesome Dove*…" Vincent tuned to look at everyone. "The greatest western epic of all time by the way. Like Jake says, 'I'd damn sight rather be killed by my friends than by a bunch of damn strangers.' Don't you think Erik feels that way, too? You'll be doing him a favor, believe me."

162

Jeff reached the knife out hesitantly and then drew it back.

"Grab his hair with you other hand," Vincent instructed helpfully.

Jeff did.

"There you go. Now pull the head back and up to expose the ceratoid artery."

He did and then laid the knife under Erik's chin.

"No, no, no," said Vincent. "That's the windpipe. It will cause him to die slowly from asphyxiation. Do you want that for your friend?"

Jeff shook his head.

"Then right there," said Vincent, pointing to the side of the neck. "Either side works, and it only takes one. You cut that cleanly, and within five to seven seconds, he'll pass out when his brain stops getting blood. It's not a bad way to go, really."

Jeff was still holding Erik's head up by its hair. His knife hand trembled.

"You can do this," said Vincent. "I believe in you, partner."

The knife went down quickly and forcefully. Blood spurted out in a thick burst and then fountained onto the floor. The others in the room uttered groans and cries.

Jeff dropped the knife and stepped away.

"Good job," said Vincent, giving the man a giant bear hug. "Well done indeed. I'm proud of you."

Vincent holstered his pistol and turned back to them all with his hands on his hips. "All right then. Break's over. Time to get back to work. You need to clean this place up first, and then get to work."

"Work on what?" asked Jeff woodenly.

"Good question," said Vincent. "What is it you all used to do? Before the end of the world."

"We made rockets," the tall woman said tonelessly.

Vincent smiled. "I want you to make me a rocket."

Chapter 2 – Words of Advice

Ernest Givens looked nothing like he had weeks before when Sergeant Booker had visited him. Neither did his home. Both were now tidy, neat, and respectable. He had also gotten rid of all the alcohol the first few days. It had been rough not drinking after that, but it gradually got better.

He was still stunned by the amount of public support he was encountering. People really were ready for a change. The events of the past six months scared them greatly, and there had even been several protests, peaceful so far, about the currency fiasco and electricity rationing.

There was a knock on his door. He looked at his watch. Jenny, his volunteer campaign assistant, must've been early.

Opening the door, he was shocked to find Reggie Phillips standing there.

"Mister President?"

"Sorry to drop in like this," said Reggie. "I would have called, but most of the phones don't work anymore and I didn't have your number anyway. I hope you don't mind."

Ernest pulled the door open. "Not at all, come on in and have a seat. I have to warn you, I'm on my way out soon."

"It's no problem, this shouldn't take long."

"Would you like some hot tea," offered Ernest. "I just made some."

"Yes, thank you."

Ernest set out two cups on the living room coffee table and poured hot tea into each. He found Reggie looking at the pictures on the wall.

He pointed at picture of Ernest and his unit in Afghanistan. They were all smiles. Of course…they had just arrived and hadn't taken any losses yet. "I envy you that."

"You shouldn't," Ernest said. "Lots of memories and great friends, but also loss and pain. I lost my family, my friends, very nearly my sanity. What you see here is all I have left."

"Yet you've helped a lot of people," said Reggie. "What you did on the Long Walk will be told for generations...if we last that long."

Ernest looked at his watch again. "I'm sorry, but you're going to have to get to what this is about. I have to leave soon."

"Certainly, I apologize. Can we please sit?"

Ernest nodded, and they both sat across from each other and their cups of tea.

Reggie took a hesitant sip before setting it back down. "I want to tell you that I've been impressed with what you've done so far. The people obviously like you and you're a natural leader."

"You're worried I'm going to win," Ernest said with a smile.

Reggie shrugged and sipped his tea again. "I'm sure you would make a great president." He pointed at the picture again. "You've been a leader enough to know the burden it carries. You're not coming in blind or with naïve ideals."

"The people want a change."

"They always do when things are going badly," said Reggie, "but not all change is good. So often the average citizen thinks that

166

leadership is about better or worse, various degrees of satisfaction on a linear scale."

"And what do you think it is?"

"In our case, with the JP? It's about survival and non-survival."

Ernest shook his head. "That's too easy of a justification to do whatever you feel is necessary and then say it was better than the alternative afterwards. The theoretical end that never occurs can't justify whatever means you decide is best."

"Maybe," Reggie accepted, "but we are hanging by a thread here."

"And whose fault is that?" asked Ernest. "Not even talking about Fulton and the disgraceful relief effort, what about the fuel currency fiasco? What about the food lines? What about the malaria epidemic?"

"All terrible," said Reggie. "Many botched decisions and I take responsibility for most of them, but remember, we've just come out of a long war. Our country was occupied by an evil dictator, and I don't use that term lightly. All in all, we can count our blessings."

"Tell that to those in Fulton or the people who trusted in your paper currency. Better yet, tell that to parents of hungry children this winter because we don't have fuel for the tractors in the fields."

"You are very good at identifying problems," said Reggie, "but as you know, being a leader is about solutions. You've gathered quite a following by pointing out where we went wrong, but what will you do to fix things if you become president?"

Ernest was silent.

"You need to think about it, for everyone's sake. There is a good chance you'll win and you need to be prepared. You've gone pretty far on anger and frustration, but you better have a plan."

"And you're here to help me with that?" asked Ernest sarcastically.

"No. I'm actually here to ask you to tone things down. Everyone is on edge, and much of your talk has come close to causing people to do things they might regret."

"You can't lay that on me, most of them are angry about things that happened under your watch."

Reggie sighed in frustration. "I'm not here to cast blame or defend my actions. I'm talking about what is best for everyone. If you win, great. I'll be a loyal citizen and help you in any way possible. I promise you that. If I win, I'll continue to do the best job I can, but neither matters if we blow ourselves apart as a nation."

Ernest thought for a few seconds and nodded. "Okay, I hear you, but I'm going to keep telling people the truth."

"It's not as much about what you tell them as how you tell it."

"What do you mean by that?"

"One way gets them looking towards the future and solutions while the other causes them to burn with anger and look for people to blame."

Ernest smiled. "One way lets you off the hook whereas one doesn't."

Reggie dropped his head in frustration. "Fine. See it that way if you want, but let me ask you, which way is better for the people?"

There was a knock on the door followed by Jenny sticking her head in. "Ernest, it's me, you ready?"

"Sure, come on in."

The pert former advertisement executive strode in and froze at the sight of Reggie. "What's *he* doing here?"

"I was just leaving," said Reggie, standing. "Thank you for the tea."

"I appreciate what you're trying to do," said Ernest, "but it's time for a change. Everyone knows it."

Reggie smiled and nodded, walking towards the front of the small house. "Maybe so." He was at the door when he turned to look back. "One more word of advice."

"What's that?"

"Pick a vice presidential candidate. Believe me, the burden is heavier when you carry it by yourself."

"Goodbye, Mister President," said Ernest.

Reggie walked out and closed the door softly behind him.

Chapter 3 - Grieving

They buried Bethany Taylor in a small field near the cabin they shared. It was a place they had been happy for a short period of time. Nearly two years of stress, uncertainly, and chaos, but also happiness. The ceremony was attended by nearly everyone in New Harvest who could make it. Bethany had known and helped most all of them.

Nathan realized that practically all of these mourners, people who were close to Bethany and were his neighbors, were strangers to him. His time was spent elsewhere. Most of the people he knew well could not make it.

Even their son Joshua was not at his mother's funeral. He almost certainly did not even know she had died.

He endured the funeral and muttered condolences woodenly, willing it to be over. Nathan was relieved when it was over. When he didn't have to shake hands and thank people and pretend to welcome their intrusion into his grief. There was a hole in his existence that he knew would never be filled.

As the days went by, he settled into a sort of routine. He spent time with River, his mother, and Alexandra. He also tended and expanded Bethany's vegetable garden. Grief was ever-present, a pit that he walked around trying not to fall in, but the days went by if not peacefully, then tolerably.

Fishing became his alone time when people didn't worry about him. He had discovered if he was sitting alone doing nothing, people fretted over him, whereas if he were doing the same thing with a pole in his hand, no one cared. Besides, he liked fishing, and they all needed the protein.

He found himself thinking about things purposefully for the first time in years. Not just about family and what they had all been though, but the new world they inhabited now. He worried about what type of world River would grow up in, and if there was a chance she could be happy.

Happy was a relative term, he learned the hard way. Before N-Day, happy had much different connotations than after. Happy now equaled the basics: food, shelter, security. Everything else was now a fairy tale.

This is how it has been throughout most of human existence, he thought. *Brief periods of civilizations and decency surrounded by wanton lawlessness and chaos. We could easily descend into the later here if we're not careful.*

Nathan again looked out to his right. There in the distance he could see the dam. The dam that produced free electricity that kept the darkness away. That was the only thing really keeping the night at bay, he realized.

Sure, there had been civilization before electricity, but they didn't expect it. Didn't know what they didn't have. Happiness is relative, after all. Without electricity, life is harder, and most people in the JP weren't ready for that.

Nathan heard someone coming up behind him, but didn't turn. It was likely his mother coming to check on him, pole in hand or no.

Colonel Carter sat down on the driftwood log beside him and looked out over the still water.

"Luke," said Nathan. "You didn't bring a pole."

"I'm sorry about Bethany," he said.

"Thank you. It meant a lot you were at the funeral."

"It's a hard thing losing a wife," Luke said wistfully.

Nathan turned to look at him. "I didn't know you were married."

Luke nodded and smiled. "Long time ago. Met and married at my first duty station. She was coming to pick me up at the airport. My unit was returning from a security rotation in the Sinai. Drunk driver ran a red light and killed her. I waited at the airport for hours while she lay on a table at the hospital and fought for life. By the time they connected the dots and got me there, she was already gone."

"Damn," said Nathan. "I'm sorry."

"God, how we loved each other."

Nathan was silent.

"That was twenty-three years ago, but not a day goes by I don't think of her. Miss her."

Dropping his head, Nathan thought of Bethany.

Luke laid his hand on his shoulder. "But it does get better. It doesn't hurt to think of her anymore. I don't focus on all the times I let her down, but on the good times we had. And I remember how she loved me, how we loved each other."

Nathan shook his head and quickly reeled in his line. He looked at the hook. "Look at that, some damn fish picked my pocket." He re-baited the hook and cast again.

"I know it's hard," said Luke, "but we need you to come back. You're still the Chief of Defense."

"I'm not going to come back," said Nathan. "It's time to focus on my family."

"By fishing and gardening?" asked Luke.

Nathan turned to him angrily. "By being there for them. Since I've come to the JP, I've done everything that's been asked of me. No matter what the cost. Just this once I'm saying no."

"The president's struggling without you."

"He'd still be struggling with me."

"Joshua sent a report."

Nathan froze and turned to look at him. "What did it say?"

"That Huntsville is likely a serious threat. That our favorite madman Vincent Lacert might be in charge down there."

"Good God, no."

Luke nodded. "The Creek also told him that Huntsville forces hit the Milan Depot and took or destroyed everything. Killed our people down there."

"Bastard," said Nathan. "I wish we could have killed him before he got away."

"Nathan?"

He turned to look at him. "Yeah?"

"Weren't there tactical nukes at Milan? Isn't that where the one came from that David used?"

Nathan shook his head. "Don't worry. After Fulton, I made sure they were rendered inoperable."

Luke looked at him in surprise. "Seriously? Then we're not in as bad a spot as I thought."

"He's still a threat, and who knows what assets Huntsville has? I would have thought the Russians or Chinese would have targeted that place, but I guess not."

"There's something else."

"What?"

"They ran into a guy named Simon. He says he's been holed up in some secret underground bunker for the last two years. The bunker is filled with supplies and weapons and other such things."

Nathan shook his head. "I used to get excited about that sort of thing; now it just fills me with dread. Maybe this world will be better off when it's all back to spears and clubs."

"He mentioned talking to someplace called Cheyenne Mountain. Said it's a high-level military survival headquarters for the U.S. Government. Sent a girl, Jessica, north who knows the whole story; got people debriefing her now, but we won't know what we've got for sure until we talk to this Simon fellow."

"We've been hearing rumors of something like this on the shortwave broadcasts."

"Think it's legit? That there might be some sort of U.S. Government remnant still out there functioning?"

Nathan shrugged. "Still out there? Probably. Still functioning? I doubt it. They're likely holed up somewhere no better than us, maybe even worse off."

"Evidently, they're communicating with other locations."

"They've got comms with other places then," said Nathan. "Not surprising."

"How many places you figure?"

Nathan shrugged. "Who knows? Lots I bet. Does it matter?"

"Sure it does. That's the United States Government we're talking about."

"No, it's not. It's a bunch of survivors like us. There is no United States Government anymore, and if there is, we likely want nothing to do with it."

"Why would you say that?"

Nathan turned to him. "Who's your current congressman? Senator? Hell, who's the president?"

"I don't know."

"Right. I doubt there is one. If they have any type of government I suspect its very militaristic with little if any checks or balances. Little if any representation or public say. What we have here is likely much better."

Luke looked out over the water again. "Regardless, you need to come back. Things are happening, and I'm afraid they're going to get bad."

"They're already bad, count me out."

"But you're the Chief of Defense," said Luke.

"You do it," said Nathan. "I was planning on having you take over for me anyway."

Luke stared at him for a few seconds. "Okay, fine. But that means I'm in charge."

"Exactly."

"So no more coddling Joshua."

Nathan turned to him in surprise.

"Your son is a good combat leader and we're short of those," Luke explained. "I'm going to put him where he's needed, and that's in charge on people at the point of crisis."

"Come on, Luke. I've already lost one son."

"He's a soldier and an officer. You know what comes with that."

"I forbid it," said Nathan.

"I'm the Chief of Defense," said Luke. "He'll go where he's told or be courts-marshaled."

Nathan sat and thought for a long time. Finally, he turned to Luke. "You're an asshole."

Luke smiled. "Glad to have you back."

He stood and walked away.

Nathan reeled in his line and saw an empty hook. He re-baited the line and cast out over the still water.

Chapter 4 – The Bunker

Trailer and Simon led what felt like an invasion into Mississippi. In addition to Joshua and his people, there were several dozen Creek on horses.

Billy Fox had been happy to give Simon a horse as a gift. Not having any experience with horses, Simon soon found that he liked them and that strange woman Susan spent several hours teaching him as much as she could.

They even presented Trailer a mule he had named Wildcat. Although Trailer's feet only cleared the ground by a few inches, his massive weight did not appear to bother the mule in the least. Despite its name, and the typical mulish reputation, the animal was surprisingly docile and agreeable.

It was impossible for them not to draw attention along the way. Several towns reacted in panic, throwing up barricades and ringing the town's church bell or lighting a prepared signal fire.

"This is what it must have felt like to be a Mongol or Hun," Trailer said.

"No Mongol or Hun ever rode a mule," said Conrad.

"That's because they were shortsighted," Trailer answered. "If the massed hordes of Mongols had been riding herds of mules, they would have conquered the world."

Their presence not only alarmed people along their route, but also Simon's fellow inhabitants at the bunker when they finally arrived after several days.

"Lewis, it's okay," said Simon into the intercom. "Open up. They're friends."

"Did you forget that you fixed the surveillance cameras?" asked Lewis. "I can see all those people with you. Armed people that look none too friendly."

"They're from the JP... Well, some of them are."

"You were supposed to go spy on them, not invite them back for dinner."

"We both know we're running out of time here," said Simon. "When the fuel goes bad, the generators will fail. When the generators fail, we can't live here anymore even assuming we don't get trapped inside. The JP says we can come settle in their lands. We can make a new home."

"In return for what?"

"For opening up and letting them take what they need from the stocks inside," Simon answered.

"What?" said Lewis. "I'm signed for all this stuff."

"Come on," said Simon. "No one is coming. It's just us here. This is our best chance."

"No," answered Lewis.

"Let me try," said Conrad, stepping up to the microphone.

Simon stepped aside and looked up at the camera angrily.

"Lewis? It's Lewis right?"

"Yeah, that's me."

"Cool, my name is Conrad McKraven. Do you have cameras all around this facility?"

"We sure do."

Conrad nodded. "Can they see over by the fuel supply point? The concrete pad over there where the trucks used to come to deliver diesel?"

"They do."

"Good," answered Conrad. "Here's what I'm getting ready to do. I'm going to go to that pad, unscrew the intake pipe, and start dropping matches down in there until you either open the door or something interesting happens."

"You're bluffing," said Lewis.

Conrad laughed and started walking towards the fuel pad.

"Simon, stop him," said Lewis.

Simon walked back over to the intercom. "How am I supposed to do that?"

"Shoot him or something."

Simon turned to see about thirty armed persons with weapons in their hands staring at him curiously.

"I don't think that's a good idea."

"Well, you better do something fast. That maniac is unscrewing the pipe now."

"Open the door," said Simon.

"No! Stop him," said Lewis. "You, shut up, I know what I'm doing," he said away from the microphone.

"Please, Lewis open the door."

"He's holding a match over the pipe!" said Lewis.

"You better open the damn door."

Shockingly, the door clicked open.

"Hey, Simon," said a new voice, "this is Austin. Door's open. Please don't blow us up."

"Door's open!" Simon screamed, and the cry was echoed around the side of the hill.

"He dropped the match!" Simon heard Lewis scream in the background.

"Oops!" screamed Conrad, running down the hill. "My bad!"

"We're dead," muttered Trailer, closing his eyes.

Everyone held their breath. Nothing happened. Joshua pushed past Simon and opened the door. He motioned several of his soldiers through, and the Creek followed.

Conrad came running up.

"What the hell?" asked Joshua.

Conrad was shaking his fingers. "Couldn't help it, damn match burned my fingers."

"You stay out here and guard." Joshua ordered.

"Come on, now," protested Conrad. "It was an accident. At least get me something nice, like a flamethrower."

"I'll stay, too," said Trailer. "Gotta keep an eye on Wildcat. Someone's likely to try and steal her."

"You know she's not a she," said Conrad.

"In her mind, she is," said Trailer.

Joshua and Simon walked inside, leaving the two big men to their conversation. They found one of Joshua's men holding a rifle over three men on their knees.

Simon turned to Joshua. "What are you doing?"

"Let them up," Joshua ordered, and the soldier lowered his rifle.

The three men stood slowly.

"Joshua Taylor," said Simon, "meet Lewis, Derek, and Austin."

"Pleased to meet you," answered Joshua. "Simon tells me you have family in here."

Lewis rubbed a swelling bruise on the side of his face as he turned to Simon incredulously. "You *told* them?"

"Don't worry," said Joshua. "We're not going to hurt them or anything like that. We'll need you all to load up your families with supplies into a few vehicles and come with us north."

"Assuming the fuel still works," said Derek.

"It still works," said Austin, "otherwise the generators would have failed. But it may be close to the end."

"Can I trust you men not to do anything stupid?" Joshua asked. "I don't want to have to have my men follow you around. We just want to get what we can and be gone."

"And you'll let us settle in the JP?" asked Austin. "Us and our families?"

Joshua nodded. "Likely put you in New Harvest. It's a former national park created by the hydroelectric dams. Lakes on both sides. It's where I live, really pretty."

"Wow, going outside again," said Derek with wonder.

"And having electricity," said Austin.

"We can take with us what we want?" asked Lewis.

"Whatever you can carry or get into one of the cargo trucks Simon says are down below," answered Joshua. "I recommend some guns for

181

hunting, but clothing, food, batteries, medicine, light bulbs, ammo, stuff like that will trade at a premium up north. Take as much of that as you can."

The men stood and stared at each other.

Finally, Austin stuck his hand out towards Joshua. "Thank you."

Joshua took it, and this seemed to break the paralysis. The other two also shook hands and then went to get their families ready.

They wandered the vast cavernous halls of the giant bunker and realized there was no way they could take everything. Joshua would have loved to drive north with a fleet of brand-new tankers and armored vehicles but knew that wasn't practical. Without fuel, they were simply immobile guns. Instead, they focused on loading up the cargo trucks with weapons, ammunition, radios, supplies of all sorts that were difficult to find.

Joshua had imagined some sort of fight with the Creek over who got what, but he quickly realized that wasn't going to be the case. There was so much of everything that each group could take what they wanted.

They all stayed at the bunker for two days while they explored and loaded up. Simon dismantled the satellite antenna and packed it along with all the radio and communications gear into one of the trucks. Everyone put on new clothes from the vast stocks, even Trailer, and no one seemed to care that the only color was camouflage. Most of the medications were past their shelf life, but they took them anyway.

The morning of the second day, the Creek departed. Joshua and Don made a promise to each other that neither the JP nor the Creek would try to come back for more supplies here without the other.

Simon had managed to rig a failsafe to open the door should the generators shut down for good before the next visit. It felt odd to leave the valuable facility filled with priceless supplies unguarded, but it was the best option for now, Joshua decided. He said his farewell to the departing Creek and secured the bunker. Their fifteen truck convoy pulled away north with several riders in front and more in the back leading the extra horses by ropes.

"Time to go home?" asked Conrad.

Joshua shook his head. "Not yet. Second and third squad will take this stuff north along with the civilians."

"What about the rest of us?" asked Conrad.

"You and I will go with first squad to Huntsville. We still need to find out what's going on down there."

Conrad looked at him curiously. "We already have a pretty good idea. You sure you're not looking for an opportunity to get a little payback against a certain pretty blond fellow? If so, that's the sort of thinking likely to get us all killed."

"Not at all. We just need to complete the mission. We don't yet know their intentions."

"I should probably come with you," said a voice from the doorway.

They turned to find Trailer standing there, his head sticking in through the door.

"Why would you want to do that?" asked Conrad.

"'Want' is too strong a word," Trailer answered. "Our new home and the ability to live in the JP is based on an agreement you made on behalf of your government, right?"

"Yeah."

"What are the chances they would honor that if something bad were to happen to you?" Trailer asked.

They may not honor it even with me there, he thought. "I see your point."

"I don't think we need your help," said Conrad. "We're all big scary soldiers with guns. If we need someone to change a light bulb without a ladder, we'll give you a call."

"You know how to get there?" asked Trailer.

"We got maps," answered Conrad.

"I suppose you do?" asked Joshua.

"Drove those roads for years," Trailer answered. "I doubt you want to waltz in there on I-65. Maybe a more subtle approach would be best."

"He has a point," said Joshua, turning to Conrad.

Conrad stared at Trailer for a few seconds. He finally threw his hands up. "What the hell. At least maybe the mule will come in handy."

"Okay," said Trailer, rubbing his hands together. "Now we just need to talk about payment."

Both looked at him while the big man grinned.

Chapter 5 – Rumble of War

The convoy from Mississippi arrived in New Harvest and created an almost festive air in the former park. Anytime people saw vehicles running, it was a novelty, and getting fresh supplies was a big deal, especially when it involved items no one knew how to make anymore.

Nathan nearly choked when he discovered that Joshua had promised nearly two dozen strangers JP citizenship and a place to live in New Harvest. That was going to be a challenge. They were already short on houses and, technically, the JP had closed off immigration. Nathan realized that this would take some behind-the-scenes paperwork.

Nathan directed the convoy to store the contents of the vehicles in the Kentucky Dam facility under the justification that it was the most secure facility the JP had. This wasn't technically true—the uranium enrichment facility in Paducah was more secure by far—but Nathan really wanted such valuable resources close to him. Nathan intended to stay close to home from now on, regardless of his responsibilities. Reggie reluctantly agreed to allow Nathan to work from New Harvest, and they established a phone and fax line to communicate.

He and Luke Carter were in a room looking at a map on the wall. Different areas were shaded and certain magnets were placed to indicate military units or key locations.

"Doesn't look too good," commented Luke.

Nathan sighed. "No. Milan Depot is gone. We've confirmed that. Fortunately, we have a new source of supplies."

"Which we have to share with the Creek."

"Right," grunted Nathan. "Huntsville could be a problem. We don't know for sure, but it wouldn't hurt to be ready."

"Think they would go through the Creek Nation to get to us?" asked Luke.

"If I were them, I wouldn't," said Nathan. "I'd just go around and cut up between them and Memphis. Better yet, I'd conclude a separate peace with the Creek Nation so I wouldn't have to worry about them."

"Surely, the Creek wouldn't do that," said Luke. "They have a treaty with us."

Nathan shrugged. "You're probably right, but it doesn't hurt to think of things that could go wrong. The Creek might see it as justified given how many treaties have been broken with them through the centuries."

Luke walked over and put his finger on Huntsville. "But *why* would they attack us at all? We're not bothering them. They seem to be somewhat organized and have food and electricity. Why come after us?"

"Not sure," said Nathan, "but Milan shows they are. Or they think they can come in and take from us without any consequence. I strongly suspect that reports of Vincent Lacert being in charge down there might be true. If that's the case, he'll come after us, because I don't think he ever lets go of a grudge."

"I wish we had reached out to them before Vincent took over, if in fact that's who's in charge."

"Either way, they've attacked us," said Luke. "We can't let Milan go unanswered. They killed our people and stole from us."

"We don't even know their strength or capabilities yet."

"With any luck, Joshua will help us in that regard."

Nathan gave him a frown. "You know I don't like him being down there."

"I know, but he knows what he's doing. Besides, he has Conrad to look out for him."

Nathan blew air out of his mouth. "I'm not sure that's a good thing."

Luke shrugged and turned back to the board. "WTR is still in shambles. We forcibly disbanded all their military forces after Fulton. In hindsight, that might have been a mistake."

"We couldn't trust them."

"I know," said Luke, "but the WTR is becoming the wild west with gangs and crime and whatnot. Each county down there at a minimum needs the authority to organize its own county regiment, just like in the JP. They will also at least serve as a speed bump if Huntsville does invade."

"What about our own forces?"

"If there were an opposite term for 'high alert,' that would describe them right now."

"Because of planting season?"

"To some degree," answered Luke. "Everyone is also kind of sick of fighting after the last couple of years. It's become harder and harder to get recruits, especially with the JP blocking refugees. That used to be a prime source of soldiers." Luke looked sheepishly at Nathan before adding, "Malaria is hitting everyone pretty hard, too."

Nathan nodded, trying not to think about Bethany. He stared at the board instead. If he prepared for a conflict that never came, he would be seen as wasting resources and looking for another war. On the other hand, if he didn't prepare for the conflict and it came, they could all be in serious trouble.

"Go ahead and issue the word to recall all regular forces. Bring them up to full strength if possible," ordered Nathan.

"What about the regiments?" asked Luke.

"They're not under my control unless the Executive Council gives me that authority or the president declares martial law."

"You could at least advise them to get ready for something."

Nathan grimaced. "That's going to go over well."

"None of this is going to go over well," Luke said. "Nevertheless, it's necessary."

Nathan nodded, and Luke left the room. Turned to his desk, Nathan began writing on a piece of paper. He now found it much easier than typing something on a computer and then trying to find a printer that worked.

CONFIDENTIAL REPORT
EYES ONLY FOR: Jackson Purchase President Reginald Philips
SUBJECT: Imminent Threat to the South
FROM: General Nathan Taylor, Chief of Defense

Mr. President,

We have been able to confirm with a reasonable degree of certainty that the attack on Milan Depot came from elements based out of Huntsville. It is possible that these forces are led by the former JP Chief of Defense, Vincent Lacert.

Although the stocks at Milan did include tactical nuclear weapons, I can confirm that they were rendered inoperable by my order prior to this raid. I have also placed the supplies and weapons obtained from Mississippi in safe storage at the dam.

Today I have ordered the JP Regular Military put on active duty. It is my intention to bring them to the highest state of readiness as soon as possible given the threat to our south. Unlike in previous conflicts, we cannot count on fuel-driven vehicles to quickly transport our troops where they are needed nor to provide supplies. Our movements have to be thought out and planned. We must anticipate enemy movements ahead of time.

Considering this necessity, I intend to take the following actions in the next few weeks after the units have been fully mobilized:

1. Begin moving units south along the Tennessee River using barges. This will be more difficult than it may sound considering the barges will not be powered and will be moving upstream. Still working on details.

2. Coordinate with the Creek for safe passage of our forces through their territory. This might be tough, but I believe they will cooperate.

3. Secure a military alliance with the Creek to fight this common enemy. They will likely argue that Huntsville is no enemy to them, but I will try to reason with Billy Fox in that regard. He will certainly want something in return.

I would ask that you do the following things in support of this campaign:

1. Order the county regiments mobilized and brought to full strength.

2. Have these elements secure key areas, such as bridges that regular forces currently guard. This will allow for the relief of the regular forces.

3. New Harvest still does not have a county executive or regimental commander. I know this is not a top priority, but it needs to happen given the importance of the Kentucky Dam, which falls within the New Harvest area. I can provide you with recommendations for the regimental commander if you like, and I have taken the liberty of assigning my most trusted staff officers to fill the position on a rotational basis.

4. Authorize/order the Tennessee counties to organize their own regiments. I know this will be a tough one to sell, but they need some defensive infrastructure.

I fully understand the political sensitivities of taking these actions on the eve of an election, but feel the threat is too great to do otherwise. Please advise soonest if you disagree with any of the above actions.

Respectfully,
General Nathan Taylor

Nathan read over the memo a few times, knowing this would cause Reggie no end of trouble. He didn't like it, but saw no way around it. Walking over to the fax machine, Nathan sent it to his president.

Chapter 6 – The Speech

The Paducah Spring Farmer's Market had slowly grown into the biggest trade fair on the Ohio River. Paducah fenced off a portion of the waterfront, and hundreds of sellers set up stalls selling and trading fruits, vegetables, crafts, clothing, tools, pottery, and anything left over from before N-Day that was now valuable.

People from within the JP made the journey, bringing their wares, and camped out in communal camps around the waterfront in an almost-festive air. Along the waterfront, barges and boats from up and down the river came to sell and trade. This particular market was especially well attended because of the recent harsh winter, and people wanted to see the Brazen Memorial, which was within spitting distance of the market.

Ernest Givens came to shake hands and kiss babies, as politicians always had. Although he was a natural leader, he was not a natural smoozer, so talking to masses of people in a never-ending series of superficial engagements was not easy for him. It was made easier by the fact that he was well thought of, genuinely liked, and he knew many of the people there.

At some point, a group of supporters pressed him into saying a few words. Ernest initially refused, but the cry for him to speak grew louder and louder. Someone found a wooden table for him to stand on, and even before he knew what was happening, he was hoisted up onto its surface. He was surprised by the number of people that were looking at him and cheering. He could also see how devastated the city still was from the last two years.

Finally, the cheering died down. "I feel like I'm up for sale here," he said, and the crowd laughed.

"Seriously, everyone. This market is fantastic. People getting together and trading fairly with each other. The best thing is it's not run by the government. You did this all yourselves."

There was a loud round of applause.

"Before N-Day, everyone thought the government had to be involved to make things happen. That every problem was theirs to solve, but that wasn't true then and it isn't true now. I would say more government sometimes even makes things worse.

"As I'm sure most of you know by now, I'm running for JP President." There was another instance of clapping and cheering. "I expect to make a decision on a vice presidential running mate soon and will let you know. In contrast to myself, I'll make sure they're someone who actually knows what they're doing."

People laughed and held their hands up. Bottles of homemade liquor were passed around liberally.

"I want you to know that I deeply respect President Reggie Phillips." There were some groans and boos. "Hear me out, please. He recently reached out to me, and I can see he's a man who genuinely cares for the JP and everyone in it. The problem is he's surrounded by people who do not necessarily feel the same way. He is a tired, old man rundown by the pressures of the job. Let's face it, who wouldn't be? I would bet if he loses the next election, the first emotion he will feel is immense relief. He was our first president and has done the best he can and should be commended. But it's time for a change."

Ernest noticed that the crowd was growing even larger. Those who had been trading stopped what they were doing to come hear him speak.

"I don't have to tell you that things are not necessarily going the way they should. I'm not just talking about all the terrible tragedies that have occurred over the last two years. What about this election? I would love to address you all by radio as my opposition does regularly, but I am not allowed. I would love to sit in those Executive Council meetings to see how the sausage is really made, but I am not allowed. I would love to try and help, but I am not allowed. The question has to be asked, why?"

They had become nearly silent.

"I'm sure most of you have heard about the recent decisions and executive orders placing the military back on high alert and calling up the county regiments. Why, I ask? Do we face some other grave threat? Not that anyone knows. So why is President Phillips doing it? A better question, why have his people convinced him to do it?"

Ernest let the question hang in the air.

"Doesn't it seem a little coincidental that this is all happening so near the election? I've served in countries all over the world where shadow democracies beat their chests proudly about freedom and will of the people, but in the background, it was all about maintaining their power. Does anyone really think President Phillips will step aside quietly? Let me ask you a better question, does anyone really think Nathan Taylor will go quietly?"

There were grumbles and angry words.

"I've been down to Fulton, and I've seen the devastation. I've seen the camps filled with people, vomiting their intestines out in agony while their skin falls off. These were just normal people, like you and I. Who has ever been called to answer for that? No one."

People were becoming more agitated, and Ernest felt a sort of euphoric energy flowing through him.

"I've been to Murray State University and seen the giant crater there. A site of learning and research where they were working on refining oil so we would have a sustainable source of fuel. It's all gone now, just like the fuel reserves that backed up our currency that they promised would be good. Anyone here had money stolen from them by the government?"

More hands went up and angry responses.

"I have to ask, why? Not why our leaders have done these things. That's obvious. They have exercised unchecked power for so long that they no longer consider the long-term consequences of their actions. No, the question is why do we allow it?"

There were angry voices at the edge of the crowd. A stall in the back was knocked over and it appeared a fight had broken out.

"Now it's not just enough to point out the problems; we also have to look for solutions," Ernest began, but the crowd had begun to undulate, and people began to push and shove each other.

"Please everyone, just remain calm," he yelled out, but he could no longer be heard above the din of people. There were now fights and yelling and pushing. Ernest saw a woman fall to the ground while people walked over her.

"Stop, listen to me! Everyone calm down!" Ernest yelled, but the crowd surged forward and knocked the table over that he was standing on. He fell backwards onto the concrete and found himself in the middle of a large wave of people.

He saw an open space near the water and crawled frantically in that direction through panicking feet. Ernest was stepped on numerous times and saw others around him fall themselves. He rushed towards the open area offered by the river and plunged into knee-deep water to get away from the mass of struggling people. Able to finally stand, he carefully made his way to the Brazen Monument and climbed up on its lower levels to get out of the water and people.

Looking out, he saw chaos everywhere. There were fires, looting, and fighting. Several of the boats nearby were being swamped with people. He didn't think it could get any worse until he heard a gunshot. This was answered, and then the shots were going off like a popcorn machine.

Ernest hid behind the monument waiting for it to be over. His face was close to the stone and he looked up to see names. They all blurred together until one stood out as if carved from eternity itself.

Major Beau Myers.

This is not what that good man died for, Ernest thought. *They are not responsible for what they are doing. They are so afraid and desperate they are like children, lashing out at everything.*

This is all Nathan Taylor's fault. The outsider who came in and controlled Reggie Phillips. The man who sent his sadistic son to do his dirty work. The man who even now would steal the election.

Ernest Givens would make him pay.

He clung to the monument as the city burned again.

Chapter 7 – Skyline of Fire

Downtown Paducah and the waterfront burned with fire and frustration for nearly twenty-four hours before police and military could re-establish control. The city had barely started to rebuild from the last assault it had faced before this latest destruction.

Nathan had rushed from New Harvest with every soldier he could gather and quickly established a headquarters tent near the epicenter of the conflict. After a bloody night of conflict, dozens of civilians were dead and hundreds more hurt.

Reggie made his way into the tent. Several state police officers shadowed him as security. He was flushed and sweating

"You shouldn't be here," said Nathan. "It's still pretty hairy. You don't look so good either."

"This is where I should be, Nathan. And, as far as my appearance, just a little cold, I'll be fine."

Nathan nodded. "That's for approving use of the McCraken County Regiment. I brought some troops with me, but they weren't enough. We need more police and firefighters, too. Most of the fires are out, but we keep getting flare-ups."

"I'll see about making it happen."

Nathan pulled Reggie over to a corner of the tent where they were unlikely to be heard. "There are strong indications the city is going to explode again tonight."

"Why?"

Nathan shrugged. "That's just the way these things work. Violence begets violence. Some people just love smashing stuff. Everyone's still upset about the currency fiasco. We'd be having runs on banks if we still had banks."

Reggie nodded, thinking.

"We need to institute martial law," said Nathan.

"That seems a little extreme," Reggie said.

"I don't think so. With martial law, we can enforce a curfew, and the military forces can enforce the law and have arrest authority."

"How did it start?"

Nathan cursed. "Ernest Givens. Giving some sort of rabble-rousing speech right over there." He pointed towards the river. "He stirred everyone up. Seems like he's good at that."

"Where is he now?"

"No one knows," Nathan answered. "I think we should issue a warrant for his arrest."

"We can't do that. A judge can though."

"Good luck finding a judge and getting that done quickly," said Nathan. "Besides, that guy is super-popular here. Everyone involved in getting a warrant was either on the Long Walk or had a relative on it. They're not going to issue an arrest order."

"My hands are tied," Reggie said.

"Not if you declare martial law," said Nathan. "You can order his arrest and hold him for thirty days without charges."

"That would run through the election."

Nathan sighed. "I know, but we can't have him running around inciting people to violence. Just hold him for a few days and let him go when things calm down. I've got my hands full prepping for Huntsville and can't handle all of this as well."

"Speaking of having your hands full, have you made a decision yet regarding my offer?" asked Reggie.

Nathan's face fell. "I'm sorry, really, but I have to decline. I need to be there for my daughter. As a matter of fact, the only reason I'm still the Chief of Defense is because you said I could do it from New Harvest."

"I understand. You don't have to explain anything to me."

"I'm presuming you have a backup?"

Reggie nodded. "I think Valerie Cutchfield will accept."

"The MSU President?"

"Yes," said Reggie. "She's smart, capable, and relatively young. Something I am not anymore."

"I am sorry," said Nathan.

Reggie put his hand on his shoulder. "I understand."

"So, martial law?" Nathan pressed. "I took the liberty of drawing up the order. All it needs is your signature to go into effect. There's also an arrest warrant for Ernest Givens, just to get him off the streets for a while."

"I don't like this. People will see it as me trying to influence the elections."

"Then postpone the elections, too. You can do that under martial law."

Reggie shook his head. "That never goes well."

"Look," said Nathan. "I understand this is terrible timing and could very well cost us the election. At this point I don't care. I'm afraid we're in danger of losing *everything*."

Reggie shook his head sadly before walking over and signing the first document. "I'm not signing the arrest warrant, not yet."

"But he caused all of this," said Nathan.

"You're telling me he held a gun to the head of every single person and made them riot?"

"Of course not."

"Then, they're responsible for their own actions," said Reggie. "He may have contributed to all of this, but I doubt he set out to intentionally cause a riot."

"I'd feel safer with him behind bars," said Nathan.

"I would, too," said Reggie, "but the answer is still no." He then rubbed his head and began to shake.

"You okay? You don't look so good," Nathan said, noticing his friend's color.

Reggie closed his eyes and sat down in a nearby chair. "Just a cold, I think."

"Go on home. Get some rest. We'll take care of things here." Nathan stared hard at him. "Seriously, I'll get someone here to take you."

"Perhaps I will," answered Reggie as a lethargy rolled over him.

The unsigned arrest warrant rolled off the table and onto the floor.

Chapter 8 - Reconnaissance

Joshua ordered his men to establish a base camp in a secluded location north of Huntsville. There, they left their weapons, most of their supplies, bicycles, and Wildcat.

Trailer, Conrad, and Joshua walked south alone. They re-donned their old clothes and concocted the cover story of being from WTR and were looking for seasonal labor before returning back home. Now that tractors were mostly dead, and draft animals scarce, human backs were critical to planting and harvesting.

Huntsville itself was like many formerly prosperous cities after N-Day. The outskirts were most of the times abandoned and often stripped of useful items. Sometimes, whole neighborhoods were burned wastelands where sparks had started fires that raged unchecked by those who could put them out. Sometimes, residents from safer areas close to the town center came out during the day to tend gardens hidden in the back of abandoned houses. Inside of these vast vacant areas was often a transition zone where you started to see people and signs of habitation. This transition zone was also usually where any defensive perimeter would be located.

A few blocks from the city center where most people still lived and traded, they were stopped, searched, questioned and released. Trailer did most of the talking, and within minutes, the guards went from stern and suspicious to casual and helpful.

"You seem to have a way with people," Joshua said to Trailer after they had walked away.

"It's the height I think. People are initially put off by it, but when they realize I'm not going to eat them, they relax very quickly. Plus, I'm funny as shit."

"I guess we'll just have to take your word on that one," said Conrad.

Walking through the streets, they found people subdued and quiet. Everyone seemed to be going about their business without the normal amount of banter. Few of those they passed would make eye contact.

"This seems like an odd place," said Conrad.

They turned down a side street that led to a large square. In the middle of a square was an individual hanging by his neck. The man didn't look like he had been up there long.

"That was this morning," said an old woman, sweeping the front of a nearby shop that appeared to sell cloth and homemade clothing.

"What did he do?" Trailer asked.

The woman shrugged. "Who knows? I can't keep track anymore. Drugs or stealing or talking bad about the Reaper. They'll probably be a different one up there tomorrow morning. Walk a few blocks south and you'll probably see more of the same."

"Reaper?" asked Conrad.

She stopped sweeping and looked them up and down. "You must really be new. Stay around here long enough and you'll see him. My advice is hunker down and hope his eye doesn't fall on you. There's a reason he's called the Reaper."

"Thank you kindly," said Conrad. "We're just going to go somewhere else now."

Walking south, they did see more bodies. One seemed to hang at nearly every intersection.

"We've at least learned they're not short on rope," said Trailer.

"Don't be so hasty," said Conrad, pointing off to their left. "That one was hanged by a dog chain."

"Damn that had to hurt," said Trailer.

"Yeah," said Conrad, "it was the *chain* that made it hurt. Otherwise being hanged would have only been uncomfortable."

"You hear that?" asked Joshua.

Conrad shook his head.

"Banging, maybe," said Trailer. "Like someone's building something."

"We know it's not a gallows," said Conrad. "They don't bother with them here in Huntsville."

Walking further south, they passed through old neighborhoods with stately homes surrounded by abandoned cars and unkempt lawns. By starts and stops, they tried to vector in on the sound and climbed steadily upwards until they eventually found themselves on a small hill overlooking the city. The Tennessee River wound in a lazy curve to the south. There were several children and old men sitting on the hill as well, all looking east towards the sounds.

Below them was a large fenced-in area delineated as much from the surrounding city by its barriers as its orderliness. Neat uniform buildings sat between roads unclogged by abandoned vehicles. The people they could see moved with purpose and not slowly. There were an unusual amount of uniformed personnel.

"Hey, old timer," said Trailer to a black man sitting in a lawn chair. "What is that place?"

The man shielding his eyes looked up at Trailer. "That's Redstone Arsenal, treetop. Used to work there, I did."

"Yeah? What'd you do?"

"Drove a forklift mostly, but it was one of those big ones. Had to be to pick up those thruster parts."

"Thruster parts?" asked Joshua.

The old man looked at Joshua. "Yeah, like for rockets. Nearly every rocket NASA sent out of this atmosphere was either designed or built right here. Same for the military."

"What are they building down there now?" Conrad asked, looking at a group near a large concrete pad.

"Hard to say for certain," said the old man. "They're assembling it in pieces, but it's obviously too small to be one of the big Atlas or Deltas. I'd guess one of the smaller Minotaurs or Falcons."

"Are we talking rockets?" asked Joshua.

The old man turned to look at him again. "Hell yes we're talking rockets. Did you think we came up here to see them assemble sewer pipes?"

"Are you sure?" asked Trailer. "That could be anything down there."

The old man chuckled. "Yes, I'm sure. I've helped assemble rockets for forty years."

"What would a Minotaur or the other type of rocket you named carry?" asked Conrad.

"Falcon," said the old man. "They're smaller, newer, less expensive rockets. Mostly to put satellites into orbit."

"Why would someone want to do that?" asked Joshua.

"Course it could also be used like a SCUD missile," the old man said. "Maybe do a little pre-emptive strike on those bastards in the JP. They're going to hit us if we don't take care of them first."

The three men looked at each other before turning again to the old man.

"Let's say it was used as a SCUD," Joshua asked. "How accurate would it be?"

"With a GPS on board?" the old man laughed. "They could put it right up your ass as long as you stand still and we get the right grid coordinates. Those GPS satellites are still orbiting up there you know. The satellite telemetry is likely off a little without constant adjustment, but not enough to really matter."

"I think maybe we need to go," said Conrad. "Probably seen all we need to see, wouldn't you say?"

Joshua nodded.

"Don't sit up here until you burn, old man," Trailer said as they walked away.

"Screw you. I'm going to stay here and watch another launch. It's the most beautiful thing in the world."

Joshua turned back. "Excuse me. How long does it take to prep one of those rockets for launch?"

The old man shrugged. "Before, you could get it ready in a week to ten days. But that was with heavy machinery. There also used to be mountains of bureaucratic mandated safety procedures, so if they ignore those…who knows?"

They made their way back north away from the sounds of the rocket construction.

"We have to destroy it," said Joshua. "Do it now before they can complete the rocket."

"I'm not a soldier like you folks," said Trailer, "but that sounds really dumb."

"For once, I have to agree," said Conrad. "There's obviously tight security and there's just three of us. Maybe if we could get mortars onto that hill we could hit it, but how would you manage that?"

"And who's to say they wouldn't just build another rocket?" Trailer said.

Conrad nodded at Trailer. "Another good point, you're bating a thousand right now."

"But what if they have something bad?" said Joshua. "What if they have a nuke or chemical weapons or something like that?"

"Now where would they get such a thing?"

"Milan," answered Joshua. "My father told me that's where the nuke that destroyed Fulton came from." Joshua closed his eyes and sighed. "That's why Huntsville hit Milan in the first place, I bet. Vincent Lacert would have known about the nukes as well. He snuck one north to take out the dam, after all."

"Good reasons for us to get out of here quickly before we're all sharing a lamp post," said Conrad. "I agree something needs to be done, but we need help."

"First, we have to get out of here," said Trailer.

"Is that going to be a problem?" asked Joshua.

"Maybe. We did come to find work and it seems odd we would leave so soon, even if we didn't find it." Trailer thought. "We'll need to go out a different way at least, so we don't hit the same guards. A different story as well."

"It might be too late for that," said Conrad.

"What do you mean?" asked Joshua.

Conrad pointed back towards the hill they had just walked down. Now the old man they had met was talking to two men in uniform with guns. The old man was pointing in their direction.

"Okay," said Trailer, walking away from the hill quickly. "Escape plan B."

The two fell in beside him.

"What's escape plan B?" asked Joshua.

"Get out of here and hope we don't get caught," said Trailer.

They did and…they did.

Chapter 9 – Radio Link

Nathan made his way up to Kentucky Dam as quickly as he could. John Downing had sounded positively agitated and that was saying something. The former TVA director turned Kentucky Dam Nanny-in-Chief was not what anyone would consider emotional.

John had told him that Simon was doing something on the top of the dam involving communications. He wanted to know if Nathan wanted John to have the security elements stop him. John had sounded hopeful when he suggested this.

"Just hold on," Nathan said. "I'll be up there as fast as he can."

"Okay, but realize he's just going to keep on doing what he's doing until you get here."

"How much damage can he really do to a two million-ton concrete structure?"

"You'd be surprised," John said. "Most of the weight is at the bottom; it's relatively vulnerable up top."

"John," said Nathan, growing exasperated, "if you think Simon is going to destroy the dam with his monkeying around before I get up there, you are authorized to stop him by any means necessary."

"Got it," said John, sounding satisfied.

Nathan had an idea what Simon was up to, but since Nathan didn't really know Simon, he thought maybe it prudent to see just exactly what he was doing. Besides, he hadn't been to the dam in a while and

River appeared to be asleep for the rest of the afternoon. She saved most of her wakefulness for the hours between midnight and dawn.

He stifled a yawn and returned a soldier's salute as he strode across the top of the dam's surface. He could already tell what John wanted him to see. Simon had climbed nearly fifty feet up into the air where he had attached himself to a tall metal lighting tower. Below him, Jessica was passing him pieces of equipment back and forth using a tow rope. Projecting up above Simon's head for about five meters was a series of long metal rods with plastic metal bulbs on them that Nathan knew from his time in the military meant it was a radio antenna array.

John Downing stood around the area pacing and looking up at Simon. "He's going to mess something up," John told Nathan as he walked up.

Wires and cables ran down the lighting tower to the ground, and as he walked up, Simon began his slow and careful descent.

"If you're trying to get cable television," said Nathan, "you're wasting your time."

Simon frowned. "No. I'm working on setting up communications with Cheyenne Mountain."

"You sure that's a good idea?" asked Nathan. "More importantly, don't you think that's the sort of thing you should have asked someone beforehand if it was okay?"

Simon froze, and it was obvious wheels were turning in his head. "Maybe so," he finally admitted. "Who should I ask?"

"I would have been a good start," said Nathan.

"Or me," said John. "I actually told you to stop."

"Did you?" asked Simon with what appeared to be genuine confusion.

"He did," confirmed Jessica.

"What do you plan to tell these people at Cheyenne Mountain?" asked Nathan.

"Give them a general situation report," said Simon. "They're on the same side as we are, after all. It's possible we could all help each other."

Nathan grunted, non-committal.

"Anyway, I've set up the radio, transmitter, and encryption module downstairs to keep it out of the elements," said Simon. "Want to send a message?"

"I don't know Morse Code," muttered Nathan.

Simon looked away sheepishly. "This will be an encrypted voice link channel assigned specifically for Site Conway."

"Voice link?" asked Nathan. "I thought you only had Morse Code capability."

"That's what I wanted everyone to think," said Simon. "Lewis was always such a control freak and hovered over everything, even in Morse Code. If it were voice, he would have been insufferable. Besides, voice would have allowed those guys at Cheyenne Mountain to tell us more quickly stuff to do."

Nathan smiled. "I'm impressed. You sandbagged your capabilities to control the situation."

"I guess so," answered Simon. "So, do we send a message? Do you want to talk to them?"

Nathan paused and thought for a minute. He certainly didn't intend to allow these shadowy remnants of a demolished nation to exercise any control over the JP. On the other hand, they might be able to share useful information with each other, and information, especially now, was power.

"Let's try it," said Nathan. "They might not even answer, but take my lead. If I say kill the transmission, it's over."

Simon nodded and hooked a few final cables to each other before walking purposefully down several flights of stairs. Nathan, John, and Jessica followed.

They went into a small room that had previously been a closet. A metal conduit pipe had been cut open to allow cables to run from the room upwards.

"What did you do?" asked John, aghast.

"It's just an air conduit," said Simon. "No need to worry."

John looked at Nathan, stunned. "Do you see what he did?"

"Perhaps you should take care of other things right now," said Nathan. "I've got this, I think."

John shook his head, threw both hands up in the air, and stormed off.

Simon turned to a large piece of communications equipment and hit several power switches. He then punched a long series of numbers from a small book into what Nathan presumed was the encryption module. After a few seconds, the spinning lines all stopped and faced the same direction.

"I think we're good to go," said Simon, adjusting the speaker and microphone.

"Control, this is Site Conway," said Simon. "Do you read me?"

Static.

Simon repeated his message.

No answer.

"Who knows if they're monitoring this channel?" asked Nathan. "You said each site had its own assigned frequency?"

Simon nodded while staring at the transmitter worriedly.

"Well," sighed Nathan, "if they thought your voice encryption didn't work, which they would since you only used Morse Code, they might have taken that frequency off the network."

"Control, this is Site Conway," said Simon. "Do you read me?"

There was a break in the static. "Authenticate, Site Conway," came a young sounding voice.

Simon remembered his five-digit code. "I authenticate: 3-8-6-7-6."

"Authentication confirmed," replied the voice. There was then a long pause as if the person at the other end didn't know what to say. "How you doing?"

"Swell," said Simon. "We were directed several weeks ago to conduct a recon near the western Tennessee-Kentucky border. I'd like to provide a report."

"Hold on," said the voice. "Let me go get the shift commander."

After several minutes of silence, a no-nonsense voice came back on the line. "This is Lieutenant Commander Porter. Who is this? And don't give me any shit about Site Whatever or your identification code, this is a secure channel."

"Uh, this is Simon Cushter. I've been communicating for the last couple of years with you by Morse Code."

"Okay, so you must have found a way to fix the secure voice capability?"

"Yeah," said Simon slowly, "that's what happened."

"So, I hear you were able to go up north and check things out for us?"

"Actually, I'm there now," answered Simon, missing Nathan's shaking head.

There was a long pause. "What do you mean? Aren't you at Site Conway?"

"We had to abandon Site Conway," said Simon. "The fuel was going bad and we were afraid we'd get trapped when the generators failed."

"That's already happened at a few locations," said Porter.

"What?" said Simon. "And you didn't think to tell us?"

"So where are you now?" asked Porter.

Nathan was motioning for Simon to let him speak.

Simon slowly slid away from the microphone.

"Hello?" asked Porter. "You still there?"

"Lieutenant Commander Porter, this is General Nathan Taylor. I am the Chief of Defense of the Jackson Purchase...nation, I guess you would call it. I understand you want to learn about us."

Another long silence. "We've heard rumors of something like that. Several people have picked up your radio broadcasts and gossiped about them on the shortwave lines."

"People always talk," said Nathan.

"Tell me about the nuclear explosion," said Porter.

"You first," said Nathan. "Who are you and where are you?"

214

"That's info you likely could have gotten from Simon there if you wanted it badly enough."

Nathan frowned. "If you are implying we are torturing him to get his cooperation, you are mistaken. We have welcomed him into our community."

"If that's true, have Simon provide me with his pre-assigned safety code phrase."

Simon looked confused as he leaned towards the microphone. "Uh, there was no safety code phrase."

"Correct answer," said Porter. "Which proves that you really are not under duress or that you're an idiot not to make something up."

"He's not an idiot," said Nathan, taking the microphone back. "So anyway, tell me a little about yourself."

"I presume you actually are a military man and haven't just taken on that title?" asked Porter.

"Yes," said Nathan. "I was an active duty officer when it happened."

"Okay, so you understand what I mean by Northern Command?"

"The major geographical combatant command responsible for North America."

"Correct. NORTHCOM's headquarters since the days of the Soviet Union has been in a secret location, which is designed to withstand a nuclear holocaust."

"It's not too secret," said Nathan. "Everyone knows it's at Cheyenne Mountain near Fort Carson, Colorado."

"That's classified…but correct," admitted Porter.

Nathan laughed. "You'll have to write us both up."

"Anyway, we're here. Doing what we can to ensure the survival of the United States."

"And just how are you doing that from inside a mountain?"

"Communications like this mostly," Porter answered. "We took three direct nuclear hits topside, so it's still not safe to go outside, according to the radiation meters."

"Who's in charge there?" asked Nathan.

"I think it's my turn to get an answer or two," said Porter. "Tell me about the nuclear explosion."

"It was from a low-yield tactical nuclear weapon."

Porter sounded surprised. "And it was set off intentionally?"

"In a sense," said Nathan. "Call it part of many smaller wars that happened after N-Day."

"Are there more of these nukes out there?"

"You tell me," said Nathan.

There was a pause. "Honestly, no one really knows for sure. Everyone has lost track of what was where. Most of the information we used before N-Day was either on the Internet or secure servers. Most of it is gone now. So, let me rephrase, do you have more nuclear weapons?"

"No," said Nathan, feeling this was important somehow.

"Good," said Porter. "Do you still profess loyalty to the United States of America?"

"What?" asked Nathan.

"It's a simple question that as a military man I'm sure you understand."

"There is no United States of America anymore," said Nathan.

"Thankfully, you are wrong. It will take time, but the U.S. Government will reassert control. It starts with small pockets all over the country doing their part. Can we count on you?"

"Count on us to do what?" asked Nathan.

"Whatever we say, of course," said Porter.

Nathan slowly reached over and cut the power on the radio.

They were all silent for a few seconds.

"What does it mean?" asked Jessica.

"It doesn't mean anything," said Nathan. "We're not going to start taking orders from someone we don't know that's two thousand miles away and can't even walk out their own front door."

Nathan shook his head sadly. "It means that we're on our own, same as before."

Chapter 10 – The Alley

"Did they see us?" asked Joshua as they moved quickly away from the hill.

"They didn't have to see us," said Conrad. "All they need to do is look for a seven-foot-tall black guy."

"And a bald-headed troll," said Trailer.

"Let's keep moving. Maybe we can get some distance from them," said Joshua.

"But to where?" asked Trailer. "Are we looking to blend into crowds or find isolated locations where we can hide if need be?"

"Hey there!" said a voice behind them. "Stop! We want to talk to you."

They looked back to see the two men in security uniforms and carrying batons coming down a side street after them.

"I think hiding is best at this point," said Conrad. "We're not going to blend in with someone chasing us."

"Just keep walking fast," said Joshua. "Don't run yet. Maybe we can lose them."

Turning down a narrow alleyway, they saw another smaller path at the end. They hurried down to the end and rounded the corner to find a blank wall. Looking around, they saw there was no exit. Nearby windows were boarded up. Only a small dumpster to one side provided any cover.

Conrad peeked back down the alley. "They're coming this way," he whispered.

"Stand over there," Joshua told Trailer, pointing at the wall.

"Just out in the open?" he asked.

"Yes," answered Joshua and turned to Conrad. "Get behind the dumpster here."

Trailer shook his head, but backed up against the wall nevertheless. "I don't think I like this plan."

"Don't worry," whispered Conrad to Trailer. "Whatever happens to you, we'll be fine."

Trailer showed Conrad his extended middle finger.

There were voices from the alley, and then suddenly the two security personnel rounded the corner at the sight of Trailer.

"Howdy, boys," Trailer said.

"There he is," said one of the men.

Trailer smiled. "Here I am. What did you all want to talk about back there?"

"Where's your two friends?"

"We split up," said Trailer. "I don't think they were as keen to talk to you as I was."

"Let's take this one in," said one of the men. "We'll put the word out for the other two."

His partner nodded. "Turn around, get on your knees with your hands interlocked behind your head and lean forward until your forehead is resting on the wall."

"Come on now," said Trailer, "is that really necessary?"

"It is," said the first security personnel, pulling out a large pair of plastic flex-cuffs from his belt.

"Damn," said Trailer, turning around and getting on his knees. "I hate this part."

Both men walked forward, and one was about to reach out for Trailer when his partner happened to glance to the left and saw Conrad and Joshua crouched down. "What?"

Conrad launched himself forward at the nearest man, pinning him to the ground, while Joshua lunged at the man with the flex-cuffs.

He dropped the flex cuffs and swung the baton viciously at Joshua's head.

Joshua jerked his head back and stepped out of the way. He felt the wind of the swing on the tip of his nose.

The man looked to swing back in the other direction, but found there was sudden resistance. He looked up to see that Trailer had stood and held the end of the baton securely in his massive hand.

Trailer pulled hard on the baton with one hand while punching forward at the man's face with the other. The security man's face made a sound like an omelet hitting the kitchen floor. He crumbled to the alley and didn't move.

Conrad was rolling on the ground with the other security person, who evidently had some experience with wrestling. Although Conrad kept trying to use his superior size, the other man was using grappling techniques and nearly had Conrad pinned.

"Get the undercut," encouraged Trailer. "No, the other side, get your arms under his."

Joshua looked back and forth between the two men. "Shouldn't we help him?"

Trailer shook his head. "No, he's fine." Looking back at Conrad, he said, "Come on now, you got this. Don't gas yourself out. Breath."

The man finally got Conrad on his back and put the big redhead in a chokehold. Conrad looked up with a red face. "Help, goddamnit!"

Trailer shook his head in dismay. "So embarrassing," he said as he brought the baton back and then struck the man swiftly at the base of the skull.

The man collapsed and smacked his face on the pavement.

Panting, Conrad pushed the man off of him and slowly climbed to his feet.

"I'm not being critical," said Trailer, "but maybe you need to work on that a little."

Conrad took a wild swing at the big man, but missed and spun, losing his balance. Crashing loudly into the dumpster, he fell on his back and lay there panting.

"I stand corrected," said Trailer, smiling, "you're a freaking kung fu panda."

"Can this wait?" hissed Joshua, looking back up the alley.

"Sure," shrugged Trailer. "My time is your time, boss."

"Asshole." Conrad climbed gingerly to his feet.

"Okay," said Joshua, peering down the alley and seeing no one. "Let's take their uniforms. The smaller one should fit me and the bigger one should fit you, Conrad."

"Uh, what about me?" asked Trailer.

"Go knock out a guard your size," said Conrad. "We'll wait here for you, promise."

"Even if we did find you a uniform," said Joshua, "it wouldn't do any good. People who are seven feet stand out no matter how they're dressed."

"Sooooo, I just hide in the dumpster a few weeks until you come back with the cavalry?" asked Trailer.

Joshua looked at the small dumpster. "Wouldn't be room. That's where we're going to put the knocked out guards."

"I think I get it," said Conrad, smiling. He began putting on the uniform over his other clothes and tossed the flex-cuffs to Trailer. "Put those on."

Frowning, Trailer looked back and forth between both men. "Wait a minute. Are we seriously going to go all *Star Wars* here?"

"You got it, Chewbacca," said Conrad.

Joshua nodded as he changed as well. "Hopefully, it will work as well. I'll be Han Solo."

"Bullshit you will," said Conrad. "You're the young wiper-snapper, Luke Skywalker. *I'm* Solo."

"Fine," said Joshua, "you can be Han."

Trailer cinched the plastic cuffs on his wrists. "Something tells me I'm going to regret this."

Chapter 11 – Sickbed Visitor

Reggie couldn't stop shivering. The cold wind blasted across his body as he stumbled through knee-deep snow. There was nothing to hear but the howl of the wind, and he could see no more than a few feet in front of him through the driving snow.

Grandfather's cabin must be up ahead. It was stupid to go hiking this time of year, but if I can just get back to shelter, it will be okay.

Reggie noticed that it was getting darker. Soon it would be night and nearly impossible to find his way. Looking down, Reggie realized he was in his slippers and robe.

No wonder I'm shivering, he thought.

Ahead, there was a banging noise. Maybe the cabin was close and someone was trying to guide him in by sound.

More banging and then voices. One of the voices was Brazen urging him to hurry. That time was running out.

With a sudden start, Reggie realized he was dreaming and struggled up out of the dream.

"He's resting right now," Janice told someone in her you-shall-not-pass voice.

"I need to talk to him, ma'am. When will he be awake?"

"I don't know," she answered. "When he wakes, if he's better, I'll give you a call at the police station."

"It's okay," Reggie started to say loudly, but it came out in a whisper. It felt like there were fishhooks in his throat. Reaching over with a shaking hand, he took a long drink of water from the glass on the nightstand beside his bed.

"I'm awake," he finally managed to call out, and the voices stopped.

"Congratulations," Janice told the unknown someone. "You woke him up. He needs rest."

"It's okay, Janice," said Reggie. "Go ahead and show them in."

His wife walked in and placed her hand on his head, and he shivered. "You've still got a fever, even after taking the aspirin."

A man in police uniform stood worriedly in the doorway. "I'm really sorry to bother you, sir."

Janice turned and pointed a commanding finger at him. "Go make yourself conformable in the living room. I'll call you in when he's ready."

The man vanished.

"As protective as ever." Reggie smiled.

"I have to be," she said, soaking a washcloth into a small bucket of water beside the bed. She wrung most of the water out and then laid the cool cloth across his forehead. "You don't have to see him. He'll come back later."

"I got to get up to go pee anyway," said Reggie. "You know how my prostate is."

Janice held up a small bedpan. "We got this left over from when I was bedridden after...my leg."

"No," Reggie said, forcing himself to sit up, and he instantly felt a sensation of dizziness. "I'm not ready for that yet."

"Suit your stubborn self," she said, helping him to his feet and guiding him towards the bathroom. When he came out, he carefully made his way into the living room. As usual, he always looked up at the ceiling's corner to see the iron poker head that was still imbedded there. If it hadn't come off during one of his upswings, it would likely still be embedded in Ethan Schweitzer's skull.

More the pity, he thought.

Reggie saw the man sitting nervously in the couch and recognized him now as the new Mayfield police chief. "You're Norton, right? I'm sorry I don't remember your first name."

"Just Norton," said the man rising. "That's what everyone calls me."

"Please sit," said Reggie, waving him back down. Janice helped him into a cushioned armchair across from Norton. She then grabbed a blanket from the nearby quilt stand and bundled it around him.

Reggie smiled. "Janice, can you bring us some mint tea, please? I think my throat would appreciate it."

"No problem, dear," she said and then stepped out into the backyard to clip some mint from the garden.

"So what's this about?" asked Reggie.

The man looked like he didn't want to talk now that he was here. Finally, he sighed and said, "Ernest Givens."

"Somehow that doesn't surprise me. What's he up to now?"

"He's still campaigning heavily."

"As he should," said Reggie. "There's an election coming up."

Norton looked pained. "Yes, but he's getting everyone all riled up. I have to devote most of my officers to keeping the peace during his daily speeches, and we have to ignore other more pressing matters. Even with the extra security, the crowds always get a little out of control."

"How out of control?"

"Three hurt this morning. One of them a policeman who had his forearm broken by a thrown brick."

Janice came back in and set two cups down with fresh cut mint sprigs covered in steaming hot water. "Here you go."

"Thank you," both men said in unison as she left the room.

Reggie took a careful sip of the hot drink and then set it back down. "Forgive me for asking the obvious, but have you requested that Mister Givens stop doing what he's doing?"

The police chief nodded. "Says he's not going to stop, no matter what I say."

"That sort of stubbornness and determination is at times admirable. Maybe even the core trait responsible for allowing him to save so many people."

"Maybe," answered Norton.

"What did the mayor tell you to do?" asked Reggie. "I presume you went there first?"

Norton shook his head, frowning. "He told me to come ask you."

"Of course he did," smiled Reggie. "What do you recommend?"

Norton started to answer and then closed his mouth. He dropped his eyes and looked away. "I don't know, sir."

Reggie stared at the man for a few seconds and then set the hot cup down. "You know there are stories about Ernest Givens."

"I know," said Norton. "The Long Walk seems to be all anyone is talking about."

"Yes, but also his organizing of a resistance movement here when Schweitzer's forces were in control. Have you heard those stories?"

Norton nodded, but looked away.

"There is one particular story I heard not too long ago. It was about Ernest's group ambushing and taking supplies not far from here. Supposedly, he convinced all the occupation people to come over and join his resistance. All accept one."

The police chief fidgeted.

"This man refused to change sides, yet Ernest spared him anyway and let him go. Now, most would have said that was a stupid move by Ernest considering that the man would likely go report everything he knew about what had just happened."

Norton looked at the floor.

"That man was you, wasn't it?"

The police chief looked up angrily at Reggie.

"I imagine you are flooded with a surprising number of feelings. Guilt maybe for being part of the occupation force. Maybe gratitude for what Ernest did. Certainly some sense of—"

Norton cut him off. "All of those things and none of them. What does any of that have to do with him now?"

Reggie shrugged. "Well, you *are* the chief of police. I have to assume you are well qualified and come to this job with plenty of experience. Am I right?"

"Yes, I supposed so."

"So, when I ask the chief of police what he thinks we should do about someone causing trouble in his town, a reasonable person would expect an answer. For you not to have one tells me there's something else going on."

Norton sighed and sat back on the couch a little.

"You don't owe him anything, you know."

"I owe him my life," said Norton.

"There it is," said Reggie. "You feel like you owe him because he didn't kill you when he could have. Some would say *should* have."

"Yes."

"But you have a greater obligation. You owe the citizens under your care much more than you owe Ernest Givens. Don't you agree?"

Norton looked down and clenched his hands together before nodding.

"So, let me rephrase my question. If this were anyone else but Ernest Givens, doing what he is doing now, what would you recommend we do?"

Norton thought for a few seconds. "Find a way to arrest him. Maybe charge him creating a public nuisance or inciting violence, but those are misdemeanors. I can't hold him for very long on those charges. He'd be out the next morning for his daily rally."

"Unless we arrest him and hold him indefinitely," said Reggie.

"On what charge?" asked Norton.

"No charges," sighed Reggie. "We're still under martial law. I can have him arrested and held for thirty days without charges, as Nathan Taylor recently reminded me."

Norton looked taken aback. "Are you sure you want to do that?"

"I'm pretty sure I *don't* want to do that, but I see little choice in the matter. Do you see other options?"

He shook his head.

"Okay, draw up the warrant and I'll sign it," Reggie said. "You can have one of your men bring it by. I suggest you arrest him at his home instead of in front of hundreds of rabid supporters."

Norton nodded and stood. "I understand, sir. I really appreciate your time." He turned to Janice, who was standing in the doorway. "Thank you for the tea, ma'am, and sorry for waking the president."

Janice just smiled and nodded back.

The police chief was nearly to the door when he looked back at Reggie. "I often wonder why he didn't kill me. I would have him." He looked at the poker head in the ceiling. "I suspect you would have as well."

Before Reggie could answer, the man was gone. A fit of shaking hit Reggie again.

"Now back to bed," Janice said. "This is not going to end well if you don't get some rest."

Reggie thought that it wasn't likely to end well regardless.

He climbed back into bed and resumed the fight for his life as the *plasmodium vivax* parasite raged through his body.

Chapter 12 – Tertian Fever

Nathan walked into his home greeted by the furious screaming of his daughter, River. He went to the sound and found her lying in her crib, face red and fists clenched. Nathan reached down and picked her up, trying to sooth her with soft words and caresses.

He walked from room to room, looking for his mother or Alexandra and found no one.

They left my daughter here alone, he thought and felt such a flush of anger…then he froze in place, not even hearing his daughter for a few seconds.

Striding out of his house and across the space separating the cabins, Nathan burst into his mother's residence without knocking. "Mom, where are you? You know River was over there screaming her head off alone? Mom?"

There was no answer. He searched her house, but didn't find her.

Nathan walked out and approached Joshua and Alexandra's home. Maybe they were both over there. As he got close, he heard the now-unusual sound of a motor vehicle racing down the dirt path. It stopped in front of the house he was walking to and Doctor Bobby Wilson hopped out, medical bag in hand.

"What are you doing here?" asked Nathan. "And how did you manager to get a car?"

"From my understanding, your mother made such a ruckus, even throwing your name around, that they felt they had to."

"For what?" Nathan asked.

"Something is wrong with Alexandra."

"The baby?" asked Nathan with dread.

"I don't know anything yet," said the doctor. "Why don't we go in there and have a look at her?"

Nathan nodded and followed the doctor inside.

"Is that you, doc?" his mother called out. "It's about damn time." She saw Nathan as well. "I've been trying to call you to..." Her eyes fell on River, and the color drained from her face.

"Oh my God," she said, putting her hands over her mouth. "I'm so sorry."

"It's okay," said Nathan, feeling his anger drain away. "She's pissed, but otherwise fine. What's going on here?" He stopped talking when he saw his daughter-in-law. The normally energetic Alexandra lay on her side and appeared to hardly be breathing. Her skin had taken on a dead yellow tone, and there was dried vomit around her mouth and on the blankets covering her. Her extended belly felt taut while the rest of her was flaccid and lifeless.

His mother turned back to Alexandra. "I don't know. She's had a fever and chills, even some convulsions. Now she's unconscious and I can't wake her."

Bobby began to examine Alexandra. He pulled up her eyelids and shined a small penlight into each eye. He listened to parts of her body with a stethoscope. He then pressed on parts of her body, and she moaned loudly when he pressed under the left side of her ribcage.

"What's wrong?" asked Nathan.

Bobby shook his head. "I don't know for sure. I'd need to take blood and run some tests."

"How long will that take?" asked his mother.

"A few days at least," said the doctor. "We no longer have the lab equipment we once had."

"Does she have a few days?" asked Nathan.

Bobby frowned and refused to answer.

"What do you think it is?" Nathan asked.

"We're seeing lots of cases like this. They're not exactly alike, but I think she's going into organ failure. Her liver seems to be the worse off."

"Why?" asked Nathan's mother.

"I suspect it's because she has untreated malaria," the doctor explained." The parasite travelled through her blood stream until it lodged in her liver and began to reproduce. Now those viruses are maturing and being released back out into her body to attack other organs."

"We've been hearing rumors of malaria," said Nathan's mother, "but it mostly infects the old and very young. Alexandra's strong."

"Actually," said Bobby, "a lot more are probably infected, but are able to fight it off. Even those untreated will likely have relapsed at some point. I suspect, like Bethany, she is more vulnerable due to her pregnancy."

"Could it infect the baby?" asked Nathan.

"I'm not a pediatrician, but the baby should be okay as long as the mother is okay."

Nathan snapped his fingers. "We got a bunch of meds from that bunker in Mississippi the other day. Maybe one of those could help."

Bobby shook his head. "She needs antibiotics. I went to the dam to check out what they brought in when I heard about it. All of the antibiotics are decades out of date. Seems like the only thing they kept the bunker resupplied with over the years was generator fuel."

"So what do we do?" asked the mother.

Rubbing his hand on his head, Bobby sighed heavily. "If I knew it was malaria, I might give her some of the new antibiotics they've developed over at the Murray State Biology Department. I have some with me now in fact."

"Good, let's do that," said Nathan.

"Hang on," said Bobby. "I don't know for sure it *is* malaria."

"But you're pretty sure, right?" asked Nathan's mother.

"Yes," Bobby sighed, "but the other complication is the fact that she's pregnant."

"What are you talking about?" asked Nathan.

The doctor held a stethoscope to Alexandra's belly. "Currently there is a live baby in there. I can hear its heartbeat. I have absolutely no idea what kind of side effects these homemade untested drugs will have on the baby."

They all looked at Alexandra's belly.

"What do you think will happen to her if we do nothing?" asked Nathan's mother.

"I suspect the parasites will continue to infect her body. Her white blood cells likely can't keep up and her liver is almost shot now. Once her liver goes...it won't be long after that."

"But she could recover?" asked Nathan.

"Sure," said Bobby, shrugging. "Anything is possible, I guess."

"Do you think she will recover on her own?" asked Nathan's mom.

"No," Bobby answered.

"So," said Nathan, "we're faced with the decision of either giving her the medicine that might save her life and also harm the baby or not giving her the medicine and hope that she will recover on her own."

The doctor nodded.

Nathan's mother looked at the doctor. "So, what are we going to do here?"

"I can't make that decision," said Bobby, "especially when it involves an unborn baby. Normally, the next of kin decides if the patient is incapacitated."

"Joshua?" said Nathan. "But he's still in the south. There's no way he could get back here in time."

"Then it needs to be one of you," said Bobby. "I doubt she has time for us to go track down other relatives."

Nathan looked at Alexandra and then at River, who had fallen back asleep. He thought of what Joshua would think if something went wrong. He thought of David and couldn't get his dead son out of his head.

"I can't do it," said Nathan.

Bobby pointed at Alexandra. "Imagine this is Bethany, Nathan. What would you want done then?"

Nathan shook his head. "No, there has to be another way."

The doctor dropped his head.

"Give her the medicine," said Nathan's mother.

They both looked at her, and she nodded.

The doctor slowly opened his bag and filled a syringe from a vial. He then injected her with a large dosage of a clear liquid.

"There's nothing more we can do now," said Bobby.

"Yes there is," said Nathan's mother. She slid to her knees beside Alexandra. She placed a hand on the woman's head and another on her stomach.

She began to pray.

Chapter 13- Finding a Place

Ernest Givens lay uncomfortably on the thin mattress. He stared at the cold bare walls of the Mayfield City Jail and still found it hard to believe he was here.

As a former army non-commissioned officer, he had visited plenty of jails in his time. Typically, it was to come take control of soldiers who had gotten too drunk in public. Most police tended to give soldiers a bit of a pass instead of formally booking them and allow their chain-of-command to come take them away. Usually, it was understood by all, including the soldier, that dire punishment of its own would be forthcoming through informal NCO channels.

Several times he had come down for soldiers charged with DUIs, and in those cases, there was nothing he could do. Once, he even had a soldier charged with manslaughter after a bar fight ended badly. Sergeant Major Givens had said that however low he sunk in life, he would never end up on the wrong side of those bars.

Yet here he was. Ernest looked up and down the jail cell hallway. Some were quiet like he was, but others were loud and boisterous. Especially in the communal drunk tank filled with people the police thought needed to sober up before being released again.

How did I end up here? he wondered. *Am I making a big mistake with this whole president thing?*

Ernest lay still and thought about this question. Something told him it was important on some level. He eventually decided that it was in the JP's best interests that someone ran in opposition to the incumbent. It wasn't healthy for democracy to have the sitting leader just get re-elected year after year as a simple formality. He had seen plenty of countries around the world with 'free elections' where there was only one candidate who received ninety-nine percent of the votes. *Who does that one percent vote for?* he always wondered.

No, should someone run was not the key question. The question that mattered to Ernest was if he was the man for the job, and he already knew that he didn't know. Hell, less than a month before, he had been a total mess on the verge of blowing his own brains out.

Someone has to run against him, he thought. *I didn't ask for this. People came seeking me out. If no one else is going to step up, then I have no choice.*

There was a presence outside his cell and Ernest realized that he had dozed off. He opened his eyes and saw a man standing there in a police uniform with a grim expression.

"Police Chief Norton," said Ernest, "I see that you were obviously raised properly."

"What's that supposed to mean?"

"Why, being a good host and coming to check on your guests."

Norton looked self-consciously at the other prisoners who were watching and listening to him. "You know it didn't have to be this way."

"You're right," said Ernest, sitting up on the edge of the bunk and swinging his feet to the floor. "You could have *not* arrested me."

"You were getting people hurt. Inciting violence and mischief."

"Are those the charges? Inciting violence and mischief?" Ernest thought for a second. "By the way, I've never been read my rights or charged yet. Now that we're on the subject, I want a lawyer."

"Me too," said a belligerent voice down a few cells. "I want a lawyer."

"Shut up," said Norton without looking at the man down the hall. "You haven't been formally charged," explained Norton, "because we have up to thirty days to do that under martial law."

"Ohhhhhhh," said Ernest, smiling. "Now it makes sense. Now I know why I'm really in here."

"You're in here because of why I just told you."

"Don't you think it's a little convenient that right before the election the sole challenger to the man in power is arrested and held without charges? Reggie Phillips surprises me. I thought he was more of a 'let's play fair ball' sort."

"It was me who recommended you be detained," said Norton. "The president asked for my recommendation, and I gave it to him."

"And I guess that's all it takes anymore," said Ernest, rising from his bunk to approach the bars. "Two men just get together over, what, beer?"

"Tea."

"And decide to make their problems go away by locking it away."

"It's legal," insisted Norton.

"It's only legal because you say it's legal," said Ernest. "Where are the checks and balances that are supposed to be in place? Who approved the president's order on martial law? What judges say what is legal and what is not?"

"It's not like that," Norton said. "The president is a good man."

"Probably so," admitted Ernest, "but total power changes people. The JP is quickly headed down the path of totalitarianism."

"Right on," said several inmates, and there were other words of agreement.

"You know that I fought against Ethan Schweitzer's totalitarianism," Ernest said, moving closer to Norton. "Remember that?"

Norton nodded, his face tight.

Ernest spread his hands wide to take in his surroundings. "And is this what all that was for? You know I'm not a criminal."

"I ain't no criminal either," said the belligerent voice again.

Norton ignored the voice and kept his eyes locked on Ernest. "Why couldn't you have just kept quiet?"

"I did," answered Ernest. "For a long long time, but those days are over."

"So are those of you running your mouth," said Norton abruptly. He looked around, the spell broken. "It's almost lights out," he told them all.

"Hey, Norton," said Ernest.

The man turned back to look at him.

"You ever think about that day?"

"What day?"

Ernest smiled. "You know damn well what day I'm talking about."

"No, I don't think about it."

"You're lying," said Ernest. "I bet late at night you think about it all the time. Maybe even in your dreams you're walking away from me, waiting to hear that gunshot you know will be the last sound you hear. Actually, you wouldn't hear it, because the bullet would travel much faster than the sound, but dreams are funny like that."

"Good night," said Norton, walking away to catcalls from the other prisoners.

Ernest sat back with his head against the wall.

"Hey, man," said a voice across the hall from him.

Looking outward, Ernest saw a small Hispanic man. "Yeah?"

"He called you Ernest and you talked about running for president." The man paused. "Are you really that same Ernest Givens? The guy from the Battle of Paducah and the Long Walk and the Resistance?"

"I guess I am," answered Ernest with a wry smile.

"So why you deciding to run for president?" the man asked.

Ernest noticed that nearly everyone in the jail cell was now paying attention. *Hell*, he thought, *these are potential voters, too.*

So he told them. He talked about the injustices he had witnessed and his fear of key individuals holding power. Ernest expressed misgivings about the lack of transparency and how there were too many forgotten citizens. He expressed outrage over the continued wars and broken currency promises. He told them how Reggie Phillips was no longer the man to lead the JP and how if they continued on their current path for much longer there wouldn't be much left.

And they listened.

There was one pale, thin, former meth user sitting at the end of the hallway, Spence Pruitt.

Somewhere between his sophomore and junior years of high school, Spence had gone off the rails badly. Before he had been an A's

240

and B's student gifted in art and music. He had followed the rules and respected his teachers and parents.

Then Lisa happened. She was sexy and fun and always seemed at ease. Taking notice of Spence, they had quickly fallen in together. Spence had always been a secluded loner and girls were a mystery. Lisa broke down all his barriers and didn't care if he didn't know what to do or say. Lisa became the only really important thing in his life. The center about which all other things diminished in importance when compared to her. He had loved her more than he had ever loved anything in his whole life.

But she had not felt the same. It became obvious that he was simply short-term entertainment for her. Even after Spence had learned she was sleeping around, he had forced himself not to believe the rumors, even when he knew they were true. She tried less and less to hide her other affairs as she grew more bored with Spence. Others could see that he was a discarded play toy to her, but Spence couldn't accept the loss of the center of his universe. If nothing else mattered as much as her, how could anything matter without her?

His parents had seen what was happening and tried to talk some sense into him, but he would not listen. Finally, she had publically rejected him in the most humiliating fashion possible. Spence had run away for awhile and then fallen in with a group of boys he had known when he was younger. Soon his life was characterized by booze and pot and not caring anymore. Spence had joined them.

His grades, interests, and relationship with his parents had deteriorated. They had tried to talk to him and pull him back in, but Spence no longer cared about what happened to him, and his self-pity didn't allow room for him to care about others. Before long, he was staying away from home for days at a time and was smoking meth nearly every day.

Several more times they tried to help, but he still wouldn't listen to their anguished entreaties. It was only a few days before N-Day when he saw his parents last. He had agreed to go with them on a beach vacation down to their old spot in Gulf Shores, Alabama. He remembered it fondly from his time as a young boy, running and playing in the sun and sand and crashing waves. They had all been happy then. His parents were willing to spend money they didn't have to try and draw him back.

The morning they were supposed to leave, he rejected them for the last time. Lashing out with all his anger, resentment, and humiliation, they became the target of it all. The more hurt their faces became the more he poured it on. When his mother started crying, he had smiled and reveled in the power he had. It was only when he lay bleeding on the ground that he stopped.

Looking up, he had seen his father shaking and crying himself. That caused Spence to pause. He could never recall seeing his father cry. The small, powerful, professional welder massaged the hand he had used to strike his son. He looked like he had wanted to say something, but then turned away, herded his distraught mother into the car, and drove away forever.

After N-Day, Spence had smoked meth like it was part of some race he wanted to win. When the basic chemicals used to make meth ran out, he switched to anything else he could find to buy: crack cocaine, oxycodone, marijuana, even ecstasy. When those had finally run out, he had smoked or snorted anything with even the mild promise of temporary oblivion.

After six months, there was nothing left. He sat in his parents' house staring at himself in pictures displayed prominently all around the house. With a painful breakdown, he truly realized how much his parents had loved him and what he had done to them.

Spence had tried to hang himself using an electric extension cord from the ceiling fan in the den, but it had crashed down onto his head, knocking him unconscious. When he awoke, he discovered that he was sitting in a pool of his own urine and that the ceiling fan had smashed the display case containing all his mother's treasured Hummel figurines.

Her favorite had been the one he had cut grass for months and saved to buy her. A small boy holding flowers with a slight smile. A boy that looked like Spence.

Now it sat in pieces.

How much more damage can you do? he heard her voice say.

Spence had laid there in the glass and his own piss and cried, for everything.

Since that day he had tried to go forward, but he didn't seem to know how. What little manual labor was to be had he tried to get, and it was barely enough for him to feed himself. Always an artist and musician, he found creativity just too much work now. One day blended into the next seamlessly, and Spence waited for something, anything to happen.

He had not intended to go to the Givens Rally. Spence had come to the courthouse to renew his ration card when he heard the crowds and voices. After getting his card from the county clerk, he had wandered down to hear what was being said.

Not much of it made sense, and Spence found his mind wandering as it did these days, but he liked the energy. The feel of being around masses of humanity. He could scream and yell like they did without even knowing what it was about. For the first time in a long time, he didn't feel alone.

When people started punching and smashing, Spence didn't hesitate. He joined in with gleeful abandon. He grinned foolishly and laughed with near hysteria as he kicked and punched strangers. He took his own fair share of kicks and strikes in return as one look at his face would attest, but he had hardly felt them. It had been liberating, like a shade pulled up on a dark room.

Now he sat and listened fascinated to what Givens said. The man was really talking to them, like they were important and he cared what they thought. Givens even locked eyes with Spence several times.

Spence began to smile, a lightness filling his chest. He knew what he needed to do now to make everything right.

Chapter 14 - The Return

Joshua, Conrad, and Trailer had been able to make their way out of Huntsville in their new disguise with surprising ease. They had of course drawn plenty of attention on the way, but figured everyone just assumed they were taking the unfortunate Trailer out into the nether regions of the city to execute him and leave his body as a sign for others.

After linking up with the rest of the squad, they continued north through the Creek Nation and up into JP. Their going was slow because Wildcat wasn't nearly as fast on straightaways as the bicycles were, but she made up for it on hills, quickly outpacing everyone with Trailer mocking them all the way. They had taken to placing most of their extra gear on her substantial rump and towing the three-wheeled cargo bicycle in tough spots.

Joshua sensed something was wrong when he approached the New Harvest headquarters. People greeted him, but dropped their eyes, some even saying they were sorry for his loss. Joshua began to get a premonition, a certainty, that his father was dead. He had come close to losing him before, and now he was gone for good.

He raced ahead of his comrades to the large sturdy cabin that served as the New Harvest administrative governance building. He found his father with Colonel Luke Carter and couldn't help giving Nathan a hug.

"Glad you made it back safely, son," said Nathan.

"I need to talk to you about what we found out," said Joshua, looking at Luke.

"That can wait," said Nathan. "I'm afraid I have some very bad news to tell you."

Joshua stiffened. "What?"

"I'm sorry to tell you that..." Nathan stopped and looked away before continuing. "That your mom got malaria. Everyone did what they could, but it just hit her so fast. She wasn't able to fight it off. I'm sorry, son. She died earlier this week."

Joshua just stared at him.

"Did you hear me?" asked Nathan.

"Mom's dead?" Joshua shook his head. "I don't understand. I saw her just before I left."

"I know," said Nathan. "It took me by surprise as well. She was the finest woman I've ever met and I certainly didn't deserve her." Nathan's jaw clinched, holding in emotion. "Anyway, she's gone now. I'm sorry."

"When was the funeral?"

"Earlier this week," said Nathan, putting his arm around his son. "She was proud of you. I hope you know that."

Joshua nodded. "Can I go see her?"

"Yes," Nathan sighed. "I'm afraid that isn't the end of the bad news."

"Oh, hell, what else?"

"Alexandra got malaria as well."

"She's not...dead, is she?"

Nathan shook her head. "She recovering, but..."

Joshua didn't wait to hear the rest. His father yelled for him to stop, but Joshua ignored him. He sprinted across the paths and under shaded forest clearings until he leaped up the steps of his home. He burst in to find his grandmother sitting in their living room sleeping.

She awoke, startled at the sound of him coming in. "Oh, Joshua," she said, putting a hand over her heart.

"Where is she?"

"Shush," she said. "Alexandra is sleeping. She needs her rest, but the doctor said she's going to be okay."

"Can I see her?"

His grandmother nodded sadly.

Joshua walked in their bedroom and was stunned by how pale and thin Alexandra appeared. She actually looked vulnerable for the first time he could ever remember. Alexandra was the strongest and fiercest person he had ever met; she even frightened him sometimes when she went off alone to hunt. He took a deep breath and grasped her hand, finding it cool to the touch.

She opened her eyes and looked up at him. "You're here."

"Yes, I'm here," he said, bending down to kiss and stroke her forehead. "I'm so sorry I wasn't here before."

"Did they tell you?" she asked as a tear rolled down her cheek.

He nodded. "But you're getting better now. That's all that matters."

She closed her eyes and shook her head. "They killed our baby."

Joshua stared at uncomprehendingly. "What are you talking about?"

"The medicine they gave me. I miscarried."

Looking from his wife back towards the living room where his grandmother sat he didn't know what to say.

She grasped his hand and looked at him with fire in her eyes. "As soon as I have my strength back, I'm going to kill that woman."

"What are you talking about?" asked Joshua. "Who?"

"Your grandmother. She's the one who told them to use those untested antibiotics on me."

"Grandma?" Joshua said, again looking towards the living room. "You don't mean that."

Alexandra nodded. "Yes. I've been thinking about it. I'm going to let her run and then hunt her down like a frightened rabbit. Once I catch her, I'm going to field dress her like a deer and cut her throat. Might even eat her heart. You know the Iroquois used to do that to enemies they vanquished in battle."

"You don't know what you're saying," said Joshua.

"It wasn't her decision to make," said Alexandra angrily.

"Well, if those drugs saved your life, I would have told the doctor to give them to you as well."

She pulled her hand from out of his. "You wouldn't."

Joshua nodded. "I wouldn't have sat here and done nothing and let you die."

"Get out."

"Alexandra."

"Get out!" she hissed.

Joshua did.

****

Conrad and Trailer came into the headquarters after Joshua had already left.

"Gentlemen," said Conrad, saluting both Luke and Nathan.

Nathan waved the salute away. "Have a seat, Conrad. Thanks for bringing my..." he trailed off as he looked at the huge form of Trailer ducking under the doorframe to come into the room.

"Who's your little friend?" asked Luke.

Nathan was pointing at him. "You're... Aren't you Horace Trailer Smiley?"

Trailer sheepishly nodded.

Nathan smiled widely. "You were one of my favorite players. All-Conference your freshman year and then you got hurt. Ankle, wasn't it?"

"Knee," said Trailer. "Had to have it scoped."

"Damn shame," said Nathan, shaking his head. "You were a lock for the NBA for sure."

"That's what everyone says," Trailer muttered through a forced smile.

"Are we done with basketball memories?" asked Conrad. "Because I think the antichrist is getting ready to try and kill us all."

"You're talking about Huntsville?" asked Luke.

Conrad nodded. "We're pretty sure Vincent Lacert, now evidently known as Reaper, is in charge there."

Nathan frowned. "We suspected that. Not good news."

"It gets worse," said Conrad. "He's building a missile."

"A missile?" asked Luke. "Like a big one?"

"Big enough to hit the JP, I'd bet. Worse yet, they cleaned out Milan." Conrad looked around at them. "Joshua said you told him there were tactical nukes in Milan."

"They're non-functional now," Nathan said. "After what happened with David, it didn't feel right to leave them sitting down there. I didn't want to move them up here so I asked some of the professors from MSU to go down there and render them safe."

Conrad seemed to deflate. "Thank God. I just kept thinking of Vincent Lacert with a nuclear-armed missile and what he could do with it."

"He *does* still have a missile," added Trailer. "It's probably still big enough to pack some punch."

"What do you think he plans to do with it?" asked Luke.

"Lacert?" asked Conrad. "If I know him at all, death and destruction for everyone else. He'll likely hold a grudge for everything that's happened to him since Missouri."

"Which means he'll be looking at us," said Nathan.

"So what do you want to do?" asked Luke.

Everything depends on his intentions, thought Nathan. If Lacert is content with his own little kingdom, then things might be okay. Relations would never be good, but the JP might be able to peacefully co-exist with Huntsville.

Then again the man might have revenge in his heart. Or maybe he thought of himself as some sort of modern-day conqueror ready to lay claim to the land around him.

"We need to know what the man intends," said Nathan. "Not conjecture. We need to know with certainty."

"Don't see any way to find that out unless you go down there and talk to the man," said Luke.

Nathan sighed and looked around at them.

"Oh, hell," said Conrad.

"Luke's right. I need to see him with my own eyes. Get a feel for what he intends." Nathan turned to Conrad. "You know the man...better than most from what I understand. Go set up a meeting for me."

"Oh, hell," said Conrad. "I was afraid you were going to say something like that."

Chapter 15 – Offer of Empire

Nathan and Conrad walked through a small deserted park in Southern Tennessee. A cold spell had descended several days ago, and sharp wind and drizzle blew about their exposed faces. The park had been Conrad's idea and arranged through several messengers sent back and forth. It was an open area where Nathan and Lacert could talk privately, but not a good location for an ambush, as each side would be able to watch closely from standoff distance.

"Don't trust him," said Conrad. "No matter what he says."

Nathan looked at him quizzically. "Of course not. I barely trust you."

"Thanks...I guess," said Conrad. "Anyway, I only spoke to him through messengers, but if I know him at all, he has an ace up his sleeve."

"What was that like? Talking with your old boss?"

Conrad shrugged. "It wasn't like we were close even then. I did his dirty work to stay alive; that was all it was. I knew even before your son came along I needed to find a way out; he just helped provide it."

Nathan tensed at the thought of Joshua's burns and pushed the image away.

"There he is," said Conrad, pointing unnecessarily to the tall blond man walking across the grass towards them.

There was something about the man that impressed Nathan immediately. Some inner vitality or sense of power. A man who couldn't help but draw the attention of everyone when he walked into a room. He was not overly attractive, nor large, nor striking in any other way. He was simply…more.

"Let's go," said Nathan, walking forward with Conrad following closely behind. Lacert had stopped in the middle of the park and held his hands behind his back. He stared calmly at Nathan with those icy-blue eyes.

"Perhaps you should leave us, Conrad," said Lacert when Nathan stopped a few paces away. "You were never really the discussion type, more of an action person." Lacert turned back to Nathan. "Besides, men in our position should be able to speak freely with each other. Privacy makes that possible."

Nathan turned to Conrad and nodded.

Conrad hesitated and stared hard at Lacert before turning to Nathan. "I'll be right back there if you need anything. And don't forget what I said." He then strode away.

"It seems odd that the two of us have never met," said Lacert, looking down on the smaller man.

"That was probably to your benefit," said Nathan, "considering you tortured my son."

Lacert spread his hands out to his side. "Yet here I am now, just the two of us. What is it you imagined you would do to me if we ever met?"

"I've imagined plenty," said Nathan softly.

Lacert smiled. "I like a man with imagination, probably the reason Conrad and I never were closer. I see you two are buddies now, but you should know he played a not insignificant part in what happened to your son... Well, one of your sons. The other I understand went out in a blaze of glory, you might say. That's got to make you proud."

"Don't talk about my sons," said Nathan evenly.

"I'm not blaming here. That boy did me a favor. Saved me the trouble of killing Ethan Schweitzer myself. But setting off a nuke? That's some cold-blooded shit right there. Most inventive method of suicide I've heard of in awhile."

Nathan felt his heart racing and forced himself to remain calm. He unclenched his fists at his side and took a deep breath.

The tall man chuckled and nodded. "I see that we are much alike. You'd prefer to settle this here now, maybe like the ancient warriors of old. We could be the champions of respective armies fighting to the death on a field of glory. That would save everyone a great deal of bloodshed, wouldn't you agree?"

"What are your intentions with that rocket you're building in Huntsville?"

"Ah," said Lacert, "you know about that? That saves me the trouble of having to explain to you my position."

"What position is that?"

"Why, peaceful, of course, yet we are concerned about very aggressive neighbors to our north. It is only prudent we take certain measures to defend ourselves."

"I would say you were the aggressors," said Nathan. "You attacked the Milan Depot, killing our soldiers and stealing our property."

"Well, after Fulton, "Lacert smiled, "who could blame us? Once you start setting off nukes, it seemed only prudent to secure them before they are used on us. Now those nuclear weapons are safely in our hands."

"They won't work."'

Lacert pointed a finger at Nathan. "It was you, wasn't it? You are the one who sabotaged them."

"We both know if your threat was to put a nuclear warhead on the tip of that missile and send it at us, that's now impossible."

"I have a lot of very smart, geeky people here," said Lacert. "They used to be responsible for putting things in space. Who's to say they couldn't fix a warhead?"

Nathan stared hard at the man. This was the crux of the problem. Could Lacert launch a nuke at them or not?

Unless we're willing to surrender, Nathan thought, *our response is the same. Resistance.*

"I see you're thinking about it." Lacert rubbed his face. "Boom!" he yelled out theatrically and laughed maniacally.

"What is it you want?" asked Nathan. "I presume you have some purpose in what you are doing?"

"See, I knew you were the right man to deal with. Of course I want something. Can't you guess?"

"Electricity," sighed Nathan.

Lacert waved his hand at Nathan. "Oh no, we have dams of our own. Not as big as yours, but enough to meet my needs."

"Then what?"

Lacert looked away as if thinking. "We're all on the cusp of something...new. Everyone keeps trying to get things back the way they were before, but that's a dangerous route to take and an illusion. We can never go back."

The wind picked up and blew leaves around their feet.

Lacert looked back at him. "Three hundred years ago this land was nothing but wilderness, yet they built a nation from it. It's more than that now. The potential is there."

"For what?"

"An empire." Lacert smiled, sweeping his hand around him. "It's out there, just waiting for us to claim it. The things we could build will be the new world."

"With you in charge, I suppose," said Nathan.

Lacert shrugged. "Why not? Someone has to be. That is the way most leaders came to be throughout all human history. Power is the ultimate qualification for more power." He smiled at Nathan. "But I will need some good people to help me along the way. Men with imagination, like you perhaps. The rewards for loyalty would be impressive, I promise you."

"So you want us to join you?" asked Nathan. "Just abandon everything we've built and follow you as our beloved dictator?"

"President is fine," said Lacert. "People are used to certain titles; the label is not terribly important. And if you look at it objectively, you have no choice."

Nathan shook his head and chuckled. "What makes you think you could force us to do anything? I think you've overplayed your hand, my friend. We're stronger than you, we're in a better position than you, and we will not be bullied by a power-hungry maniac."

Lacert's smiled slipped away. "I assure you, there will be consequences."

"What consequences?" asked Nathan. "Bullshit on your fixing the nukes. And you only have one rocket."

"How do you know we don't have more rockets? Or can't build more?"

"Make reparations for Milan and stop building rockets and maybe we can find a way to co-exist peacefully."

"I don't *want* to co-exist peacefully. There is too much at stake." Lacert brought his fists up in front of his face. "There is just too damn much potential, don't you see that?"

"You can't force us to submit. Keep this up and you'll force us to destroy you."

"Not everything hinges on nukes. Even without nukes, those rockets can still pack a tremendous punch, enough to level a city block. I can put one anywhere I want; those GPS satellites are still up there in space working overtime."

Nathan felt his heart rate speeding up again. "You're threatening us? Are you sure you want to do that?"

"Imagine a missile obliterating your hometown. Mayfield, I believe it is? Or maybe Paducah or Murray? All that suffering would be your fault. Death and destruction and misery for no purpose."

"You're never going to stop, are you?" said Nathan. "N-Day only gave you an ideal opportunity. First, it's the Missouri Alliance. Sadistic criminals with you as their warlord. Then it's Ethan Schweitzer's master of atrocities, and now you're somehow here again. Doing everything you can to burn the world down."

"No," said Lacert patiently. "Not burn the world down. Build it up again, better than before."

Nathan waved his hand at Lacert's troops behind the man. "How did you get to this place? By making the world better? You didn't have to kill or torture anyone."

Lacert shrugged. "Sometimes you have to break a few eggs, as the saying goes. No job is without its complications."

"I think we're done here," said Nathan. "You have our terms."

"'Terms, is it?"

Nathan thought of the JP and its upcoming elections. The fragile peace with the Creek Nation and enemies on all sides. A people straining to survive. What would Lacert do to them if he got the chance? Could they even resist him? Would they have the will to resist?

"Yes, make reparations for Milan and destroy all rockets," said Nathan before turning to walk away.

"You're making a mistake," said Lacert, actually sounding amused.

I've made a lot of mistakes, thought Nathan, *but this certainly isn't one of them.*

The bolt of lightning streaked across the heavens in the distance followed by a deafening crack of thunder. Before Nathan could get to cover, the dark sky opened up, and he was drenched in cold, icy rain.

Chapter 16 – Deal With the Devil

It was beautiful country, peaceful most of the time. Sunlight played off the rippling river and a gentle wind blew through the tall grass.

Susan closed her eyes and willed the image she had seen at Chicoca's funeral to come to mind. The image came to her often unbidden, late at night in the stillest of hours, but during the day she had to force herself to remember.

She saw the bend of the river where the dead bloated bodies were stacking up, carrion for ravens and wild dogs. Shadowy figures in rags walked among the dead lying about in the fields, squatting occasionally to do who knew what around one of the corpses.

And there was the camper on the edge of the river. Susan opened her eyes and looked at Chicoca's old residence. It had already been sitting there, sealed up nicely, when the Creek had arrived. The elderly couple lying in the camper's bed held hands. They were remarkably preserved in the sealed-dry environment.

"Poison," someone had said, and Susan couldn't place the voice, but the horror of it had stayed with her. She had stared at the dried faces of the man and woman as they brought them outside. The most horrible thing of all was that they looked somehow at peace.

Closing her eyes again, the memory of the vision returned. The image itself wasn't much worse than the things they had seen along the way. One lonely scene of death and loss among thousands. No, it was the utter sense of finality and despair that had pervaded the vision. As if she were getting a glimpse into the last moments of a gasping, dying world with no hope of recovery.

And there sat that dirty gray camper with blue curtains drifting out of the shattered windows.

Susan opened her eyes and stared at Chicoca's old home. It was certainly similar to the one in the dream, but not exactly. This camper had cheap plastic blinds instead of curtains, and the surface was more white than gray.

Of course she could be remembering everything wrong or changing the memory to ensure it wasn't her new home. To ensure she wasn't imagining this beautiful land being turned into a wasteland. Maybe someone got rid of the cheap blinds and put in blue curtains. Maybe the camper got moved. Maybe it was a hundred years from now or more.

"And maybe you're going bat-shit crazy," she said to herself.

The door to the camper opened, and Billy Fox walked down the stairs towards her.

"What do you do in there anyway?" Susan asked.

Billy shrugged. "It helps me think sometimes. To be close to where he was. I've started to think of it as my office."

"Some big, badass Creek Indian you are with your *office*."

"Anyway, it's hard to think with you out here staring a hole into the trailer. I didn't realize you were in such a hurry to have this meeting."

Susan looked away. "It's not that."

"You're thinking of the vision again, aren't you?"

"Hallucination caused by heatstroke, you mean? Yeah, I was thinking of that."

"Visions are difficult to interpret sometimes...or so they tell me. Never had one myself."

"It wasn't a vision," Susan insisted. "It means nothing."

"Then why do you keep thinking about it?"

Susan was silent, and both of them looked towards the sounds of approaching voices.

"You know what this is about, don't you?" asked Billy.

Susan nodded. "And you know how I feel. We need a time when there is no fighting. I mean, how much land is enough?"

"Just what is ours."

"Yours? You mean because it was Creek land three hundred years ago it's always supposed to be yours? What about the people before you who had the land? It's all just a matter of who has the power to take and hold it."

"I couldn't agree more." Billy Fox smiled. "For the first time in those three hundred years, the Creek have the strength and opportunity to reclaim what has been lost. I will not let that opportunity pass."

"What about the cost?"

"That is not our way," Billy explained. "We do what we must and the cost will be the cost."

Susan opened her mouth to argue, but nothing seemed to come out. She realized that she was exhausted in body as well as spirit. "Let's just get this over with."

Billy nodded and clasped his hands behind his back.

They turned to see a tall serious man approaching them flanked by several Creek braves. Susan recognized him as the man who had come down with Nathan Taylor to propose peace only months before.

"Luke Carter," said Billy, warmly holding his hand out.

The man shook it and then turned to Susan and did the same.

Billy indicated a group of camp chairs outside of Chicoca's camper that were in the shade of a small awning attached to the vehicle's side.

Susan, who preferred to be just about anywhere other than near that trailer, forced herself to follow the two men and sit with them.

"I suppose you know why I am here," Luke said.

"Possibly something to do with Huntsville and that raid in Milan we told you about?" asked Billy.

Luke nodded. "We've learned that a very dangerous man named Vincent Lacert has seized power down there. He intends to move towards conflict with the JP."

"Is this the same Vincent Lacert who was the former JP Chief of Defense?" asked Susan.

"It is. Prior to Fulton's...well...destruction, he was arrested and imprisoned. He subsequently escaped and fled. No one knew where until recently. Seems like he has established himself well as the leader of this group that includes a great deal of resources and people. We know he is building rockets with the intent of launching them at us."

"And you want to strike him before he strikes you?" asked Billy.

"Of course," said Luke. "We tried to talk to the man, but it was fruitless. He is intent on causing as much pain and destruction in the world as he can. We will need to move to prevent him from harming our people."

262

Billy leaned back in his chair. "A prudent course, I guess. How does this involve us?"

"We are allies," said Luke. "We sat right here not long ago and smoked that peace pipe thing."

"That signified we would not fight each other," Billy explained. "Not that your fights would become our fights or vice versa."

"Let me explain something to you," said Luke, leaning forward. "This man is very dangerous, and he is right on your doorstep. He will not stop until he has everything under his sway. That is just the way he is."

"Maybe so, maybe not," said Susan, "but we've had enough of war. What do you want from us?"

Susan's declaration seemed to take some of the wind out of Luke's sails.

"Tell us what your plan is," said Billy. "Let's start from there."

Luke hesitated for a moment and looked from one to the other. "We plan to attack Huntsville and destroy their ability to threaten us. We mean to get rid of Vincent Lacert any way we have to."

"Any way?" asked Susan pointedly.

Luke's jaw tightened at her implication. "We do not intend to use nuclear weapons if that is what you were implying."

"That is a comfort," said Susan, "given that Huntsville is right on our doorstep, as you mentioned earlier."

"So a long siege is what you have in mind?" asked Billy.

"If need be. We'd prefer to be able to find a weakness in their defenses that can be exploited, but we are assuming the worst."

"That will take a lot of people. To surround an entire city, that's got to be, what? Twenty, thirty miles?"

"Thirty-eight," said Luke.

Billy whistled. "Wow. That's a lot of perimeter and a ton of people you're going to need to bring down there."

"And we don't have the fuel to drive them like before. We're going to have to use barges to float them down the Tennessee River."

"Up the river, you mean," said Susan. "The current runs north."

"Yes," said Luke. "We'll have draught teams pull the barges south from shore."

"That means through our territory," noted Billy.

"One of the things we had hoped you would be able to help us with," said Luke.

Billy rubbed his face. "This is not our fight, yet you want us to take actions that might draw us into this conflict?"

"Allowing us passage down the river and through Creek lands is not the same as drawing you into the conflict."

"You said 'one of the things we could help with,'" said Susan. "What else?"

"We're going to need to be provisioned. That's a lot of troops that will need food and some supplies. Our logistics can't support that distance, and we prefer not to pillage and live off the land like armies did in days of old. We'll pay you for everything, of course."

"We'll talk about that in a minute," said Billy. "What else do you want from us?"

"Just one more thing." Luke paused and looked back at the masses of Creek braves of horseback returning from hunting. He then turned back to them. "We need cavalry."

"Horses?" asked Susan.

Luke shook his head. "No. It takes a lifetime to train a horseman. We need the Creek. We'll bring what troops we can, and it will be a great deal, but there is no way we can bottle up thirty-six miles. We need cavalry to screen and harass most of the perimeter. To keep them bottled up and afraid to come out from behind their defenses."

"No," said Susan.

Luke looked first at Susan and then at Billy. "Our people will be doing most of the fighting and taking the majority of the casualties. The Creek will simply be—"

"No," Susan repeated. "There is no reason we should be drawn into this conflict."

Luke turned to her angrily. "You say 'we' like you're an Indian, but you were an Air Force officer once. You can't stand on the principle of 'my people' and 'how we have suffered.' You're not even a Creek."

"Yes, she is," said Billy seriously. "And if you wish to have any hope of gaining our support, you will recognize that fact."

Susan stared at Luke before turning to Billy. "We should remain neutral. There is no reason for us to become involved."

Billy was silent and nodded finally.

"So that's it?" said Luke. "You're not even going to let us pass down the freaking river?"

"What would be our incentive to do so?" asked Billy.

Luke appeared taken aback. "You would get our gratitude. In the future we would come to your aid, of course."

Billy scrunched up his face and shook his head. "Remember, we're Native Americans. We have pretty bad experience relying on promises from the government."

"Well, what do you want then?" asked Luke.

"Only one thing," said Billy, leaning forward with a smile. "And you can even keep you payment for any provisions."

****

They stood side by side and watched Luke Carter being escorted away.

"You did well," said Billy.

"I can't believe they agreed to it."

"They had no choice," said Billy. "They need us for this to succeed. They're in a tight spot, not just with Huntsville, but back home."

"And you really think they'll just stay neutral if the Creek take all of Northern Alabama in exchange for that help?"

Billy nodded. "I'm not one for trusting promises, but they can't risk a war with us as well. They'll follow through, even if they regret it afterwards. Besides, they're having enough trouble without trying to govern even more lands."

"Like we can do better?" asked Susan.

"That's the difference," answered Billy. "We're not trying to govern our lands; we just live on them, taking freely of what the earth gives us."

Susan snorted. "Does that include taxes from non-Creek?"

"Of course it does. They benefit as well. As long as they pay their taxes and live in peace, we leave them alone and they live without fear of getting murdered or enslaved. They live under the umbrella of protection we provide."

She kicked at a rock. "I've never heard of Indian tax collectors. Ruling over non-Creek like the Roman Empire or something. I thought this was all about regaining ancestral lands."

"It is, but times change, and we must as well. My ancestors would have massacred or driven off all non-Creek. This way is more…productive for everyone, wouldn't you agree?"

Susan shrugged. "I suppose."

"You played your part like a pro," said Billy, smiling.

"I did take drama in college my freshman year."

"Really?" asked Billy. "Were you in any plays?"

"Mostly minor roles," Susan said, "although I was the devil in *The Screwtape Letters*."

Billy looked at her critically for a few seconds before shaking his head. "I don't see it."

Susan shrugged. "That's the magic of acting. You can be anyone simply by making yourself believe you are that person. Sort of like your prophetess."

"You're not pretending; that's who you are."

"And a Creek."

"You heard me back there," said Billy. "You are one of us. We adopted you into the tribe. That can't be changed."

Susan looked away.

"At some point you really need to let go of all this guilt. It does no one any good and is frankly getting old. You need to realize that nothing that has happened is your fault."

She started chuckling and spread her arms to indicate the world around them. "Billy, that's where you're wrong. *Everything* that's happened since that day is my fault in some way."

Susan Who Brought the Fire From the Sky turned and walked down towards the bend of the river that contained the camper.

Chapter 17 – Wheeler Dam

Joshua opened his eyes and gazed at the setting sun. He had tried to sleep, as it would be a long night, but he had never been a day sleeper.

Evidently, most of the men and women under his command didn't have the same issues. He could hear their snores over the steady drone of crickets from the nearby Wheeler Lake.

He looked back up into the woods and could see a few signs of their camouflaged vehicles. Although his father had impressed upon him the importance of the mission, the fact that he had been given actual running vehicles and a good amount of working fuel told him more. Given the distances they had to cover from the JP, southeast around Nashville and Chattanooga and to the east of Huntsville, there was no way they could have been in position to coordinate the attack without the vehicles.

Conrad McKraven slipped down beside him. "Saw you were awake."

"How is everyone?"

"Good. A third are on watch and the rest are either eating, resting, or pumping up the boats."

Joshua nodded. It was the largest military force he had ever commanded, nearly two hundred soldiers, and they would need all of the two dozen inflatable boats they had brought with them.

"Is everyone clear on their roles?" Joshua asked.

Conrad pulled out a canteen and drank deeply before answering. He pointed towards Wheeler Dam in the distance. It straddled the Tennessee River and provided electricity to Huntsville and the surrounding areas. "I'll take half the soldiers and attack the north end of the dam and you'll get the south. We'll meet in the middle."

"When?"

"You don't have to quiz me. I know the plan."

"Say it anyway," said Joshua. "If not for your sake, then for mine."

Conrad sighed. "Midnight. That's when the JP main forces west of here will begin their main assault on Decatur. Jason Green's forces will be conducting an extremely dangerous raid on the solar array in the Huntsville Botanical Gardens."

"All of these missions are dangerous."

"Yeah, but he got the short end of the deal. He actually has to sneak into the outskirts of the city and destroy the array and then run out before he gets caught. Poor devil."

"He volunteered for the mission."

"That doesn't make it any less crazy," said Conrad. "Also, doesn't say much for Green's sanity."

"Someone has to do it," said Joshua. "Once we cut off their electricity we can start the siege in earnest. We'll unload most of our troops on the barges at Decatur Harbor while the Creek keep them bottled up to the north and east. They'll run out of food soon enough, and without electricity, they'll be more likely to talk."

Conrad shook his head. "Not Lacert. I would tell you more, but you know the man. There's no need. He'll let everyone in there starve and won't think twice about it."

"I know," said Joshua, absently rubbing his scarred head.

"You know," said Conrad casually, "as your deputy on this mission, maybe I should stay with you. Lieutenant Grubbs is more than capable of leading the assault on the northern part of the dam."

Joshua turned to look at him curiously. "Still here to protect me, are you? My dad put you up to this?"

"No one had to put me up to anything," said Conrad. "You're family has lost a lot lately. No need to lose more. Besides, your wife and mine are friends, and they talk. Alexandra is worried about you."

Joshua stiffened at the thought of his wife talking to someone else about him. Then he remembered her grief at the loss of the baby and his anger melted away. It was good she had someone to talk to, especially with him being away. He shook his head. "There's no truly safe place anymore. Even back in the rear, there're diseases and other craziness. I'd rather be out here where I can see the enemy."

"I agree with you there," said Conrad, looking at the darkening sky. "Speaking of which, the moon will be close to full tonight. With any luck, we'll get some cloud cover."

"Any reinforcements arrive at the dam?"

"Not that we've seen. Still about fifty to sixty guards. A few medium machine guns, but mostly light stuff."

"Let's not underestimate them," said Joshua. "Surprise is everything, and if we can't take the dam, we need to at least disable it."

Conrad nodded. "The demo team knows their role and will plant the explosives as soon as the objective is secured."

"Make sure they only blow the control equipment and stay away from the main part of the dam. Don't want the blast weakening the dam

271

walls. That's all our JP forces needs: several hundred tons of water rushing down on their moored barges."

"Actually, that's what I would do," said Conrad, thinking. "Might even be what Victor would do."

"What do you mean?"

"Well, if he knows he's surrounded and that troops are landing downstream from the dam, why not use the water to disrupt them? He doesn't necessarily have to blow the damn; he can just open the sluiceways as far as they'll go."

"Another reason for us to get control of that dam."

"Right," said Conrad. "I'll go check on things again."

Joshua nodded and thought about his wife far to the north.

****

A quarter to midnight on a cloudy evening, close to two hundred nervous soldiers slipped quietly into inflatable rafts with their combat gear and began to paddle west along the broad flat surface of Wheeler Lake. One group hugged the northern shore while Joshua led the other across the lake to the southern shoreline. From there, they would make their way towards the southern side of the dam.

Initially, they had considered simply attacking the dam from land at each end, but someone evidently had been thinking of such a threat, and there were new fortifications and obstacles along the land approaches. Most of the guards' attention appeared to be focused towards landward approaches, but that wasn't saying much. What guards they had seen in the two days since they had arrived were obviously not expecting any sort of trouble. They spent their days in leisurely boredom.

That's about to change, thought Joshua.

At the southern edge of the lake, he looked back at the ten boats behind him and motioned for them to proceed west again. The sound of the paddles dipping into the water made Joshua cringe, but he realized it couldn't be helped and likely wasn't as loud as he imagined.

As they approached, the dam's surface loomed ahead of them. It wasn't as big as Kentucky Dam, but it was still impressive. A long, tall wall of concrete and steel stretched across the dark water's surface. At each end of the dam were large concrete structures that housed the machinery that sent electricity to waiting homes and people. Incredible. Something that no one would even consider building today. Something the likes of which might never be built again.

The shore came on so suddenly that it surprised Joshua. He stuck his paddle out ahead of them to keep the underside of the boat from scraping loudly along the bottom of the shore. Slipping into the water carefully, he motioned for everyone else to get out before they carried the boat up against the base of the dam's edge where it would hopefully be difficult for anyone to spot in the darkness. The other boat teams did the same.

Joshua dispatched the security team first. They would make their way silently south through the forest and set up a position along the road that crossed over the dam. Their job was to stop, or at least delay, any possible reinforcements that might attempt to come help their embattled colleagues. Conrad's group would be doing the same along the road to the north.

As the security team melted into the darkness, Joshua gave final instruction to the support team who would take up a position to provide flanking fire on the guard posts and fortified positions. This was the largest element and contained most of their heavier machine guns and grenade launchers.

That left Joshua sitting silently with two dozen handpicked men and women. They were the assault team. Their job would be to clear the dam of any resistance the support team didn't take care of. They would hopefully link up with Conrad's forces at the center of the dam. If not, they at least needed to stop the flow of electricity.

He looked at his luminescent watch, a gift from his father that was synchronized with dozens of other watches in the JP forces. Joshua felt some comfort in knowing that a great number of friends and comrades were staring at their watches now as well.

Watching the seconds tick away, Joshua said a silent prayer for his people and his family. He then pulled out the parachute flare, removed the safety, and slapped the bottom edge of the tube forcefully.

With a whoosh sound, the flare shot up into the air and opened with a loud *pop* and flash of light. A brightness like a small sun lit up the area, and harsh light began to slowly drift to the ground, suspended by a small parachute. Soldiers on the dam looked up and pointed while others started yelling a warning.

Machine gun fire opened up from their support team soon followed by small arms and grenade launchers. Joshua could hear similar sounds coming from the north.

Joshua looked at his watch, and after ninety seconds of this sustained fire, he pulled out another flare and popped this one as well. This time a dimmer red flare lit up the sky before descending towards the lake's surface.

"Let's go!" Joshua yelled and led his men and women up from the surface of the lake's shore and around behind the makeshift fortifications. The support team firing had ceased, and he could now hear cries of the wounded ahead of him. He scanned for any threat while several soldiers used wire cutters to make a path through the concertina wire strung before them.

As the last strand was cut, Joshua charged through, and a blast erupted from his left. He felt something strike his backpack and let his momentum carry him forward to roll onto the ground. Looking back, he saw the JP soldier behind him fire a burst of gunfire into a man who had been hiding behind a barricade with a shotgun.

"Fan out!" ordered Joshua. "Clear the area up to the edge of the dam. Move quickly."

They did, and he heard occasional sustained gunfire and even isolated pops that told him they had found someone wounded.

"We're all clear here, sir," said a female sergeant.

Joshua nodded and blew three quick blasts on the whistle hanging around his neck. This was the signal for the support team to move forward and set up a defensive position to hold the south side of the dam.

"Follow me," ordered Joshua, moving north towards the road that ran across the top of the dam. They climbed over a burning truck. Two men, who were maybe enjoying the cab's warmth when the attack happened, sat inside. One was clearly dead, but the other stared at them with wide eyes, blood pooled below his leg, the sharp white of his shattered femur poking through the skin.

Joshua continued forward and heard a pistol shot from behind him.

There were several more bodies in their path, but not as many as he would have expected. Sustained gunfire came from the north side, and Joshua realized that Conrad's forces may have had more resistance since an attack on the dam from the north was more likely than from the south.

Creeping forward out into the dam, Joshua felt suddenly exposed. There was nothing but the broad flat expanse of the lake to his right and a sheer drop-off to the Tennessee River below. He unconsciously picked up his pace.

There was a sharp *slap* sound behind him followed by a flash and *pop* ahead of him. Joshua turned to see the soldier following him fall to the ground, blood leaking from a dark wound in the man's abdomen.

Joshua and the soldiers with him dropped to the ground as several more shots rang out in their direction. He turned on the red lens flashlight attached to his rifle and shined it ahead. He saw three men, two working intently on something on the ground and another one pointing a rifle at them.

Joshua shot the man with the rifle in the face. Shots came from behind him, and the other two men fell.

As a medic came up to work on their fallen soldier, Joshua and several others moved forward to the three dead or dying bodies. There was what appeared to be a radio transmitter of some sort as well as several bags of tools and snippets of wire. A coil of rope and a roll of duct tape lay off to the side.

"What the hell were they doing?" asked someone.

"Shush," said Joshua, shining his light across the dam. He heard something from the northern direction.

There were three sudden flashes of red.

Joshua answered with two of his own.

"Coming forward," said Conrad. "You skittish bastards, take your nervous little fingers off your triggers."

They lowered their weapons as Conrad and a dozen soldiers made their way forward.

"Report," said Joshua.

"We've secured the north side of the dam. Took three casualties; two were light, but one's not likely to make it."

"Any signs of reinforcements?"

Conrad shook his head, looking down at the equipment and tools at their feet. "What's this about?"

"Not sure," answered Joshua. "They were working on it when we arrived."

Conrad poked at one of the tool bags with his foot. "Looks like electrical wiring and stuff." He then gazed at the radio transmitter. "Now why would they want to transmit anything out here?"

"Maybe they were trying to tell Huntsville they were under attack," suggested someone.

Conrad stared intently and then walked over to the lake side of the dam and shined his light down towards the water.

"What are you looking for?" asked Joshua.

He didn't answer, only went to the opposite side and shined his light down. Conrad raised back up and pointed downward. "That."

Joshua and dozens of eyes peered over the edge. In the dim red flashlight glow, they could see a small bundle, about a foot square, duct taped to a metal support against the dam's surface. The bundle was about thirty feet below them. A small radio with a wire stuck out from the side of the bundle.

"Is that what I think it is?" asked Joshua.

Conrad nodded. "My guess? They were setting it up to be remotely detonated using this transmitter, but we interrupted them."

The clouds had finally cleared and the bright moon cast calm light over the surface of everything. Joshua was staring at the blinking next to the bundle. "Maybe we didn't completely interrupt them. The transmitter would have given them a longer range, but if someone knows what they're doing, it might still be set off."

Conrad leaned over again. "Yeah, that looks like a standard walkie-talkie. Might be set to go off if someone breaks squelch on that frequency."

They all looked around at each other in sudden realization.

"Could be nothing," someone said.

"Get the demo team up here!" screamed Conrad back towards the north.

Joshua was visualizing that bomb going off and killing all of them as tons of water washed downstream. A wall of water that would swamp, and maybe even flip, those flat barges carrying hundreds of soldiers at Decatur. It would be a catastrophe and signal possible defeat.

"No time for that," said Joshua, handing his rifle to Conrad.

"What are you doing?" asked Conrad.

Joshua moved to the edge of the dam and looked down before lifting one leg over and then the other.

Conrad realized what he was planning too late. He moved forward to grab Joshua, but he now held a rifle in each hand. A lifetime of training kept him from dropping either weapon.

Looking down, Joshua saw the bundle and then slipped off. He plunged downward intending for his feet to hit the bundle and knock it off the wall, but he was too far to one side. Joshua grabbed a hold of the bundle, and he lay there suspended for a fraction of a second before the tape and wires holding the bundle to the metal support pulled away with a ripping sound.

Joshua hugged the bomb to his chest as he dropped down, plunging into the cool water and darkness of the river.

Chapter 18 – Bastion of Decency

It had been a very long time since Trailer had been inside what he would call a real home. Even before N-Day, he had lived out of the cab of his semi-trailer truck with the occasional vacation in a rundown hotel or rest stop. He hadn't minded; it was the life and it kept him moving.

It was the pictures that got to him. Strolling around the small neat rooms of Reggie Phillips' house he saw that they were precursors to larger stories, in a sense similar to covers of books promising tantalizing tales.

Simon and Jessica were in the living room talking to Reggie who had graciously invited them over for dinner after hearing of their ordeal from Nathan Taylor. Trailer stuck his head in and saw an elderly dignified man who looked hollowed around the eyes, as if he could use more rest. Simon and Jessica sat closer to each other than was strictly necessary on the large couch.

Trailer ducked back into the den chuckling to himself. He wished Simon and Jessica well, although it would be a miracle if either of them let their feelings be known to the other any time soon.

There was a small crash in the kitchen.

"I'm fine," came a resigned and slightly disgusted voice.

Trailer stepped in to see Janice Phillips bending down awkwardly on her artificial leg to pick up a cookie sheet of cooked biscuits.

"Here, let me help," said Trailer, closing the hot gas oven. He then grabbed a dishtowel and placed the hot sheet on the stovetop before gathering the hot biscuits.

"I'm sure they're still fine," said Janice, blowing off the biscuits and placing them back into the pan. "I won't tell if you won't."

Trailer popped one of the hot biscuits in his mouth and crossed his chest.

"A man after my own heart," said Janice with an approving nod. She placed a series of casserole dishes in the oven and set a timer. "Should be ready in a bit. How are you doing?"

The question made Trailer pause in his chewing. It had been a long time since anyone had asked him that question. He looked down on the small woman and saw that the question was sincere.

"Okay, I guess," he finally mumbled. "You sure it's not too much? Having us here, I mean? President Phillips has only just recovered from malaria, after all."

"He's through the worst of it, besides my husband thrives on human interaction."

"I can tell," said Trailer, looking again into the hallway.

"I saw you looking at those pictures in there," she said.

Trailer nodded and felt strangely embarrassed, as if he had intruded onto an intimate moment.

She slipped her hand into his arm. "I'll give you the grand tour, although it's not too grand."

They stepped into the dining room and the picture that was difficult to ignore. It was obviously an inauguration. A powerfully built man stood with his strong jaw thrust out, his hand on a large black bible held by a man in judge's robes. In the background, a number of people stood expectantly with bright eyes. In the forefront stood Reggie Phillips.

"That was Governor Henry's inauguration," Janice explained. "Reggie was sworn in as lieutenant governor later in the governor's library. I always thought that should have been part of the public ceremony as well, but the privacy of it suited Reggie just fine."

Trailer moved to the right and stared at a man who had to be Reggie and Janice's son. A beautiful woman, two girls, and a teenage son stood around him in a garden on a sunny day.

"Our son, Trevor," she explained. "His wife, Shirley, and our three grandchildren. Connor is the oldest and the girls are Megan and Elise."

Trailer saw the tears in her eyes, but couldn't resist asking. "What happened to them?"

Janice shrugged and wiped her eyes. "We don't know for sure. Trevor worked for the state department at the U.S. Embassy in the Netherlands. Europe got hit pretty hard from what I understand, but not the Netherlands. Brussels of course was crushed, being the headquarters of NATO and the European Union. The Hague is only a few hours away from there, so..."

Trailer nodded. "Lots of people made it. Nathan Taylor told me he lived between D.C. and Baltimore, and that area was supposedly leveled."

"I know," she said and took a deep breath. "I imagine them out there somewhere. Still alive...but regardless, we'll never see them again."

Trailer didn't have to ask what she meant. With the evaporation of governments and total devastation, getting a transatlantic flight or cruise from Europe was as likely as teleportation.

She steered him by the arm to the next photograph that needed no explanation. "Our wedding day. My daddy wouldn't come because Reggie had refused to tolerate his bullying. My father wasn't a bad man, but he was used to getting his way in everything. He was the county sheriff for nearly thirty years before he was killed in a silly drunken brawl out at the Hilltop Bar. Reggie, even as a young man, was respectful. He didn't back down. The first time I saw him stand up to my father, something I'd never seen anyone do, I suppose I fell in love with him."

Trailer turned to look into the living room at the man. Even in his own home he wore a coat and tie. Trailer glanced down at his worn pants and shirt and felt the need to go freshen up.

"He's a good man," said Janice from far away, "but he's worn thin. It's not in him to turn away when he can help, but there's not much left I'm afraid."

His eyes caught on the sharp piece of iron sticking out of the corner of the ceiling. "He might just surprise you."

She chuckled. "I see you heard that story. In fact it did surprise me. Surprised the hell out of me if you'll forgive me for saying. I thought he had killed that man. Might have killed those other two men who were guarding him. I never heard and never thought to ask, but I know my husband. We've been married for a long time and I've never seen him this worn down."

"Maybe he should take a break."

"I would love that." She smiled. "So would he, I think, but who is there to replace him? I know I'm biased, but my husband is special. He has a gift and that gift is getting people to put aside their petty differences and work together. There are plenty of men who are smarter or better leaders or even wiser, but I don't think there's anyone else who can do what he does."

Trailer stared at the man on the couch. He was listening carefully to something Jessica was saying. Reggie Phillips would have looked at home giving a university lecture or as a courtroom judge, not someone who could nearly beat a man to death in his own home with a fireplace poker.

"We've lived here most of our life other than the six years in Frankfurt before...well, before." She sighed. "We raised our son here and played with our grandchildren. I suspect we'll die here."

"We all die somewhere," Trailer said. "There are worse places than home to do so."

"Indeed. So much has been lost in the last two years, but here...in the JP...so much has been saved. People are still neighbors. We have families, community, but people are scared and near the breaking point."

Trailer thought about the places he had been and the things he had seen. The depravity and desperate measures people had sunk into. He looked around at the electric lights and clean carpet. Janice smelled like shampoo and lotion instead of the typical sweat and fear that had become the standard scent of humanity.

You all are living in a fantasy world, thought Trailer. *It's nice, but it's a mirage. Hot water and ovens that work and even clean drinking water straight from the tap. This little oasis can't stay this way forever; eventually the real world will get in and then where will you be?*

Janice was staring at him expectantly when the oven timer began making a ringing noise. She clapped her hands together and turned towards the kitchen. "Excuse me, I'll be right back. You're not going anywhere, are you?"

Trailer looked around the room at the pictures and all the clean surfaces and the nice furniture. The extra tall ceilings where he didn't even have to duck were even better. He mentally contrasted this with what he knew was just outside on the borders, mere miles away.

Going anywhere? Good question...am I?

Is this the last bastion of goodness and decency or a sinking ship?

He turned to look at the gentleman in the other room. The one who had made him feel at ease and important at the same time. So much rested on those thin old shoulders.

Janice carefully walked in carrying a large platter with a cooked ham on it, and Trailer grabbed it from her and set it on the table.

"Thank you, dear," she said before turning to the living room. "Dinner's ready, everyone. Come enjoy it while it's hot."

Come enjoy it while we still can, thought Trailer.

Reggie turned and looked at him with his hollow, knowing eyes.

Chapter 19 – Running the Course

General Nathan Taylor walked into the hastily assembled headquarters northwest of Redstone Arsenal. Couriers ran in and out of the building, carrying messages back and forth to the field units. The busy room became still as weary eyes and dirty faces fixed upon him.

Nathan saw a sergeant major sucking in breath to call the room to attention.

"As you were, people," he said, and some of the tension seemed to leave the room. Nathan walked over to stand beside Luke Carter and stare at the map board. He already knew what he would see, but much of being in command was about presentation and show.

"We're in a good spot," Nathan told him loudly enough for others to hear. "Resistance was heavy, but we're where we need to be."

Luke nodded. "The Huntsville forces have pulled back to here, here, and here," he said while pointing to positions on the map. "They've abandoned their outer perimeters, and much of the city suburbs are in our hands, but that means urban warfare."

Nathan didn't have to ask what that meant. Street-to-street and house-to-house fighting. Enemy snipers killing from a distance and then falling back to repeat the process. Booby traps and explosive tripwires in doorways. The sort of warfare that caused an inordinate amount of civilian casualties and made atrocities from frustrated and tired soldiers all the more common.

"The whole northwest outskirts"—Luke circled and area with his finger—"are in flames. We've pressed the civilians into service to help put it out. We're not sure if the retreating enemy started the fires to slow us down or it just happened."

"Doesn't matter too much at this point. Is all the power cut off?" Nathan asked.

"As far as we can tell. No electricity getting in from Wheeler Dam or the solar arrays at the botanical gardens, so that means our teams must have been successful. We secured the Decatur Dam this morning. They still have diesel generators, but that's it."

"Have all the teams reported in?"

"Not yet," said Luke, "but that's to be expected. Cell phones don't work down here and our radio batteries are mostly shot. The best bet is that Joshua's and Chris Green's teams are okay. The fact that they were successful is a good sign. Green should be on his way back here, whereas Joshua's orders were to secure and hold the Wheeler Dam facility."

He imagined his son out there and prayed he was okay. Nathan thought of how angry Bethany would be if something happened to their remaining son, and then he remembered that she was dead. His stomach sank, but he kept his face neutral. It was frequently like this. The pain and the loss hitting him fresh, numerous times a day. He would think of a tidbit he would like to tell her, or something she would enjoy, and he would have to remind himself that she was no longer waiting for him at home.

"Sir?" asked Luke, seeing his faraway look.

"The shelling on the Decatur Harbor stopped, so I'm presuming we were successful in taking those mortars out."

"We were. Seized six eighty-one millimeter mortars and hundreds of rounds. Ironically, all of it was from Milan."

Nathan shook his head. "I imagine a great deal of what they are using to kill our people came from there." He looked around the room to make sure no one was listening too closely before leaning over to whisper to his deputy. "What are our casualties like?"

Luke pulled a notebook from his pocket and whispered back. "About nine hundred wounded and two hundred fifty dead. Most of those were from that barge that took the direct mortar hit. Lots of drowning. I just went over to the field hospital an hour ago and Doc Frazier tells me that the death rate is going to go up fast. We just don't have the medical staff or supplies to deal with this amount of casualties. He said for shattered bones in the arms and legs they just have to amputate since surgery isn't an option and gangrene will likely set in."

Nathan hissed, thinking of an old grainy photo he had once seen of piles of severed limbs outside a field hospital tent. "It's like the damn Civil War for God's sake. You'd think we could do better than that."

"I don't think so," answered Luke. "We don't have antibiotics any more. Infection sets in and they're dead fast. It's the only way to save lives."

"This is going to be tough," Nathan whispered, looking at the map again.

Luke nodded. "It will take weeks, maybe months to starve them out, especially if Lacert prioritizes rations to the soldiers. A full assault will result in significant casualties. The Creek are reporting mass

288

desertions, but that is along the perimeter and mostly families just trying to get away. The key nut to crack is Redstone Arsenal."

"Because that's where they're building the rocket."

"Exactly. And every day that goes by without them being defeated is more time for them to finish and launch it at us, or even build more. It's a poor long-term strategy for Lacert, since we'll still starve them out in the end, but all the while he might be raining down rockets on the JP."

"I'm not sure our soldiers would sit still for a long siege in that situation."

"I don't either," said Luke. "The army would mutiny and either desert, try to make a separate peace with Lacert, or throw themselves against his guns senselessly."

"So what do we do?"

"Take out the rocket for starters," Luke said, pointing to a spot on the map south of the Huntsville Airport and north of the Tennessee River. "That's the hill from where they first spotted the rocket. It's the best place for our mortars to range the rocket. We can probably destroy it from up there. Of course they can likely make more, but it buys us time."

Nathan looked at all the territory between their current perimeter and the hill. "That's a pretty deep advance. It will take us a while to get there."

"Unless we throw everything behind it, hold everywhere else, and push hard in a narrow advance."

"Excuse me, sir," said a voice from across the room.

Nathan and Luke turned to see a young female staff officer with a bloody bandage around her upper arm.

"Yes?" said Nathan.

"We've got a man outside from Huntsville carrying a white flag. They seized him near Indian Ridge. Says he's a messenger from Vincent Lacert." She held up a heavy plastic trash bag with distaste. "He was also carrying these."

Luke went over and took the bag and looked inside. He stared silently for several seconds before holding the bag open for Nathan to look.

Leaning forward, Nathan saw three severed heads. "Ours?" he finally asked.

His deputy nodded. "I recognize one as Sergeant Hayes. He was one of Green's squad leaders."

Nathan carefully closed the bag and handed it to a nearby staff officer. "Put these in a safe place for burial later." Nathan turned back to the front of the tent, his face tight. "Show this messenger in."

Grabbing Nathan by the arm, Luke looked around the room. "You sure you want to do this here? Maybe something a little more private would be better."

Nathan shook his head, his lips tight. "The rumors are going to be flying anyway. Having the meeting out in the open will save us the trouble of having to clean up those false rumors afterwards."

"Okay. Just realize whatever gets said is going to spread like creamy peanut butter before breakfast."

A middle-aged man with waxy skin and premature gray air was pushed into the room by two sentries. His hands were bound together in

290

front of him. He looked scared and tired, but was doing his best to project an appearance of calm.

Staring at the man, Nathan had an urge to simply pull his pistol and shoot the man in the head.

The messenger must have seen something in Nathan's look because his calm demeanor slipped slightly. He looked around before saying in an overly loud voice, "My name is Captain Harry Giles. I'm here on behalf of General Vincent Lacert to protest your senseless aggressions against us."

Nathan pointed in the direction where the staff officer had taken the bag of remains. "And I suppose the point you're trying to make by bringing…that bag…is that you have some of my soldiers?"

"We do. Thirty-three men and women survived the battle with our forces before being captured. I'm afraid some of their wounds are serious and time is critical if they are to survive."

"I would be outraged if I didn't already know who I was dealing with," said Nathan. "It shouldn't surprise me that the same man who hangs, tortures, and mutilates captured prisoners would not hesitate to cut off heads or withhold medical care."

"I'm afraid that may only be the beginning if you do not withdraw your forces."

Nathan was silent for several seconds, resisting the urge to look over at the map. The map that clearly translated into casualties and death for his people. Finally, he nodded. "We'll withdraw as soon as several conditions are met. The first is an immediate cessation of hostilities."

"Of course," answered Giles, spreading his hands wide. "That is what we want."

"Second, I want all prisoners returned to us, starting with the group taken at the botanical gardens."

"We can discuss exchanging prisoners after your forces are back across the Tennessee border."

Luke looked at Nathan and shook his head slightly.

Nathan knew what he was thinking. Lacert only wanted them to go away so they could get breathing space. Once the JP army marched away, it would be damn near impossible to get most of those part-time citizen soldiers to return to a painful and difficult siege.

"Was there anything else?" Giles asked.

"Yes. We will begin our withdrawal as soon as we see that rocket on the launch pad destroyed as well as any other rockets you are currently building."

The man shook his head sadly. "That's going to be difficult, as they are part of critical protective measures. The rockets are purely defensive in nature."

Nathan chose not to swing at that slow-pitch bullshit softball. "You will also return everything seized from Milan and make restitution for the losses suffered there as well as those that have been killed or wounded in this war."

Giles looked stunned. "You can't seriously believe General Lacert would agree to these terms?"

"We don't believe he would live up to any terms," said Luke. "We have some history with the man and understand how unpredictable and dangerous he really is."

"You have no idea," Giles answered, stepping forward a step. His calm was now nearly gone. "Please, for all our sakes, let's figure something out. Don't send me back with that message, or we're all dead."

"You're scared of him," said Nathan.

Giles looked at him incredulously. "Hell yes, I'm scared of him. Some of the things he's done, well…let's just say I have a family to think of in there. Pull your forces back and, with time, we can find another way."

"Another way to what?" asked Luke.

"To end all of this."

Nathan stared at the man for a long time, finally recognizing that he was as much a prisoner as Green's men. Most of the Huntsville soldiers and civilians were likely in the same situation. "Here's the other way. You bring me Lacert, alive or dead, I don't care which, and it's over. We stop fighting, blow up the rockets together, and then go on our way. Simple as that."

"Simple as that?" asked Giles in a high-pitched voice. "Do you know what happened to the last group that even considered something like that? Them and all their families, even a little girl, were covered in gasoline and burned. We all had to watch." He shook his head. "I'm not going to risk that, not my family. No one will."

"You have to," said Luke. "He's just a man, and fear is his power over you. Take him out before it's too late."

Giles hung his head and asked in almost a whisper. "Is that all?"

"Yes," answered Nathan and looked at the guards. "Make sure he gets back to his lines safely."

The room stood silent as the messenger was escorted out. Staff officers peered at each other with wide eyes.

"Back to work everyone," ordered Luke Carter.

The paralysis broken, they quickly returned to their duties, and the room became a beehive of activity once more.

"What now?" asked Luke. "I don't recommend waiting for them to bring us Vincent Lacert."

Nathan walked back over to the map and jabbed his finger at the hill sitting between the airport and the river overlooking Redstone Arsenal. "There. We have to take it, whatever the cost. Anything else will only prolong the conflict and cost more lives in the long run. Put everything we have into taking that hill so we can destroy the rocket. Then we have time to lay back and starve them out if we want."

"When do you want to do this?"

Nathan looked outside at the afternoon sun and the growing shadows on the ground. Most of the fighting would be done for the day except for sporadic sniping and the occasional raids. Tired men and women on both sides sitting down to some food and shelter, grateful they had survived another day and not sure about the next.

Was Joshua out there somewhere, sitting down by a fire to eat or lying in a ditch somewhere hurt and already growing cold?

"Sir?"

"Dawn," answered Nathan. "Let's not let this go on another day."

Luke looked at him, startled. "Dawn? That's not much time."

"I know. I'm afraid we don't have much of it," answered Nathan and walked out of the command tent, not knowing how prophetic his words were.

****

In the dream, Nathan and his family were back in Southern Arizona. The rugged mountain and terrain of the high desert were stunning in their brutal beauty. He knew it was a dream, but also that he was happy. Happy again to be with his family.

Bethany stood on a high outcropping. As always, she had a camera up to her face and was taking the perfect picture. Nathan could hear Joshua and David behind them exploring at their leisure and he resisted an urge to remind them to watch out for rattlesnakes.

They know, he thought. *They're grown men.*

But they're not. Nathan turned and saw his boys as they had been many years before. Young and carefree. Boys on an adventure without cares or concerns. How it was meant to be.

"Come look at this," cried Bethany.

Nathan turned and walked to stand beside her. He gazed out on the wide valley below them. Cacti that had bloomed frantically after the last rain had turned the normally brown and red landscape into a mosaic of color.

Without looking away from the scene, Bethany took his hand. "Isn't it wonderful?"

Nathan nodded.

"And it will be gone in a few days," she said. "Such is life, I suppose. We enjoy the beauty while we can before it's gone. All beauty and goodness runs its course and then is gone."

Joshua walked up beside them, except he was older now. Nathan could see the scars on his head and arms. He was carrying a baby boy in his arms.

"I'll go check on David," Bethany said with a smile.

"Don't," said Nathan, grasping her hand. "Stay here a little longer."

She pulled away gently. "I can't. David needs me."

Nathan watched as she strode down the hill and out of sight. He turned back to the valley and saw that the light had faded and it was growing darker. The flowers below were wilting and dying by the millions in time-lapse speed.

Joshua looked at him sadly, the baby now gone.

"Wake up, sir," said Joshua, his voice growing excited.

"What?"

"Something has happened. You need to wake up," said Joshua, and suddenly, there was no Joshua, just an officer bending over and shaking him.

"What is it?"

"The rocket…it's…"

Nathan didn't wait for him to finish. He jumped up and ran outside to find others staring into the sky at the impossibly bright ball of light lifting up slowly into the sky. The deep rumble of the rocket's engine sounded like prolonged deep thunder in the distance.

"Where's it going?" asked someone, a tinge of panic in their voice.

I just killed a whole bunch of innocent people, Nathan thought, his stomach sinking.

They stared up into the sky, mesmerized, until the light disappeared into the atmosphere.

All beauty and goodness runs its course and then is gone.

****

The Minotaur II rocket was originally a Minuteman Intercontinental Ballistic Missile, but with the end of the Cold War, many of these ICBMs had been repurposed for other uses. The Minotaur II was a solid, compressed fuel, three-stage rocket designed to lift payloads of nearly a ton into low-earth orbit and had been extremely successful at this mission.

The Minotaur that lifted off from Huntsville was only a single stage rocket, as it didn't have near as far to travel as the edge of the earth's atmosphere. Two hundred thousand pounds of thrust lifted the rocket with its eight-hundred-pound payload upwards on a north-by-northwest heading.

The rocket's engines cut off in the earth's thermosphere, approximately one hundred fifty miles above the ground below. At the peak of its parabolic arch, the rocket now began its long drop back towards the earth and its target, which was two hundred fifty miles north of its launch location.

Gravity pulled the rocket downwards while the tailfins made miniscule adjustments based on the global positioning guidance systems. The guidance system's altimeter recorded the shrinking distance between the rocket and the ground, and when this distance had diminished to less than one thousand feet, the payload's proximity fuse was activated.

The radio transmitter began transmitting a 180-megahertz signal at the onrushing ground and analyzing the refracted patterns reflected back. The wave patterns became more and more compact until the pattern indicated the payload was at the exact height predetermined for detonation.

At three meters the fuse triggered the detonator and eight hundred pounds of high explosives packed into a specially designed shaped charge activated in a brilliant burst of energy and light.

****

John Downing stood out on the top of the dam. He often found himself there early in the morning. He liked to see the sun reflected off the surface of the lake held in place by the mass of steel and concrete he stood upon.

He hadn't known shit about dams when N-Day happened. Sure, he understood the basic principles of how dams and hydroelectric power worked, but most of what he had learned had been self-taught. It had been surprisingly simple. John's father had owned an auto repair shop until he died at the age of forty-two from a heart attack. John had worked with his father and learned how to assess and fix problems. He liked machines; they never lied.

John had wanted to be an engineer. After his father died, they had lost the house and things had become difficult for them. Still, he had done well enough in school that with some scholarship targeting his disadvantaged economic standing had allowed him to attend Georgia Technical University, one of the best engineering schools in the world.

It had been a catastrophe almost from the very beginning. He was smart and inquisitive, but his Kentucky public school math preparation had been sorely lacking. The other students in his classes were far ahead of him, and his professors grew frustrated with him. It wasn't long before he was so far behind his confidence was crushed.

By his second semester, he had changed his major from mechanical engineering to management, much to the relief of his advisor. John had only felt a sense of failure and loss.

It wasn't until years later he realized that if he'd gone to a different school, perhaps one that wasn't filled with the best and the brightest, he might be an engineer now. Maybe if he had gone on to one of the small state universities, things might have been different.

John Downing had still been highly successful, one of the reasons he had been appointed Director of the Land Between the Lakes Park. The first week after assuming his new post, he had toured the dam facilities and been mesmerized.

After N-Day, John had no doubt about what was critical. When the dam's managing director had vanished, John stepped in. Let all the rest of it fall about into rust and dust, but the dam was something special and magical. Electrical power from the sheer kinetic energy of blocked water. Sustainable power that could still be relied upon and outlast them all maybe. Something that would hold back the coming darkness for a little longer.

Let all the rest of them chase after other things; he knew his purpose and it was the dam.

He even felt like it spoke to him sometimes. Not in a crazy, needing psychiatric help sort of way, but in him sensing that something was wrong. Most of the remaining engineers no longer responded to his suggestions with skepticism. When he said a turbine didn't sound right or that the bearing needed to be checked, they did what he said because most of the time he was right. When he told them to check the transmitter lines on a relay, they did it without question.

John closed his eyes in the pre-dawn light and listened. He felt the steady but faint hum of vibration through his feet and hands. A content purr of activity, everything working as it should.

He opened his eyes with a small smile and gazed up into the sky. This was the best time of day, the rising sun casting a beautiful kaleidoscope of colors onto the western horizon. Everything was calm and he could be alone with his thoughts. This was when he was reminded of how fortunate they all were, and that the sacrifices they had all made were worth it. That the JP was special, maybe the most special place left.

His eye caught on a speck in the sky. It was a dark object floating…no, not floating. Falling.

It grew and grew as it came down closer. John saw it was oblong. He thought at first maybe it was an airplane, but soon saw that it had no wings. Only a tail.

A rocket?

John stared in amazement as the object grew and grew, and he began to hear a whistle as it cut through the cool, early morning air. Soon the whistling stopped.

He didn't even bother to turn away, only grasped the rail in front of him firmly.

John Downing closed his eyes sadly just before the explosion vaporized him.

****

The explosion sent a shock wave across the surface of the water and the damn. Windows for miles around shook; many imploded.

Everything on the surface of the dam was either obliterated instantly or thrown outwards to fall down the far side of the dam.

At first, an onlooker might have thought the dam had survived without significant damage. The surface was still intact and the water still flowed, but there were growing stress fractures in the surface. Those fractures were spreading and cascading at a speed that would have been too fast for the human eye to follow.

A large concrete section along the top of the dam crumbled and slid down the steep slope of the dam's riverside surface. Soon thereafter, a faint trickle of water began to flow over the top of the dam through this gap. The trickle became a stream; the stream became a flood. Soon more chucks of concrete and rebar were torn loose and thrown downriver.

When the dam finally crumbled, it happened quickly. The center part collapsed upon itself and the millions of gallons of pent-up water rushed through and surged into the riverbed beyond.

Those that lived downriver of the dam had little notice of the deadly wall of water headed their way.

They were all focused on the lights going out.

Part III

Deepening Shadows

Chapter 1 – Uncovered Memories

Alexandra ignored the sharp pain in her back and scrubbed the piece of laundry even harder against the old wash board. Joshua's blue denim shirt was starting to wear through in places.

Blue, she thought. *They dress baby boys in blue.*

She hissed at the unwanted thought and scrubbed even harder.

Benjamin. That would have been his name, the voice said. It was the name she had never uttered out loud, not even when they buried him. The little body wrapped in a towel had fit into a shoe box.

Alexandra screamed and threw the wet shirt away from her. She then kicked the wash tub, stubbing her toe painfully. Ignoring the pain, she put her hands to the tub and, with another angry scream, pushed it over onto the ground.

Panting, her hands clinched, she stared at the pooling muddy water as it ran over her shoes.

There was a thin shrill noise from high above, almost like a train whistle. It grew louder and deeper in timber, and she looked to the north where the sound appeared to be headed.

The explosion caused her to stagger backwards. She tottered on unsteady feet and then did fall onto her butt. Sitting there in the wet grass, she suddenly remembered listening to the radio the morning of N-Day and finding out the world had overnight slipped off its foundation.

Pushing herself to her feet, Alexandra raced down to the lake's shore where several other people had gathered. The lake curved out of sight, but they could see a black cloud of smoke billowing upwards to the north.

"We all thought it couldn't get any worse," said a voice to her left.

Alexandra turned to find Joshua's grandmother standing there staring out over the lake. For the first time since losing her baby, she didn't feel the urge to pull the knife at her belt and drive it into the neck of the old woman beside her.

"That was a bomb," someone from the crowd said. "A big one."

"Was it another nuke?" a small girl asked.

"No," said a wrinkled man with intense eyes.

The small group turned to the man. "How can you be so sure?" one of them asked.

The man smiled. "Because if that had been a nuke, we'd all be dead now."

"Look at the water!" the little girl yelled, pointing.

They turned and saw that the normally placid lake surface was now flowing steadily north. Although the dammed river still moved along its old bed through the dam's concrete bottleneck, the movement was usually imperceptible.

Now the water began to rush northwards.

"It's going down," said Alexandra, looking at what had once been the shore. Now slime-covered rocks and limbs that had recently been covered in water were shining in the dim evening light.

"Did they open all the dam gates?" someone asked.

Everyone stood silently and watched as the water steadily receded. Surprised, fish flapped in the mud.

"Go get 'em," a man told his two sons who raced out into the mud to grab the fish and throw them up onto shore. "There's more over there," he told them, and soon others were out scrambling to pull in the stranded fish.

Alexandra stood rooted and wondered where Joshua was now. She realized that she hadn't even told him goodbye before he left. At the time, she hadn't cared if she ever saw him again, but she cared now.

They watched as regular-edged surfaces began to emerge from the water off to their right. Thin upright stones, coved in slime, placed in lines. The partial remnants of a rusty fence ran around the stones. Further down what looked like a roof was appearing.

"I heard about this when I was a child," Joshua's grandmother said. "Looks like they took the church steeple and bell when they were forced to leave."

Alexandra turned to look at her. "What are you talking about?"

The woman pointed. "That was a church with a graveyard…before they built the dam back in the thirties."

"People lived…there?" She pointed out towards the much shallower water.

The old woman nodded. "This used to just be a river valley. People lived and worked and farmed here. Then the government came in and pushed them out."

"They were forced to leave their land?"

"Not all of them. Some accepted the government offer to buy their land. From my understanding, it was good money in the dark days of the Depression. Plenty were glad to get it, I imagine, but not all. Some just wanted to stay on their land. My grandparents were some of them."

"What happened?"

"What always happens," she answered. "Men showed up with guns and made them leave, and they never saw their home or land again. I always wanted to see it."

Alexandra stared at the receding water. "Well, you might get your chance now."

The woman waved her hand to the east. "Their farm was somewhere over in the Cumberland River valley."

People were coming up out of the riverbed as long shadows crept down the valley. They carried gasping fish in shirt tails and buckets. They made their way to their homes to clean the fish for dinner.

"Going to be dark soon," Alexandra said.

"In more ways than one," the old woman said, turning away. "I better go make sure the lanterns are in order. I think we may have seen our last burning light bulb for a while."

Alexandra turned again to look at the thin ribbon of black smoke to the north and shuddered. She then faced to the south and gazed at the darkening shy.

"Where are you, Joshua?" she surprised herself by saying out loud.

Alexandra realized that she wanted him back home desperately.

Chapter 2 – Evening Swim

Joshua hit the cold water and pushed the bomb away from him. He tried to swim away from the dam, but his boots and gear filled with water and started to pull him downward.

Forcing himself to be calm, Joshua stopping thrashing in the water and shrugged out of his tactical vest. With a pang of regret, it pulled away from him and dropped downward. As he bent down to unlace his boots, he felt his feet touch the bottom of the shallow river. He quickly unlaced his boots and pushed them off as his lungs began to burn. With a last tug, his boots were free, and he kicked himself upwards to the surface.

Breaking free with a gasp, he heard Conrad yelling from the surface of the dam. "That was a damn foolish thing to do."

"It worked, didn't it?" yelled back Joshua, treading water. He noticed that the surface of the lake was now lit brightly by lights from the dam.

"Maybe the water shorted out the radio; maybe it didn't," Conrad responded. "For all we know, the blasted thing is waterproof and just sitting there below you waiting for someone to push a button on their little walkie-talkie. I expect the blast pressure would blow your asshole up through your mouth."

Joshua started swimming hard for shore. Some of his soldiers met him there and pulled him out. Someone wrapped a green blanket around him, and he began to towel off.

Conrad trudged down the shore towards them. "You do know the demo team was only like fifty feet away when you decided to go all stupid on us?"

"No, I didn't know that," answered Joshua, looking around at his soldiers' feet. "Anyone have an extra set of boots that might fit me?"

Someone retrieved their backpack and tossed him a pair of worn boots that looked to only be a size too big. A dry shirt and pair of socks were also passed his way. Joshua changed while Conrad stood nearby cursing and grumbling to himself.

"Sir?" a voice said and Joshua looked up to see one of the men assigned to watch the road. "Two of those Indians are here on horses. They heard the commotion and came to check it out. Say they want to pass along some news since they're here anyway."

"The Creek," said Conrad to the soldier. "Bring them on in."

Several minutes later two men on horseback made their way down to the shore. "A fine night for a swim," one commented, looking at Joshua.

"Indeed it is," Joshua answered with a smile. "I hear you have news."

The other rider nodded. "We've scouted for at least twelve miles all around here; there's no Huntsville forces."

Joshua looked at Conrad. "This may have been all of them."

"Doesn't mean they can't be sending reinforcements," said Conrad.

"Not with Huntsville surrounded," said the first Creek. "Between the JP forces and the Creek patrols, it would be pretty hard for anything to get through."

Looking west, Joshua began calculating the distance.

"Our orders are to secure and hold the dam and power plant," Conrad reminded him.

Joshua looked at him and grinned. "We've already done that. A small force can keep an eye on things here, watch the prisoners, and tend to any wounded." Joshua then remembered his responsibilities as a leader. "Did we have causalities?"

"Yes," answered Conrad, looking around at the soldiers staring at him. "Five dead so far and sixteen wounded; three of those aren't expected to make it."

Joshua lowered his head and nodded solemnly. "Nothing we can do for them by sitting around here. We can leave all the medical folks along with a detachment. They should be able to hold things."

"Unless the Huntsville forces mount a counterattack to retake it. They surely like their electricity as much as we do."

"There's nothing between here and Huntsville except friendlies," said the Creek.

"See," said Joshua. "The fight's at Huntsville and it's going to be a tough one. Chances are they're going to need everyone they can get."

Looking around at the dam, Conrad shook his head. "I don't know about this. Maybe we should send a courier or find a way to send a radio message. Let them know we have secured the objective and ask for further orders."

"Since when have you been one to ask headquarters for orders?" asked Joshua. He turned to the soldiers around him. "Good job, people. We've accomplished our objective, but there's still a battle being fought in Huntsville where they probably need our help."

311

"Damn right they do!" yelled a woman, holding up her assault rifle.

"So…what do you say? Everyone up for a little traveling?"

There was a chorus of cheers.

Joshua looked at Conrad with a smile. "It's out of my hands. They all want to go help." He turned to the gathered soldiers. "Go get ready to move out."

Conrad watched as the soldiers strode away to prepare for the next mission. "It's not a goddamn democracy, and you damn well know it," he grumbled.

Taking his rifle back from Conrad, Joshua walked up the shore towards the Creek. "Thank you," he said, shaking their hands. "Let us know if anyone comes near here."

The two riders nodded and turned their horses to the west to canter away.

"I know it's not a democracy," said Joshua, turning back to Conrad. "My orders are to move west towards Huntsville within the hour. Leave a detachment here and be prepared to move fast. Is that authoritative enough for you?"

Conrad stared at Joshua for several long seconds before turning away. The big man cursed under his breath as he walked towards the dam.

Shaking his head, Joshua turned back towards the river and spotted a dark shape bobbing on the surface of the water nearby.

With a start, he realized it was the bomb he had pulled off the wall of the dam. Joshua walked quickly after Conrad, throwing furtive glances back over his shoulder.

Chapter 3 – Lights Going Out

Ernest Givens, only recently reacquainted with regular sleep unaided by large quantities of alcohol, didn't appreciate being woken. He had learned to sleep with pieces of cloth stuffed in his ears. Even nights were never truly quiet in the jail block, but the noise coming through the makeshift plugs was unusual.

He pulled the cloth from his ears and heard angry voices and breaking glass. It was dark in the cells, but that was not unusual. There was supposed to be hall lights on all the time, but power outages were regular.

Something I'll fix when I'm the JP President, he thought.

Ernest looked down at his wrist to see what time it was forgetting that they had taken the watch, along with all his other personal items, when they had admitted him to these fine guest rooms.

"What's going on?" Ernest asked no one in particular.

"Don't know," said a voice in the cell to his right. "Started about an hour ago. Lots of people outside and they don't sound too happy. Even sounded like they were trying to get into the jail earlier."

A lynching? he wondered, but then dismissed the thought. None of them had committed any crimes so grievous as to rile up people to murder.

Ernest rolled out of his bunk and walked to the bars of his cell that faced the central hallway. He looked towards the guard room and saw shadowy light and hushed voices.

313

"Norton!" yelled Ernest. "You out there? Norton!"

"Shut up, back there!" screamed an authoritative voice. "Chief Norton's busy."

"Busy with what?" yelled Ernest. "Tell us what's going on."

"I said shut your damn mouth, or I'll shut it for you."

There was several seconds of silence.

"Norton!" Ernest screamed out and then began chanting it. "Nor-Ton! Nor-Ton! Nor-Ton!" The other prisoners took up the chant, and soon it was a loud clamor of voices that echoed in the concrete halls.

A guard strode towards them with a tight jaw and a baton clinched angrily in his fist. His other hand shined a large flashlight in the cell.

Ernest moved back away from the bars as the man approached, but didn't stop his chanting. He smiled at the angry policeman who pointed his baton at him.

"You really want it to go down this way?" the man asked.

Ernest kept chanting, but gave the man the middle finger of each hand, one for each syllable. Soon the entire floor had taken up the middle finger accent to the chant.

"Open up cell three," the man called out.

"What?" came a high voice.

"I said open up cell three, you dumb shit," the officer said.

"How?" the high voice responded. "We don't have electricity."

Ernest smiled at the man. "I guess he's not the only dumb shit, is he?"

The officer strode angrily away as the prisoners on the floor laughed and hooted. A minute later, he returned with a ring of keys and fumbled in the dark between the key ring, flashlight, and baton.

314

Ernest stopped chanting, but everyone else kept up their call for Norton. "What are you planning on doing once you come in here, officer?"

The man dropped the keys and angrily picked them up again. "I'm going to shut you up, just like I said."

"I've shut up, officer. No need to come in here."

The man banged his baton savagely against the cell bars. "It's too late for that." He resumed his search for the proper key, and Ernest noticed that the man's hands were shaking.

"What's happened?" Ernest asked.

The man smiled in triumph as he inserted a key and turned. The sound of the gate unlatching caused everyone on the floor to suddenly become silent.

"Shut and lock that door!" yelled Norton, walking towards them. "Now!"

The officer turned to look at Norton in surprise and then back at the cell in disbelief as if he had awoken and wasn't sure how he had gotten to where he was.

Ernest walked forward, pulled the cell door closed before reaching through and taking the keys from the man's lifeless hand. He turned the key in the lock, pulled them from the keyhole, and tossed them to the approaching Norton.

The police chief caught the keys and put them in his pocket. He then took the flashlight from the officer's hand. He tilted his head towards the exit. "Trevor, get out there and help. Try not to hurt anyone. Keep in mind these are our neighbors. They're just scared."

Trevor nodded and, without a glance at Ernest, walked away.

"What's going on?" Ernest asked him. "Why are they scared?"

Norton stared at him for a long time, and Ernest didn't think he was going to answer. "The power's gone off."

"So? The power goes on and off all the time."

Norton sighed and looked towards the exit again. "The power has gone off forever."

There was several seconds of silence before one of the other prisoners asked, "What do you mean, forever?"

"The dam," Norton said, turning to look at them all. "It's gone. Someone blew it up somehow. Killed no telling how many people who live downriver."

"But they can fix it, right?" asked another voice.

"No," said Ernest with a faraway look and resignation. "There's no fixing something like that, not anymore."

Norton nodded, pointing outside to the angry voices. "Something everyone is starting to realize. The days of electricity are over."

"It's not just that," said Ernest, nodding. "Their days of pretending nothing has changed are over."

"And the only way they can deal with that terrible thought is to lash out and destroy."

"They're rioting?" asked Ernest.

Norton nodded. "Smashing windows that can never again be replaced. Trying to set buildings on fire. My people are trying to restore sanity, but I'm not sure that's going to be possible. No matter what, it's going to be a long night."

"You may have to lock them up, for their own good," Ernest said. "Before they hurt themselves of someone else. If they were drunk, you wouldn't hesitate."

Norton looked around at the cells that were at least half full.

Reading his thoughts, Ernest spoke softly. "No one in here has committed a violent crime. None of us are a threat. These are extraordinary times, and I'm guessing you're going to have to put a lot of people in here to restore order."

The chief looked at him and then the other prisoners, his mind obviously working. There was a gunshot outside.

"You know I'm right," Ernest said.

Norton sighed and then walked to the center of the cell hall. "Listen up. I'm paroling all of you temporarily. I expect to see each of you back here first thing in the morning three days from now. If you want to run, go ahead and keep on going right out of the JP and don't come back. If you think you want a life here, you better behave while you're out and come back without my officers having to track you down. Everyone understand?"

There were nods and murmurs of accent.

Moving to the end of the hall, Norton began opening cells, and the men walked hurriedly away.

"What about our personal affects?" one of them asked.

"You'll get them when you're officially released," Norton said. "This is just a temporary thing. Now get out of here before I change my mind."

Ernest watched as the men walked out in the dim light. The strange, thin, young man, Spence, didn't immediately exit when his door was opened. Instead, he walked over to Ernest's cell.

"I know what needs to be done," he said. "You don't have to remind me. Consider it done."

"What are you talking about?" asked Ernest.

Spence nodded knowingly. "Don't worry. I was listening and I heard you. I know what needs to be done. I *listened.*"

"What?" Ernest said, shaking his head, but Spence walked away, smiling knowingly back over his shoulder until he was out of sight. Ernest was wrenched out of his thoughts by the sound of his cell door being opened.

"You made the right decision," Ernest said. "I'll remember this when I'm president. You'll be—"

"Shut it with that crap," Norton said softly. "It'll be a miracle if there even is a JP in a week. Now get out before I decide to beat the shit out of you in a failed jail break."

Ernest looked from the man's dangerously calm face to the long flashlight held tightly in his fist like a club. Walking slowly, Ernest made his way out of the cell and around the chief. Not looking back, he strode down the dark hall through several sets of open security gates, and then outside.

Into chaos.

Chapter 4 – Desertion

Nathan Taylor felt like a butcher. He sat on the hill overlooking Redstone Arsenal in silence. Whenever someone sought to approach him, Luke Carter intercepted them and sent them away.

He wasn't by any means unfamiliar with warfare. Major Taylor had served multiple combat tours and was a veteran of low-intensity conflicts in places most people couldn't find on a map. Still, the sheer scale of the carnage was something he hoped he would never see again. Nathan feared he would be seeing those images in his mind for the rest of his life.

Touring battlefields had been one of his pastimes as a history buff. When stationed in the United States, Nathan had taken his family to Shiloh, Gettysburg, Antietam, and a score of other Civil War battlefields. When they were in Europe, they had visited the Somme, Normandy Beach, and Verdun. Nathan had tried to imagine how a general felt sending wave after wave of soldiers into certain death in order to win a battle.

Sadly, now he knew.

"General," said Luke from his elbow. He pointed to the right and handed Nathan a pair of large binoculars.

Nathan looked through them and saw what looked like an old telephone pole being pushed upwards against the perimeter wall of the embattled compound below. A man in JP uniform was attached to the crossbeam of the pole with what appeared to be spikes through his forearms and feet. Although he could not hear the man's screams, his face clearly showed the agony he was in.

"Do we have any snipers nearby?" Nathan asked.

"Just down the hill," Luke answered.

"Do it."

Luke nodded and moved away. A moment later, there was a single rifle shot. Looking through the binoculars, Nathan saw that the man now hung limp with a neat red hole through his forehead.

"They'll be more," said Luke, moving up beside him again. "Likely some of Green's men or maybe others they've captured."

About to reply with some angry retort, Nathan found he couldn't speak and put the binoculars up to his face to conceal the emotion. *I never wanted any of this,* he thought. *At least Joshua isn't here.*

"I think we weakened that section of the west wall," Luke said, pointing.

"There has to be a better way. We can't just keep sending waves of men against them."

Luke shrugged. "That's been the nature of siege warfare for millennium. It's either assault or starve them out. And we can't wait to starve them out, not with other possible rockets."

Nathan turned to look behind him at their primary camp where the men and women were resting after the last assault. It had taken all of his abilities to keep the army from splintering after the rocket was fired. They still did not know where it went, or what damage had been done, and most wanted to go home to ensure their families' safety. Nathan had convinced them of the need to eliminating the means to fire more rockets. He had also been forced to appeal to their desire for vengeance against the Huntsville forces.

"Assault or starvation," Nathan said. "There is also another way."

"Harry Giles didn't look like the sort to foment rebellion. Think what you want of Lacert, but he's a master at instilling fear in others. To wait for someone to take him down from the inside would be a mistake."

Nathan nodded. "So more assaults?"

"Yes. We focus on the western perimeter closest to the rocket launch pad. We support with artillery as best we can. Meanwhile, we've got sappers digging tunnels under the north wall. Once there, we can plant explosives and blow a hole in their defenses."

"How close are they?"

"About twenty-five more meters to the wall," said Luke, "but they've hit rock. The diggers will have to go around if they can."

"And if they can't?"

Luke shrugged. "They start over with a new shaft."

Nathan swore and his knuckles turned white on the binoculars.

Running to their rear caused them both to spin around. A panting young lieutenant drenched in sweat ran up to them both and saluted quickly.

"What is it?" asked Luke.

The young officer gulped in air for several seconds before he could speak. "The McCracken Regiment, sir. They heard that Paducah was hit...by the rocket. Their commander told them...they..."

"What is it?" asked Nathan.

"They're leaving, sir," the man finally spat out. "The whole regiment took one of the barges at gunpoint and is loading up now. They say they're going home."

"They can't be allowed to leave," Luke told Nathan. "If they do, word will get out, and then we've lost the army. It will simply melt away."

Nathan shook his head. "Damn fools." He turned to Luke. "Take two of the active regiments and stop them."

Luke raised his eyebrow in question.

"Use force if needed. Try to get them to see reason, but don't let them get away."

"Yes, sir," said Luke, saluting Nathan. He grabbed the young lieutenant by the elbow, and both jogged down the hill to the main camp.

Just when I thought it couldn't get any worse, he thought.

Nathan saw a bright flash from the top of a building near the center of the encircled base below. He put the binoculars to his eyes and looked at the building. On the roof, there was someone with binoculars looking back at him from just outside of sniper range. A man with long blond hair.

Grinning at him.

Chapter 5 – Fly in a Jar

Jason Green had always known he wanted to be a soldier. His father had been a soldier, a man who had fought valiantly and been hideously wounded in Vietnam before returning home.

His father had not been the brooding or distant type. He was just a man who loved his family and tried to live the best he could. Jason had always been surprised when other kids had asked, "Why does your daddy look that way?" Jason often forgot that his father appeared different from others.

His mother told him a story once. She said that when she went to the Walter-Reed burn hospital where her husband had been evacuated to after being stabilized in Japan, she hadn't recognized him. She had walked the ward looking at faces after concluding that the bed number the orderly identified must be a mistake.

Finally, he had opened his eyes, seen her looking around in frustration, and called her name. He smiled sadly at her because he knew what he looked like. After their helicopter crashed in that remote jungle, he had burned over sixty percent of his body before the crew chief managed to drag him out of the cockpit, burning himself badly in the process.

Many men would, and some did, avoid or hide from their wives. Some drove them away in self-pity masquerading as selflessness. "You deserve better," or "How could anyone love someone like me?" But not his father. He knew his wife loved him, and he loved her. It had not always been easy, but they had built a life and a family.

One day, Jason came home crying with a bloody nose. "What happened?" his father asked.

"They called you a freak," Jason said, looking away from his father's hideously scarred face. "They laughed and made fun of you."

His father had stared at him silently for a few minutes, thinking. Finally, he said, "Follow me. I want to show you something."

Jason followed the man out to the garage and over to a far corner. His father moved several boxes of clothes out of the way, revealing a long wooden footlocker. He lifted one corner of the box up and pulled out a key lying underneath and then used the key to open the padlock on the box. He lifted the lid and stood aside.

Staring down, Jason moved forward uncertainly. On top, there was a green flight suit with captain's rank and his father's name. Underneath were dozens of black and white photos. Jason gazed at each of them in wonder realizing the smiling young man in all the pictures was his father, before he was burned.

Underneath the photos was a folded American flag and a packet of letters. His father reached down and took those away. "Forgot those were in there," he said with a smile. He then pointed down at a long thin metal box. Jason pulled out the box and opened the top. Inside were curiously shaped folders.

"Open them," his father said, and Jason noted the smile was gone. Now he looked sad and a little hesitant.

In wonder, Jason pulled out and carefully laid on the concrete floor three Purple Heart medals, two Bronze Star medals, and a Silver Star medal.

"That last one is the kicker," Jason's dad said, pointing to a larger folder with a large box attached.

Pulling it out, Jason opened the folder slowly and stared. Even at a young age, he understood what the Medal of Honor meant. He ran his fingers across his father's name and felt as if he was going to faint. He read the citation with wonder and then opened the box. Inside was the unmistakable inverted five-pointed star attached to a pale blue ribbon containing on word: *Valor*.

"It's yours," his father said. "If you want it. Maybe it will help you more than it has me."

Jason looked at his father is shock.

"Whenever someone laughs at your father, remember that award and look at it."

In the years to come, Jason looked at it often and not just when someone gazed at his father with disgust or pity or amusement.

There was a dull pounding noise from high above and Jason realized he had been asleep. He didn't want to open his eyes or smell the fumes or feel the coldness.

"Wake up, wake up," says a loud voice from above.

Jason finally peered up out of the large metal fuel container they had imprisoned him in. A blond-haired man with blue eyes looked down on him from the small opening twenty feet above. Next to him was another covered pipe going up further to vent excess fumes.

For a moment, Jason could imagine what the man saw. A pitiful creature lying naked in a foot of gasoline, filth floating around him. Twice a day, someone came and a Ziploc bag filled with water and another with food was dropped inside. Both would splash into the gasoline, and Jason would eagerly consume their contents. During the first few days—or weeks, it was hard to judge time—he had tried to keep his waste in the bags, but had eventually given up. Now he lived in a urine, feces, gasoline cocktail.

"Brother, it's hard to see, isn't it?" asked Vincent Lacert. He then pulled out a cigarette lighter and opened the top. A thin, incredibly bright flame appeared above Jason.

Jason Green imagined that Vincent had produced the lighter in an effort to terrorize him, but he just smiled upwards. He knew he was never getting out of his current prison alive and he had always wanted to be like his father. Maybe burning ran in the family.

"Poor soul is deranged," Vincent said to himself, looking down with interest. "Wouldn't you like to get out of there?"

Green laughed. He started to speak and had to cough and spit a wad of foreign material into the liquid around him. "You can't really expect me to believe you're ever going to let me out of here?"

Lacert shrugged. "No, not really. You'd be surprised though by how many people do believe just that very thing." He looked down the slick walls of the container. "Honestly, I'm not sure how the hell we would get you out of there even if we wanted to. Clean up is going to be a bitch for someone."

Green shook his head. "This is the worst interrogation ever."

"Oh, I don't want anything from you. I'm just bored right now and thought I'd come down and check on all the little flies in jars."

Lacert stared at him expectantly, and Green resisted the urge to ask about his men and women. He knew that was what the man wanted. To torment him with threats or stories of torture. Even through the thick walls he had heard the screams.

"Other than entertainment," asked Green, "what is it exactly that you want?"

"That's a very good question and one so few bother to ask. I want to be king and destroy all those who stand against me."

"King of what?"

"Everything, of course. What king worth his salt is content with less?"

Green laughed. "Is that all?"

Lacert looked surprised. "You think that's expecting too much?"

"For a psychotic deranged egomaniac like you...not at all."

"My thinking exactly."

Green coughed again. "What I meant was, what do you want with me?"

"Maybe you'll come in handy. If nothing else, you're a curiosity to me. I've always been fascinated by how people die. Some take forever to finally breathe their last breath whereas others just roll over and give up after hardly anything. You just never know."

"I'm ready to die," Jason surprised himself by saying.

"Really? You look like you still have a lot left in you. Unlike your soldiers." Lacert laughed. "Those sad sacks are definitely ready to die, let me tell you."

Green just stared back.

"You sure you're ready?"

Green closed his eyes and tried to go back to sleep.

"Well, okay then," said Lacert. "If you're sure, I guess you're sure."

Opening his eyes, Green saw the man let go of the lighter in his hand. It tumbled down in slow motion. Green followed it with his eyes, expecting the flame at any moment to ignite the thin gasoline fumes floating around the inside of the container. When the lighter was nearly to the level of his head, he reached out a hand and snatched it out of the air while closing the wheel on the flame.

Lacert chuckled. "Guess you're not so sure, after all." He then closed the metal lid above.

Jason pulled the lighter close into his chest, thought of his father, and went back to sleep.

Chapter 6 – Appeal to Calm

"You sure this is going to work?" asked Trailer, looking at all the wiring running into Reggie Phillips house.

"Of course it's going to work," answered Simon. "Nothing more to it than simple electronics."

Trailer turned his head towards the front of the house and thought the situation was not as simple as Simon seemed to think. Thin ribbons of smoke still climbed into the sky from several downtown buildings, and reportedly over fifty people sat in the county and city jails this morning.

"How are we looking?" asked Reggie, stepping slowly out into his backyard to look down at them.

Simon didn't bother to glance up from what he was doing. "We're wired into the main radio transmitter downtown, which is connected to their radio tower out in Hickory. The station's generator should give us more than enough power for a broadcast. As long as someone doesn't run over or cut the wires running from the station, we should be okay. I didn't have time to bury them or string them up high on the poles."

"Thanks, Simon," answered Reggie. "You did great. Worst case, we can always move the broadcast down to the station."

"No," answered Janice from behind them. "You're still healing and weak as a puppy. I only agreed to this because you *wouldn't* have to leave the house. Worst case, you simply talk to those people out there who are trampling all over my flowers and save the radio broadcast for another day."

Jessica's lithe form slid around the corner of the house. "People are starting to get restless in the street. Two men had to be separated after they started yelling at each other."

"Are we ready?" asked Reggie.

Simon looked at his watch. "Almost. Tim Reynolds is supposed to turn on the generator at noon. We still have a few more minutes."

Reggie nodded and walked through his house and towards the front door. Janice followed and, at her request, Trailer would stand beside her husband. She seemed to think the presence of the huge man would deter anyone from doing anything stupid regarding Reggie. Simon and Jessica would stay in the backyard and would have their hands full making sure the radio broadcast went off without a hitch.

As Trailer walked through the front door behind Reggie, he felt a tension and buzz in the air. He had played dozens of basketball games at Rupp Arena in Lexington before twenty-five thousand fans and in other packed arenas around the country. On those nights, the energy in the air had seemed to make his hair stand on end. It was a good feeling.

This was not.

People let off glaring at each other to turn frightened and angry faces towards Reggie. Voices started yelling the minute he walked outside. They all pressed toward the front porch, mashing everyone tightly together. At least three hundred people were gathered around them and more were streaming in from the street.

"What's going on?"

"When's the power going to come back on?"

"How we supposed to make it through the winter without heat?"

"Does this mean we've lost the war?"

Reggie held his hands up for calm, but the voices just kept rising. Trailer reached around towards the inside of the door for his cudgel, but Reggie's hand stopped him. "Just give them time," he said to Trailer. "They're scared."

"I think maybe *we* should be scared," Trailer responded. "This could turn out really bad."

Reggie smiled. "I know. The important thing is to not *look* scared. That would cause them to do something they would regret. Try your best to just appear bored."

"Bored?" Trailer asked, but Reggie had already turned away. Trailer leaned back against the front door frame, yawned, and looked at his watch.

Again, Reggie was holding his hands up for calm, but it didn't appear to be having any effect.

"Perhaps we should go back inside for a while," said Janice hesitantly. "At least until things calm down. Maybe ask the police to come?"

Reggie shook his head. "We don't want people thinking there's a reason to have police. Especially after last night. This at least needs to have the appearance of a peaceful gathering."

Jessica stuck her head in from the house. "Simon says power is up. You're good to go whenever you want." She was then gone again as fast as she had appeared.

Reggie looked at the microphone and portable transmitter mounted on a small wooden table in front of him. He definitely didn't want to begin a live broadcast throughout the JP with angry crowds in the background drowning him out. For the first time, Reggie started to have doubts that his plan was a good idea.

He raised his hands again for calm against tumult of noise and heard a persistent voice above the rest.

"Everyone, just shut up," the commanding voice said. "Let the man speak for God's sake. Kim, tell your brothers to shut their fool mouths with that racket. Yancey, enough of that now, you've yelled enough for one day. Give it a rest, people."

Reggie looked and saw the voice was coming from Ernest Givens, who stood out in the middle of the crowd. He kept yelling at people and calling them by name, which seemed to startle them into realizing what they were doing. Slowly, the noise died down to a slow, deep grumble.

"Thank you," Reggie called out weakly over the crowd and smiled at Ernest in gratitude.

Ernest nodded back.

"What's going on, Reggie?" asked a voice in the front in a pleading voice. Other voices started to join in.

He held his hands up. "I know there are lots of questions, but people are out there waiting by their radios for the answers just like you are. Let's get this started, and I promise we'll let you ask questions towards the end."

Reggie saw hesitation and some resentment. "I need your help people. We'll get through this together just like we have with everything else, but I need you to work with me. Can I count on you?"

There was a few nods and then a growing number of "Sure, Reggie," and "No problem," or "We're with you."

Nodding, Reggie pulled his prepared remarks from his sport coat pocket. He unfolded the paper and pressed it firmly flat on the table beside the microphone.

"You ready?" Trailer asked, reaching for the transmitter broadcast switch Simon had showed him.

"No." Reggie smiled and nodded at the switch.

Trailer flipped it, and the light changed from red to green. He then plugged a thick cord into the front of the transmitter so whatever Reggie said would be amplified to a large set of speakers set up in the front yard.

"Hello, everyone," Reggie began and coughed. "This is Reggie Phillips broadcasting from my home in Mayfield. This will not be the normal weekly broadcast."

He paused and looked down at his notes. There were several key points, not a word-for-word speech. Reggie realized he didn't know how to go on. Peering out over the crowd, he saw expectant frightened faces of mothers, fathers, and children. He imagined families all over the JP gathered around their radios having heard the rumors.

"Yesterday, we suffered a horrible attack from an aggressive force to our south centered at Huntsville, Alabama. Our military forces have successfully surrounded these enemy elements and are in the process of defeating them. If there were any question before, we now can be assured that Huntsville and its irresponsible leaders pose a direct and dire threat to the JP that must be eliminated."

"But what happened to the electricity?" a voice called out. "Did they really blow up the dam?"

He lips tightened, and he nodded. "From what we can tell, they managed to launch a rocket from Huntsville that hit the dam, doing significant damage to its structure and shutting down the power turbines."

"How long until its fixed?" someone else asked.

Reggie paused. They had all heard the rumors that the dam would never be fixed, that it couldn't be fixed, not with the limited technology and resources they possessed now. In this case, rumor was fact. He wanted to lie to them to gain time, let the people adjust to the idea of no electricity, but he couldn't do it.

"It is very likely," said Reggie slowly, "that we will not be able to repair the dam."

There was a hush over the crowd and stunned faces as their worst fears were confirmed.

"Nearly every technician and scientist in the JP who might have been able to fix things was killed in the attack. The dam itself can be repaired, but I've been informed that the machinery and electronics that run the turbines were damaged beyond repair."

"Where are we supposed to get electricity from?" someone asked.

"Nowhere," said Reggie more forcefully than he had intended. "Except for occasional uses of generators, our days of electricity are over."

There was growing angry murmur in the crowd. Someone yelled out, "And how long for that with all the fuel going bad!"

Reggie pushed on. "In the rest of the world, there are plenty of people who have survived since N-Day without electricity. Hell, our descendants lived in the JP for hundreds of years without electricity and prospered. This is indeed a setback, but not the end. We will find a way to survive and move forward."

People were staring back at him with stunned faces. He imagined they were thinking that they would never again be able to use that portable heater, or have electric lights on in the house, or use their telephones. Their world had just changed, and Reggie imagined the same stunned looks on the faces of people listening on their battery-powered radios around the JP.

"Now more than ever," Reggie continued, "we need to come together as a community. Look around you." Several people did. "These are your neighbors. People you can rely upon to help you in the days ahead, as you will help them. That is the strength of our community. That is why we will survive and go forward and make a place for our children and grandchildren to live and thrive. This is not the end, everyone."

"It is for you," yelled a thin young man who had pushed forward to stand only a few feet from Reggie's microphone. "We know the truth. The problem is you and people like you. I *listened*. I *know*." He then pulled a heavy revolver from inside of his long shirt, pointed it at Reggie, and pulled the trigger.

With a blast, Reggie fell backwards through his doorway, knocking Janice over, her crutch flying out behind her.

The thin man stepped up onto the porch with a tight grin on his face. He pointed the gun at Reggie again and smiled.

That smile was obliterated by a massive powerfully thrown fist slamming into the man's mouth. Falling backwards off the porch, the man dropped the gun and used both hands to clutch at his ruined face.

A heartbeat later, Trailer was on top of the man pounding him furiously in the face with powerful blows.

Screaming and panic gripped the crowd as it ran in all directions. People tripped and fell as others ran over them or pushed children out of the way. Tension and fear that had built up over the last few hours was released in a flood of panic as everyone ran aimlessly away.

"Somebody help him!" yelled Janice from the front of her house.

Ernest Givens hadn't moved since the shot was fired. He stared at the massive black man pounding a clearly unconscious Spence in the face. Looking up, he saw an old woman with one leg lying under Reggie in their doorway. She was holding her hands over a bloody hole in the man's chest.

Ernest felt himself move forward and put his hands over Janice's. He saw that Reggie was struggling to breathe, and blood dribbled from his mouth. He heard a wheezing sound coming from the man's chest.

"It's a sucking chest wound," Ernest said. "We have to form a seal so he can at least breathe."

"What happened?" asked a small woman from the inside of the house.

Ernest looked up at her. "Get me something plastic. Anything that will form a seal."

"Plastic?" she asked, staring at all the blood on the front porch.

"Now!" he hollered at her, and she ran back inside with a start.

Feeling around to the back of Reggie, his fingers probed a ragged hole in the man's back and his heart sank.

"Will this work?" the girl asked, holding out a roll of plastic cooking wrap.

Ernest grabbed it from her hand without answering. He ripped Reggie's shirt off to expose bare skin and then pealed some of the sticky plastic off the roll. Placing it over the hole in the man's chest he wrapped it around to the hole in the back and then around again while Janice helped to lift him upwards. Ernest then stripped off his own shirt and tore it into two strips. One he packed around the front wound and the other on the back, and then he used the plastic wrap again to hold it all in place. That done, he leaned Reggie back down into Janice's lap. A thick pool of blood covered the porch surface.

"Is he going to be okay?" asked the girl from the doorway.

Ernest looked up. "Blankets. Get me blankets."

The girl darted back inside.

Reaching out, he felt the man's neck. The pulse was weak, but still there and he appeared to be breathing more normally with the wounds closed.

A shadow fell over Ernest, and he looked up to see a towering black man with bloody fists. The man stared down at Reggie while taking ragged gasps of air. Ernest turned back to Spence and then quickly away. There was nothing left of the young man's head except a thin smear of blood, bone, and brains on the grass.

Reggie's eyes flickered open, and he looked at Ernest.

"Hang in there," said Ernest. "Help is on…" He had started to say that help was on the way, but that wasn't true. There was no way to fix the damage done to Reggie even if help were on the way.

The old man pointed a weak finger at Ernest. "Remember what I said." He then dropped his hand and closed his eyes.

Reaching out, Ernest felt for the pulse again and found it weak.

"Do something," Janice pleaded.

"He's lost too much blood," Trailer said emotionlessly above them. "Best say your goodbyes, ma'am."

Janice bent her tear-stained face forward and began whispering in her husband's ear while stroking his hair. She stayed that way for several minutes until she lifted her head and looked at them all. "He's gone."

"Here's the blankets," said Jessica, coming back. "Hope this is what you were looking for."

Ernest stood and took a blanket from the girl's hands and then draped it over Reggie and pulled it gently over his face. He then bent down and lifted Janice out from underneath her dead husband. She clung to him on her one leg a moment more than was necessary.

"Thank you," she whispered, "for trying."

Ernest felt all the air go out of his body and looked back at the remains of Spence lying there in the grass. The young man in the jail who had seemed to listen to what he said with an unnatural intensity.

Janice tottered forward to the microphone and pulled it downward to her level. "This is Janice Phillips speaking to anyone still out there listening. My husband, Reggie Phillips, has just been shot, but he'll be okay." Her voice was strong and firm. "I plead with you all in his name to remain calm and do what he would have urged you to do. Help each other and remember who you are." She stepped away and knelt down beside her husband's corpse.

Trailer reached down and turned off the transmitter and saw Simon standing on the grass nearby. He held a bundle of loose wire in his hands. "I heard the pop and thought the transmitter had blown."

"Horace," said Janice, and Trailer turned to her. "Please help me get him inside."

Trailer moved forward and carefully lifted the man, trying not to disturb the blanket covering him.

"Carry him into our bedroom please," she said.

Moving gingerly so as not to bump against any walls, Trailer made his way down the hallway with Janice now on her crutch following. He laid the corpse gently on the quilt covered bed and stepped back. Janice moved forward and sat down on the edge of the bed.

"I was always afraid it would end this way," she said softly.

"I'm so sorry, ma'am," answered Trailer.

She smiled and took his hand. "Thank you." Turning back to Reggie, she said, "I need you to do something. Not for me, but for my husband's legacy."

"Yes, ma'am. Anything you want."

"Everything he's done, everything he's sacrificed"—emotion caused her to pause—"will have been for nothing if things just fall apart."

"What do you want me to do?"

She looked back at him. "Go find Nathan Taylor. As fast as you can. My lie about him being alive will buy you some time, but not much. Tell him what has happened. He'll know what to do." Janice then pulled herself up on the bed and curled up next to her dead husband. "Please leave me alone now."

Trailer nodded and backed out of the room, closing the door behind him. Making his way down the hall, he found Simon and Jessica standing there waiting for him. There was no sign of the man who had tried to save Reggie's life.

"What do we do now?" asked Jessica.

"Stay with her," Trailer said. "Both of you. Watch over her and make sure she eats. Give her some time with him, but then he needs to be buried."

"Where are you going?" Simon asked.

"South," he answered. Trailer retrieved his cudgel from beside the front door and his pack from behind the couch in the den. He then walked out back and untied Wildcat. Leading the mule around to the front of the house, he saw what remained of the man who had shot Reggie.

He looked down at his blood-covered hands and then at the small pile of spilled blankets on the porch that Jessica had brought. Trailer walked over to the pile, unfolded a blanket, and laid it gently over the smear of Reggie's blood on his front porch.

Trailer then led Wildcat to the south, making sure it stepped on the headless body in the front yard on the way.

Chapter 7 – The Execution

Joshua and his soldiers felt the strange tension as soon as they drove through the Huntsville outer defenses. The guards checked them out and let them inside with unusual somberness.

"What's going on?" Conrad asked a woman with sergeant's rank. She was supervising a group of civilians clearing away debris from a building damaged from artillery.

She shaded her eyes to look at them. "Just get here?"

Joshua nodded.

The woman hooked a thumb over her shoulder. "Keep going that way and you'll find out. Outside headquarters from what I understand. For once, I'm glad I got this detail. I'd rather be anywhere than there." She turned away from them and walked towards a man who was attempting to slack off.

"Lucky for us, that's where we're headed anyway," said Conrad.

Joshua and his small convoy of men and women drove slowly through roads cluttered with broken concrete and abandoned vehicles. Several times they were forced to stop and ask for directions, their operating vehicles serving as credentials to their legitimacy.

Finally, they reached a road between two large buildings. A long flatbed trailer had been pushed across the road as a barricade, and several soldiers stood behind it with weapons nearby. A man in uniform walked towards them. "Roads closed. No vehicles in here today. Didn't your commander tell you?"

"We just arrived," Conrad said, looking over the man's shoulder at the mass of soldiers in formation around a central open square. "What's going on?"

The soldier shook his head. "You picked a good time to show up. Get to see those traitors get what they deserve. My buddy helped build the gallows so at the very least there's to be a bit of hanging."

"Hanging?" asked Joshua. "What for?"

"You really don't know?" the man asked and saw their confused looks. "The McCraken Regiment mutinied. Tried to steal a barge and head home. Leave all the fighting and dying for the rest of us." The man smiled. "Some mortars dropped near the barge and snipers showed them the error of their ways, and they gave up quick enough. They learned that General Carter doesn't play."

"We need to get in there and talk to my father," said Joshua.

The man shook his head, looking at the rank on their shoulders. "Sorry, sirs, my orders are to let no one in after the formation call. You might be able to see the show if you climb up to one of the high stories of a building around here."

Conrad leaned forward. "Son, we're not here to enjoy the show. We need to get to headquarters. Captain Taylor here needs to report to his father...General Nathan Taylor."

The man's eyes widened with understanding. "Oh...sorry, sir, I didn't know. I guess I could let you through, but not your vehicles, and your soldiers need to stay here."

"Not a problem," said Joshua, getting down out of the truck. He turned to the vehicles behind him. "Find a place to bed down for the night and get some food. After that, send someone to headquarters to find us." Joshua then turned to Conrad. "You're with me. Let's go."

They walked past the barricade and around the back of formations of soldiers. Huge squares of men and women stood in combat gear with weapons at the ready, their commanders out front of each formation with their unit flag held by the assigned bearer. They all faced another block of soldiers, who were unarmed and hatless without any leader in front of them. These soldiers appeared downcast and many wore bandages.

They stood in formation, facing a wooden gallows erected at the south end of the large clearing.

"This doesn't look good," said Conrad.

"Over there," said Joshua, pointing to a nearby building off the courtyard with guards posted outside. "That has to be headquarters."

They walked around the back of the formation, and as they approached the headquarters entryway, a group of officers walked out, led by Nathan Taylor and Luke Carter. Nathan stopped in his tracks.

"Son, what are you doing here?"

Joshua saluted his father. "Sir, reporting that we have accomplished our mission and await new orders."

Nathan returned the salute. "Your orders, I believe, were to hold the objective and guard it until further notice."

"We're still doing that, sir," said Conrad. "The Creek tell us there's nothing around that dam for miles. We left a detachment that should be plenty sufficient."

"I see," said Nathan, looking at Luke who shrugged. He turned back to his son. "I'm glad to see you are okay, but I wish you weren't here to see this unpleasant business."

"What business?" asked Joshua.

Nathan turned to Luke. "Go ahead and prepare the prisoners. I'll be along shortly." Luke nodded and moved away. "Everyone, give us a minute," Nathan said, and the small group of officers moved away from them.

Joshua nodded at Conrad who followed Luke. "I heard there was a mutiny?"

Nathan sighed heavily. "An entire regiment tried to desert in the middle of everything. We couldn't let that happen. Fortunately, General Carter was able to get them to surrender with minimal casualties."

Looking out over the McCraken Regiment, Joshua saw men with looks that ranged from shock, to fear, to defiance.

"Surely you're not going to hang them all," said Joshua, pointing at the gallows.

"No. Just the officers. Ultimately, this is their fault and their responsibility."

General Carter walked to the center of the compound and stood at attention. He bellowed, "Army. Atten-tion!"

Each unit in unison came to attention with a loud echo of boots. The condemned regiment remained slouched in its current position.

"Bring forward the condemned!" Luke ordered, and a small door was opened to a shack off to the side. A line of shackled men in uniforms without rank were marched out and lined up before the gallows.

Joshua gasped. The line kept going on and on. "Surely not *all* of them," he said to his father. "There has to be fifty men there."

"Sixty-two to be exact, and five women," answered Nathan.

"You're going to hang sixty-seven JP citizens?"

Nathan turned to him with an angry stare. "You think I want to do this? Everything is on a razor's edge right now. I'm holding this army together by sheer force of will. It would take nothing for it to collapse, and then everything could be lost."

"I understand, but couldn't you just lock them up?"

"Where?" asked Nathan. "And for how long? I think I've been more than generous." He pointed his finger at the mass of dejected soldiers standing before the gallows. "Every one of them rightly deserves to be hanged for their mutiny, but I've ordered them pardoned. There has to be some consequence for this action, or others might take the same course in the future."

Joshua looked back at the men standing before the gallows. "It just doesn't seem right."

Nathan snorted. "Nothing about this is right." He saw Luke looking at him and nodded. Luke Carter in turn pointed to an officer standing near the gallows.

The officer stepped forward and read from a piece of paper. "Officers of the McCraken Regiment. You have been found guilty of mutiny and sedition during a time of war in a trial by a court-martial. You have been sentenced to death by hanging." He then turned to several soldiers standing near the prisoners. "Guard Detail. Bring forward the first line."

Ten men were marched forward and up the steps of the gallows to the ten nooses waiting for them. Once they were standing in front of the nooses, they were turned to face the crowd. The first man in the line yelled out, "This isn't right! Someone stop this!"

Carter nodded, and a guard behind each prisoner placed a hood over their heads.

"Don't do it," pleaded Joshua. "There has to be another way."

"I wish there were," said Nathan.

A chaplain stepped up onto the center of the gallows holding a large Bible.

There was a murmur to their rear and cries of pain. Despite being at attention, soldiers started to turn and look at what was going on.

"Stop right now, or I'll shoot," came a voice.

Joshua looked and saw a huge black man. He carried a large cudgel with a fresh smear of blood on one end. He was dusty and walked with slumped shoulders and led a mule that looked just as tired.

"Don't shoot!" Joshua yelled out. "Hold your fire."

Looking up at the voice, Trailer adjusted his advance and approached Nathan and Joshua. When he was in front of them, he dropped the reins of his mule and leaned forward with both hands on his cudgel. "I have news," he said.

"It can wait," said Nathan, turning back to the gallows.

Trailer's big hand reached out and grasped Nathan's shoulder and forcefully turned him back around. There were several gasps of surprise from the vast formation of soldiers. "No, it can't."

Nathan stared hard and him. "What is it?"

Trailer gazed around and then leaned forward and in a soft voice said, "Reggie Phillips is dead. He was assassinated four days ago."

Nathan shook his head. "You're mistaken. I've talked to people who heard the radio broadcast. He was just wounded."

"No," said Trailer. "I was there with him. He's definitely dead. Missus Phillips sent me to tell you. Said you would know what to do."

Looking back at the gallows, Nathan saw that everything had stopped and all eyes were on them, wondering what this is about.

"Whatever you decide to do," Trailer said, leaning back up, "I suggest you do it quickly. I get the feeling things are about to come apart."

"Dead?" asked Joshua in a whisper. "Are you sure?"

Trailer just nodded.

Nathan stood staring at the ground for a second, and then shook his head. He walked up to the front of the gallows and stood in front of the prisoners. "Colonel Bowers. As commander of your unit, you are invested with trust and authority to do the will of your nation. You have violated that trust and put your nation in peril. For that, you are sentenced to die." Nathan paused and looked the other prisoners. "Officers of the McCraken Regiment, you have proven yourselves unworthy of leadership. I hereby commute your sentence of death, but strip you of all rank. From this point forward, you are privates."

He turned around to the McCraken Regiment. "You soldiers will be subject to hard labor and duty until you have proven yourself worthy of trust. Officers will be appointed over you from outside of your unit. Any further instances of rebellion or desertion will be dealt with most harshly," Nathan said then nodded at Luke.

Carter looked up at the gallows. "Guard detail, remove all the prisoners from the platform with the exception of Colonel Bowers."

"You can't do this!" yelled out Bowers. "You don't have that authority!"

The chaplain moved to the condemned man and spoke to him for several minutes and prayed before exiting the platform himself.

Carter pointed at Bowers, and a noose and a hood were placed over the man's head and tightened into place. To the man's credit, he stood up straight and kept quiet. Nathan then nodded when Carter and the guard detail looked at him.

A man pulled on a lever and ten trapdoors opened, with only one body falling to a jerk and a swing.

"Commanders, take charge of your units and return to duty!" yelled out Carter. He then marched over to stand with Nathan, Joshua, and Trailer. "That was unexpected, but not unwise," Carter said.

"President Phillips is dead," Nathan told him. "I must return immediately. I'm relinquishing command to you."

If Luke Carter was surprised, he didn't show it. "What are your orders, sir?"

"Destroy Lacert and his forces," Nathan said.

"What about them?" Carter asked, tilting his head towards the regiment and the line of prisoners.

Nathan looked around and saw Conrad. He motioned him forward. When the big man was standing before him, Nathan reached out a hand, and Conrad took it. "Congratulations, Colonel."

"Congratulations? Colonel?"

"You're now the acting commander of the McCraken Regiment."

"What?" said Conrad and Joshua in unison.

"Effective immediately," said Nathan. "You are to take your orders from General Carter."

"You mean I'm supposed to assume command of a unit where the commander has just been executed and all the officers stripped of their rank? A unit that has already tried to desert? A county regiment made up of volunteers from a county I'm not even a part of? Hell, I'm not even from the JP!"

"I admit the position is not without its challenges," said Nathan.

"Challenges," said Conrad. "Every soldier in that unit is going to hate me."

"What, you're worried they won't like you?" asked Carter.

Conrad looked flustered. "Well, yeah," he finally said.

"If it makes you feel any better," said Joshua, "nobody likes you anyway. Besides, I'll be there to help you."

"No, you won't," said Nathan. "You're going back to the JP with me, and don't waste time arguing with me."

"What am I supposed to do for new officers?" asked Conrad.

"I'd pick people you can trust," answered Nathan.

"Our people," said Joshua. "The detachment we brought with us. It's going to be tough, but they're loyal to you."

"Damn," said Conrad. "I did *not* see this coming."

"No one did," answered Joshua, shaking the man's hand. "Take care of the troops." He looked over at the dejected soldiers of the McCraken Regiment. "All of them."

"We better go," said Trailer.

"Our vehicles will make better time," said Joshua and then looked at Wildcat, "although you might have to leave your mule."

Trailer looked at the mule and then at Conrad. "Mind taking care of her for me?"

"Not at all," said Conrad. "Might make her the new unit mascot. And she's not a she by the way."

"To me, she is," answered Trailer.

"Take a company of soldiers with you," said Luke. "You might need them on the way."

"Or when you get there," quipped Trailer.

Nathan nodded. "We'll do that, and thanks."

"Anything else before you go?" Carter asked.

Staring at the gallows, Nathan said, "Yeah, bury Bowers, but don't let anyone touch that. Leave it up as a reminder."

Chapter 8 – Committee Meeting

Joshua fought coming with him, but Nathan wanted his son to have nothing to do with what was coming. He sent him instead on a meaningless mission to try to assess the damage to Kentucky Dam. Nathan already had a very good idea of the damage.

Nathan was on his way to see Janice when he heard of an emergency meeting of the JP Executive Council and knew that was where he needed to be. A veteran of numerous meetings of the like, he knew what would be happening there. Even in the best of times, they were gatherings of difficult men trying to push self-serving agendas at each other in return for future favors.

When Nathan arrived at the USECO plant in Paducah where the meetings were typically held, he saw a small group of citizens held away from the main bunker complex by a squad of local police. Both groups parted without a word as he and his men strode into the facility.

It was evident they were running the generator. The facility would have been as dark as a cave without them. Nathan wondered if the vast underground complex would get much use when the fuel finally all went bad. Maybe it might be useful as storage as long as folks had an ample supply of torches or lanterns run on rendered animal fat oil.

Before he even reached the meeting council room, he could hear angry voices. There was plenty to be angry about, Nathan admitted. Fuel reserves going bad, the hydroelectric dam destroyed, an unpopular and costly war in the south, malaria ravaging the population, and now the only clear leader assassinated with no line of succession in place. He was about to make their problems worse…or better, depending on how they chose to look at it.

"We must hold immediate elections," one voice was yelling. "That is the only way to resolve this situation."

"Elections now?" asked another voice. "Are you crazy? With the people's mood the way it is? They would go for some radical that could doom everything."

"Besides, how could we organize an election without a means to inform people?"

"We should govern by Executive Council until elections can be held," said someone else. "We can meet once a week or maybe twice a month to address any issues."

"That'll be really efficient. With all that's going on we're going to govern by committee through bi-monthly meetings?"

"Well, what do you suggest?" someone asked.

"We select someone in this room as the interim president," another suggested. Other voices seemed to agree to this idea until another squabble broke out about which of them would assume the position.

Nathan strode into the room along with a half dozen soldiers. It took several seconds for members of the committee to notice him. When they did, the room slowly grew still.

"There will be no interim president," said Nathan. "President Phillips declared martial law, which is still in effect. As the Chief of Defense and senior member of his cabinet, I will govern in his stead until the election can be held."

"And when will that be?" asked Wayne Lotts of Marshal County.

Nathan turned to him. "To be honest, I don't know. The sooner the better, as I want this position about as much as you want me to have it, but it's not real high on my priorities right now."

"The Chief of Defense is not in the line of succession," said Brad William of McCraken County.

"There was no clear line of succession established," Nathan answered. "Everyone assumed having a vice president would be enough, but that position has been vacant since Ethan Schweitzer took over as president. In the absence of clear procedures, and the existence of martial law, I'm assuming authority."

"You're declaring yourself president?" asked Lotts incredulously.

Nathan shook his head. "I mean to have little authority as I need to keep the peace and win the war. After that, I'll step aside."

"How do we know we can trust you?" asked the Paducah Mayor Leslie Mitchell.

Nathan smiled. "Because if I really wanted to seize power in a coup d'état, I would have come in here and killed all of you."

They looked at the soldiers nervously.

"But I don't want to be in charge. I never have. My intention as much as possible is to govern through you people. The Executive Council meetings are a good idea, and let's plan on meeting once a week. Anything I can hold off making a decision on until that meeting I will try to do so."

"And if you say a decision can't wait?" asked Williams.

"Then I'll do what I believe is best and inform you afterwards," Nathan answered. "Winning the war is the top priority right now."

Mitchell moved up to the front of the room. "Maybe we need to reconsider our priorities in light of recent events."

"How would you suggest doing that?" asked Nathan.

"The war is obviously not going well," continued Mitchell. "They have shown with the rocket attack that they have weapons we do not. What is to prevent them from raining bombs down on all of our towns and cities?"

"Nothing," answered Nathan, "except our soldiers destroying their capability to do such a thing."

"Perhaps we should be courting them as an ally rather than an enemy," said Mitchell, turning to the rest of the room for support. "War might not be the answer."

Nathan fought to control his anger. Mitchell had run like a coward when Paducah had needed him on several occasions, yet he appeared to lack the basic ability to feel shame. Any other man would have resigned.

"Under any other adversary, I might agree with you," said Nathan, "but we are dealing with a bloodthirsty madman named Vincent Lacert. Maybe some of you remember him?"

People in the room looked around at each other nervously. Several had actually had the unfortunate experience of meeting the man.

Nathan continued on. "The security of the JP, I would say even the continued existence of the JP, depends on removing Lacert from power. Once that happens, maybe we can reassess relations with Huntsville."

"And we're just supposed to follow your lead in the meanwhile?" asked Mitchell.

"No. You're supposed to do everything within your power to keep people calm and productive. Enforce the curfew and rationing. No riots, no demonstrations, no large gatherings of more than ten persons except for family events, funerals, education, or religious events."

"Does that include us?" asked Lotts, looking around at the two dozen people in the room.

Nathan stared at them silently for a moment. "It does indeed. Like I said, we will meet once a week, but you are not to meet without my permission or presence."

"And if we do?" asked Williams.

"Then I'll have you arrested and your position filled with someone of my choosing."

Mitchell sucked in his breath. "You wouldn't dare, not even you."

"You would give me no choice," explained Nathan. "This is martial law, which means extraordinary measures for unusual circumstances."

"I hope you realize that you'll have to answer for everything when this is all over," said Williams.

Nathan nodded. "That is my hope. It will mean we will have survived long enough for there to be a reckoning."

A soldier walked in from outside and whispered in Nathan's ear. "I'm sorry, gentlemen. I have urgent business elsewhere. Please gather your belongings before you leave."

"You're kicking us out?" asked Mitchell.

"This meeting is over," answered Nathan. "We will meet again at noon on Monday. Until then, these facilities will be secured and guarded. Now please leave and remember what I said about your duties."

"Like we could forget," quipped someone as they filed out of the room. Some glared at him while others refused to acknowledge his existence.

When the room was empty, Nathan was about to turn off the lights when he glanced to where Reggie normally sat. In the chaos of the meeting, the president's chair had been overturn and was lying on its side.

Nathan walked over slowly and carefully picked the chair back up and slid it under the table. He patted the leather of the headrest and missed his friend.

He then walked out of the room, turning off the lights.

Chapter 9 – One Moon

Conrad felt the cold wind from the north. It was only early autumn, but this winter promised to be bad. Especially with the electricity gone and the fuel on a ticking clock of diminishing usefulness. *At least the cold weather should help keep the malaria in check*, he thought.

He had believed being a JP outsider would be a detriment when he took over command of the McCracken Regiment, but it had actually served him well. Someone else from the county would have been driven and pulled by family and community loyalties, whereas a commander from another county would have been looked upon with suspicion. His soldiers he had placed in leadership positions as officers were another matter, but the regiment was showing signs of recovery.

He had worked with Carter to get the unit off punishment details and to start patrolling outside the wire in small elements. If there was a dangerous mission, Conrad volunteered for it and made sure his soldiers knew they were taking the most dangerous assignments. He hoped with time they would again regain their pride and could look at soldiers from other units without ducking their heads.

It hadn't been easy or without setbacks. There were still numerous disciplinary issues. Colonel Bowers obviously hadn't believed in leading by example, and even before the attempted desertion, the regiment had been characterized by laziness, lack of discipline, slovenliness, and an inability to accomplish basic missions. Colonel Bowers had been chosen as a successor to the martyr Brazen and bragged about how he was going to bring a military mindset to the position. It was now obvious that Bowers had only sought to enrich himself and gather power in order to domineer others and make himself feel important.

The local populace was another problem. At first, they had welcomed them as saviors from the brutal system of governance established by Vincent Lacert. Although the JP troops were under strict orders to treat civilians with courtesy and respect, given enough time, tempers and frustration had frayed at the fabric of questionable discipline. Looting was the most common infraction, but one man had killed a local while drunk and several others had teamed up to abduct and rape a woman. Carter had ordered them all shot.

Conrad found that he spent most of his time dealing with such issues. The locals had learned that he cared enough to keep his people in line, which meant they came to him with constant complaints, all of which had to be investigated. Most of them were baseless, but on occasion, he was sorry to find out that war didn't just bring out the best in people.

Which was why he was going to see Carter. His quartermaster had been caught withholding supplies from the troops and selling them to the locals on the black market. Conrad would have likely never found out, except he had complained to Carter about the lack of supplies and was told to examine the books. That he should have enough of what he needed. What he had seen didn't add up.

He could have handled the situation on his own. The man had already been removed from his position, lost all rank, and been put into a line position where everyone knew what he had done, but Carter said to keep him informed of such issues. It was a shame that when their primary goal was to defeat Lacert's forces, most of their efforts were on keeping control of their own troops.

Walking into the headquarters, he saw that Carter was meeting with several of the Creek scouts. Carter had deep black circles under his eyes and his uniform appeared to hang on him like a trash bag. Conrad got himself a cup of horrendously bad chicory coffee and stepped over closer so he could hear some of the conversation.

"What is that supposed to mean? One more moon?" Luke asked.

"It means one month," explained the Creek patiently. "The Creek will return north in one month, whether this is over or not."

"I met with Billy Fox myself," Luke said. "He agreed to support us throughout the campaign."

"This comes from Billy Fox. He said this campaign has already gone on twice as long as expected. You can't expect us to stay here indefinitely, not with winter coming on."

Luke took a deep breath and slowly let it out. "Listen, without the Creek, we can't keep the Huntsville forces cut off. They can sneak out between our thin lines and get supplies. Hell, they might even be able to flank us. I understand where you're coming from, but we just need a little more time."

"That's what you've been saying for weeks."

"And this is a little more time," said the other Creek. "One moon."

"Okay, I'm all ears," Carter said. "You got any recommendations? Their defenses are too solid to take in an assault. What little artillery we have doesn't have the range to do more than harass them, and we don't have enough of that. We could probably starve them out, but the whole time they might be raining down rockets on all of us, including the Creek."

"They have no reason to bomb the Creek."

"Not until you went to war against them with their adversaries."

The Creek looked at each other and then back at Carter. "One moon." They then turned and left.

A gust of wind came into the room as the door opened, and a piece of paper flew around on the floor. Conrad stared at it, remembering the cold north wind that had been blowing for several days.

Carter stared after them. "One moon indeed. Go take your damn moon and smoke it. Hell, smoke it in a sweat lodge or whatever the hell you do. I hope you choke on it.

Conrad grinned. He had never seen Carter so flustered and knew the man had to be exhausted. "When's the last time you slept?"

The man turned slowly to look at him. "I can't remember. I'm not sure it matters if we can't crack those defenses or smoke them out into the open where we can fight them. Our supplies are going to start running out soon, especially if the Creek stop helping us."

"Wait a minute," Conrad said, setting his cup down. "That might work."

Carter ran a hand through unruly hair. "Conrad, I don't have time for games. What do you want?"

"Smoke them out. You said it yourself. It might work."

"It was a turn of phrase," Carter sighed. "What are we supposed to use to smoke them out?"

"Smoke," said Conrad, smiling.

Carter just looked at him expressionlessly.

Pointing outside, Conrad talked quickly. "That wind. It's been blowing steadily south for days. We could build huge fires to the north and let the smoke play havoc with them. If nothing else, it might obscure a major assault if we wanted to make one."

"If the wind doesn't stop or change direction," Carter said. "It's also going to take a ton of combustible material to make that much smoke, and green wood doesn't burn readily. All that material has to be placed close to the walls to have any effect, and you'll have to keep feeding it even if we're lucky enough to keep a sustained wind in the right direction. The whole time those tending the fires will be getting shot at from the Huntsville forces."

"Sure, it won't be easy, but give us the green light and we'll make it happen. It's not like there's any better ideas floating around here."

"I don't know," Carter said, shaking his head. "That's a lot of effort for something that might not even work and could get a bunch of people killed."

"You're right. It was a dumb idea. We'll go with your plan instead. What was your plan again, sir? I believe it's the whole 'wait and see' strategy? I understand its showing some promise."

"Do not screw with me," Carter warned with a pointed finger. "Not now."

"Just let me try it. I have everything I need…well, except for some trucks to transport the wood and maybe some tires, chainsaws, and a bunch of fuel to pour on the wood and to fuel the trucks. Other than that, I have everything I need."

Luke closed his eyes and sighed. "Fine. Talk to the quartermaster. Tell her I said to give you everything you need. Let me know a few

361

hours before you're ready and I'll get a couple of regiments to provide covering fire."

"Thanks," said Conrad, turning to leave.

"You better hope the wind doesn't change direction," said Luke, "or all that smoke will be blowing in on us and a bunch of pissed off civilians."

"We definitely don't want that," admitted Conrad.

Chapter 10 – Condolences

Ernest Givens found himself standing on the street staring at the Phillips' house. He had started walking to clear his head, not really planning on going anywhere in particular.

It's a small town, he thought. *You walk long enough and you pass by everywhere.*

Still, he wondered if maybe this wasn't his destination all along.

He could still see the trampled grass and flowers, although someone had picked up the trash and done their best to right the planters. Ernest wasn't sure how long he stood there, but he finally heard someone ask, "Can I help you?"

Startled, he looked up to see the small dark-haired woman who had given him a blanket on that terrible day.

"Oh, it's you," she said with neither welcome nor rudeness.

"Is Missus Phillips here?"

The girl hesitated and then went inside. A few minutes later, she came out again. "She's sitting around back in the garden. Go around the side." The girl looked like she wanted to say something else, but went back inside. Ernest caught the glimpse of the man who had been setting up the radio that day looking through the curtains at him with the woman at his shoulder.

Good, he thought. *Reggie's wife isn't alone and she isn't without those wanting to protect her.*

He walked around the side of the house and into the backyard. Janice sat in a lawn chair with a small table nearby. Her back was to him. Her crutch was on the ground, and the woman's dark brown dress covered the leg stump from view. Without turning around, she said, "Pull up a chair and sit for awhile."

Ernest looked around and saw several worn chairs against the side of the house. He grabbed one and placed it near the woman, then sat carefully while studying her face.

"This has been my home for nearly forty years," she said abruptly. "Sure, we spent time in Frankfurt, and even some in DC, mores the pity, but this was always home. It's been a good home, but it's seen a great deal of violence."

"I'm very sorry for your loss, ma'am."

Janice went on as if she didn't hear him. "That madman came to kill Reggie and ended up hurting me instead. Right over there." She pointed towards the back porch. "That was how I lost my leg. Then not a few months later"—she chuckled—"would you believe my gentle Reggie near beat Ethan Schweitzer to death with a fire poker? You can still see the poker head stuck in the dining room ceiling. I suspect if it hadn't come off, Reggie would have beaten him to death."

"I'm sorry," Ernest mumbled, not sure what to say.

"And now this. Some might make the conclusion that this house is cursed, but I don't think that is the case. These are just troubled times, and Reggie chose to take on the mantle of responsibility. For him, there really was no other calling. If he hadn't been the JP President, he would have been something else."

"I'll be running for president," Ernest said without thinking. "When they have elections again, that is."

She looked at him for the first time. "That's good. Reggie always said this place needed good leaders, and that's more true now with him gone."

"I mean, I was running for president…before. I was running against him."

The woman turned an amused smile his way. "I know. He told me all about you. There was little we didn't share with each other."

Ernest was silent for a while. "What did he say about me?"

She looked back ahead. "That you were a man seeking his place in the world. Someone who knew there was something more they were supposed to do, but wasn't sure what it was."

"And he thought my place wasn't as the JP President."

"He never said that. I could tell he liked and admired you a great deal."

Ernest shook his head. "I find that hard to believe."

"Why? Because you were adversaries in politics? Reggie didn't want to be president. He would have welcomed someone to take over, someone worthy. The way he was worthy." She turned to look at him again. "Is that you, Mister Givens? Are you worthy of that responsibility? The way my husband was?"

He stared at her before turning away from her gaze. "Honestly, I don't know."

She chuckled and looked back at the freshly turned earth at her feet. "That's not the worst answer, I guess."

"You should know, I don't agree with everything your husband did."

"Neither did I, but I trusted him. I trusted his intentions. They were always honorable. Time will identify mistakes and critics will pick over him like vultures on a carcass, but he gave his whole heart and soul to the people he served. He loved them."

"I don't think that's the sort of person I am."

"It could be." She smiled. "You are who you want to be, not who you happen to be."

Ernest was silent.

"You know he's watching and listening to us now, don't you?"

Looking around, Ernest realized with a start that the freshly turned earth at her feet was in the dimensions of a grave. He resisted the temptation to stand up and move away. "Is that where he's buried?"

Janice nodded. "Seemed only right. I'm sure I'll lie there beside him soon enough. I've seen enough for one lifetime and don't care to experience too much more without my Reggie. I just wish I could see my boy and grandbabies again."

Ernest looked at her with concern. "You're not planning on doing anything…"

"Rash?" she asked. "No, nothing like that. The Good Lord will take me away when he's ready to take me away, but I do pray that He hurries up about it."

He sat there silently for a few minutes before lifting himself out of the chair. "I guess I should be going."

"Tell me why I should vote for you, Mister Givens."

"Excuse me?"

"I still got a vote. Tell me why I should use it on you. My husband had to answer that question all the time."

"Because I'm the best man for the job," Ernest stammered. "I'm highly qualified. I've got…"

She waved a hand at him. "No, no, no. Not your resume. Why should I trust my life to you? Why should any of us trust our lives and the lives of our children to you? You do know that's what it ultimately comes down to, don't you?"

Why? Ernest wondered. *Why indeed.* He thought of how he had ended up here and the things he had been through. All the good men and women he had known in his life. He thought of his home and the community he had grown up in.

He looked off at the sky. "I don't know if you should vote for me or not. I just know that this is my home and I don't want anything bad to happen to it. I want what's best for my neighbors and I want to do a good job."

"Not bad," she admitted, pursing her lips.

"Does that mean I have your vote?"

"I haven't decided yet"—she smiled—"but you will have my prayers."

Ernest stood there looking down at Reggie's grave and thought of that madman, Spence. *I didn't cause this,* he thought. *I didn't want him dead.*

"Goodbye, Mister Givens," she said. "I wish you the best in the dark days ahead."

Ernest nodded and walked slowly out of the yard and back to his lonely home.

Chapter 11 – Smoke and Fire

Conrad looked at his watch nervously. Although he had consciously displayed outward confidence to his unit, underneath he feared failure could tear what little stitching that held the thin fabric of morale together loose.

"Teams are in place, sir," said a staff officer near Conrad who nodded while looking back over his shoulder. Hidden along streets were ten heavy dump trucks loaded with wood, tires, and other combustible material that would burn and smoke for days. These loads had been soaked in fuel to make them easier to light. The drivers and co-drivers for these vehicles had the most dangerous assignments despite the thick sheets of protective metal placed over their windows.

"Inform HQ that we're in place," Conrad ordered, and the officer began cranking on an old TA-312 radio that operated without electricity. A thin wire ran from the end of the radio to a similar one in the headquarters nearly a mile away. "Wildcats in position," the man said into the radio.

Trailer's mule had become the regiment's unofficial mascot. Hard-working, never complaining, and oblivious to any abuse, the animal seemed to exemplify the regiment's new mindset. Some of the soldiers had even taken to calling themselves Wildcats.

Looking at his watch again, Conrad counted down the seconds and then peered up into the dark early morning sky. After a few seconds, he saw a flare rise up high into the air to illuminate the ground around the embattled Huntsville northern perimeter with dark shadows. The steady wind blew the flare away from them but not before concentrated JP mortar and artillery fire began to rain down near the walls and barricades facing them.

The barrage only lasted a minute and a half, they didn't have the shells to sustain a longer bombardment, but Conrad hoped it was enough to keep the defenders head's down and, with any luck, it might have actually killed some of those stubborn bastards.

"Covering fire," Conrad yelled, and his regiment, along with three other regiments, began firing at the perimeter in front of them. Staring intently at his watch, Conrad counted off exactly sixty seconds. "Cease fire!" he ordered.

The order was relayed, and the McCracken Regiment stopped firing at the enemy perimeter in front of them while the other three regiments kept up their sustained shooting along the edges of the objective.

"Delivery Teams, forward!" Conrad ordered. Another staff officer relayed the command, and a second flare arched high into the sky. The sound of heavy trucks rumbled from behind them.

Conrad waited long anxious minutes for the first truck to appear. "Where are they?" Conrad asked no one in particular. "They were ordered to move fast." He waited another few minutes, but when he did not see the trucks, Conrad stood up with a curse and made his way back towards the sound of vehicles.

What he found was a line of heavy dump trucks, their headlights covered in cloth to keep them from being easily targeted by enemy mortars. The front vehicle was leaning heavily to its front right, its driver side tire flat. The heavy unbalanced load in the rear of the vehicle threatened to tip the dump truck and blocked both lanes of the road.

Conrad ran up to a group of soldiers trying to get a heavy jack under the front of the truck. "What the hell is going on? We need to be moving!"

A sergeant turned to him angrily, ignoring Conrad's rank. "We're driving around in the goddamn dark and these roads are covered in debris. No one should be surprised that we popped a tire." He shined a flashlight at the tire to emphasize his point, and Conrad saw a long sharp piece of metal sticking out of the tire.

"How long to fix it?" Conrad asked.

The man laughed. "I really don't think you can lift this bitch with a full load. We've got to be talking twenty tons at least, not even counting all the metal added to the cab to stop bullets. We'll likely have to fully unload her and then may still need a heavy wrecker."

Looking back, Conrad could see the line of vehicles with drivers standing around smoking and talking. He could hear the sustained firing in the distance. "Back up, people! Everyone back up! Find another route."

He walked down the line yelling at soldiers to get into their vehicles, and when he reached the last vehicle, he found it abandoned. "Where did the driver go?" Conrad asked several soldiers standing nearby.

"He went that away." A soldier pointed off vaguely to the east. "Said while everyone was stopped, he was going to go take a shit."

Conrad suppressed a scream of frustration. "Do you know how to drive this thing?" he asked the group of nearby soldiers, and they all shook their heads.

Climbing up into the cab of the large truck, he said softly, "How hard can it be?" Conrad sat there looking at all the lever and dials in dismay. He hopped back down and ran to the front of the column and saw the man he had spoken to still trying to get the jack raised. "You!" he ordered. "Come with me."

The man stopped what he was doing, shrugged, and with exaggerated slowness climbed out from under the truck.

"I presume you know how to driver these things?"

"These *things* are Oneida four-axle standard dump trucks configured for hauling rock and gravel from the quarry to the north. And I know how to do more than drive them."

"Great," said Conrad. "Follow me, and if it's not too much trouble, can you hurry the fuck up?"

Conrad finally got the soldier to jog after him to the last vehicle where they both got into the cab. "What's your name, soldier?" Conrad asked as the man started the vehicle.

"Sergeant Cleaves," the man answered.

"Well, Sergeant Cleaves, we need to get moving and deliver these loads before our covering fire runs out, or we'll be sitting ducks."

"Sure." The man started backing the truck up slowly, his head out the window peering to their rear. Once at an intersection, he peered left and right. "Which way?"

Conrad looked at him, startled. "Don't you know?"

Cleaves held his hands up off the wheel. "I'm not one for exploring the town."

"Just pick a direction," Conrad said, "and head south. Eventually, we've got to run into the enemy."

Cleaves turned left, and Conrad looked back to see other trucks backing up and then following them. Peering through the cut slits in the metal over the front windows, they could now see by the morning light.

"At least we can finally see where we're going," Cleaves said.

"And the enemy can see well enough to shoot at us."

The man turned to look at Conrad. "You're one of those glass-half-empty sorts, aren't you?"

"Turn right," Conrad ordered at the next intersection, and they found themselves on a narrow road with several abandoned vehicles along the sides of the road. "Just push on through," Conrad ordered, "don't worry about scraping the paint."

"It's your call," Cleaves said. "If I get a bill, I'm sending it to you."

The truck weaved from one side of the road to the other trying to avoid obstacles, and the squeal of screeching metal could be heard on both sides of the road. Looking to their rear, Conrad confirmed the line of trucks was still following them.

"Uh-oh," Cleaves said, slowing.

Looking forward, Conrad could see out into the open 'no man's land' between the JP and Redstone perimeters. Blocking their path was a barricade designed to provide cover for friendly troops and deter attacks from enemy. Several old cars have been pushed together with sand bag and large stones piled around the opening and inside the vehicle. Surprised soldiers were staring back at them from the rear of the barricade.

"Bust through it," Conrad said calmly.

"Bust through it?" asked Cleaves. "This isn't some monster truck. We're fully loaded and she could tip on us."

"Just do it!" ordered Conrad. "And make sure it *doesn't* tip on us."

Cleaves sighed and grumbled under his breath. He aimed the truck for the point where the two vehicles came together and shifted down into a lower gear before pressing the accelerator to the floor. "Here we go," he said, while reaching up to secure the seatbelt over his shoulder.

Conrad grabbed his seatbelt to do the same while staring at soldiers running to get out of their way. With a crunch and a shudder, twenty tons of truck and loaded wood slammed into the two vehicles, and they spun out of the way like tops.

"That wasn't so—" Conrad's words were cut off as the left wheel went up high on something and he felt the truck tilting dangerously to the right.

"Crap," commented Cleaves as the vehicle tilted up to nearly a thirty degree angle. "Hold on," he said, turning the wheel hard to the right and directly towards the side of a building along the road.

The right front wheel hit the curb, and incredibly, the dump truck for a split second only had one wheel touching the road. The tire reconnected with sidewalk as they plowed over a street sign. Conrad had just enough time to cover his face before the truck slammed into the side of the building and smashed back down on all four wheels before rocking up onto the other side. Finally, it settled flat with a crash.

Conrad sat there for a second and realized the vehicle was no longer running. Rubble from the building they had run into started to fall down on the hood of the truck and roof of the cab.

"She didn't tip," Cleave said cheerfully, giving Conrad two thumbs up.

"Let's get out of here! That building's getting ready to fall on us."

"Let's see if we can," the man answered and tried to crank the vehicle. It sputtered while Cleaves talked to the dump truck using endearments that made Conrad feel like he should give them some privacy. Cracks ran up the side of the building's masonry, and it gave forth a deeply ominous grinding noise. Finally, after a long wheeze and sputter, the engine turned over and roared to life.

They backed away from the building as the wall collapsed against the side of the truck and the roof slid off in front of them where they had just been.

"That was close," said Cleaves.

Looking backwards, Conrad saw that the other trucks were still behind them.

He also didn't hear covering fire anymore. Looking at his watch, he realized their window for executing this mission had passed. The sun was rising in the east and throwing dim rays of light through gray clouds. Sticking his head out of the truck again, he felt for the north to south wind and found it.

"Let's go," Conrad ordered, pulling his head back in.

"You sure?" Cleaves asked.

"Absolutely not, but let's do this anyway."

Shrugging, the man turned the wheel carefully back to the left and began pressing the gas. Within a minute, they were completely beyond their own lines and into the cleared area around Redstone Arsenal. They could hear pings in front of them as bullets began to strike the truck's armored windshield and radiator.

"Faster," Conrad ordered. "If they hit our tires, we're done."

"I have to follow the road. And this one is none too straight. This isn't an all-terrain vehicle if you haven't noticed."

"Do you ever say, sir?" Conrad asked.

"No, sir."

Conrad looked through the slit in the metal as he felt the road sloping down. Their objective was the near side of the gulley in front of them. The trucks were supposed to veer to the right and left before the small bridge crossing the ditch and drop their loads in a long line parallel to the enemy's perimeter. "We're close enough," Conrad yelled. "Turn right."

Cleaves reached outside the window and pulled down a heavy slab of metal over his side window before turning the vehicle. Conrad looked back and saw the next vehicle turn in the opposite direction. The next in line followed the lead vehicle.

"That's far enough," Conrad said. "We want the fires to be close together to create a solid mass. Let's back up and dump the load."

The driver nodded, and as he began to back up, a loud beeping noise ensued. Conrad heard more bullets hitting his side of the vehicle, and he reached out and pulled the metal slab down on his side. He jerked back as the slab slammed against the door with a wince and saw there was a line of blood along his arm.

"Got you a graze," said Cleaves, stopping the vehicle. He reached for the dump lever and pulled it backwards. There was a loud squeal of metal and a pneumatic whine. "Uh-oh," the man said.

"What's wrong?"

Cleaves looked back through the cab's rear window and gazed up while pulling the lever again. "We bent the cab frame over the lip of the bed when we crashed into that building back there. She won't lift up."

"Well, let's just—" Conrad's words were cut off by a blast and roar of heat that threw them forward. His head and arms flew forward while his body pressed painfully into the seat belt. His body then snapped back hard against the seat as the truck settled back onto the ground.

Cleaves rubbed blood from his face. "What was that?"

Conrad looked behind them at the flames that were enveloping the dump truck's bed and creeping around to the sides of the cab. "One of their bullets or flares or something must have ignited the gasoline on the load."

The driver reached forward to crank the vehicle, but Conrad grabbed his arm. "We got to leave it. We would be cooked before we made it back." Smoke was starting to fill the cab.

Cleaves nodded and tried without success to unbuckle his seatbelt. "Damn thing's jammed."

Unbuckling his own seatbelt, Conrad pulled his combat knife from a boot sheath and sawed through the nylon strap. Smoke was billowing around them and both men were coughing.

"If it's not too much trouble," coughed Cleaves, "could you hurry the fuck up?"

Despite himself, Conrad laughed and yanked on the webbing as he cut harder. With a final tug, it came loose, and both men reached for their door handles and tumbled out onto the grass and the blessed oxygen.

Smoke billowed up in all directions, and bullets were striking the ground and their truck. Conrad darted to the rear of the vehicle where Cleaves was already heaving in great gasps of air. The heat of the truck threatened to force them out from behind its cover into the open. Looking off to the right, Conrad could see nine huge bonfires and the last of the trucks pulling back through friendly lines. Huge columns of smoke billowed into the enemies' faces, yet gunfire was still coming from that direction.

"Ready to make a run for it?" asked Conrad.

Cleaves nodded, wiping soot off his face.

"On three. One. Two. Three!"

Both men took off at a run up the side of the little ditch and tuffs of dirt flew up around them as bullets hit the soft soil. Conrad could see soldiers of his regiment cheering them onwards and firing towards the enemy. He pushed himself harder, and then noticed that he was alone. Looking back, he saw Cleaves lying on the ground.

Skidding to a stop, Conrad turned and ran back to find the man groaning and holding a thigh that spurted bright red blood.

"Shit, shit, shit," Cleaves kept saying.

Conrad pressed his palm forcefully against the spurting blood while striping off his belt. He let go of the wound to wrap the belt around the thigh and immediately got a hot stream of blood in his face. Conrad closed his eyes and worked by feel.

Once the belt was around the thigh, he wiped his eyes of blood and looked around for something to torque the belt tight with. Seeing nothing, he felt his pistol digging painfully into his side. Conrad drew the weapon and brought it towards Cleaves.

"Don't you think that a little premature?" Cleaves asked through pale lips.

Putting his knee against the wound and the belt above it, Conrad pressed the take-down leaver and pulled the slide off the weapon. He dropped the grip and placed the slide through the belt and began to twist.

"Stop it! No!" Cleaves immediately began to scream and fought against Conrad.

"I know it hurts, but if I don't do this, you'll bleed out."

"I don't care! Stop it, you bastard!" He fought for a few more seconds and then went silent.

Reaching up to the man's neck, Conrad found a weak pulse. He pulled Cleaves belt off and used it to secure the slide in place so the tourniquet wouldn't move.

Looking up, Conrad saw soldiers eagerly waving him forward. They seemed to be moving in slow motion, and he realized he couldn't hear anything. Turning back to the blazing masses, Conrad saw huge piles of billowing black smoke. Through this haze, bright flashes of gunfire appeared along the wall and tuffs of dirt flew up around him. He felt a hard punch against his shoulder and fell back. He lay in the grass staring at the gray sky. Reaching over to his shoulder, Conrad felt wetness. He pulled his fingers away and towards his face, seeing blood.

Noise suddenly filled the world, and time speeded back up. Conrad rolled over onto his stomach and pushed himself to his feet. He reached down and grasped the inert Cleaves by the shirt sleeve and pants leg of his unwounded side and, with a groan, lifted the man up onto his shoulders. He scuttled as fast as he could towards safety.

It seemed to take forever, and he found himself just looking at the ground in order to keep from tripping and falling over anything. Conrad knew if he fell, he'd not likely have the strength to get up again…at least not carrying Cleaves.

He felt hands on him and the load was falling away from him. Conrad looked up into friendly faces helping him. Several soldiers put Cleaves on a stretcher and took him away. They forced him to sit and someone was tying a bandage around his shoulder.

Conrad peered back towards Redstone Arsenal and saw gigantic bonfires spewing forth black smoke that the wind blew steadily into the faces of the enemy. He could also hear cheering. Not only from his own soldiers, but up and down the JP lines.

The other regiments were cheering. Cheering the Wildcats.

Chapter 12 – Ruins

A gray dark sky hung over Nathan, matching his mood. A brisk northern wind threatened to push him closer to the sheer edge where the drop would be nearly fifty feet to the rubble below.

The sight of the dam had depressed him. The once gently curving surface of the dam was now a jagged V with water pouring angrily through the gap. The once majestic structure had become no more than a set of rapids on the otherwise placid river. He could see the makeshift memorial that had been erected to the dam workers who lost their lives in the attack. The plywood board contained the names of twenty-seven men and women who had been working at the dam when the warhead detonated; many of their bodies yet to be recovered.

Although the rocket had caused most of the damage, all of the munitions and ammunition Nathan ordered stored inside the vault from Site Conway had contributed to the destruction. Even now, small smoldering fires burned beneath him, and thin tendrils of smoke made their way out through cracks in the damaged concrete.

There were voices and the sounds of children playing on the other side of the gap across from him. People had come to see the damage and possibly convince themselves that it wasn't as bad as was said. After seeing the dead remains of the once mighty structure, there could be no illusions about its recovery.

Children played and laughed, climbing around the ragged crater in the dam's surface. Adults looked on more somberly, but the children seemed oblivious to the enormity of the destruction around them.

"That's our future there," a soft voice said behind him.

Nathan turned to find his mother standing there, hugging a fleece around her. He wanted to give her a hug and receive comfort in return, but it somehow seemed wrong in this place. Instead, he turned back to the destruction. "I'm afraid the future of the dam is as nothing more than a curiosity. Something future generations will come to look at and hear stories about."

"I'm not talking about the dam," she said, moving up beside him. "I'm talking about the children. Many of them are so young they barely remember the old world. They don't know they're supposed to be devastated by the loss of electricity. They'll grow up in a world without it and think nothing of their loss."

"Assuming the world is safe enough for them to grow up."

"The world has always been a dangerous place."

"Not like this," Nathan said, turning to her. "You don't know. I've been out there. There's death and starvation and disease. Men who'll rape and torture and kill you as amusement. Cannibals, gangs, murders, animals walking around in the skin of man."

"All the more reason we have to maintain what we have built here. The loss of the dam isn't the loss of everything."

Nathan smiled. "I wish I could believe that, but I don't think so. In all my travels, in those months it took to fight through to get here with the family, the only thing different about this place and those is what we're standing on."

"Surely, it's not just that."

"Yes, it is. We had electricity, and what goes with it, and they didn't. Without that, I'm not sure what is going to happen to the JP. Hell, there may not even be a JP come spring."

"Just have a little faith," she said, putting her hand on his shoulder. "It isn't all on you."

He put his hand over hers. "How did you get here anyway?"

She pointed back the way she had come. "A group of us road up from the camp on bikes together. Everyone wanted to see the dam and Joshua let me know you were going to be here."

"Joshua. How's he doing?"

"I should ask you," she replied. "You see him more than I do."

Nathan shook his head. "I don't know how to read him anymore. It seems like just a few minutes ago he was a kid and now he's this grown man with responsibly."

"I think everyone's going to start growing up faster, just like in generations past. The concept of childhood is a luxury we may not have any longer."

That made him think of his baby daughter. "How's River?"

"Took you long enough to ask. She's doing fine. Needs her father though. It would be good if you came around more often."

"Is Alexandra watching her?"

"Yeah. I can't decide if having the baby around is helping her get over her own loss or just making the pain fresher."

"How are you two getting along?"

His mother smiled. "She still wants to kill me in my sleep, but we're figuring things out. Having Joshua back for a bit helps, I think. They're still trying to sort out how to be a family."

Nathan nodded, wondering what had become of his family. "I'm going to do all I can to keep us out of danger. When things go bad, they'll go bad in a hurry. Stay close to him; he'll know what to do."

"What do you think is going to happen?" she asked, putting her hand on his arm.

"I don't know," he answered. "Maybe nothing, but I spend my nights thinking about worst case scenarios when I should be sleeping."

"You need a vacation."

He bent his head back and laughed. "What do you think this is? I'm neglecting my duties right now. A war is going on in the south, martial law just barely keeping hysteria at bay, and oh yeah, I now have a bunch of assholes calling themselves the Pirates of the Mississippi raiding up and down the river."

"Pirates of the Mississippi? I thought the JP destroyed them in the spring."

"Evidently not. Or maybe some other group is also a big Johnny Depp fan. Anyway, our western border is easy pickings along the river right now with everyone down south fighting that madman."

"It's a shame about Reggie," she said.

Nathan turned back towards the river. "It's a shame about a lot of things."

"Come on," she said, pulling on his arm. "Come with me, see your daughter. It's been too long."

"I can't," he protested. "I need to get back."

"Either be her father or don't," she shot back at him angrily. "If you're not going to be there, then give her up to Joshua and Alexandra to raise her as their own, but make a decision soon. For the child's sake."

He hung there indecisive and thought of Bethany. She was gone, but he still couldn't bear to do anything that might make her ashamed of him.

"Come on," she said more gently, pulling him away from the destruction.

He took one more look behind him at the ruin and followed her home to his family.

Chapter 13 – Desperation

"You haven't been released from the hospital yet," said General Carter, pointing a finger at him as he walked into the room.

"Colonel McKraven reporting for duty, sir," said Conrad, saluting.

"No," answered Carter, ignoring the salute. "You're still recovering. Get back in bed."

"It's only a flesh wound, as they used to call it in those old Monty Python movies," Conrad answered, lowering his salute. "Besides, it's so boring in the hospital tent. It's full of sick people."

"I mean it," said Carter, pointing at him again.

"Sir," interrupted a ruddy-faced aide to their side. "There's a man approaching from Redstone under a white flag."

"Escort him in," Carter said.

"And make sure you search him first," hollered Conrad after him. "Remember who we're dealing with here."

"What do you think they want?" asked Carter.

"To surrender, of course," answered Conrad. "I told you we'd smoke them out."

"I like your optimism, but I doubt the smoke alone has worked. The wind has already changed direction and the weather looks like it's going to dampen our beloved bonfires."

"We should still keep them going as long as possible. If nothing else, the smokescreen makes it easier for the sappers. They can drill vertical air shafts without fear of discovery."

"Good point," Carter admitted.

"Sir," said the aide, walking back in with two guards and a middle-aged graying man. "Captain Harry Giles."

"We've met," said General Carter. "Welcome back, Captain."

Giles inclined his head slightly. His eyes were hollowed and his skin looked stretched too thin. "General Vincent Lacert sends his greetings. He proposes a truce in order to discuss terms for an agreement."

"Surrender?" asked Conrad. "I guess that smoke got to them, after all."

The man shook his head. "No, although I will admit the smoke has become quite annoying."

"Then what are we to discuss?" asked Carter.

"The details of an agreement that would end the conflict between our two peoples."

"General Taylor presented you his terms the last time you were here," said Carter.

"Yes," the man said. "General Lacert found those terms unacceptable, but he is a reasonable man and is amenable to compromise. He is willing to return half of the equipment and arms acquired at Milan Depot and agree to not infringe upon sovereignty of the Jackson Purchase again. He is also willing to accept a prisoner exchange, should you wish it. Captain Green and his soldiers are been treated well, but wish to return home."

"You expect us to believe any of that?" asked Carter.

"I can't speak to what you believe or do not believe, but I sincerely urge you to accept this offer. People are suffering on both sides."

"I believe you," said Conrad, staring at the man intently. "This might come as a surprise to you, but I once worked for Vincent Lacert. I know what it means to fall under his authority. Always living in fear, not knowing when his displeasure could bring pain or shame to those you love. Wanting a way out but not daring to look for it."

"Then you know better than most why this must end," said the man, his eyes shining. "He was always bad, but he's gotten worse every day. He trusts no one and seizes anyone he suspects and tortures them until they confess to what he tells them to confess to. Just agree to the terms."

Carter stared at the man intently for nearly a minute. "I'm going to give you a way out, Captain."

"Thank God."

"Not so fast," Carter said. "I'm rejecting this offer. Tell Lacert that the original terms still stand."

"Don't you know what you're doing to us?"

"Here's the way out of your dilemma; bring me Lacert alive or dead."

The man looked at him in shock. "You say that like it's a real possibility."

"You bring him to me and all is forgiven. We simply march away and leave your people in peace. Perhaps we'll even be friends going forward."

"No punishments or reparations?"

"No. Just an exchange of prisoners and everyone goes on with their lives as best they can. I think you will agree that will be an easier thing to do without Lacert around."

"Don't think people haven't thought about it, but no one dares. It's like he can sense our thoughts."

"He can't," said Conrad. "He just suspects everyone equally. It's your own guilt he sniffs out. He's just a man."

"Do you really know what you're asking of me? I've got a family."

"Then think of them," said Carter, "because if you do not do this…when my soldiers finally breach your perimeter after weeks of frustrating siege…I'm going to turn them loose."

"What do you mean?"

"It means I'm going to let them ravage you and your families. We'll burn everything to the ground, and those that survive, after my men are done with them, will be sold at the slave markets down south."

"You wouldn't!" the man said.

"Why wouldn't I? You have the ability to end this. Do it or suffer the consequences." Carter turned to the guards. "Escort Captain Giles back towards his lines."

The man stared at him in shock as he made his way out of the room.

"Would you really do all of that?" asked Conrad after the man was gone.

"I haven't decided yet. Ask me again when we get there."

"I hope he's more resourceful than he looks," said Conrad.

"Desperation is a resource," added Carter turning to Conrad. "Better go tend to your fires."

Conrad saluted and left.

Chapter 14 – Light of Release

Vincent Lacert knew what his subordinates thought of him and it was just what he wanted. He had learned in his lifetime that fear is the chief tool to bend others to your will. This was one of the few things his abusive alcoholic father had taught him before sixteen-year-old Vinny had finally managed to kill the worthless bag of flesh.

He didn't necessarily *wish* others harm for harm's sake; he simply didn't believe they were the same as him. His thoughts, desires, feelings, and ideas were all superior to anyone else's. It was right that they fear him, because he was the closest thing to God on earth that these people would ever experience. Even minor setbacks like the current JP siege couldn't change that. He had experienced setbacks before and still came out on top. Vincent Lacert knew he would always win in the end. How could he not? He was more worthy than anyone else.

Vincent opened his brilliant blue eyes and realized he had been dozing; for how long, he didn't know. He stared through his office windows at the turbulent sky. That was right as well. The very weather matched his mood. His eyes drifted around the room that had previously belonged to the facility director. The walls and shelves were bare and clean; all the false mementoes and sentimental keepsakes from the old occupant had been tossed out somewhere.

Now it was clean and bare. He had cleaned house, just like he did wherever he went.

Perhaps that's what I need to do now, he thought. *Clean house again. They have failed me, after all.*

Yes, he smiled. *I'll start with the top down. Make an example of them and their families. That should serve to motivate others on what happens when they do not adequately serve me. They should know that I deserve more than just their best, I deserve their…everything.*

Vincent knew that his offer would not be accepted. When Harry Giles returned, he would carry valuable intelligence about his enemy and their mindset. He would also have planted a seed in the minds of others in the JP camp who were not so enthusiastic about the siege. There would be whispers of his offer and the fact that there was a way out, a way to go home. After all, hadn't an entire regiment already tried to depart?

Giles would tell him what he needed to know, and then he would do a little house cleaning…starting with Giles. The man was a talented administrator and speaker, most lawyers were, but he still will have failed Vincent for the last time. He could not suffer such continued shortcomings. If the man could convince juries to let rapists and murderers to go free, why couldn't he get the JP leaders to do what he wanted? It was obviously a lack of motivation, something that simply could not be borne.

Looking at his watch, he realized that Giles should have returned hours ago.

"Guards!" he yelled, and two soldiers obediently opened the double doors and stepped in. Each came to attention with a crisp salute. They were both familiar, but he had never bothered to learn their names. Why should he? Their very existence was meaningless outside of what they could do for him.

"Both of you go find Captain Giles and bring him here, by force if need be."

"Yes, sir," they both exclaimed and departed, pulling the doors shut behind them.

He turned back to the window and looked at the sky. At least the wind had stopped. That confounded smoke was simply billowing straight up into the sky. As soon as the next rocket was completed, he would make them pay for what they had done.

One of the prisoners they had captured and vigorously interrogated said the assault to lay the bonfires had been lead by Conrad McKraven himself. The sheer audacity of the man's betrayal made Vincent shake when he thought of it.

How dare he go against me. Conrad knows what I'm capable of. I'll make him regret ever living.

There was a sound of boots on the floor outside and he awaited the knock on his door. He was startled when it opened without his invitation. Vincent immediately leapt to his feet, his fury about to be unleashed, but it died in his throat in confusion.

It was Harry Giles standing there, but his guards were gone, and he was accompanied by about a dozen other officers.

Vincent's hand dropped to the butt of the pistol at his waist.

Several of the men with Giles raised their weapons and pointed them at Vincent.

Vincent smiled. "I knew you all were stupid, but I never thought you were *this* stupid. What do you think is going to happen to your families? To your wives? Your little kids? I'll make them scream until their little voices give out. I'll peal the flesh from their bodies and make their mothers sew the skins into boots for me. I'll whore out the whole damn lot of your women for all the world to see!" he screamed.

"We already rescued our families," said Giles, pulling a pistol from his own belt. "That's the last time you're going to threaten my family."

"Didn't General Carter say we had to bring Lacert to him?" one of men behind him asked nervously.

"He said alive or dead," answered Giles. The small man then raised the pistol at the man and shot Vincent Lacert in the forehead.

The body crashed back against the desk chair and then both fell into the floor. Giles walked around the desk to stand over Vincent and look down at his body. A look of stunned surprise was frozen on the man's face.

And his eyes were no longer as blue.

****

Jason Green stared at the flame in his hand. It was beautiful. It brought light to his dark world. It was the release when he summoned enough courage to grasp it. He had lost track of time. Years would pass and then some extraterrestrial being would carve a hole in the sky and food and water would fall from heaven. Then they were gone.

All of the universe was nothing more than the small container he occupied. The gasoline. And the lighter. The flame. He couldn't even remember how he had gotten it.

The flame. He stared at it. It cast a beautiful glow of light and warmth.

Maybe I'm already dead, he wondered not for the first time. The thought was not as frightening as before. It would explain a great deal.

There was a deafening noise in the sky, and Jason reached his arm up to shield his eyes. The hole appeared, and the brilliant heaven light appeared. A face looked down and stared at him.

"Damn," the voice said. "There's another one in here. Looks almost dead."

"Well, you better get him out," replied a voice from further away. "Giles was very specific. Don't want anything to derail the truce with the JP."

Truce. JP. Memories began to flood back.

"Captain Jason Green," he croaked.

The man in the sky hole grunted. "Hang in there, asshole. We'll get you out." He looked around the inside of the smooth container surface. "Although I don't rightly know how."

"I'm sure we'll figure it out," whispered Green.

He closed the lighter and dropped it into the gasoline around him.

Chapter 15 – A Fresh Start

There was a steady drum of voices in the USECO executive council room, but Nathan did his best to tune them all out.

It's almost over, he thought.

He had been able to lift martial law several weeks previously after the JP forces' victory in the south. The terms Carter had settled on hadn't been popular; people wanted to punish them for destroying the dam, at the very least make them pay for the cost of the war, but Nathan wouldn't second-guess Luke Carter who told him it was the best deal they were likely to get. To count their blessings it was over and to move forward. He had told the man to get it done and he had.

Besides how could you ever put a monetary cost to the dam? Something the likes of which the world may not see again for centuries, if ever.

True to his word, Nathan was overseeing elections. Each county was monitoring its own results and sending those results to the USECO facility for a final tally. Right now it looked like an even race between Ernest Givens and previous JP President Paul Thompson who had come out of solitude—and some would say disgrace—to run. The polls had closed hours before, and they were only waiting on the Paducah results to be able to declare a winner.

Nathan looked up at the bright lights above him. A month ago, he would have fretted at the cost of such extravagance, but now knew it didn't matter. If they didn't run the generator, the fuel would soon be worthless anyway.

Almost over, he told himself again.

The room became suddenly silent, and Nathan looked up to see the election commissioner approaching him with a piece of paper. Nathan took it and stared at it for a long time. He then folded up the note and began writing on another piece of paper. When he was done, he folded it, placed it into an envelope, which he sealed, and then wrote a name on the outside. Nathan stood and walked towards the door.

"Who won?" someone on the council yelled after him.

Nathan ignored them and strode purposefully up the long concrete ramps and hallways out into the open air. There he found Joshua leaning against a car he had requisitioned just for this purpose. His son was smoking a pipe while reading a paperback book.

"Since when do you smoke?" he asked.

Joshua shrugged. "I don't know, just something I picked up along the way."

Nathan felt like he should say something else, as if maybe this was an open window to reconnect with his son. An opportunity he shouldn't let pass, yet he couldn't think of anything to say.

Instead, he held out the sealed envelope to Joshua who took it, read the front, and nodded. Joshua tossed the paperback book into the passenger seat of the muscle car and got inside, cranking the engine with a throaty roar.

Joshua put on sunglasses, grinned at Nathan, and gave him a peace sign. He then stomped on the gas and flew out of the facility parking lot on squealing burning tires.

Nathan stood there and listened to the sound of the engine fading away in the distance.

****

Ernest Givens wanted a drink. He wanted one so badly that he could close his eyes and actually taste the vodka or rye or even the borderline poisonous rotgut they made in homemade stills now. He didn't have the shakes or the sweats like before when his body actually needed alcohol, but his mind craved the release. The stress and uncertainty would fade with just a little drink.

He shook his head and was thankful he had gotten rid of all his booze a long time ago, otherwise he wasn't sure he could resist the temptation. He looked at his watch and saw that the polls had been closed for hours. Of course his watch could be off. No one really knew for sure what the correct time was anymore.

Ernest walked outside and stood on his porch. An old lady who sat on her own porch across the street gave him a thumbs up. "You win yet?" she called out.

"Don't know," he yelled back.

"Well, you better," she said. "I had to walk all the way down to the high school to vote, and these bones don't move the way they used to."

"Thank you, Missus Tucker."

"You can thank me by getting the electricity back on."

Ernest cringed inwardly. People still thought the dam was something that could be fixed. Damn the war with Huntsville. Even after all of that, and everything they had lost, the JP had just walked away with nothing. He was sure Nathan Taylor would claim they had eliminated a dire threat in Vincent Lacert, but men like Nathan would always be seeing dire threats in order to justify their actions. There were always going to be dire threats.

With Reggie's death, Ernest had had plenty of time to reassess the former president, and his overall verdict of the man had changed. Reggie Phillips had been in a host of difficult situations and done his best. Given everything that had gone on, he hadn't done too bad by them, Ernest admitted. His one major failing was in trusting Nathan Taylor and allowing that man to get whatever he wanted.

Everything bad that had happened over the last two years could be laid at the feet of that one man. Nathan probably meant well in his own mind, but he was so sure of himself that he couldn't be bothered to consult others. This was exactly what several of the county executives and mayors had told him when they came to talk to him after realizing he might actually win. They said they wanted to make sure he knew they were willing to work with him. Unlike Nathan Taylor, who was impossible to even reason with.

There was a loud rumble in the distance, and Ernest thought his ears were playing tricks on him. He had owned an old Camaro when he was a teenager and the sound the engine made was distinctive. As it drew closer, he knew he was right. Someone was actually driving a car. Not only that, but a gas guzzler at a time when gasoline and everything else was rationed.

A black Camaro in desperate need of a wash and wax job pulled up in front of his house. A young man with a scarred head and arms leaned out of the driver's window to look at him.

Joshua Taylor, Ernest thought. *I should have known only Nathan Taylor wouldn't hesitate to waste resources for whatever he thought best.*

"You're Ernest Givens, right?" the man asked.

Ernest nodded, and Joshua turned off the car. He got out and pulled on a cap, careful to cover up the pale puckered skin where hair would never grow again. Walking towards Ernest, he stuck out his hand. Surprised, Ernest took it.

"We met once," Joshua said. "Not too long ago, but it seems like a lifetime."

"Up north," Ernest said. "You and your father had just crossed over the Ohio River."

"And you had just brought all those people from Paducah safely home. I don't think people are ever going to forget about that."

"Thanks," said Ernest, uncertain what to say.

"Oh," Joshua said as if remembering why he was there and pulled an envelope from his back pocket. He handed it to Ernest. "Nice to see you again," he said while turning back to the car.

He held the envelope in his hand. "What's this?"

"A note from my father. Congratulations, by the way." Joshua got back into the car, put on his sunglasses, and with a roar pulled off down the street.

Ernest stared after him and then slowly opened the letter.

President Elect Ernest Givens,

Let me be the first to congratulate you on your victory. I've taken the liberty of scheduling your inauguration for one week from today at the Jackson Purchase Committee Building at the old USECO plant in Paducah. This has been where the last two elected JP Presidents have been inaugurated, but if you wish to change the date or venue, that can easily be arranged.

Until that time, I will continue to execute the authority given to me by the late President Phillips. I remain at your disposal if you wish to meet to discuss any matters in regards to the Jackson Purchase. Following your inauguration, I plan to resign immediately as the JP Chief of Defense, and will retire from any sort of public life or service. I can recommend General Luke Carter as a more than able replacement, but the decision is, of course, ultimately yours.

I wish you the very best in the days ahead and pray our fledgling nation can begin the process of healing with the war to the south ended. I feel we need a fresh start. Like most, I am daunted by the challenge of doing so without the many benefits of the Kentucky Dam, but I am confident in us as a people to survive and prosper.

Sincerely,

General Nathan Taylor

Ernest read the note again and then gazed off into the distance. The enormity of the challenges that lay ahead began to descend upon him. Nathan Taylor had made a catastrophe of things, and now he was going to step aside. It would be up to Ernest to muddle through the quagmire he had created.

He was right about one thing. They did need a fresh start.

Ernest crumbled the note in his fist.

Chapter 16 – Branded

It's almost over, Nathan thought again and remembered all the times before change-of-command ceremonies. It had been with regret that he had given over the mantle of command to another, but it had also been with relief as the weight of responsibility slid to another.

He had intentionally kept the inauguration crowd small. Ernest Givens hadn't given him an invite list, which had made it easy. Large crowds came to see this historic event, but Nathan had the police keep them back on the roped-off parking lot where they could see and hear the speeches, but were not too close.

Even so there had already been trouble. The Elins and the Cambry's, two large McCraken County clans, had already nearly started a riot when a simmering and long-standing family feud between them burst into open fighting. One man was stabbed, but the police were able to separate them before firearms were involved. Both groups had been sent away, and now the crowd was at least peaceful, although a thin sheen of electric-like tension seemed to hang over them. It felt as if a spark could pop off at any moment igniting their discontent and frustration.

He noticed that the mayors and county executives hovered around Ernest like he was some sort of royalty. They were obviously courting his favor and several of them looked over at Nathan with knowing, vindictive smiles.

Pouring vitriol into their ears about me, he thought. *Let them. Soon it will be over and all of this will be someone else's problem.*

There was a policeman at Nathan's elbow, and he was pulled out of his thoughts. "Sir, the Creek delegation is here."

Nathan nodded and began moving in that direction. He had invited officials from neighboring states to see this event, including the Pennyrile Communities, former West Tennessee Republic representatives, and even Huntsville to much consternation. Most had not wanted the Creek Nation there, but Nathan had insisted.

At the parking lot, he saw a group of what looked to be thirty mounted warriors gathering in a nearby field where a small stream flowed. They were dismounting and bringing water to their horses with small buckets. The crowd parted on its own for these warriors, and the Creek Chief Billy Fox, accompanied by Susan Rivera, Jasper Timmons, Mindy—the one they called Little Lion—and two large Creek braves, came forward. All were dressed simply for traveling and were unarmed, Nathan noted thankfully.

Nathan walked to them and greeted Billy. "What? No headdress?"

"I didn't want to scare anyone," he responded with a smile. "It was kind of you to invite us."

"Nonsense. The Creek have proven a valuable ally to the JP."

"And vice versa," answered Billy. "We have already started claiming and taxing land to our south. We appreciate the JP staying neutral and ignoring Huntsville pleas for assistance. Many of the Huntsville leaders have since come around to recognize the benefit of falling under the Creek Nation."

Nathan looked around. "Maybe it would be best if you didn't mention that at the moment. That was under Reggie's administration. It's not common knowledge and might be unpopular."

Billy's face clouded with concern. "The JP isn't thinking of backing out on its agreement, is it? That would be most unwise of you."

"No," answered Nathan. "The agreement still stands and it was official. Just let the new president get his footing. He'll have a lot to deal with."

Billy nodded, and Nathan shook Susan and Jasper's hand. "Good of you to come."

"We are honored by the invitation," answered Susan and looked back at the large gathering of horses and warriors. "The Creek have brought gifts for the new president as a sign of our respect and friendship. Will there be an opportunity to present these?"

"There will be an official celebration dinner later here," Nathan said. "It will be a much smaller affair. That is when I would recommend presenting them."

"Will you be there?" Susan asked.

Nathan shook his head. "My official duties end at the conclusion of this ceremony."

She looked at him with something like sadness and finally nodded and turned to Mindy. "Then I think we should present you with your gift now."

The little girl walked forward, pulling a looped leather bag from around her shoulder. Reaching inside, she pulled out a long thin shape wrapped in a strip of deerskin. Nathan took it with both hands reverently and began to unwrap it. Beneath the folds was long smooth wood and bone beautifully carved with animal shapes.

"It is the peace pipe we smoked last spring," Billy explained. "The one that cemented the alliance between our people's. It still carries the last tobacco Chicoca ever smoked."

"Thank you," said Nathan. It seemed only days ago that he had smoked the pipe with the Creek.

"Be sure and keep it safe on your journey," Mindy said brightly.

"Journey?" Nathan asked.

The girl looked at him with exasperation. "The long trip your getting ready to go on. Make sure you keep it safe. The pipe was Chicoca's."

Nathan started to ask what she meant but was interrupted by the master-of-ceremonies at the front podium microphone. "Ladies and gentlemen, the ceremony will begin in approximately five minutes. Please make your way to your seats."

"Electricity," Billy said with a smile at the microphone and speakers.

Pointing down into the bunker complex, Nathan said simply, "Generators."

Billy nodded in understanding.

Nathan grabbed the arm of a staffer walking nearby. "Cindy, can you please show the Creek delegation to their seats? They're up at the front." She smiled and led the delegation to seats near the front of the stage.

As they moved away, Nathan scanned the crowds and remembered his last inauguration here. It had been when Reggie had been beaten by

Paul Thompson and was giving his farewell speech. Those had been eloquent words. Thoughts that Nathan might express himself. Ideas that surely still held true if only Reggie were around to deliver them. Nathan quietly made his way to his seat and sat erect and still as the ceremony started.

He knew it would be a boring affair, but hopefully short, and he had planned it that way. James Harping, the county executive from Ballard County, and the elder statesman, had been given the honor of the introductory speech. As the event began, Nathan tuned the man out as he droned on and on about Ernest's great deeds and praise for Reggie, a man Harping said would likely join that long list of JP martyrs that future generations would venerate.

Assuming there are future generations, Nathan thought.

He was startled out of his thoughts by everyone rising. Ernest Givens stood and walked forward where he laid his hand upon a large Bible and recited the oath of office led by Doctor Valerie Cutchfield, the Murray State University President. When it was over, everyone applauded and sat again.

Harping spoke briefly again before Ernest Givens took the stage to stand in front of the podium. He pulled out a thin sheaf of papers and began to read in a droning manner. For all his many qualities, and Nathan was sure there were several, he was not a good speaker. At least not in this instance. Nathan noticed that Ernest Givens looked tense, uncomfortable, and even slightly pale.

Soon, it was over, and the new JP president stepped down to polite applause.

They then all stood for the playing of the National Anthem and saluted the U.S. flag that flew about the facility in front of them. They all remained standing as the official party on the stage departed to their rear into the USECO bunker complex.

"Ladies and gentlemen, this concludes today's inauguration," the master-of-ceremonies said. "Thank you all for coming today."

Nathan sat down heavily in his chair and let out a huge breath. It was over. There was no duty, no calling or responsibility. No one had a hold over him any longer except his family. He was finally free.

A shadow fell over Nathan, and he looked up to find a state trooper standing there. "Sir, President Givens wishes to see you in his office."

Reggie's office, Nathan thought. "Now?"

"Yes," the man said and held out an arm towards the bunker.

Nathan stood heavily and began to walk. The trooper fell in after him. "I know the way. You don't have to show me."

"I'm supposed to escort you," the man replied expressionlessly.

Why now? Nathan wondered, warning bells beginning to go off in his head.

He strode down the familiar concrete halls lit by dim lights, making his way towards the office that Reggie had never liked. As a matter of fact, he had never liked the USECO facility at all, preferring to conduct business when he could at the Graves County courthouse near his home. Nathan walked in the door and saw Ernest sitting behind Reggie's desk with Leslie Mitchell and the new vice president, Brad Williams, standing behind him. Both were fighting hard to keep smirks off their faces.

"Congratulations, Mister President," said Nathan. "It is an honor for you to call for me so early in your administration."

"Thank you," answered Ernest woodenly. "I thought it best to get this business over as soon as possible."

"If I might ask, what business?"

"You are hereby relieved of your duties, effective immediately."

"Sir, you already have my letter of resignation. I've taken the liberty of preparing General Carter to assume those duties until you either confirm him or select another."

"Luke Carter has been relieved of his duties as well," said Mitchell.

Nathan nodded slowly. "I see. Who will be the Chief of Defense?"

"Leslie Mitchell here will assume those duties," Ernest answered.

Biting his tongue, Nathan nodded his head once. "I understand. Will that be all, sir?"

"Unfortunately, no," Ernest said, staring pointedly at Nathan's hand. "You know that sentence was never commuted. President Paul Thompson signed it himself."

Nathan looked down at the EX brand on his hand and felt a ball of lead in the pit of his stomach. "That was when our president was under the control of Ethan Schweitzer. You can't uphold those decisions."

"Probably not," said Ernest, "but it does save us a great deal of paperwork and trouble. It also means we don't have to brand you. It's already been done."

Nathan stared at the man for several seconds and was conscious of the large state trooper behind him. "Are you saying…I'm to be exiled?"

"Yes," answered Mitchell. "You're to be out of the JP by sunset three days from now on pain of execution if you are not. You'll go west and never return."

Forcing himself to breath slowly, he asked. "Why west?"

"Some thought that was the best option," said Ernest, "given our equities and relations elsewhere."

Nathan smiled ruefully. "You're afraid I'll stir up trouble for you with the Creek or Huntsville."

"Among others," answered Williams. "Count yourself lucky. Execution was on the table."

"What about my family?"

"They have not been charged with any crimes," Ernest said. "They may stay or go as they like, but don't expect them to have the same privileges as when you were in charge."

"Privileges?" asked Nathan.

"I think our business here is done, Mister President," said Williams. "We have a dinner to prepare for."

Nathan stared at the three men while rubbing the brand on his hand. "I sincerely hope you have a successful and uneventful term."

"Thank you," said Ernest. "We all agreed that will be much more likely without you around. The trooper will show you out."

Dismissed, Nathan turned and walked out the door and up the hallways into the light.

He could feel the burden, so recently lifted, settling back upon his shoulders.

Chapter 17 – Goodbyes

Joshua stood outside and stared up at the roof of their little cabin beside the lake. A wind storm the night before had blown a large limb down and it had ripped some of the shingles away. There were other trees that were too close to the house and those could threaten the cabin if there was an ice storm. First, the fallen limb had to come off and the roof repaired before the next rain.

He saw things around the cabin that he hadn't noticed before. The front railing leaning. Peeling paint that needed to be replaced. Nails that had worked their way out of old wood. Things neglected in all the time he had been away.

Looking towards the house, he saw Alexandra move around purposefully in the kitchen. He slowly climbed the steps and opened the door. He heard River wailing for her breakfast and Joshua found his wife in the kitchen, transferring breast milk from a hand pump to a bottle. Thankfully, Candice Roger next door had a baby several months before and was willing to share her milk, although it had been easier to store when they had refrigeration and electricity.

Alexandra glanced up at him and then back at what she was doing. "She eats more than ten grown men."

Joshua waited for her to finish and then followed her into the second bedroom where she picked River up from a crib and put the bottle in her mouth. The crying stopped. Alexandra bounced the baby.

As she fed her, Joshua realized that his wife's face looked relaxed when she held the baby.

We lost our baby, he thought. *She's had to deal with that alone, without me.*

"Did you hear about my father?" he finally asked.

Her calmness vanished as her face tightened. She nodded.

"He's with the Mennonites now, buying wagons and teams. Quite a few people have decided to go with him. They're actually fashioning the wagons from old pickup trucks. Using large tractor tires and such. Should make them much easier to maneuver and more reliable as well."

"Good for him."

"Of course, Grandmother is going. She's already there with him. Luke Carter and Jason Green as well. Seems like no one is too high on military folks right now."

She bent down and kissed the baby's head.

"Conrad and his family are going, as well as some of the new folks: Simon, Jessica, and the big guy Trailer. They're gathering in Mayfield and will be heading out tomorrow."

Alexandra's lips got tight, but she didn't say anything.

"He plans on taking River," Joshua finally said.

His wife pulled the baby closer to her. "Why? He hasn't shown a lick of interest in her since his wife died. Besides, exile is no place for a baby. Where are they going to get milk?"

"Dad talked to Doctor Wilson, and he said goat's milk should be fine at this stage."

"Goat's milk? On some dangerous trail? What if the baby gets sick or they're attacked? What then?"

"I suppose they'll find a way to deal with it. Babies went on Oregon Trail wagon trains all the time."

She snorted. "A wagon train, is that what it is? So tell me, where are they going? Oregon?"

Joshua shrugged.

"Well, they're not taking River."

"Alexandra," Joshua pleaded.

"No!" she hissed at him. "It's no place for a baby. Out there, she could get sick. She could...could even..." Her face started to contort into fear.

"We could go with them," he said.

Her anger returned with a sarcastic smile. "There it is. I've been waiting to hear how you were going to follow your father like you've followed him everywhere else. Never mind that this is our home."

Joshua sighed. "I'm not sure this is our home anymore. Not after everything that's happened. Everyone will know me as Nathan Taylor's son and David Taylor's brother. That may not be a good thing."

"Well, I'm not leaving, and neither is River," Alexandra said.

"My sister is not our baby," Joshua said.

"Maybe not, but she's more mine than his. If he wants her so badly, he can come and try to take her from me," she declared fiercely.

"Alexandra, can you please try to be reasonable?"

"Sure. Here's reasonable for you. I'm not leaving. So the choice you have to make is whether you're going to go with you father or stay here with your wife."

Joshua choked down an angry retort and ran his hand over his head. He felt the angry scars and remembered what he looked like in the mirror. Alexandra didn't seem to see the ugliness and he didn't feel ugly when he was with her. He wondered why he had stayed away so long. The army didn't own him, and duty was his father's calling, not his. Closing his eyes, he imagined the difficult farewell he would have to make.

"That's no choice at all," he said. "My place is with you."

Her glare softened in surprise. "Really? You'd say goodbye to your father and grandmother and possibly never see them again to stay here with me?"

"You're my wife," he answered. "My best friend. Where else would I want to be?"

She came over and pressed close, the baby between them, and gave him a kiss. "Thank you," she whispered.

"I guess I should get to work on that roof," he said.

She shook her head. "We'll be leaving anyway. Better start packing instead."

"What are you talking about?"

"I always said I was going to leave Kentucky after high school anyway and never got the chance. Besides, I don't like the vibe of this place anymore. You're right about it maybe not being safe for you. And the hunting has become terrible. Too many people scaring off the wildlife."

"So what was the last five minutes about?"

"I needed to know where your heart was. More than that, I wanted *you* to know where it was."

"So, it was a bluff?"

Her smile slipped. "I don't bluff."

Joshua looked around at the inside of their cabin. "So what now?"

"You still have any gas in that Camaro outside?"

"A little."

"Let's pack up and get to Mayfield. We're going to need a wagon and supplies of our own."

Joshua nodded and started towards the back room.

"And Joshua," she said. "Make sure we take every weapon we can get our hands on. We're going to need them."

Chapter 18 – Leaving Home

Four makeshift wagons, each pulled by a pair of mules, approached the long bridge over the Mississippi River leading west out of the JP. Each wagon had at least two passengers, and several spare mules as well as a dozen horses were tied to the backs of the wagons. A pair of goats also trudged along by tethers.

Nathan had traded everything he could for the wagons, animals, food, and supplies. He judged it should be enough to last them a few months at least. He had also asked Luke Carter and Jason Green to steal several machine guns, rocket launchers, explosives, and a large stash of ammunition in addition to other combat items. These were hidden in special compartments between the wagons' axles installed by the Mennonites. Each large pickup truck turned wagon had a camper top on the back to protect their contents and the passengers from the worst of the weather. Other supplies, such as spare tires and parts, were roped to the top of the campers.

A rider galloped back east along the road and stopped in front of Nathan in the seat of the first wagon.

"There's a group gathered at the edge of the bridge," Green said. "Couple of state police cars as well. About what we expected, but not nearly as many."

Word of Nathan's exile had been spread by Ernest's subordinates. Although it had been a popular decision, scores had not been happy about the way Nathan was being treated. Many friends and neighbors

414

came to see him and his family off. Hugs, gifts, and tearful farewells were exchanged.

Several of the visitors had warned them of the organized protest awaiting them on their way out of the JP. Most of the slander and stirring up against Nathan appeared to be coming from the new Chief of Defense Leslie Mitchell. The man and his minions were energetically and publically laying all the JP's current faults and hardships on him.

"How nice of them to see us off," said his mother from beside him.

Luke had ridden up on a horse beside them as well as Trailer on Wildcat. "We expecting a fight already?" asked the big man.

"Maybe," answered Nathan, reaching back to ensure his assault rifle was ready behind him. "Best pass the word to everyone to be ready."

Carter nodded and rode back towards the end of their wagon column. He would inform Joshua and Alexandra in the wagon behind them, Simon and Jessica after them, and then Conrad's family which was bringing up the rear.

Green checked his own assault rifle strapped behind his saddle and then rode up ahead of them again. Nathan flicked the reins over the rumps of the mules.

Within minutes, they could see the crowds themselves. A couple dozen were on each side of the road along with a state police car, its lights flashing. Several old vehicles and bicycles and even a couple of tethered horses were nearby.

They were looking at the approaching wagons, and Nathan could hear murmurs. Four police officers stood and watched them approach with arms crossed or thumbs resting in their belts. People looked at them with suspicion and distaste. Nathan stopped the wagon in front of the first police officer.

"Come to give us a send off?" Nathan asked.

"Just told to make sure you depart when and where you were supposed to."

Nathan didn't like the look on the people's faces. "We're leaving. There's not likely to be any trouble, is there?"

"Shouldn't be," the man said, but there was a suppressed grin on his face.

"All right then," said Nathan. "Let's go."

Later, none of them could have said where the first rock came from, but it startled them. As if it were a signal, the crowds began yelling at them and throwing rocks.

Nathan saw a rock strike the neck of the mule to his front right. The animal squealed in pain, trying to back up, while its partner kept moving forward. The axle tongue twisted, and the wagon itself began to lift off the ground on one side. "Easy!" yelled Nathan, pulling tightly on the reins as more projectiles flew around them. One struck the side of his leg painfully.

There was a prolonged burst of automatic gunfire and the crowds dove to the ground.

Nathan managed to get the team under control and looked up to see Luke Carter pointing a smoking AR-15 at the police officers. "Is this how you want it? We got nothing to lose here. I'll shoot every damn one of you, pick your pockets for breath mints, and be on my way. It's your call."

"You better get these people under control," added Nathan to the stunned officers, the rifle now pointing at them as well, "or we can't be responsible for what happens. I'll not let anyone here harm my family, even if that means a bloodbath."

One of the officers finally moved towards the crowds. "Step aside, people, and let them pass. Anything else gets thrown and you'll spend the night in jail, I promise you." The other three officers quickly followed their companion's lead.

Carter rode up beside Nathan. "This isn't how I wanted to remember this place."

"Me neither," answered Nathan, looking down at the brand on his hand. It reminded him of the last time he was thrown out of the JP and how Brazen had come to help him.

His mother was looking behind them east and there were tears in her eyes.

"It's not too late," Nathan said. "You can still stay if you want."

She shook her head. "No. This is for the best. Just feels sad to be leaving home. I've lived here all my life."

"I know. I'll find us a new home out there. Someplace to start over. To build a new home."

"Well, we'll never get there if you don't stop talking and get moving," she said.

Nathan smiled and slapped the reins on the rumps of the mules. They clattered across the Mississippi River and out of the JP forever.

Epilogue

Lieutenant General Teddy Smits read the reports in front of him just as he had the day before that and the day before that and every day for the past two years or more. There was little else to do in Cheyenne Mountain, and it was important to establish a routine or you'd lose your cornflakes. At least that's what the shrinks said.

The intel reports were pretty much limited to radio intercepts and some satellite imagery at this point. Although they had contact with some other isolated outposts, they had discovered that these elements were extremely unreliable. Several had stopped communicating over the last few months.

The Jackson Purchase communication had been promising for all its brevity, but no one there would answer their calls now. Site Conway was obviously lost. It wasn't the first and wouldn't be the last, Smits knew.

Smits put aside the report about the latest Alaskan Free State broadcast and shook his head at the next report in the small pile. It concerned Admiral Young, the former Seventh Fleet Commander. After launching everything he had at China at N-Day—plus one, as had been his orders—Young had moved with his fleet to Australia, which provided sanctuary. Since then, he had urged any and all remaining U.S. naval ships to come to him and dozens had.

Recently, the man had gone a step further and held presidential elections. He bragged that he had received nearly one hundred percent of the "American" vote—all from sailors and marines serving under him. Smits now claimed to be the U.S. President and to head the government from the U.S. Embassy in Canberra.

"What is it?" he growled at the knock on his door.

A uniformed officer stepped in and closed the door. Smits noted the man looked unusually nervous. "Yes, Commander Porter?"

"Sir, I just reviewed the report on the latest radiation levels around Cheyenne Mountain."

"And?"

"Still dangerously high, sir. Around twelve kilo-rads, which is not surprising considering we took five hits within a twenty-mile radius."

"So…no change?"

"No, sir."

"Okay, thank you," said Smits, turning back to his reading.

"But the techs keep saying the levels should have dissipated by now. Twelve kilo-rads is far too dangerous to go out in radiation suits. After this much time, it should be below five hundred rads, they say, but all the sensors agree, and they can't all be wrong. One or two maybe, but not dozens."

"Yes, commander, we've been over this. The big brains can't figure out why is hasn't lowered, but all are in agreement. We can't crack the seal on the facility."

"Exactly, but one of the techs realized that all of those sensors feed into one relay control module. He also noticed that twelve kilo-rads was exactly the level which the radiation peaked on N-Day, plus five. It was virtually impossible for the levels not to have gone down at all."

Smits looked up with a sigh. "Commander, what are you trying to tell me?"

"The relay module burned out, sir. It was overloaded. Once we replaced the module, we got different radiation level results."

"And what are they now?" Smits asked, leaning his chair back on two legs. He thought how fantastic it would be to have a cigarette.

"They range from between ninety to one hundred twenty rads."

All four chair legs slammed to the floor. "Have you verified this?"

"We've checked everything at least ten times. The new readings are accurate, sir."

Smiling, the general looked up at the ceiling. "This means we can go outside."

"Yes, sir. The techs say we don't want to be playing in the dirt or drinking any of the water around here for a good long while, but going outside for short periods should result in minimal exposure."

Smits rubbed his face and smiled.

"With your permission, sir, I'd like to lead a reconnaissance around the mountain. Possibly even to the bases near Colorado Springs."

"Agreed," Smits answered. "Take a detachment and go in NBC vehicles just in case. Make sure we have good comms. Short recon only, three or four hours at most."

"Yes, sir," the man smiled and departed.

Smits knew what Porter was smiling about. None of them had felt the sun on their faces or smelled fresh air in years. He looked back down at the report on Admiral Young. President indeed. This changed everything.

Closing the folder with the intelligence reports, he put them aside and typed on his computer. After several minutes, he found the folder he wanted.

Continuity of Operations.

The ambiguous title was typical government understatement. It was in fact a plan for the reestablishing of the United States after it had suffered a crippling nuclear, meteorological, or biological attack. Cheyenne Mountain was designed to be the center of any recovery from catastrophic devastation. Not only did the hollowed-out mountain facility contain resources and people to rebuild, it had all the knowledge of where hundreds of smaller unmanned facilities existed around the country.

Seeds for an American rebirth, he thought.

Smits smiled. "Time to take our country back."

Author's Note and Acknowledgements

Thank you for reading *Shadows of Before*. I sincerely hope that you enjoyed the story and ask you to take the time to leave a review so other readers may know if this book is for them or not.

Please consider signing up for my reader's newsletter at https://dl.bookfunnel.com/nm7lm5ldjy. You can unsubscribe at any time. For signing up, you will immediately receive a free book in addition to the latest information on new releases and free giveaways.

I began writing the *Land of Tomorrow* series in January 2010 and published the first book *Glimmer of Hope* in September 2012. The second book *Children of Wrath* followed in October 2013, and the third book *Paths of Righteousness* in June 2014. When I finished this third book, I had intended it as the end to the *Land of Tomorrow* series, which I had always envisioned as a trilogy.

As the months passed, I began to think about the characters in this series and wonder what had become of them. New characters like Simon and Trailer began to come to mind, and I realized I wanted to write their stories. To discover what had become of them in this new dangerous world.

I was also encouraged by several readers who urged me to write more books in the series. To them, I am grateful, as writers are always inspired to write by those who want to read. To those readers and others who have enjoyed these works, thank you.

As always, gratitude is due to my wife and sons for allowing me to seclude myself to write. Without them, none of this would be possible. Thank you.

As I said before, I sincerely hope you enjoyed reading this story. I don't yet know for certain where it will lead from here, but I have some ideas. All I know for sure is that it isn't over yet. Nathan and his band have left the safety of the JP and set out on a very dangerous and deadly road.

Let's see where it will lead them…

Ryan King - 15 November 2017